God-Fearing Criminals

J.M. Burt

iUniverse, Inc.
New York   Bloomington

iUniverse books may be ordered through booksellers or by contacting:

iUniverse
1663 Liberty Drive
Bloomington, IN 47403
www.iuniverse.com
1-800-Authors (1-800-288-4677)

Because of the dynamic nature of the Internet, any Web addresses or links contained in this book may have changed since publication and may no longer be valid. The views expressed in this work are solely those of the author and do not necessarily reflect the views of the publisher, and the publisher hereby disclaims any responsibility for them.

ISBN: 978-1-4401-6522-1 (sc)
ISBN: 978-1-4401-6521-4 (ebook)
ISBN: 978-1-4401-6520-7 (dj)

Printed in the United States of America

iUniverse rev. date: 11/12/2009

DEDICATION
For Marie
** She gave the most **
** She gave herself **

and

Jonathan & Noel
and
Karen "Missy"
** We crossed the realms of time and space together **
** on our way home **

A MEMORIAL

Joseph and **Doshia Mae Burt**

Ferman and **Lula Belle Kent**

They shall mount up with wings as eagles;

They shall run, and not be weary;

And they shall walk,

And not faint.

- From the Book of Isaiah 40, vs. 31.

A NOTE OF THANKS IN PASSING

To the ladies at EBS Business Services, Inc.:
Jannie Barrett, Charlene Meyer, and Shelby Balius
for their gracious help and support.

I owe a Debt of Gratitude to Andrea Long, My
Publishing Services Associate, at iUniverse Publishing. If
Patience is a Virtue, it is surely one of her Many Gifts.

Author's Comments

This book is a work of fiction. Names, characters, places, and incidents are either the product of the author's imagination or are used fictitiously, and any resemblance to actual persons, living or dead, business establishments, events or locales is entirely coincidental. I have chosen to use Dawson and surrounding counties in North Georgia as the setting for my story. They too are used fictitiously and I have used them only because I am a product of that time and place.

God-Fearing Criminals

Part 1

First of all
there must be a
story to tell.

CHAPTER 1

The cold December rain started falling late on Monday afternoon. Falling as a light mist at first, the rain intensified during the night until Tuesday morning broke to a steady downpour that had drenched and soaked everything exposed to the falling torrent. By daybreak, every ditch and gully was running full of muddy red and yellow water, flushing streams and branches full and out of their banks.

William Tate McClure was hoping the late fall spell of Indian summer weather that had taken hold before Thanksgiving would last for a few more days. But as the rain began to slack off by mid morning, a cold wind began gusting out of the Northwest.

The clouds, no longer laden with tons of water, lightened to a blue-gray color and raced along in ever changing patterns. They rode the crest of a wind that was rapidly changing a rainy day into what would be a frigid night.

The mild days and cool nights of Indian summer were being blown away, and Will knew that North Georgia was in for the first cold snap of the coming winter.

The sudden change of weather could not have come at a worse time as far as Will was concerned. His forty-year-old wife of twenty three years was expecting, the birth of their fifth child at any time.

Carrie's pregnancy had not been an easy one. She had supposed herself to be – past my time – but in early March after a spell of dizziness and nausea that lingered on for more than a week, she asked Will to hitch the mules to the wagon and carry her the five miles to the home of Dr. Victor Henry Holden, Jr. Dr. Holden's office was located in his home, as were the offices of almost every country doctor of that day.

The day rarely passed that Carrie did not think back to that raw and windy March morning when Will assisted her onto the burlap bag covered seat of his wagon, wrapped her in an old quilt and drove the five cold and windblown miles to Dr. Holden's office.

Since the days of billowy nausea had started, Carrie made every excuse, and used every reason that came to mind, to convince herself that she was not pregnant. All of her other pregnancies had been accompanied by huge appetites and high spirits. There were many nights when she was filled with such an inexhaustible supply of energy that she would lay wide awake in her bed, impatiently waiting for daybreak to come.

Surely then, Carrie reasoned to herself, this nausea and discomfort must be the result of the pain and depression that she had been warned would accompany menopause. But the uneasy suspicion remained. Try as she might, she could not completely push the fear of a change of life pregnancy from her mind. At least, Carrie thought to herself as Will turned the team into the driveway that lead up to Dr. Holden's house, I am about to find out, one way or the other, very soon.

Carrie noticed immediately the examination that Dr. Holden gave and the tests that he preformed were the same as the previous ones when his diagnosis had always been another pregnancy. She did notice that he seemed to spend more time thumping around on her stomach and back, and listening here and there with his stethoscope. But when he finished and sat down in his fathers battered old desk chair, his diagnosis was the one that Carrie most dreaded to hear.

"Well Carrie, from the way you and Will have been acting I don't suppose that you're going to be very happy to hear this, but you're fixin to have another baby. Though I expect that you were fairly well satisfied that was the case." Carrie made no attempt to answer though she did think to herself, 'at least there is some relief in knowing for sure.'

Vic opened his office door and looked out into the hallway that served as his waiting room. "Come on in here Will and let me tell you what I've found out."

Will and Carrie were among the first to use the young Dr. Holden as their family doctor, after an introduction during the dinner hour of May Meeting at Shoal Creek Baptist Church. Out of the relationship, a life long friendship and respect was developed between Will and Victor's two families. Before he married it became almost a weekly custom for Vic to come by the McClure home for Sunday dinner.

They hunted and fished together as often as possible, and it was during these outings that Will introduced Vic to the corn malt taste of sweet mash corn liquor, as well as the fruity taste and smell of apple and peach brandy.

When Will stopped just inside the door of Vic's office, glancing nervously from his wife to Vic, Vic knew that his friend was in no mood to discuss anything. His only concern at the moment was for his wife.

"Will, I hope you haven't put that rockin chair away, because it looks like your wife is fixin to need it." said Vic.

Will did not appear to understand Vic's attempt to explain Carrie's condition and also to put him in a better humor at the same time. "Why, is Carrie bad sick?"

Vic replied, "No Will, your wife is pregnant and it looks to me like after already having four babies, both of you ought to recognize the symptoms, and you certainly ought to know what causes it."

Will did not reply for a long moment. He stood turning his hat round and round by the brim, finally dropping his hands to his sides and clearing his throat before he spoke. "Well, that's not exactly the news we were hoping to hear Vic, but there's not much that can be done about it now is there."

Vic was not only surprised that they seemed so devastated by the news of a late pregnancy, but his patience was beginning to wear a little thin. "Now the both of you listen to me. Carrie's not the first woman to get pregnant during the change of life, and my guess is that she won't be the last. I have always dreaded for the day to come when there will be no more babies around our house waiting for me to get home in the evening and climbing up in my lap at the supper table. Why I think that's one of life's greatest blessings. I didn't have the greatest childhood myself. I was the only child, and my daddy was gone a lot. We just never did have the chance to do a lot of things together. Fact of the matter is, I came to realize just how important those things are, when I spent a lot of Sundays at yours and Carrie's house before I was married." Vic felt sure, that if nothing else registered, they both had to know that.

"Anyhow, I hope that neither one of you will let your old age keep you from enjoying one more baby, because I think I can guarantee you one thing. This baby will be the last one you will ever have to worry about."

Vic pulled open one of the drawers of his desk and removed four packages of the large white calcium tablets that were now the required supplement to every pregnant woman's diet. "Now Carrie till you get over this morning sickness you'll need to take these with a little something to eat. Only this time I want you to double up on them. Take four a day instead of two. Two before breakfast and two before supper. I want you to get out of the house every day that you can and walk around a while, and I want you to lay down every day right after dinner* and take a nap. You've got to get plenty of rest Carrie, and you might as well get started on it now or you might wind up having to stay in the bed a lot more than you want to later on."

Vic sat quietly for a moment before he continued this time with just a hint of humor in his voice. "I am depending on you to do that Carrie and if you don't I am depending on Will to let me know." Carrie knew he was expecting an answer. "All right Dr. Holden, I'll do everything you tell me to, the best I can."

Vic shifted his attention to Will. "Will, I want you to find some good corn still beer and keep enough for Carrie to have a glass full of it every evening before supper. I think that it will help to settle her stomach, and I'm pretty sure it'll make her sleep better.

"I'll stop by in a week or two to see how you're doing Carrie, and I better not catch you out doin your washin and using a battlin stick. Better get her on home Will. She don't need to be out in this cold wind no more than you can help"

Carrie remembered that Will had hardly spoken on the seemingly endless trip home. She remembered the aloneness and sadness she felt as she sat huddled against Will, wrapped in the old quilt that her mother had helped her to quilt before she and Will were married. She remembered again the grinding jolt of metal wagon wheels on rocks, the jangling rattle of trace chains, the mules tails blowing out to one side in the cold gusting March wind, and she also remembered that she had cried.

CHAPTER 2

When Dr. Victor Holden, Sr. returned from the war, he returned a very sick man. He was sick not only in body, but in mind as well. As a result of severe bouts of depression, his mental state was affected to the degree that he was no longer able to make the day to day decisions and diagnoses required of a practicing physician. Dr. Holden was aware of his condition as was his wife Maude. But out of a sense of loyalty to his older patients, he continued to provide them with medical care, but on a very limited schedule. Dr. Holden began, more and more, to depend on the fortifying effect of alcohol.

It was also Maude who provided him with the solution to his greatest inability. Due to the agony and suffering from his battlefield experience, he returned to his practice unable to deliver babies. Whenever a request came for Dr. Holden to attend at a delivery, Maude referred the caller on to Cora and Nora Perry. Sending word, by way of explanation, that Dr. Holden was unable to come due to his health, and that he recommended the use of the Perry sisters.

During the time that Dr. Holden was on active duty for the Confederacy, Della Perry delivered every baby born in the Amicalola Community of Dawson County, Georgia. She was assisted in the work of "her calling" as she referred to it, by her two daughters Cora and Nora. While they were as yet early teenagers, Della carefully instructed and meticulously trained each of her daughters in the practice of midwifery. At the same time Della had to satisfy herself that they were not at all "squeamish" about dealing with blood and gore that usually accompanied childbirth at that time.

Della also had to teach her daughters the proper way to care for the body of a mother or child who died during childbirth, and their duty to comfort the remainder of the family. "And especially the little ones'" Della always admonished her daughters, "fix them something to eat, and stay with them until some more of the family gets there."

When Dr. Holden returned from the war, Della sent word that she was no longer able to carry on her work as a midwife, but that her daughters were trained and capable of carrying on her practice. She assured Dr. Holden that they were available first of all to assist him as they were needed, but if not; they would carry on her practice if they were called.

The following Sunday after church Maude walked with Della out to the edge of the churchyard where their horses were hitched close beside their buggies. Without revealing Dr. Holden's condition, Maude told Della that for the foreseeable future he was unable to make house calls, and for that reason, he would refer all baby delivery calls to Cora and Nora. With no thought on their part, of having done so, that short conversation gave meaning and direction to the remainder of Cora and Nora Perry's days.

CHAPTER 3

Dr. Holden paid a heavy personal toll as a result of his dependence on alcohol. His daily intake of liquor increased until before two years were out, he had completely surrendered to the mind numbing effects of alcoholism. The realization that he could not hold out until his son, Victor, Jr., completed his internship at Emory Hospital, and come home to take over his practice, seemed to end any desire that he had to continue his lifelong work.

On one occasion, Maude found him sitting in his office with an open jar of whiskey setting on his desktop. He was rocking slowly back and forth, staring at the ceiling with open unblinking eyes. Tears arose in his eyes and coursed a trail down each cheek. When she laid her hand on his shoulder a faint smile of recognition trembled at both sides of his mouth. "Maude, how lonesome I was for you. I would have given up everything I had, if I could have come home long enough to see you and our boy for a while."

He fell silent for several minutes, slowly rocking back and forth, before he continued. "When a fight broke out early in the morning it wouldn't be long before we could hear the wagons coming. We'd go out and help the drivers unload the ones that were alive, and they would take the dead one's on to be identified and buried. We'd take the one's that had to have arms or legs amputated and send the rest on to be sewn up or have broken bones set. Cuttin them boys all to pieces was terrible. We knew that some of them was goin to die and the rest of them would be cripples for the rest of their lives. We weren't doctors; we were a pack of damn butchers.

"But Maude, the thing that I couldn't stand was that smell. It was awful and it was everywhere. My clothes reeked of it, even when I took a bath and put on clean ones. I would wake up in the middle of the night and the taste of it would be in my mouth. I got to where I didn't think I could stand it for another day, and then I woke up one morning and I couldn't smell anything. Honest to God Maude, I thought to myself how lucky I was not to be able to smell anything."

He reached out with a trembling hand and picked up the jar of crystal clear liquor. Two weeks later Victor Jr. was called home from Emory Hospital in Atlanta for his father's funeral.

All through the afternoon and late into the evening they came. On foot, on horseback, riding in wagons and high-top fancy buggies, they came to pay their last respects to the only physician who had ever provided many of them with medical treatment. Victor and his mother received the large number of families, old soldiers and fellow doctors from the war and many of his old patients. Old patients, whom they felt were as much in need of their sympathy, as was their desire to extend it.

During a quiet moment as the crowds began to thin, Victor and his mother were standing together beside the open casket. Trying to comfort his mother as best he knew how, Victor asked if she had any idea what had been the final cause of his father's death? Maude stood looking down at her husband for a long moment before she answered. "Well Victor, you know that he never got over the war, and when he came home he was never able to resume his practice of medicine. He was already drinking a lot, and there toward the end, he got to drinking more and more. I really don't think that any kind of disease killed your Father. It seemed to me that over the last few months he just lost interest in everything. I think that he died simply because he had no desire to live any longer."

CHAPTER 4

When Dr. Holden's son, Victor Holden, Jr. returned home to the Amicalola Community in Dawson County, Georgia to reestablish his father's medical practice, he was met by considerable surprise and doubt. Surprise that he had returned and doubt that he intended to stay. But Victor understood that during his short visits home, he had given none of this friends, nor even his own family, any indication that his intention was to return to the North Georgia Mountains and to eventually carry on his father's practice.

Looking back now on those first footloose months and weekends in Atlanta, Victor remembered that there was very little commitment on his part to anything. That frivolity had lasted until one Monday morning when the Dean of Medical Students called Victor into his office and confronted him with two police reports, and the school record of his attendance and grades for the first three quarters of his freshman year. Victor remembered the slightly amused expression on his face and the friendly glint in his eyes. His voice carried no such expression, and Victor quickly realized that he was in a perilous situation.

"If it wasn't for the fact that I knew your daddy, I'd throw you out of Emory Medical School and send you home this morning. -- Do you understand that Mr. Holden?"

"Yessir"

"No, Mr. Holden, I don't think you do. What I mean is, not only have you violated the rules of this school, which by your signature on this copy of the rules you agreed to abide by; but in addition to that your attendance is barely permissible and your grades are not sufficient to maintain a passing average.

"Mr. Holden, I am going to give you one chance to stay in this school, and one chance only. If at the end of your freshman year of study, there is another mark against your conduct, and if you do not have perfect attendance from now until the end of this school year, and if your grades, from here on out, are not sufficient to give you a passing grade point average for the whole year, I will send your father a complete copy of your records with a personal letter telling him that you have failed your freshman year of study, and I will recommend that you not be permitted to enroll for your sophomore year of study. ---Mr. Holden, do not offer me an excuse, it will avail you nothing."

"Yessir – I mean no sir – I won't."

"Mr. Holden, you are dismissed."

"Thank you, Sir."

Some five years later, while Victor was doing his intern work at Emory Hospital it was this same Dean of Students that sat on a Board of Physicians, and offered Victor an opportunity to remain at Emory as a staff physician. Then during the final days of his internship, Victor received an invitation to join a prominent group of physicians as a junior member of their medical firm.

But the opportunity to remain at Emory, or in Atlanta where Victor had come to enjoy the restless energy of a rebuilding city, was not to be. While Victor did spend some trying days and sleepless nights, when made, the decision was to go home. He knew that, now more than ever, he was needed at home. By his mother as much as by a medical practice that was already there and established, waiting for a practitioner to come. And so it was a joyous bonus that during the last days of parties and promises and farewells, Victor realized just how much he wanted to go home.

CHAPTER 5

Carrie knew when she awoke before daybreak on Wednesday morning that she was about to give birth to the child of her troubled pregnancy. She had felt a change in the baby's position and during the night the pain in her back and hips had increased. Daybreak brought a pale yellow sunrise with ragged clouds being pushed across the sky by a cold gusting wind blowing out of the Northwest. But the morning sun did nothing to raise the frigid temperatures that overnight had fallen into the mid-teens, causing a crust of ice to form on every water filled mud puddle.

Neither did the morning sun and clearing skies raise Carrie's spirits as they usually did. The dull aching pain moved even further down into her lower back and it seemed even into her hip joints. Then, just after midday, she experienced what she felt was her first birthing pain and along with it a rush of fear that surprised even her.

With the exception of her first pregnancy, Carrie had never had to deal with fear. She knew from past involvement about the suffering and danger of early childbirth. As a young girl she learned early the meaning of 'known only to God' etched on a small tombstone. She accepted the risk of bearing a child and the danger of seeing it live through childhood in the early years of her and Will's marriage. But even now, after the long days and sleepless nights of this final pregnancy, her resolve to deliver this baby out of her body and safely into the world had not wavered. The fear that troubled Carrie at the very core of her being, and the fear that she would not name, was that something was wrong with her, yet to be born, child.

CHAPTER 6

Carrie breathed a sigh of relief and felt a lift in her spirits when she looked out the front window and saw the red spoked wheels of the high topped black buggy that belonged to Cora and Nora Perry. Nora was handling the reins to their little dark red mare as they came wheeling up the driveway and into the yard at the side of the house. She applied the foot brake and pulled easily back on the reins. "Whoa Babe. Stop right here please." Cora began folding their lap rugs and gathering their bags and boxes together prior to stepping down from the buggy. Just as she started to stand a strong gust of cold wind rocked the buggy causing the little mare to take a step into the wind to steady her footing. The buggy lurched forward throwing Cora backward into her seat. She spoke to the animal in a voice much sharper and louder than Nora had used. "Stand still Babe, we can't get down with you dancing all over the place."

Then to Nora as she pulled herself up from the seat again, "Gracious sister this weather is turning colder by the minute. Lets get in the house before we either freeze to death or get blown away."

Will came hurrying from the barn followed closely by James, the third oldest, and so far the only boy in the family. "Well Miss Cora and Miss Nora. I sure am glad to see you. I was just fixing to hitch up the team and send James after you. Looks like there's going to be a baby coming here sometime tonight for sure."

Cora sat back on the buggy seat for the second time. She spoke to Will in a voice raised enough to carry over the strong wind. "Well William, if you had only checked the Almanac you would have seen that the signs are in the privates, and also the moon came new over the weekend. Now add to that this powerful change to the weather and I'd have to say if a baby was about ready to be born, then we better get ready for it ourselves, and be quick about it."

Will took the reins from Nora's hands as he answered Cora. "If there's anybody in this settlement that knows Miss Cora, it's you, and nobody will be any happier when it gets here than I will. Besides that, nobody's going to be happier to see you than Carrie is, so get down and go in. James, you carry their things in while I put Babe in the barn and feed her. I'll put the buggy in the hall of the barn so there won't be any danger of it blowin over in this wind."

The two sisters climbed down while James held the buggy steady. Cora gathered her old cloth coat against the cold and hurried towards the house. Nora reached back into the buggy and pulled their old canvas traveler down as she spoke to James. "James I'll carry our overnight bag and you bring the two rag bags." As they walked across the yard toward the porch Nora placed her free hand on James' shoulder and gave it a friendly shake. "My goodness James, I'll bet you've grown a foot since May Meeting. Next thing I know you'll be chasing one of these giggling girls around here, and the next thing you know, if you're not mighty careful, she'll catch you." They were laughing together as they caught up with an impatient Cora waiting on the front porch. James pushed the front door open and ushered the two sisters thorough the front door and into the dimly lit hallway.

*   *   *

Neither of the Perry sisters were very handsome women. Both however had received, on more than one occasion, proposals of marriage. Though most of those proposals came from men whose wives had died and they needed a wife to care for their family, some were from older men who knew the value of an industrious, and of course, a virtuous woman. There were also invitations to marry from an occasional man who realized the advantage of being married to a woman who would soon be part owner in one of the best bottom land farms in Dawson County.

To their chagrin all offers were rejected out of hand. Cora and Nora were well aware that the offers extended were not made in order that they might be loved and cherished. Beside that, their interests lay elsewhere. There was their farm and home to care for and maintain. There was the ever-increasing demand from their practice of midwifery and also assisting Dr. Holden when he requested their assistance. There was also their life long love for Shoal Creek Baptist Church and their dedication to it. No Deacon, or any minister, ever loved their church with the simple devotion that Cora and Nora Perry loved Shoal Creek Baptist Church.

*   *   *

When Victor Holden, Jr. returned to his father's practice, his first visit was to the home of Cora and Nora Perry. He wanted to personally assure them of his desire that they continue to assist him when delivering babies. Since most babies, especially those born in the rural areas of the South were delivered in the home, both the preparations for the delivery and details for the care of the infant had to be made there. With the sisters assisting in the home deliveries Vic did not have to be involved in any of those arrangements, and to Vic that was another of the real advantages of having the assistance of the Perry sisters.

On one occasion, when Vic was at home from Emory Medical School, he voiced his concerns about home deliveries to his father. Dr. Holden gave his son a quick reply "Why hell yes Vic, where else would they be born. Nine tenths of them are born on the same bed they were planted on." Vic noticed the grin tugging at the corners of his father's mouth as he added, "just like you were."

Vic's introduction to what had now become the well known and generally accepted 'Rag Bags' of the Perry sisters did not happen until the first delivery in which he was assisted by the sisters. Nora had made the introductions to Lester Adams and his wife Alice, the mother-to-be. She also pointed out that the four children playing outside in the yard also belonged to Lester and his wife. While Vic was making his initial examination of the patient, he noticed the stack of white clothes, one on either side of the bed. He immediately suspected what they were for, but it irritated his sense of sick room order when he noted the different kinds of material and the various sizes of the cloths.

His examination complete, he turned to Cora and nodded his head indicating the stacks of cloths by the bedside. "Miss Cora, I suppose I know what the two stacks of rags are for, but I would like to know where they came from, and if they are properly sterilized for use in delivering a baby and cleaning up the mother and baby after the delivery is complete?" The answer came immediately. Cora's voice contained neither a conciliatory tone nor one of apology. It contained a note of stern warning that served to remind and inform Vic, that as the new practitioner in the community, his acceptance depended on his ability to perform the work that he was trained for and called here to do. Certainly not to complain or to accuse about the supplies that had been provided for his use during the delivery.

"Dr. Holden, they may be rags, but they are rags provided by the ladies of this community, including your mother. They have been washed and rinsed in boiling water by sister and me. And you are correct in supposing that they are to be used for any need that arises. One other thing that I might add is, we burn every piece of cloth that is used during the baby's birth and the clean up afterwards."

Nora continued in a lighter and friendlier tone. "We already have water boiling on the stove Dr. Holden, and you only have to tell us whatever else you need or want done and we'll see to it. Isn't that right sister?"

"It certainly is sister. Just exactly like we always did for your father."

The sudden anger that had flushed Vic's neck and ears, and hardened his mouth and eyes, subsided as quickly as it had risen. The realization that this was what he wanted in an assistant dawned on Vic just as he was about to vent his anger on the two sisters.

"Well thank you ladies, and yes Miss Cora and Miss Nora, my daddy always impressed upon me the fact that he never found any fault in anything you did while you were assisting him in treating a patient." Vic was very relieved when he heard the breathless gasp of immediate birthing pains coming from the patient. "Now ladies, if you're ready, I believe it's time for us to get started here."

CHAPTER 7

The sisters came bustling past James into the hallway, which ran from the front door to the back door of the house. Then without knocking, through the first door on their right, into the large front sitting room where Carrie was part sitting and part lying in a big overstuffed chair with wide heavy arms. The room was heated by a wide mouthed rock fireplace. Oak logs covered a bed of hot coals and fed the flames that swept up the back of the chimney keeping the room cozy and warm.

They both rushed to Carrie, laughing and hugging, patting her hair into place and holding her hands. They slowly eased her upright in the chair and adjusted her gown about her large unrestrained breasts and huge belly. Nora produced a length of red ribbon from an apron pocket and deftly tied Carrie's long graying hair with a bowtie at the nape of her neck. During all this time they were soothing Carrie with sympathetic small talk that women understand and respond to. Sympathy and empathy that men do not fully understand, and therefore while they happily and vainly receive it, they are not fully capable of giving it in return.

"Gracious me Carrie, have you ever seen such a spell of weather in your life? Just as mild as May on Saturday and Sunday and now everything that cain't move is about to be froze to the ground," Cora began as both she and Nora removed their long coats and heavy shawls, which had been wound about their head and necks. James, without being asked, collected all the garments and carried them back out into the hall where he hung them on large wooden pegs, which were mounted on the wall near the front door.

Cora continued. "Sister and I have been waitin on pins and needles for a week now, sure as certain that Will would come for us at any minute. I just got so uneasy about you that I told sister last night, if Will didn't come this morning, we were going to come over here and look about you."

Then Nora added, "And here we are Carrie, baby or no baby, you're going to have to put us up for the night. I'm not planning on going home on a night like this to a cold bed and no supper."

Carrie's attempt at a smile ended as only a change of expression that mirrored her extreme discomfort. "I've been hoping all day that you would get here. I believe my baby will be born before morning. I've had this awful backache all night and all day today. Now I have this dull aching pain down in my lower parts and I think I had another pain just before you all got here. As soon as Will comes in we may need to go ahead and send for Dr. Holden."

Laurel Jean, at twelve, was the youngest of the McClure children. When Carrie was forced to give up cooking and housework during the last two months of her pregnancy, it was Laurel who inherited the lion's share of the household chores. Laurel did this without complaint and for the most part by herself. Each day when they arrived home from school, James went almost immediately to the woodpile to split and stack enough firewood and kindlin wood on the back porch for the coming night and next day. This left Laurel to prepare the evening meal, get the table set, the meal on the table and, depending on whether or not Carrie felt like coming to the table, see that she had her supper.

James whined endlessly about sweeping floors and making beds, so Will did most of that after they left for school in the morning. Laurel was so terrified that James would "break every dish in the house," that she would not permit him to wash the dishes or even set the table. However, a mutual agreement was reached that her stove wood box would be kept full, the ashes taken out and dumped in the garden, and every water bucket kept full at all times. Laurel was more than happy with the agreement if for no other reason than the full water buckets.

The well that supplied the water for household use was located some fifty yards behind the house. The well was 60 feet deep, and the water was drawn from the well by means of a two-gallon water bucket tied to a rope, and pulled to the top of the well curb on a hand turned windless. Not an easy task for a twelve year old girl during the daytime, but almost unthinkable for one who was terrified of being alone in the dark, as was the case with Laurel.

James did not fully realize just how serious his agreement with Laurel was until one rainy evening in late October. To make matters worse a cold wind out of the northeast drove the falling sheets of rain against the side of the house, causing the old house to shudder and creak. James finished eating a huge supper of squirrel dumplings, hot biscuits covered with freshly churned butter and sorghum syrup, and two large glasses of spring cold sweet milk. Already tired from doing his other chores, he arose from the table and went directly to the living room where he sat reading from his geography book and drowsing by the fire.

Laurel meanwhile cleared the table and washed the dishes and pans from the evening meal. She cleaned the table and swept the floors; put the leftovers out on the back porch where James' beagles were huddled against each other for protection against the wind and rain. Then satisfied that she was finished, Laurel took the kitchen lamp with her into the living room where she set it on the flat top made when Carrie's sewing machine was stowed in its cabinet. She perched on the edge of Carrie's chair, where her mother began combing and brushing her waist length long golden hair.

She looked across at James, still drowsing by the fire, and decided it was time to enforce the terms of their agreement, and prove to her brother that if he expected her to keep her part of the agreement then she had every right to expect the same in return. "James I have used all of the water washing dishes and scrubbing out the pans. Every water bucket and even the kettle is empty. Would you fill at least two of them please? We don't even have any drinking water on the porch."

The reminder and accusation jarred James wide-awake. How could he have been so stupid as to have forgotten the water buckets, he admonished himself, especially since his sister was the one using the water out of them. Why hadn't she reminded him as soon as he had finished his supper? She has done this to me on purpose.

"Mama, can't I wait until in the morning please? I'll get up in the morning as soon as Daddy does and I'll draw all the buckets full, I promise I will." Carrie, knowing how tired her son was bound to be, and aware of the wind and rain lashing against the side of the house was ready to grant her son's pleading request. But she made the mistake of looking at her husband.

Will was not at all inclined to be sympathetic towards his son's predicament. "James, your sister has been in the kitchen ever since you got home from school. She's fixed our supper and put it on the table for us to eat. Now she's washed the dishes and cleaned up the kitchen. So if your end of the bargain is to keep the water buckets full, let's get about it. Bring that lantern in here from out on the back porch and I'll light it for you while you put your coat on."

James pulled on his heavy coat and took the burning lantern from his father's hand. Angry with his father for ordering him to do a job, which he had already agreed to do, and embarrassed by the stern reprimand, he directed a scathing look at his sister as he started for the door. Laurel, with her back toward Will and Carrie, answered with a quick wrinkle of her freckled nose and a turn of her fist that mimicked the wiping of a crybaby tear from her eye.

Carrie took her daughter by the shoulders and turned her around. "Laurel, will you turn around here and sit up straight please? How can I braid your hair with you twisting around and around like this?"

James stomped out of the door in a furious rage.

CHAPTER 8

Laurel came down the hallway from the kitchen, opened the door to the front room and jumped headlong into Nora's arms. Laurel had no living grandparents, the last of them having died just before the turn of the century. While there were various aunts, uncles and cousins who lived in and around the Amicalola community, the two people whom she loved the most outside of her own family circle of course, were Cora and Nora Perry.

That love was returned not only in full measure but, added to that, was the adoration of two women, forever childless themselves, who doted on her as if she were their own. Laurel's love was so precious to her that Nora could not resent the secret awareness that Cora was Laurel's favorite. It was enough that Laurel's love for her was perfect and true. Enough that it did not hurt when Laurel loosed herself from Nora and ran to Cora, throwing her arms around Cora's neck and kissed her again and again on her face.

"Oh Aunt Cora, I'm so glad to see you and Aunt Nora. Mama's been hurting so awfully bad today. I've been praying all day that you would come. I was so thankful when I saw you and Aunt Nora coming up the road." Cora leaned down and kissed Laurel on top of her head where her hair was parted for her braids.

"Now sweetheart you quit all that worrying and fretting. Sister and I are here and we're going to take good care of your Mama until Dr. Holden gets here." Nora dried the tears from Laurel's eyes with a newly embroidered and lace trimmed handkerchief and then pushed it down into Laurel's apron pocket. "Sister, is this not the prettiest little girl you have ever seen?"

Cora, not to be outdone pinned a red hairbow in Laurel's hair. "I know she is sister, and the smartest one I know of to boot. Is that flour I see up there on your forehead child?"

Laurel's face broke into a becoming smile. "Yes," Eagerly waiting for the next question.

"Didn't I just tell you she was smart as a cricket sister? What's them purty little hands fixin us for supper?"

Laurel counted each dish off on one of the fingers of her left hand.

"Well, let's see now. We're goin to have fried chicken and gravy, mashed potatoes, hot biscuits, syrup and butter, and coffee.

Laurel clapped her hands and gleefully added. "And I'm saving the parson's nose for Aunt Nora."

Nora gave her a playful swat on the backside. "Hush that up you little scamp. I'll give you a paddlin and put you to bed without any chicken at all."

Cora had been watching as the pain lines deepened on Carrie's face. Then she heard Will stomping the mud off his boots on the front porch. Just exactly at the right time, Cora thought to herself. "See there sister, I told you if we'd get on down here before night we might get to help eat one of James' dominicker roosters.

"Now then Miss Laurel, you and sister go on back to the kitchen and finish our supper. If I'm not there when it's ready put mine in the warming closet. I've been a cravin hot biscuits and chicken gravy all day, and I don't want mine cold." Cora turned and laid her arm around James shoulder, "James you fill every bucket and pan, you can get your hands on, full of water and get some heating on the stove right away. Sister, tell Will to come in here. We need to get Carrie in the bed now, just as soon as we can make it." Her initial orders given, Cora turned and went quickly back to Carrie's side.

"Carrie can you tell me whether or not your water has broke."

"Yes! I'm sure it has Cora. I think it was about 2 o'clock when I felt my underclothes getting wet, then, just after that, I had another pain. I hate it that I haven't been able to get washed and changed, but I just wasn't sure I could stand up long enough to do it."

Cora patted her arm and assured Carrie of her understanding. "Now, now, honey, you quit worrying about that. That's what sister and me are here for, and we'll have you and everything else ready by the time Dr. Holden gets here, which ain't going to be long now, the way things are lookin to me."

Cora noticed Will standing just inside the bedroom door. "Will come and help me get Carrie over to the bed. She'll be able to walk on her own; I just don't want to take no chances that she might get unbalanced and tip over."

With Will supporting his wife on one side and Cora on the other, they walked Carrie over to the bed and lowered her down until she was part sitting on the bed and part standing on the floor.

"Now Will bring me a dish pan full of warm water and a bar of soap. I want to give Carrie a sponge bath and get her gown on before she lays down."

As Will hurried from the room Cora began "stripping," as she referred to it, Carrie of her clothes. "Carrie do you still have one of them big tailed gowns with the split up the front.

Carrie's face lightened for a few seconds into a weak smile. "Yes, they are over there in the chest of drawers. The bottom drawer I think. Do you remember when James was born and somehow the gown got twisted around my waist? Dr. Holden got mad and ripped it all the way around the middle and threw it out in the middle of the floor."

Cora nodded her head and chuckled as she replied. "I sure do Carrie, but he didn't get the best of us did he? Soon as he left I got it up and mended it, and you had it on when he came back the next day. I know he noticed it, but he never let on and I didn't either."

Nora opened the door and Will came in carrying a large pan of steaming water. Nora was carrying a towel and one of their "Rag Bags." She handed the towel to Cora and removed a large stack of rags from the bag. These she separated, putting an ample supply of the rags on each bedside table. With her toe she pushed the bag of remaining rags under the edge of the bed where they were out of the way, yet easily accessible. Cora directed the pan of water to a convenient bedside stool.

Seemingly without taking charge, Cora began arranging the home delivery room as she knew Dr. Holden would want it. "Now then sister, you and Will go on and eat your supper with the children, while I give Carrie her bath and get her to bed. I want to be in here when she has her next pain, so that I can check the position of the baby."

Cora finished bathing and shaving Carrie and was in the process of pulling on her gown when the next pain came. Carrie caught her breath in a gasp of pain and began to fall backwards onto the bed. Without a second of hesitation Cora grasped her about the ankles and pushed her feet toward the foot of the bed, letting her head fall onto the pillows. Then as she explained to Carrie what she was doing; Cora inserted a finger into the birthing canal to check the location and position of the baby.

Cora quickly completed the simple procedure, but she averted her face away from Carrie. The wizened old eyes blinked together for a long second and her mouth compressed into a firm line of deep concern. Cora's gentle probing had not found the downy crown of a baby's head , but the spilt in the backside of what she felt sure was a larger than normal baby.

Cora busied herself arranging Carrie's gown and bedclothes until she could regain her composure.

"Dear God in Heaven," Cora breathed to herself, "How could something like this happen? After she has had four healthy babies, this one is going to come backwards. With her already weak from being pregnant in the change, I don't know whether or not she'll be able to have this baby, nor if the baby will live if we have to pull it out. The Lord help us that we can save both of them, and Lord only you know how terrible it would be to lose both of them. I need Dr. Holden here as soon as he can make it."

Nora saw the worry on Cora's face as she came thru the door bringing Carrie's supper. "Soup's on Miss Carrie and you are the lucky one. It's chicken gravy on a hot buttered biscuit for you. Sister your supper is in the warming closet. I'll stay with Carrie while you go and eat and visit for a while with Laurel and James. Have there been any pains since I went to the kitchen Carrie?" Carrie hesitated for a few seconds before she answered.

"Yes, a fairly strong one about thirty minutes ago."

"Well now that sounds encouraging," Nora replied as she turned to Cora, her eyes questioning the worry she saw on Cora's face.

"So when are you going to send for Dr. Holden sister?"

"I'm going to send Will after Dr. Holden right now sister, and then I'm going to eat my supper. Notice the time of the next pain and call me if they start coming less than twenty minutes apart."

Cora came quietly into the kitchen where Will, James and Laurel were still sitting at the kitchen table. She went straight to the "Warm Morning" kitchen stove and pulled open both doors to the warming closet. The warming closet is an enclosed metal box mounted on the rear of most wood burning stoves of that day. Mounted about twelve inches above the cooking surface, its purpose is to provide a place to store and keep food warm, especially during cold weather. The warming closet is kept warm, not only by the heat rising from the cooking surface but, by heat from the stove pipe as well.

"Gracious, gracious me Miss Laurel, that looks and smells wonderful and I'm hungry enough to eat every bite of it." Cora did not want to alarm James or Laurel any more than they already were, so she paused for a long moment before she turned and addressed Will.

"Will I want you to go for Dr. Holden now. The pains are coming about twenty to twenty five minutes apart so let's not wait any longer."

James and Will rose from the table, and hurried down the hallway to the coat pegs where they began pulling on their overcoats and hats.

"James, light both lanterns and come help me hook up the wagon."

"Daddy, why don't you let me take a lantern and go after Dr. Holden on foot? I can be a mile on the way by the time you get started in the wagon, and I can walk faster than them mules can at night. Besides that, you need to be here with Mama. It seemed to me like Aunt Cora was worried about something."

Will had noticed the same look of concern on Cora's face and nodded his head in agreement. "Very well son, make all haste you can, and tell Vic that Cora and Nora have been here since late this afternoon."

CHAPTER 9

Vic had seen only two patients in his office during the whole day. When the rain stopped and the wind began blowing the clouds away he had spent most of the afternoon in the barn repairing leaks in his feed room. Vic was amazed at how quickly the sky cleared and how rapidly the temperature fell as the afternoon wore on.

"My kind of weather" Vic thought to himself. "Carrie's got to have that baby soon so Will and me can spend a few days in the high country back of the Amicalola Falls. I'm cravin fresh deer meat for Christmas."

As Vic and Grace and their two children sat down for the evening meal they were all in a very festive mood. The children were sure that the first snow would soon follow this first cold spell of the coming winter. Everyone, Grace and Vic included, joined the lively discussion about Christmas programs at school and at church along with the preparation and consumption of sumptuous meals at family get together's, and of course, the giving and receiving of Christmas gifts.

Franklin Victor, the 'three-year-old apple' of the rest of the family's eye, had slipped down from his hi-seated chair and gone to stand by his mother's side. He lived every day in a state of frightened anticipation. According to the situation that existed at the time, Franklin was threatened that he would be omitted from, or assured of, a visit by a red suited elf during the night of Christmas Eve. His mission, as Franklin understood it, was to reward good boys and girls with toys and candy, and to punish those whose conduct was otherwise, with a bundle of hickory switches. Since before Thanksgiving Franklin's sister was constantly reminding him of his failures and his disobedience. Her threats so convincing that for some of his misdeeds he was only reassured by an unseen pat from his mother's hand.

Vic had just started on a large serving of sweet potato pie when he pushed the curtain aside and saw the bobbing light of a lantern turn off the big road and come up the driveway. As Vic waited for the rap on the front door he had little doubt as to whom it was nor the purpose of their visit. "Abigail will you answer the door please. I expect you'll find its Will McClure and I expect I'm fixin to have to go and deliver a baby."

When Abigail ushered James McClure, instead of his father, into the dining room, Vic was not much surprised, but he noticed that James seemed quite winded. Running at night was very unusual, even if you were familiar with the territory. Vic felt he needed to calm James down if it was at all possible. "Come on in here James and take some of them clothes off. How about a bowl of sweet potato pie? It's so good it'll make you swallow your tongue."

James removed the hat and woolen scarf from his head, but he only unbuttoned his coat. "Evenin Miz Holden, much obliged Dr. Holden, but I'll have to get on back home. Dr. Holden, Daddy sent me to get you. Mama's been in a lot of pain all day and Miz Cora thinks it's her time."

Immediate concern caused Grace to make the next inquiry. "James did you say that Miss Cora and Miss Nora are already there?"

"Yes mam, they got there about two hours before sundown. Miss Cora said that with a new moon last week and with all this change in the weather this week, if Mama wasn't already in labor she soon would be. Me and Daddy sorta thought Miss Cora acted a little worried when she told Daddy to come after you. That's why Daddy stayed there with them and I come after you."

Vic's hands were spread out on the table, one on either side of his pie bowl. When James finished speaking he sat perfectly still in that same position for perhaps ten seconds. Then pushing his chair away from the table and rising to his feet at the same time, he began to make immediate preparations to leave.

"James, go on to the barn and catch out Kate. Get her hitched to the buggy, and I'll be along shortly. We must make all haste to get there. I don't see why Cora has waited so long to send for me, especially if she thinks something might be wrong." James had already retied his scarf, pulled his hat securely down over his ears and buttoned his coat before Vic finished his instructions. As he pulled the front door closed he picked up his still burning lantern and hurried across the yard toward the barn.

Grace lit the lamp in the office and began checking her husband's bag as Vic pulled on his overcoat and hat. It was a chore she performed every morning, and every time he went to deliver a child, regardless of the time.

When he was ready to leave, Vic returned to the dining room and kissed each of the children, and then his wife, good bye. "Now mother, you and the kids go on to bed and get a good night's sleep. Don't worry if I'm not back by morning. I'll probably stay for a while just to make sure that Carrie's all right, and then if it's about time for breakfast, I'll stay and eat with th`em."

Less than an hour later, just before 9:30, Vic reined the buggy in as close to the front porch as he could get, and handed the reins to James. "Just give her some hay James, she's already had grain. Pull the buggy in the hall of the barn if there's room for it. I hate to start anywhere with a buggy that's all frosted over and froze to the ground."

Vic hefted his father's old dog-eared bag out of the buggy, turned and ran up the steps onto the front porch. Without knocking he twisted the doorknob and pushed his way into the hall. He quickly closed the door against the blowing cold, turned, and came face to face with Cora and Will, standing in the hallway just outside the door to the room where Carrie lay.

Cora was holding a lamp in her left hand and guarding the chimney top with her right hand. The flickering lamplight outlined the worry and fear on their faces.

Vic immediately saw their concerned faces but he did not let them see any change in his. "Will, looks like we're in for a pretty bad cold snap. Have you got a hog ready to kill so we can have some fresh meat for Christmas?"

Without giving Will an opportunity to reply, Vic continued. "Well Miss Cora, when James told me that you and Miss Nora were already here, I knew that everything would be taken care of till I could get here. How's Carrie doing?"

"Dr. Holden, she's in a lot of pain and I'm afraid I have found out why. When I was shaving Carrie I decided to check on how close the baby was to starting out. I disremember* what it's called, but the baby's going to come out backwards."

The word shot from Vic's mouth. "Breech! Cora, you mean to say the baby's goin to be born in the breech position?"

"I think it is Dr. Holden, of course I want you to check for yourself."

Vic forced his voice back to a normal tone. "Yes I'll do that, and I'm glad you discovered that problem Miss Cora. As you know that's not a good situation to have, but at least we know about it to start with."

Neither Vic nor Cora mentioned that, of the three breech-born babies that he had delivered, Vic had lost two of them.

Vic came bustling and smiling into the bedroom and over to the bed where Carrie was propped about half way into a sitting position on a pile of feather pillows. "Well Miss Nora it looks like everything's under control just like usual."

Without giving Nora an opportunity to answer, he turned to Carrie. "Carrie, I know that nobody will be any happier to get this over with than you. Cora mentioned that you were in quite a bit of pain during last night, and all day long today. Do you think that's unusually different from your other births?"

Carrie considered Vic's question for a long moment before she replied. "Dr. Holden outside of some discomfort after my water broke; I don't ever remember being in this much pain before."

"I see, well, let's check your blood pressure and pulse and then we'll get started." Upon the completion of checking Carrie's vital signs, Vic conducted a hurried examination and verified Cora's finding that the baby was in a breech position. Vic had little doubt that Carrie's extreme pain was due to the slow movement of the baby down the birth canal, while being doubled into the breech position. Vic was also aware that this breech position posed a serious threat of damage to the baby's umbilical cord, which could in turn result in severe damage or death to the child.

Vic was increasingly concerned for the safety of Carrie's child. The quickest way to remove the child from its mother was now of the utmost importance. Having made that decision, Vic knew that he must tell Carrie and explain the need for haste to birthing her child. When Vic finished his explanation of her child's condition and of his desire to hasten the delivery, he was not surprised at Carrie's first question.

"Dr. Holden, Do you think my baby's still alive?"

Vic answered immediately. "Why I certainly do, Carrie! That's why I want to get the baby out as soon as possible. Now, let's get you situated a little better here, and then" … Before he could finish a hard spasm of pain caught Carrie and twisted her almost off the pillows. Vic caught her by the shoulders and pulled her back to an upright position.

The sisters rushed to their usual place, one on either side of the bed and began to hold and support Carrie upright on the pillows.

Vic made his second visual examination. "Well Carrie you know what to do now. Take a deep breath and push down as hard as you can." Vic made another visual check of the baby's position just as the old pendulum clock on the mantel finished striking 2 a.m. He noted little if any change since he had made the first examination around 10 p.m. He was also aware that Carrie was growing weaker, that she was less responsive to the birthing spasms, and that her speech was almost incoherent.

Cora and Nora were increasingly concerned about Carrie's deteriorating condition. They were aware, just as Vic was aware, that a time of decision was at hand. Vic was also aware that if a decision had to be made, they were in favor of saving Carrie first and the baby second. Carrie was just needed too much by her husband and children. The continuation of the home meant everything. A baby's funeral was still an accepted part of raising a family in the early part of the twentieth century.

Vic's intention was, as it had been to start with, to save both mother and child. He had not given up on that plan as yet. He had one other method he was about to try. "Method or trick makes no difference just as long as it works," Vic thought to himself. He was standing at the foot of Carrie's bed, about to begin, when Carrie raised her head and glared at Vic with pain hardened eyes.

"Dr. Holden you said you wanted to get the baby out as quick as possible. That was four hours ago and the baby's still not here. I've gotten too weak to have this baby. Please Dr. Holden, do whatever is necessary to get my baby out alive."

Vic slapped the footboard of the old iron bed with both hands so hard that it shook the whole bed. "Carrie it's too late to cut your belly open and take your baby out that way, because it's already too far down in the birthin canal, or at least I think it is. Now I think you can have this baby, but you're goin to have to make up your mind to do it. Grace and me got in a little disagreement about having babies right after she had our first one. She contended that if it was left up to a man to have babies there wouldn't be but one in each family and it would mostly put a stop to what caused em. Well I contended right back that she might be right about having babies, but I had my doubts about the other.

"What I'm trying to say Carrie is that I have never doubted that carrying a baby and having a baby is mighty rough on a woman. But, I don't know that from first-hand experience because that's the part of it that the good Lord gave to the women folks to do." Here Vic paused for a moment, and then he continued, emphasizing every word. "However there is one thing that I do know about it, and that is, they are a lot easier and a heap more fun a going in than they are a coming out!"

Carrie lashed back at him in a furious rage. "That sounds just about like a man. I don't believe any of you think about anything else, you and Will McClure included. There's not a one of you that knows or cares anything about what a woman has to go through. If I was able to get my foot up there, I'd kick your damned old head off." Even before she finished her tirade, a spasm of pain caught Carrie and this one did not let up. She sat upright in the bed, throwing Cora and Nora to the floor.

A wailing screech of pain formed deep in Carrie's breast and came roaring up and out of her mouth "aaaaaaaaaaaaaaooooooooooooooh God help me, please help me."

As Vic was helping the sisters get Carrie back on the pillows, he glanced down and saw the little backside appear.

"Keep pushin Carrie, keep a-pushing, its little tail end just came through."

"I can't – I can't – I can't"

"Can't the Devil—you already have just about done it.

"Help me here Nora-- wipe its face off and clean its mouth out, why it's a little ole boy, Miss Cora, see his little spouter a stickin out."

Before Vic could hold the baby up for everyone to see, it drew in its first quivering breath, and exhaled it along with an angry blast for everyone to hear.

CHAPTER 10

Will busied himself over Carrie's wooden flour bowl. He had formed each huge biscuit and then folded it into a lard smeared baking pan. Will was in the midst of preparing breakfast for, as he put it, "The whole push of you to show my appreciation to you for gettin my boy here in one piece, even if he was bent double in the middle."

Vic was sitting on an old ladder backed chair, which was leaned back against the kitchen wall, his boot heels hooked over the bottom rung of the chair. Sitting on the kitchen worktable was a dark brown earthen jug and two glasses. The glasses were about half filled with crystal clear, sweet mash, corn whiskey. "Mighty fine liquor Will, mighty fine. Did you make it?"

Will dusted the flour from his hands into the flour bowl and together with the flour sifter, returned them both to the bottom shelf of the cupboard. "No Vic, I didn't make it. I got it from them Darby boys on the other side of the Amicalola Falls. It's sweet mash, but I don't think it's been doubled. But you're right about it though, it's pretty good liquor."

While Will was talking he had added wood to the stoves firebox and closed the damper. Then pulling the oven door open he pushed one of the two large pans of biscuits inside and quickly closed the door. "Now then, let's make some gravy and we'll be ready to eat here very shortly."

Will took the skillet in which he had already prepared a large platter of, hot pepper and sage, sausage patties, and set it back on the hottest eye of the stove. To the remaining pieces of sausage and drippings he added two handfuls of flour, and some salt and pepper. When this mixture was browned, he added two bowls of milk and began to stir. Then he asked Vic the question that Vic knew was coming. Vic was glad that it had come sooner than later.

"Vic, I noticed back there, before Carrie got so mad, or you intentionally made her mad, that Cora and Nora were gettin mighty nervous and upset themselves. Vic, was we about to lose Carrie?"

Vic took a small sip from his glass and returned it to the table before he answered. "Well, the chances were gettin kind of slim that we could save both of em, and they knew it. Of course they wanted Carrie saved, if it came down to it, and they knew that the time had about arrived to make that decision. Carrie was almost out of strength."

"Well it looks like you made the right decision Doc and I sure do appreciate it."

Vic chuckled and reached for his glass. "Yeah, I guess it was. Anyway it worked didn't it? But, I'm satisfied it was that hellacious screamin and hollerin that got the baby to movin, and that was what had to happen. As soon as she let loose with that scream that boy came a slidin out of there so fast I liked to have dropped him. I still cain't believe how fast and easy it was. There I was one minute, about to decide to pull him out anyway I could get him out, and the next minute he was outta there, squallin at the top of his lungs, and we was all a squallin with him."

Just as Will was pouring his gravy into two large bowls, Cora and Nora came hurrying into the kitchen for breakfast. Vic jumped to his feet and reached into the cupboard for two more glasses. "Come in, come on in here ladies, are they doin alright?"

Nora answered in a voice slowed by exhaustion. "Everybody in there's asleep; that big ole black headed boy included." Nora's face creased into a smile as she continued. "He was raisin all kind of cain till we got him washed and wrapped up in a warm blanket. We laid him next to his mama and he went sound asleep.

Vic poured a fair sized drink into each of the glasses. He handed a glass to each of the sisters, and gave Will's glass back to him and then reclaimed his own. "Well, his first day has been a long one, and I'm glad he won't be able to remember it, but one of us can tell him about it someday.

"Its' been a long night for us too, but everything's turned out good. I just wish that all of life's bad situations could turn out this good."

Each glass was lifted, drained and returned to the table.

There was no desire on anyone's part to celebrate the occasion, but they did feel that they had shared together a moment of time when all of the elements of life and death were present. They also shared together the belief that their efforts were not altogether responsible for the outcome of the event they had just experienced together.

Will broke into the spell of quiet reflection by pulling one of the pans of biscuits out of the oven and shoving the other pan in and closing the door. "All right, breakfast is right now ready, let's eat while it's hot."

Vic rapidly consumed a second helping of food, drained his coffee cup, and pushed the eating utensils to one side. With a dishcloth that was lying next to Nora's plate, he carefully wiped clean the area around his plate, removed the birth certificate forms from his inside coat pocket and spread them out before him on the oilcloth-covered tabletop. "Now then, let's get this boy's paperwork done so that everybody will know who he is, then I'm going to have to be getting on home. It's coming daylight."

With that Vic began filling out the forms answering most of the questions himself, inquiring of Will and the Perry sisters for the remaining information that he needed.

Born to <u>William Tate and Carrie Mae McClure</u>

A <u>male</u> child <u>at 3am</u> on <u>Thursday December 7, 1905, in Dawson County Georgia.</u>

Weight at birth_____

"How much did he weight Miss Cora?"

"I estimate he weighed a little over eight pounds Dr. Holden."

"<u>Eight pounds</u> and <u>four ounces.</u>"

"Very good, that sounds just about right."

Name, first or given_____

"What are you going to name your boy Will?"

"Well, Carrie said if it was a boy she would like to call him Ben."

<u>Ben</u>

"All right, what else?"

"That's all she said Vic, Just Ben."

"Miss Nora wasn't it your Grandpa Perry that was killed at Manassas Creek?"

"Yes, it was Dr. Holden."

"What was his given name?"

"It was Tyler, Dr. Holden."

"<u>Ben Tyler McClure</u>," Vic filled in the form.

"Ben Tyler McClure, how does that sound to you Will?"

"Sounds good to me Vic, mighty fine."

"I'll get this recorded the next time I'm in the courthouse and I'll get you a copy of the birth certificate."

Vic pushed himself away from the table and brushed the breadcrumbs from his lap onto the floor. He sat quietly for a moment looking at each person seated around the table. Suddenly his face broke into a warm smile, and he gave an appreciative nod of his head. Then almost as one they arose from the table and followed Vic out onto the back porch. They were greeted by frigid temperatures, and a thick layer of white frosted crystals that covered everything in sight. The eastern sky was a picture of moving color. The dark gray of first light brightened quickly into a light filled gold, and in rapid preparation for a rising sun, into a brilliant rose.

The wind had completely died away.

CHAPTER 11

When Carrie learned that her child was born in the breech position, and that she had been very close to being unable to deliver him, she could not rid herself of the deep-seated worry that some unnatural condition would still claim her child. The baby however, gave her no reason to be concerned about his condition. From the very first he thrived on Carrie's milk with little more than a mild case of colic. He soon adapted to his own schedule of eating and sleeping. He usually awoke once in the middle of the night, suckled hungrily from both of Carrie's breasts, and immediately went back to sleep for the remainder of the night.

Then after about three months, just when Carrie was beginning to feel comfortable with her baby, she noticed a change in his daily routine that started her worrying again about his condition. After each feeding, even the night feeding he began to cry in a small whining voice until he cried himself to sleep. After a week had passed and it seemed to Carrie that he cried longer each day before finally falling asleep, Carrie sent for Dr. Holden.

When Vic came the next day he instructed Carrie to lay the baby on the bed and to remove all of its clothes. Vic watched the baby playing for several minutes before he reached out and pressed on its stomach. After which Vic thumped about on its upper stomach and chest and then in a move that startled Carrie, he stuck his little finger in the baby's mouth for about ten seconds. Vic took the baby's temperature and instructed Carrie to put his gown back on. "No bowel trouble right," Vic inquired.

"No-none at all Dr. Holden," Carrie answered.

"You don't think there's anything wrong with him then?" she asked, as she laid Ben in his crib.

"Oh yes, Miss Carrie, there's something wrong with him all right. The same thing that's wrong with half the young'uns on the face of the earth today, and most of them can't do anything about it. In fact, a lot of them are going to die from it.

Carrie's voice rose in fear of Vic's diagnosis; "What in the name of the Lord is it?"

"He's hungry"

Carrie's mouth fell open.

"He's what?"

"Carrie, are you goin dry?"

Carrie's neck and ears flushed red.

"No, I'm not. They're both full every time he starts to nurse."

"Well all right then, but he's needing more than he's gettin, so let me tell you what to do. Take a pint of cow's milk and add boiled water till you make a quart out of it. Add a tablespoon full of honey and bring it to a boil for about fifteen or twenty seconds.

"Then try to get it about the same temperature as yours. He'll let you know if it's not. Start him out on two ounces after each feeding, and then after a week increase it up to three ounces. Just be careful not to overdo it to start with."

As Vic stepped down from the back porch he met Will coming to the house from the barn, "Well Doc, is my boy all right. Carrie's been worried about him cryin after he's been fed."

"Yeah, he's all right."

"Well I figured he was, how much I owe you?"

"Oh I don't know; bring me some peach brandy if you have some. Apple if you can't get peach."

"All right, I think I know where I can get some. Stay with us Doc, and we'll have some dinner pretty soon."

"Much obliged Will, but I better be gettin on. Will you ought to check up on that boy's eatin place, I'm surprised you can't tell when a feller's hungry."

"What?"

Vic's answer was a wide grin and wave of his hand as he wheeled the horse and buggy down the driveway.

Will turned and started up the steps to the back porch before he realized what Vic was referring to. "Well I will just be damned."

CHAPTER 12

Ben did not stay a baby for very long, or at least it did not seem that way to Carrie, who watched as her son changed in some way almost every day. Carrie soon realized that this child of a troubled pregnancy, that she had not at first wanted, became more precious to her as he grew more and more independent of her. She could not bear to wean him, even letting him continue to suckle from an empty breast, until he finally turned away from her aching nipples, and lay at her side in peaceful slumber, his mouth continuing to move in the suckling motion.

Will lingered by the fireplace, after his noon meal, bouncing Ben on his knee until he became drowsy for his afternoon nap.

Laurel and James rushed home from school and competed for his attention until they were forced away by their evening chores.

Carrie was even more amazed when Laurel began volunteering to give Ben his tub bath. They shrieked and splashed water on Laurel and on the floor until Carrie made her take him out because the water was getting cold. Then after Ben was pinned in his diaper and his long gown tied at the bottom to keep his feet warm and put to bed; someone, usually Laurel, shared some humorous incident from Ben's day.

"Laurel please sit still honey, your hair has not been washed and plaited since Saturday night and tonight it must be done. It even has the old soured smell about it tonight."

"Oh Mama, it's not that bad. The smells from the cookstove make my hair smell just as much as anything else. Besides that, washing my hair so often in the wintertime causes me to keep a bad cold all the time."

The corners of Carrie's mouth traced a smile. "I wonder if you have considered getting the water a little hotter and also to quit fooling around so long. Nobody should require over an hour to take a bath and wash and dry their hair."

"Mama, do you know what Ben did while I was giving him his bath tonight?"

"I would not be surprised at anything honey. What did he do?" Carrie asked as she continued pulling the brush through her daughter's long hair.

"He peed in his bath water."

"Oh no!" James laughed as he laid his book aside.

Carrie laughed and decided to tell her story. "Well, let me tell you what that young man did to me today. When I was changing his diaper before I put him down for his afternoon nap, he peed in my face."

Even Will joined in the laughter when Carrie recounted that incident about his son.

CHAPTER 13

It was not that the Perry sisters came to visit at the McClure home any more often than they ever did, but they did start arriving late Friday afternoon instead of Saturday, after preaching and conference at Shoal Creek Baptist Church. Cora and Nora were welcome visitors wherever they went, but especially so at Will and Carrie's house.

Nora said it best. "Well, we know which room we're goin to sleep in, so we just put on our aprons and get busy. There's always plenty to do and Carrie's not picky about gettin a little help and we don't mind helpin."

They especially looked forward to seeing Laurel whom they knew loved them both without reservation. And then of course, there was Ben. "Why sister I believe that little tyke already knows us. Look at him kick those little feet, and the way he's waving those little hands around."

But regardless of where they were, on Saturday before the third Sunday, Cora and Nora made whatever preparations were necessary to arrive at Shoal Creek Baptist Church at least thirty minutes before the start of the 2 o'clock service. The Perry family had been members of Shoal Creek Baptist Church, "Longerin any of us can find any record of," according to Cora, and, a Perry has been the Clerk ever since before the war." The Saturday afternoon service started promptly at 2 o'clock, with conference, the business session of the church, to immediately follow. There were occasions when the Saturday afternoon services were cancelled due to a funeral. This was understood because 2 o'clock in the afternoon was the usual and accepted time for a funeral. But the third Sunday of the month was preaching day at Shoal Creek Baptist Church and that did not change.

The third Sunday in May was set aside for homecoming and foot washing. Dinner was spread on a long table built in the shade of huge oaks that ringed the church yard, and for the next hour everyone ate, renewed old acquaintances, explained to each other how they were related, showed off their babies and shared the latest community gossip. The children raced around the church and into the woods, while the younger set spread blankets and sat together or paired off and walked back and forth to the spring that provided water for the church. The elderly were assisted back to their places in the church, where they sat fanning themselves in the afternoon heat, waiting for the afternoon services to start. The ladies repacked their leftovers and returned the boxes and baskets to the family wagon or buggy.

Then just before returning to the church for the start of afternoon services, several of the families called their children together and with them walked across the dusty road into the church cemetery. There they visited the family burial plot, pointing out to the children who was buried where, how they were related, and any interesting or unusual circumstances about their life and death. These stories were told and retold to children about their ancestors, from where they originated, and how they had come to be here. These stories were considered to be as important to a young boy or girl's upbringing as any classroom training they might receive. In addition to knowing something of their ancestral background, having a sense of place and a sense of belonging, was of the very first importance to these mountain people. Some of the elderly still suffered from the lingering after effects of war.

The afternoon services were started with singing. Song leaders or choristers from Shoal Creek and surrounding churches came forward and led the congregation in their favorite hymn. It was not at all unusual for one or more quartets to be present, and they were always well received.

There was always in attendance several visiting preachers, and some of those who, 'felt led to say a few words,' ended up by preaching for several minutes. As Boyd Williams, the pastor of Shoal Creek at that time, always reported to those who were not in attendance, "the day was far spent when the meeting was dismissed."

But by far the most important event in the life of Shoal Creek Baptist Church was the Summer Revival. The success or failure of its summer revival judged the strength of any church, at that time. The Shoal Creek Church was recognized as one of the stronger churches in Dawson County, and in the year 1912 the summer revival did not disappoint. The Revival always started on the third Sunday in July and continued thru the following week, with meetings at 11:00 in the morning, and in the evening beginning at "twilight-candlelight."

The baptizing service was held on the following Sunday morning, and the baptizing was done just below the covered bridge on the Amicalola River. Since the McClure farm was nearby, Will was expected to mow the riverbanks and make sure there was a good place to enter and exit the water. At the water's edge, Will dug out an area about a yard square back into the riverbank and covered it with large flat rocks. He did this especially for the young ladies having to cope with long dresses as they stepped from the riverbank down into the water. Then to complete his preparation, Will waded out into the water and drove an eight-foot Alder-wood pole into the center of the baptizing hole. He always left two smaller poles stuck into the bank at the water's edge for the preachers to use to steady themselves against the strong current of the Amicalola River. Will did not mind the work involved in making preparation for the baptizing. As a matter of fact, without ever saying so, and without ever knowing why, he always felt a great deal of personal satisfaction from doing the work.

There were fourteen "candidates for baptism," and a huge crowd of family and friends gathered for Shoal Creek's baptizing on the following Sunday morning. Cora and Nora Perry along with some mothers and other family members stood among the large group of converts that were waiting to be baptized. They were busily engaged in making sure that each person, especially the young ladies, were properly attired and otherwise ready for their baptism. Long hair was either braided or tied with ribbons down the back. All necklaces, bracelets and earrings were to be removed. "They'll get all tangled up and broke or washed away mor'n likely. Make sure you know who has your towel and change of clothes. Everybody needs to get their clothes changed just as quick as you get out of the water. Everybody knows that the water in the Amicalola River is near about as cold in July as it is in January. We don't want anybody catching their death of cold from getting baptized."

Carrie and Will did not attend the baptizing on that hot Sunday morning in July. Carrie did not attend because she wanted to have her Sunday dinner finished when their dinner guests, along with their own children, returned from the baptizing and revival closing church service. A large Sunday dinner would be needed to feed Cora and Nora Perry, Grace and Victor Holden and their two children, as well as their own family.

Will excused himself by saying that he had already spent most of his Saturday at the baptizing hole, so he wasn't much interested in going back on Sunday, even if it was for the baptizing. The real reason being that he wanted James, Laurel and Ben to enjoy the fellowship, and participate in the experience of baptizing day at Shoal Creek Baptist Church. With Laurel at the church, and a huge Sunday dinner to prepare, Will knew that Carrie would need some help if the meal was to be completed on time.

Cora and Nora came hurrying into the kitchen, tying on their starched Sunday aprons as they came. "Well Carrie, are you about give out?" Cora inquired as she began removing glasses from the kitchen safe. "I believe every preacher that was there had to say a few words before the meeting was dismissed."

Grace looked up from where she was checking each place setting and said, "Well I know I was about give out ---- about give out of patience that is. I'll bet it was ninety degrees in that church and there wasn't a fan to be had anywhere."

The men folks, as they were referred to, came filing thru the kitchen door and began taking their usual place at the table. Every person there had eaten at Will and Carrie's table on many occasions and therefore needed no direction to their usual eating place.

Will offered up his usual – "Lord we thank thee – " Sunday blessing, followed by his usual invitation when guests were present … "Now you see what's here and you know you're welcome to it, so let's take out and eat."

In the midst of bowls, platters and pans being passed around and plates filled, Carrie gave James a curious look. "James, are you not going to change out of your Sunday clothes? I don't want you to drop food or get something spilt on your best clothes."

Laurel and Nora exchanged knowing smiles, as Laurel broke the news that had already swept thru the community grapevine. "Mama, James has got him a new sweetheart, and her name is Eunice Baker."

James gave his sister a scathing look, "Hush Laurel, you don't know nothing and besides that, it's none of your business."

"I know more than you think I do. I saw you and Eunice standing out behind the church holding hands and you walked her to their wagon and helped her climb up and sit down on the wagon seat. You never have helped me climb in the wagon James. I wonder why that is?"

"That's because you can stand flatfooted on the ground and jump all the way over the sideboards into the wagon bed. Mama, will you make her hush?"

"The both of you hush and eat your dinner. I don't see any reason why you should be so touchous about it James. I've known Eunice all her life, and I think she's a very nice girl."

Throughout the conversation Will and Victor remained silent listeners. Victor was next to get involved in the discussion. "I'll tell you something else she is James. Since she is Raymond's only daughter, she is the apple of his eyes, both of them, and that's all right. There's a couple of prize apples sitting around this table today. But one other thing that you ought to be aware of, and that is, that as far as Raymond and Lettie are concerned, Eunice Baker can walk on water. Do they know that you're courtin their daughter James?"

"Yessir they do Dr. Holden. That's the reason I haven't changed out of my Sunday clothes Mama. They've invited me to go with them to the Revival at Corinth tonight. I mean they and Eunice have."

Nora faked a look of pure devastation and slowly shook her head from side to side. "Well, well, James, you can't say you weren't warned. I tried my very best to tell you. Now here you have been caught not only by Eunice, but by the whole Baker family.

Laurel averted her face away from the table, her perfectly plaited and ribboned pigtails dangling and shaking down her back. "Oh my, the chosen one."

To James' relief Cora changed the direction of the conversation.

"Speaking of walkin on water Victor, it does seem to me like an odd set of circumstances when your wife and children can make it to the baptizing, but for reasons unknown and I hope for excuses not offered, you just can't make it. I'd rather you didn't try to tell me it was too hot, because then I'll have to remind you that it's July and it's supposed to be hot."

Victor knew that he was being lectured but he did note just a trace of humor in Cora's voice. "Now, now, Miss Cora, you know as well as I do that the Good Book says that on the seventh day the Lord rested from all his labors. I was only doin the best I know how to keep that example in its proper perspective."

Grace gave her husband a good-natured pat on the back. "My dear, it is a great comfort to me to know that I have such a pious husband. And if sitting on the back porch, naked to your waist and with your shoes off, is your way of keeping the Lords example in its proper perspective, then I want everybody here to know that your wife is the last person alive that would discourage you from the practice of your convictions."

Just as Grace finished the recount of her husband's Sunday morning spell of laziness, and her tacit acceptance of his reason for it, Will finished his helping of blackberry pie, pushed his plate away and smiled at Grace from his place at the head of the table. "Grace that's about as good of a sermon as I've heard lately, and it's just about the right length too. Now I hope your husband was payin attention and you got your message across because we need a doctor around here just about every day. What we don't need is another poor prophet."

Cora stared up the table at Will and made the only comment.

"Well, I wish I may never."

But Will was not finished. "Doc, it looks to me like you're just getting in deeper and deeper all the time. If you're finished eatin why don't we go out on the front porch and see if they ain't a cool breeze comin from some direction. James it might not be a bad idea for you and Ben to come along too."

*   *   *

As a result of the union between Eunice Baker and James McClure, eleven children were born, of which nine survived. There were six girls and five boys, which included two sets of twins. Their first born was a boy named James Raymond McClure, Junior, after his father and his grandfather Baker. At the age of seventeen James, Jr. came home one night from the revival at Shoal Creek, woke his parents, and told them he had answered the call to be a preacher.

Several years later, Rev. James Raymond McClure, Jr., then serving as the pastor of Shoal Creek Baptist Church, conducted a service there that had a defining effect on the life of Ben Tyler McClure.

CHAPTER 14

On Christmas Day of 1912, Eunice Baker and James McClure were both invited to attend a party at the home of Abigail Holden. No one at the party was at all surprised when James and Eunice arrived together. They had been "going steady" since the revival meeting in July and their marriage was considered just a matter of time, or as the teenage girls called it – any minute now.

What did cause a few soft – ahhs – followed by a ripple of laughter across the room was the lateness of the hour. During the shortest days of winter, social get-togethers usually started at nightfall. James and Eunice were over an hour late arriving at Abigail's party.

Grace immediately recognized the look on their faces, and remembered the embarrassing thrill of having a secret that you wanted to tell, but didn't know how. With the easy grace of a woman's "born with" intuition, Grace linked up arms and steered the willing couple through the back door and out into the brisk temperature on the back porch. "Alright, you two, no more secrets from me – when did it happen, and who did it?"

Grace's direct confrontation left James red-faced and speechless. Eunice, already red-faced and breathless, blurted out the whole story. "We got married at five o'clock this evening, by Preacher Boyd Williams. He married us at his house and there wasn't anybody there but him and Callie. That's why we were an hour late gettin to Abigail's party."

James finally regained his voice. "That's right Mrs. Holden. We come straight on here without stoppin. We didn't want to be any later than we already were."

When Vic came looking for his wife, he was not at all surprised to find her and Eunice, laughing and hugging, with tears streaming down their cheeks. Grace made the announcement that Vic already expected to hear. "Victor, let me be the first to introduce you to Mr. & Mrs. James McClure. They were joined in matrimony at 5 o'clock this evening by the Reverend

Boyd Williams. You should feel complimented, because outside of the Reverend Williams and his wife Callie, we are the first to know."

Vic surprised James by grabbing him up into a giant bear hug and planting a kiss on his forehead. Grace was so taken aback that she could only mumble. "Well Victor, I wish I may never."

Then he gathered Eunice in his arms, kissing her on the forehead, and then tenderly once on each cheek. Vic turned and gazed at his wife through watery eyes.

"Well Victor, I've never seen you act this way before. What is wrong with you?"

"Well Grace, this is sort of a milestone for me too I guess. This is the first time that two babies, who, I delivered into the world have grown up and gotten married."

Grace slipped her arms about her husband's waist. "Victor, I'm sorry, I should have known that. But since you're about to get a little drippy about this particular milestone, I'll fetch that fruit jar full of spirit lifter that you have concealed behind my cupboard. I bet that'll restore your vim and vigor."

"Damn Right, that's the best idea you've had today woman. And besides that we need something to make a toast with. It's not everyday that we have weddings, and pass milestones, and from the sound of things, a real good party to boot."

The smile faded from James' face and he gave Vic a quick shake of his head. "I'm much obliged Dr. Holden, but I better not take any. If I was to take Eunice home with the smell of liquor on my breath, her Daddy would probably make me go home without her. You know how dead set he is against anybody takin a drink."

Vic cocked his head to one side and lowered one eyelid at James. "Naw, hell no, you ain't takin Eunice home tonight. This is your wedding night boy. You can't do nothin there."

James face and neck blushed a deep red again, "I wasn't plannin on doin anything there."

"So that means doin something about that situation before you get there. You've got to use a little initiative my boy."

"What does that mean Dr. Holden?"

"Well, the night that Grace and I got married, I was in about the same condition that you are in now. We were on our way home from the reception at the church to Grace's house where we were to spend the night. I suddenly realized that her daddy's barn was about three hundred yards from the side of the house, and that it was right beside the road, and the barn loft was filled with fresh hay."

Grace interrupted with a cool warning. "This is not true confessions Victor. I know that most men are simple minded about that subject, but you don't have to be stupid along with it."

"My Dear, having been born and raised in Dawson County, I learned long ago that the one rule to live by, is that you never reveal anything that has been concealed. But dear heart, I shall never forget the expression on your face when your mother stood behind you the next morning at the breakfast table. She picked something from your hair, threw it in the fireplace and asked, "Grace, did you brush your hair this morning? That looks like a piece of hay in your hair."

Grace plucked the glass from Vic's hand and then threw the remainder of its contents out into the yard. "All right buster, that's all for you. That only gets you a lot deeper in my doghouse than you already are."

Vic countered just as quickly. "And now James, you know where the expression, 'A dog is man's best friend' comes from."

Vic observed Eunice as she turned her face away, her shoulders shaking with laughter. 'at least somebody is enjoying my case of foot in the mouth disease.' Vic mused to himself, painfully aware that his apple brandy loosened tongue had probably earned for himself several nights of frigid refusal.

Vic handed James a keychain that held two keys. "James, I'm sure you know how to get to mine and your Daddy's huntin cabin don't you?"

"Yes sir, I do."

"I'm talkin about the short cut where you have to go down that bluff on foot."

"Yes sir, I know how to go that way too."

"I figured you did. Well, everything's there that you'll need except some sleepin clothes, and Grace'll get them for you. Take your lantern and one of mine from right over there, and ya'll take off on your honeymoon.

"Eunice, if I can get to your folks house before Callie Willams does, I'll tell them that Boyd married you and James McClure this afternoon at 5 o'clock and that you have gone on your honeymoon, and that's all I'll tell them."

James slowly shook his head at Eunice. "Boy, Oh Boy! I hate to think what your Daddy will have to say about that."

Eunice gave Grace a half wink and took James by the arm. "All right buster, you let my Mama take care of my Daddy's mad spells, and you start taking care of your wife. Let's go, shall we."

James and Eunice were barely out of sight when Vic began making preparations to leave himself. "Grace, break up the party and send them home whenever you are ready. Tell Laurel to break the news to Will and

Carrie, and that they are gone on their honeymoon. It won't take Will long to figure out where they are, and he can tell Carrie if he wants too. I'll leave that up to him."

CHAPTER 15

Just after midnight Vic returned to a quiet house. Using great care he quietly crossed the front porch, opened and closed the front door and silently tiptoed his way along the hall until he reached his and Grace's bedroom. As he was removing his overcoat he was surprised to see a dim light shining under their bedroom door. Opening the door just enough to slip thru, Vic was astonished to find his wife reclining on a pair of white satin pillows that he had given her for a anniversary present a few years before. But what really captured and held Vic's attention was his wife's gown.

Made from a deep rose material, a white ribbon was sewn in at the top, causing a ruffle in the gown at both front and back. Grace was wearing the gown so far off her shoulders that the upper swells of her breasts were bare. Vic could see the firm protrusion of her nipples just below the ribbon line of her gown. The bottom part of the gown was sewn to be loose fitting and ankle length, but was split thigh high on both sides and held together with little bow ties of the same white ribbon.

Vic leaned across and nuzzled his wife's neck and shoulders. "My beautiful wife, wearing a rose colored gown, laying on satin pillows, waiting for me to get home. If I had known that I would have run all the way."

"How do you like my gown? I made one for me and one for Abigail. She is really excited to have a new gown for Christmas."

"The gown looks terrific, but I'm a little bit more interested in what's in this one right now. Can I untie these little white ribbons on either side of your gown?"

Grace replied in a voice just above a whisper. "Why do you want to do that? You already have my gown below my breasts. Untie the bow at the top, and take it off from the bottom."

Grace's rose colored gown floated across the foot of the bed, and onto the bedroom floor. "I still think our little episode in Daddy's barn loft was kind of romantic. Do you remember Vicky?" Grace used the name that she kept secret and used only in the most intimate of times. Only she knew that it delighted her husband.

"Damn right, and that little episode, as you call it, was what convinced me that I had the right girl. Let's throw these pillows out on the floor too; they are just going to be in our way."

"My goodness Vicky, first my gown and now my pillows, that doesn't leave anything but me and the sheets."

"Forget about the sheets sweet girl, you're what I've been wanting all day long." Vic reached for his wife, but she was already moving into his arms. Her presence in his arms and the feel of their bodies pressed together immediately fired their passion for each other. Victor brought complete trust with no reservations to their lovemaking, while Grace responded by surrendering to him completely. She wanted her husband to know that she was a passionate woman. Her body urged him to proceed with complete immersion into her. Then in a final act of giving she opened herself to receive him.

"Begin Vicky – please begin."

CHAPTER 16

There was no part of Ben McClure's growing up years in which he was not able, first to enjoy, and later to find satisfaction. Though limited in scope to the daily performance of assigned chores, Ben challenged himself by bringin his own expertise to aid in the completion of the work. Will, of course, soon noticed that his son had a talent for "doing things his own way," and encouraged him, rather than correcting, or discouraging him. As Ben grew older it was not uncommon for Will to call on his son for the solution to some perplexing problem, or to give advice in the making of one of his plans. "Son how about putting on your thinking cap and give me your idea about how to do this."

At almost seven years old Ben McClure did not know about nor understand the anticipated bliss of marital events. Needless to say Ben idolized his older brother, and when he was told that James and Eunice had, 'slipped off and gotten married and took to the woods for their honeymoon,' he was not surprised. He was somewhat concerned when he heard some of James' friends say that when Raymond Baker found it out he was liable to disown his daughter and put both of them 'in the road.' Ben kept his own counsel.

They were all, of course, mistaken and even James was surprised at the outcome. Late in the afternoon, on New Years Day of 1913, James and Eunice McClure returned from their honeymoon. Carrie and Laurel were making final preparations for the New Years Day supper when they heard Ben talking to someone from where he was chopping wood in the back yard. "Laurel, see who Ben's talkin to out there. I don't think your Daddy's gotten back from the store yet."

Laurel pushed the kitchen door open far enough to look out across the back yard. "Mama, its James and Eunice," Laurel squealed and went flying out the door followed close behind by Carrie wiping her hands on her apron. During the laughing, crying and hugging that ensued, Will came driving his mules and wagon into the yard, jumped down and joined in the celebration.

Two plates were quickly added to the table, another pone of corn bread, another bowl of turnip greens, and a large bowl of pickled peaches were soon added, to complete the evening meal. Already prepared, for the New Years Day supper, was a huge metal boiler of hog back bones cut into one or two backbones joints, and boiled in the metal boiler until they were bone slipping tender. A large bowl of dried black-eyed peas cooked with another piece of backbone were put steaming hot in the center of the table. Also, already prepared and ready to sit on the table, was a large pan of unpeeled baked sweet potatoes.

As the men of the house, Ben included, washed up on the back porch, Will sat an earthen jug on the wash board and for the first time, offered James a before meal drink. "Son, try a sup of that. It's peach brandy and it's purty good. Them Crane boys, from up in Gilmer County, brought it to me for a Christmas present. They said it was doubled and no sugar was used to make it work."

Will stopped and chuckled out loud. "It's good enough that Doc Holden comes by to see me about ever other day. When it comes to brandy or sweet mash corn liquor, Doc is just like a hog after slop. You can't keep him knocked out of it."

James laughed and nodded his head, but he did not tell of Doc Holden's advice, friendship and help on his wedding day. He was amazed when he thought back over the chain of events beginning with his and Eunice's marriage just over a week ago. So much about him had changed, and in such a short amount of time. Well, James thought to himself, I'm not the only one, and I'm not the first one and I'm pretty damn sure I won't be the last one to feel this way."

James took two swallows of the brandy straight from the jug and handed it to his Daddy. Will took his usual four swallows, and offered the jug back to his son.

"Take some more if you will."

"Much obliged, but that's plenty."

Ben was not offered and he did not ask.

James felt the warming sensation of the brandy spread through his body and just as quickly, the dizzy numbing effect on his brain. He steadied himself by briefly touching the wall. James thought for a brief moment that he was going to have to sit down, but he was saved from that embarrassment by the call from the kitchen.

"Supper's ready."

And Will's quick reply, "Boys that's what we been waitin for, lets get to it."

The McClure family and their new daughter-in-law sat down to a festive New Years Day Supper. Still warmed and relaxed from his before supper drink of brandy, Will talked of his and Carrie's marriage, the hardships they encountered and the good times they experienced together. Even Carrie, after much encouragement from Laurel and Ben, told of her and Will's honeymoon trip to Atlanta.

"Well sir, it's been so long ago that I can't remember a whole lot about Atlanta. We got on the train over at Tate, Georgia and went down through Canton and Marietta before we got there. After we went past Marietta it was just road after road full of houses and them all jammed up against one another. When we got off the train in Atlanta everything smelled like coal smoke and I've never, in my life, seen so many people and it seemed like every one of them was goin in a different direction and there were about as many of them that were women as there were men."

"The next morning Will carried me to Mr. Rich's Department Store and I've never again seen the like of it. That store was either three or four stories high and every nook and cranny was stacked full of something."

Laurel interrupted. "Tell Eunice, what you bought Mama."

Carrie stopped for a moment, smiling back at Laurel, obviously enjoying the memory of that long ago shopping experience.

"I bought a blue sweater and - and a pair of silk stockings."

Laurel leaned over and hugged her mother. Then with a pat on the back and a smile that expressed love instead of ridicule said, "And she's still got both of them."

"Hush Laurel, Eunice will think neither one of us has got any sense."

Then Ben asked his mother to relate his favorite part of their trip to Atlanta. "Mama, tell Eunice about what Daddy bought for you and him on the way back to the train station."

"Well, the next mornin as we were on our way to the train station to come home, Will carried me to a drug store and bought us an ice cream in a cone. As you ate the ice cream, you also ate the cone."

As always Ben marveled at that part of Carrie's story. When Ben was much younger, he would almost always ask for a bedtime story, and when it was Carrie's time to tell the bedtime story, he would, on many occasions, ask to be told about the trip to Atlanta and the ice cream in a cone that was meant to be eaten cone and all. And it was not at all uncommon that Carrie and her son would fall asleep for the night, Carrie savoring the memory of a wedding trip to the strangely vibrant feeling city of Atlanta, and young Ben McClure, dreaming of a future of which the city of Atlanta was only a part.

"Well folks," Carrie said as she began collecting plates and tableware, "That was my first and last trip to the big city, and I've never had any great desire to go back. There has never been anybody that was any gladder than I was to get back home and sleep in a bed of my own making.

"Will, you and James and Eunice go in yonder by the fire while sister and I put things away and wash the dishes? Ben, you've set here and let it get dark and you've not brought in any water. You'll have to draw a few buckets to do till mornin, so you may as well get about it."

James leaned around his wife and patted Ben on the back. "Well little brother, I'm proud of you. I was wonderin the other day if you would take over my old job without complanin about it too much." That was followed by a startled – "oouuff" – due to a strong elbow delivered to his short ribs by his wife."

"Go on and sit by the fire lazy bones. I'm goin to help Ben bring in some water. That is, if it's all right with Ben."

Needless to say, Ben looked at his new sister-in-law with admiration in his eyes.

*   *   *

There was little if any concern on James' part, about his future relationship with his wife's parents. It was not at all uncommon for a boy and girl to "slip off" and get married without telling anyone, much less to ask for the approval of the girl's parents. Eunice had willingly and happily accepted his proposal; therefore, as far as James was concerned, he had done nothing wrong. However, since Eunice was an only child, James did not in any way want to harm the close family bond that he knew existed between Eunice and her parents.

So early the next morning, the second day of the New Year, James and Eunice had breakfast with his family, and made preparations to leave. Will offered to hitch his buggy to one of his team of mules and carry them the six miles to Eunice's parent's home, the Raymond and Lettie Baker place.

Will had acquired a second hand buggy from Dr. Vic Holden not long after Ben's birth, but he would not purchase a horse to pull it with. When Vic pressed him for a reason for not buying a horse in order to have, 'a good looking rig,' Will replied, "I never have been able to tell what a damned horse was goin to do until he'd already went and done it."

They both declined, James explaining how they had learned to enjoy walking together during their honeymoon, and Eunice telling about the day they had walked and climbed to the top of Amicalola Falls. "And besides," Eunice added, "We'll walk with Ben as far as the school house, and make sure he doesn't play hooky."

James did not add that he would prefer they were alone when they reached the home of Eunice's parents.

Walking at an unhurried pace, yet one that covered a surprising amount of distance in a short amount of time, James and Eunice arrived at the Baker homeplace just after 9 a.m. The house set well back from the road in a grove of red oak and hickory trees, which partially obstructed the view from the road as well as from the house. As they started up the front steps they heard the squeak of a well curb wheel and the sound of rope being wound on a windlass. Eunice turned to James and put a finger to her lips. "Somebody's drawing water let's go around the house to the back porch."

The bucket of water that Eunice's mother was drawing was almost to the top of the well curb when she caught sight of movement from the corner of her eye. Knowing that Raymond was in the barn, and realizing that her spectacles were on her kitchen worktable, Lettie had to quit turning the windlass and face in that direction in order to recognize her visitors. "Ooohhh, Eunice you've come home" and in a voice rising in note and decibel, "Raymond come here, Eunice has come home," and as if it were an afterthought "and she's got her new husband with her," and with that she turned the windlass loose and ran toward her daughter.

The windlass, suddenly freed from its upward pull, answered the downward pull from the bucketful of water. The windlass turned faster and faster as the water bucket dropped fifty feet straight down and hit the water below, kaaaswish! The windlass, of course, kept turning until the rope played itself out and jerked itself loose from the bent nail that held it to the windless. The rope finding itself loose from the windlass ran through the drawing wheel, down thru the well curb and joined the water bucket fifty feet below. But the lost well rope and water bucket went unnoticed … unnoticed at least for the time being, because their only child had come home. Gone for only ten days, but it was ten days of living under a shadow of doubt and fear, but the shadow quickly dissipated with her return. A return that was accompanied by a husband, but he was the husband of her choosing and therefore, James became a husband that was immediately and completely accepted. So it was that while he was as yet unaware of this good fortune, James had also come home.

CHAPTER 17

While it is oft times the case that the youngest sibling in the family is 'favored' or 'gets away with,' or 'gets his or her way with,' or 'gets by with,' whatever they want to do or not do, that was not the case with Ben. It was in fact the second youngest sibling in the McClure family who was 'the apple of everyone's eye,' oddly enough, even Ben's eye. That was of course Laurel.

The unassuming yet fetching personality of Laurel, coupled with her refreshing beauty, drew everyone to her. Even the very young and the very old, and true to her nature she responded to each of them in kind.

While Laurel's love for her Aunt Cora and Aunt Nora matured, as she grew toward womanhood, there was a special place reserved in her heart for these two old maids. She was, as she had always been, the precious jewel in the life of her Aunt Nora. And, while the love of her Aunt Cora was returned in full measure, Laurel was no longer this 'precious jewel' of her Aunt Cora's life. It was the smiling, trusting and loving face of the boy child that sometimes came with Laurel to spend the weekend. The baby Cora had been willing to sacrifice in order to save his mother's life. It was Ben.

But, little did they know that their innocent young beauty, Laurel, would soon be gone.

*　　　*　　　*

Marcus Taylor was a distant cousin of Grace Holden and a student in the law school at the University of Georgia. Having heard that Vic was an avid outdoorsman, he had written to Grace and indicated that he would appreciate an invitation to accompany Vic on a deer hunt. The invitation was extended and a mid January hunt was planned. Mark arrived on Wednesday for their hunt, which was scheduled for Thursday, Friday and

Saturday if necessary. He was over six feet tall, very impressed by Victor's practice, most complimentary of Grace and the children, but Grace was just a little disappointed in Mark. Grace's family name was Russell and while there were, of course, other families involved she had no recollection of a red headed relative, Russell or not.

The hunt was a great success. The hunt consisted of Vic, Mark, Will and Ben. Vic was well aware that if deer were to be found Will would know where to find them so he paired Mark with Will and he hunted with Ben. They left the McClure place at 3 a.m. Vic and Mark riding Vic's two buggy horses while Will and Ben rode Will's two mules. Just after daybreak they dismounted at Will's direction, and walked about half a mile and stopped in a stand of poplar trees beside a small creek. A fair sized meadow lay just on the other side of the creek. Will motioned Mark and Ben each into a location with a good view and speaking in a quiet voice instructed the two young shooters. "Don't shoot the big buck. He's too old to be good to eat. He'll be tough. Both of you pick out a young buck and let the other one know which one. Shoot him behind the eye or the left front leg. Take your time now and get us some meat." Will and Vic backed away and stood close to an almost white poplar tree.

Almost out of nowhere, the great old buck appeared, swinging his rack first one way and then the other as he tested the early morning breeze. He was closely followed by a small group of younger bucks and does, feeding some on the frost covered bushes and grass, but obviously coming to water in the creek. Ben selected his deer, an eight pointer to the left of the pack and signaled his choice to Mark. Mark nodded toward his pick and the young boy and the young man sighted in on their selection. Both shooters estimated that his target was about seventy to seventy five yards away.

The rifles cracked almost simultaneously and both reports echoed up and back down the hollows on either side of the creek. Ben's deer bolted forward about ten feet and ran with falling head and neck onto the ground. Marks's deer jumped almost vertically about five feet and fell on its side, then jumped up and ran some twenty to twenty five feet and fell, rolling along on the ground before it stopped. The rest of the small herd vanished up the hollow into the pines.

Ben turned to look at Mark, just as he broke toward his deer at a dead run. "I got it! God-all-mighty, I got it! I've killed me a deer. Come on over here and lets look at it Ben!"

Ben turned and looked at Vic with a grin on his face. Vic turned and looked at Will with disbelief on his face. "I hope to hell he didn't put another shell in the chamber."

Will, still leaning against the tree, chuckled in amusement as he answered; "I don't think he did. I don't think he took enough time to do anything but run and holler.

Some two hours later they arrived back at Will and Vic's hunting cabin with the two deer gutted and tied across the mules backs. Will instructed Ben and Mark to lay the two carcasses out on the rough plank dressing table that he had constructed between two trees. Will had located his game dressing table close beside a stream of water. The stream was fed by a spring rising out of the ground at the foot of a huge old poplar about one hundred yards from the cabin.

"All right boys, y'all help Vic get breakfast started, while I get busy on these carcasses. There's everything you'll need in that tow sack on Vic's hoss over there. I'll have you some pieces of tenderloin, outta this big boy here, in just a few minutes. Vic, drag out that fruit jar and let's wet our whistle before we get started."

The fruit jar filled with crystal clear corn whiskey passed from Mark to Vic and then to Will. When Will finished, and before the fruit jar made its second trip around the small circle, Will handed it to Ben. "Well Ben, you've killed your first deer, and you've done your part of the work gettin ready for the hunt. I see no reason why you shouldn't have a drink with us if you want one."

Ben raised the fruit jar to his lips and took one small swallow and handed it back to Will. He did not cough nor breathe heavily nor catch his breath, but Vic noticed and completely ignored the tears that gathered in the corners of Ben's eyes. This time Will took his second drink first and passed it on to Vic. Will looked at his son and then at Mark. "Ben I'm telling this to you but Mark it won't hurt you to hear it either. My daddy gave me the first drink of liquor that I ever had, and then this is what he told me."I never have thought there was anything wrong with a man, taking a drink of liquor, but it's a damn poor man that will let a drink of liquor make a fool of him."

Warmed by the morning sun and calmed by the pleasant sensation from the corn malt flavored whiskey, Vic stood quietly by and listened to Will's advice to Ben and Mark. He smiled inwardly to himself as he thought, "Well Ben this is another event in your rite-of-passage, and it's good to be here." But the pleasant moment of reflection did not last. Cold reality came with instant clarity. Vic knew in his heart that if he had been required to make the decision on the night of his birth, Ben would not be here today.

But the chilling shadow from the past faded as quickly as it appeared because this was Vic's kind of day. He was doing what he enjoyed doing, and he was doing it with the people, he enjoyed being with the most. It was for days like these and places like this that he had shunned the more lucrative practice of medicine in Atlanta or Gainesville. There had been times when Vic doubted the rightness of his decision to return to Dawson County and his father's practice. But the day that he brought Grace to his home, and realized that she too was happy to be here, all doubt was washed away. Had he not returned to the place from which he came, he would not have found Grace and they would not be a family today. His decision was forever the right one. "Will, you get your head out of your ass feller," Vic scolded himself, "You've been around here long enough to know that the sun don't shine like this all the time." ----But Victor was not thinking about the warming midday sun.

CHAPTER 18

The sun was up by two hours on Friday morning when Ben came riding his mule thru the back yard and jumped down at the back steps. Carrie and Laurel came hurriedly from the kitchen, concerned that Ben had returned sooner than anticipated and alone. The broad smile on Ben's face relieved their concern and told part of the story. The bulging burlap bags tied together and slung across the mules back told the rest.

"Hey Mama, hey Laurel, guess what,? I killed my first deer. I've got it right there in them tow sacks. Well, all of it, except what we've already eaten."

Carrie smiled as she said, "Why Ben that's wonderful. I'm proud of you."

Laurel laughed and chided her brother. "Ben are you sure that it's not like the little boy told his teacher, "We killed a bear, but pa shot it." That bought a round of laughter from all three.

Carrie spoke to her son, but it was Laurel who noted the anticipation in her voice. "Well Ben, did you get enough of deer huntin and decide to come on home by yourself?" " No Mama, Mark and me killed our deer yesterday morning. Daddy and Vic are goin to try for theirs this mornin, and you know what else. Daddy wants to have a deer meat supper tonight and he wants you to fix it. That's why he sent me on this mornin with my deer. As soon as I get it unloaded, I'm supposed to go on to Vic's house and invite Grace, Abigail and Franklin. Daddy said to tell you they would plan on being here between three and four this evenin."

Carrie addressed her daughter as she inspected the skinned and partially dressed deer. "Oh well, Miss Laurel, we'll have to put off our sewing until another day. Ben, lay it up there on the washing table, and get me some water drawn before you go on to Dr. Holden's house. Stir up the fire in the stove sister; it's going to push us to get one of those hind quarters cooked all the way through in time for supper. Ben you make haste and get back here so you can lend us a hand."

Carrie turned and went back in the kitchen for her butchering knives, giving Laurel the opportunity to ask Ben for the information she was most interested in. "Ben, what does Mark look like?"

"Well he's real tall, and he's got real big feet. I guess he's got big feet, cause he said he wore a size twelve boot. He's not too bad a'lookin feller, but he's red headed."

Laurel wrinkled her nose and rolled her eyes. "Red headed, who ever heard tell of a red headed lawyer." Laurel gave her long curly hair a toss. "Oh well, I'm sure Grace will tell me all about him, and his red head of hair."

Grace, Abigail and Franklin arrived just after two; Franklin loaded with Grace's tote bag which contained four jars of canned apples and sufficient ingredients to make two large platters of fried apple pies. "Carrie, I knew, if they killed anything this is what Victor would want to do, and so I was not at all surprised when I saw Ben coming up the driveway. My goodness, everything smells wonderful. Here Franklin, put my bag there on the table. Carrie is it alright if I use that dining table to make out my pies?"

"Of course you can Grace, and I do appreciate you doing that. I had not even thought about a dessert. I knew I had to get this rump roast to cookin or it would never be done in time for supper."

Grace gave the stove top and Carrie's kitchen worktable a quick once over.

"Mmm-mmmmm-and what else are we having?"

"Well, this here is some deer steaks that I'm rollin in a mixture of flour and cornmeal. It's got a lot of salt and pepper mixed in with it, and I'm goin to pan-fry them on top of the stove. Then I plan on broilin some more steaks in the oven, take them out before they get done, put them in the same pan with the left over cracklings, and steam fry them with a whole lot of sliced up onions. Do you think that'll be enough deer meat for them?"

Grace grinned her approval. "I'll let them speak for themselves as I am sure they will. I'll have some of all of it. Miss Laurel, when you have a free minute, come and help me roll out my dough. I've got a little bug I need to put in your ear."

*   *   *

The sun was still an hour high when Will, Vic and Mark came riding thru the hall of the barn into the back yard and stopped at the smokehouse.

Will slid to the ground and stretched for a moment before he spoke. "Boys' huntin's about like a lot of other things. If you do any good at it, it's hard work."

Vic winked at Mark and grinned. "Well your hard work has paid off for all of us Will, even if I did enjoy it."

Will began untying the deer's feet as he replied. "Well now Vic, I didn't mean to say that I didn't enjoy the hunt and the fellowship, because I sure have. It's just that these old bones are beginning to creak a little. Vic, you and Mark hang our deer in the smokehouse while I put these hard tails in the barn and give em a good feed. I think they deserve it, don't you? Then we'll see what the prospects are for some venison for supper."

Ben had spent most of the afternoon keeping the water buckets filled and the stove wood box piled high with the driest split pine stove wood available. Carrie knew that if the large haunch of venison was to be ready for supper she would have to keep her cook stove much hotter than normal. During much of the afternoon, the fire box, on her "Warm Morning" stove took on a dull red glow, and when the men gathered on the back porch to wash up, she was satisfied that her roast of venison was done.

Carrie was not in the habit of heating water for washing up before meals. But, after two days in the woods, hunting and dressing deer carcasses, she felt that a good scrubbing with hot water and lye soap was needed. So as the men gathered on the back porch, she came from the kitchen with a steaming hot, black iron kettle and a bar of cut lye soap. Will took the kettle and poured some of the boiling water into the two wash pans sitting on the washing board. "All right boys, temper it to your likin with that cold water there and wash up. Meanwhile let me see if I can find a little dram of something to sharpen up our appetites."

Vic made the introduction. "Carrie this is Grace's cousin Marcus Taylor from over in Gainesville. Mark this is Will's wife, Carrie. She's the best cook in Dawson County, and even my wife will tell you that. Whenever you get a chance to put your feet under Carrie McClure's table you're in for some mighty fine eatin."

Carrie acknowledged the introduction and the compliment to her cooking skills. "I'm glad to make your acquaintance Mr. Taylor. I've already heard quite a bit about you this afternoon. You'll have to take Victor's talk about my cookin with a grain of salt. I always try to fix plenty and I fear that he likes the amount as much as how good it is. But we are glad to have you. Supper's just about ready."

Mark bowed slightly and expressed his appreciation and added his appreciative compliment. "Mrs. McClure, I've heard a lot about you from Grace and Vic ever since I've been here. I sure have enjoyed goin deer hunting with Vic, Will and Ben, and I can't express my appreciation enough for the invitation to eat supper with you."

Vic interrupted the introduction he had started. "Ah—ha Will, I see that you did find it. Come to think of it, I am kind of thirsty."

Will set the brown earthen jug on the wash board, "It was right where I thought it was Victor. Go ahead and start. Mark you're welcome to take all that you want."

Mark took one turn and passed the second time around. Vic and Will took a second drink and Will set the jug back on the wash board and left the cork stopper out. Ben knew the stopper was left out for him, but he passed by taking a step away from the jug. Will inserted the stopper and set the jug on the porch floor beneath the washboard. "All right boys, I think supper's ready and I hope you're as ready for it as I am. Vic, show Mark to the table and we'll be right behind you."

Vic pushed the kitchen door open and motioned Mark through. "Right in there Mark and follow your nose. You can't miss it."

Just as Mark took hold of the doorknob and started into the kitchen, Laurel turned from the stove holding a heaping platter of venison steaks. Mark reacted as if Vic had goosed him in the backside. He came ramrod straight, and instead of pushing the door open to step thru it, he held on to the doorknob and started through it. Mark's left foot caught the door and kicked it into a chair sitting behind it. Making matters worse, Carrie had placed a large dishpan containing an assortment of metal mixing cups and spoons on the chair. The dishpan and its contents sailed from the chair into the wall and clattered loudly to the floor. Marks ears and neck turned a pale white, while his face reddened almost to the color of his hair. He tried an apology but it was mostly an embarrassed sputter as he rushed to gather the scattered cooking utensils.

Grace could not control her laughter as she took Mark by the arm and turned him toward Laurel. "Never mind Mark, I'll pick all those things up in a minute. I don't think that you have met Laurel. Laurel, as you have surely guessed by now, this is Marcus Taylor, my newly discovered cousin from Gainesville."

Laurel gave Mark a reassuring smile. She had no intention of causing him further discomfort. "I'm pleased to meet you Mr. Taylor, and we're happy to have you eat supper with us. Mine and Ben's place is on the bench, and the bench is on the side of the table that's against the wall. Would you like to try the bench?"

"Miss Laurel if I can get my long legs and big feet under the table and out of the way, I would like very much to sit on the bench with you and Ben."

Some four hours later and back at the Holdens' house, Mark was still in a state of excitement about Laurel. "Good Lord Grace, I still can't believe it. When I looked thru that door and saw her standing there, I felt for a few seconds, as if someone had hit me

"What do you think Grace? Tomorrow is Saturday. Do you think it would be all right to pay her a visit tomorrow evening? I really would like to see her again before I have to leave on Sunday."

Grace considered Mark's request for a moment and made a suggestion of her own. "Mark why don't you do this? ... You're in luck that Sunday is church at Shoal Creek. When you and Victor go after your deer in the morning, ask Laurel if you can accompany her to church on Sunday. Tell her that we'll come by and pick her up. We'll carry the big buggy so there will be plenty of room. Cousin Marcus, if you play your cards the right way, you might even get invited to Sunday Dinner at Laurel McClure's house." And that was almost the way that Laurel and Mark's first occurrence of –"goin together"—happened.

Laurel was careful to introduce Mark, not only to all her friends but, to every person they encountered, as they made their way from Vic and Grace's buggy into the church. She steered Mark to the center door on the right side of the church and made sure she introduced Mark to her Aunt Cora and Aunt Nora as well as the other, older, ladies of the church. They were, of course, all impressed with Laurel's new 'feller,' that he was visiting with Dr. Holden and Grace, that he was from Gainesville, Georgia, and that he was attending the University of Georgia to become a lawyer. The Reverend Boyd Williams was impressed too with Laurel's –"red headed boy friend"--. But he was shocked to find that Dr. Holden and Will McClure were both attending church on the same Sunday.

Mark was invited to eat Sunday dinner with Laurel and before he left to begin his return trip to Gainesville, he asked Will and Carrie's permission to call on Laurel during the Easter weekend.

This time it was Ben who extended the invitation but it was an invitation to attend his overnight fishing trip. "Why sure Mark, and if you'll come on Friday we'll camp out on the Amicalola River. Me and these buddies of mine put out trotlines and then fish from the bank in the Devil's Elbow if there's enough light. We'll have catfish for supper and trout for breakfast and I know how to make hush puppies and fried Irish potato patties. We'd like to have you."

Mark quickly accepted Ben's invitation, but it was to Laurel that he looked for her smiling approval. Marcus Taylor returned to Vic and Grace's house on Wednesday of Easter week, but shortly after bringing in his suitcase and greeting the family, he went on, almost immediately, to the McClure's place.

On Friday he did visit Ben's fishing party but he could not stay with Ben and his friends because Laurel was with him. Ben and his fishing buddies were drying out around the fire, their clothes drying on the bushes from setting their trotlines. They had to scramble out into the bushes to make themselves presentable before Laurel.

As promised, Ben served them his specialty for supper. Fried Irish potato patties and trout halves rolled in cornmeal and pan-fried. After Laurel and Mark were gone and Ben was sand cleaning his frying pans he remarked to Wesley Cochran who was rolling a cigarette by the fire. "I don't think it woulda made much difference if I had just fried some corn meal in the pan. They was both too busy tryin to sit in the same place."

When Mark came to the breakfast table the next morning, Vic noticed that he was in a quieter than usual mood. "Well Marcus, you're the kind of visitor that's good to have. Since you put your grip in your room on Wednesday this is the first time I've seen you."

"I know Vic and I apologize for that," and then to Grace, "Grace do you think that Laurel could ever be happy any place other than here? She seems to be so completely happy here."

Grace was careful to answer Mark's question the right way. "Oh, I wouldn't worry too much about that Mark. I dearly loved Dahlonega, and all my girlish dreams centered around marrying prince charming and raising a family in our home close to Mother and Father. Then this country doctor, from the backwoods of Dawson County, came along and changed all of that."

Grace paused here and smiled across the table at Mark, but it was a stern and knowing smile. "But Mark, this is my home now. With the exception of mother, father, some other family and friends in Dahlonega, everything I have or want is here. Vic could have stayed in Atlanta as a partner in a group of prominent physicians there, but he came back here and by the grace of God we found each other. When God answers your prayer, and then adds a blessing to it, you better thank him for it and then get busy doing something with it."

"Now Mark, the answer to your question is yes. If you'll take Laurel to Gainesville and build her a home and start a family, and if you'll get to work trying to make a decent living, then yes, you'll find that she'll work harder and sacrifice more than you will, and she'll be happy doing it. But if you think you have to run around after the elite rich, and attend every drinking and dancing party in Hall County, you're goin to find out you've got a poor wife, because she wasn't raised that way and if you persist in following that crowd and living their way, you're going to find out that you've got a long hard row to hoe."

Mark sat quietly slowly nodding his head back and forth before he answered. "Yeah, I'm sure that's right. But I had already figured out that I had to make some big changes."

Then, in order to relieve the air of intensity that Grace felt she was responsible for, she continued. "Besides that Mark, you're Methodist and I was one until my husband "rescued me" as he likes to put it. Laurel won't have any 'getting accepted or getting to know' problems. Methodists are always out looking for new prospects, especially the ones that are well connected. I had a few stiff necks that took a while for even me to get limbered up. Of course, it didn't hurt any to have it noised about the community that I was in charge of which appointment the good doctor *kept next*." That got a good laugh out of Mark and even the Doctor himself.

Mark returned for May Meeting on the weekend of the third Sunday in May. Before he left Grace and Vic's house to call on Laurel he pressed an invitation on the Holden family to attend his graduation party at the Taylor home in Gainesville. It was, of course, understood that they were to serve as chaperones for Laurel. The weekend was also to serve as an opportunity for Laurel to get acquainted with Mark's parents.

As Grace later told some of her friends, "on top of everything else" she had to accompany Mark as he extended the invitation to a delighted Laurel and to assure Will and Carrie that Laurel would be "properly looked out for."

Then came two weeks of non-stop preparation, not only for Laurel but also for Grace and Abigail, as well. The pace of which became so furious that Will probably summed it up best as he and Vic were having a drink of brandy on Will's back porch one evening. "I'll tell you what I think Vic. This thing is about to get out of hand. It's got so bad around here that I'm afraid to sit down in a chair without looking real good. I'm fearful of getting a needle stuck up my ass."

CHAPTER 19

The Holden family, accompanied by Laurel, arrived at the Taylor house by mid-afternoon on Friday. Mark's graduation party was set for Saturday afternoon at five, but a Friday evening dinner reserved for the family's close personal friends and Hiram Taylor's business associates, was planned to begin the weekend of celebration.

Mark made the introductions as they came up the steps and onto the wide front veranda that ran the full length and turned the corners on the front of the two-storied white frame house. "Mother and Daddy this is Dr. Victor Holden and his wife Grace, daughter Abigail and their son Franklin. This is my Mother Harriet and my Daddy Hiram."

While the two families were exchanging handshakes and introductory pleasantries, Grace glanced around and saw that Laurel was just then coming up the steps. Grace knew that Laurel was not shy, and just as quickly realized that she knew exactly what she was doing.

"And Mother and Daddy this is Laurel."

Laurel extended her hand, first to Harriet and then to Hiram. "Mark has told me so much about both of you that I feel as if I already know you. I'm so happy to meet you both, and I do appreciate the invitation to Mark's party, and the pleasure of visiting in your home."

Grace was both surprised and pleased at Laurel's quick but noticeable curtsy as she shook hands with each of Mark's parents. Grace noticed that Harriet seemed pleased by Laurel's gesture, but she was quietly amused at Harriet's surprise, when her husband took Laurel's hand in both of his and bowed from the waist.

Some three hours later, Laurel and the Holden's along with the remainder of the Friday evening dinner guests were assembled on the large screened porch located at the rear of the house. The two daughters of Delia, fondly known as Aunt Delia, the Taylor's cook and only full time domestic help, were serving iced lemonade and chilled apple cider as the now quite large party waited for the call to dinner. Since the gathering consisted of family and his father's business associates, Marcus used the opportunity to introduce Laurel to each person individually, and in so doing he renewed his family relationships and acquainted himself with his father's business partners.

While the refreshments were being served, and family ties rerun and renewed, Vic asked Hiram if he could accompany him to the barn out behind the house where the buggies were stored for the weekend. At the double seated Holden family buggy Vic removed the blanket and unlocked the storage box located under the rear seat. From the box Vic lifted a small oak keg and placed it in Hiram's hands.

"Hiram that's a gift sent to you from Will McClure, Laurel's daddy."

"Well now Victor, if that's what I think it might be, that's a mighty fine gift."

"It's a brand new two gallon white oak keg, charred on the inside, and its filled with doubled and twisted sweet mash corn liquor, and it is a mighty fine gift. Fact of the matter is, you're the first man I know of that got a gift like that from Will McClure that he didn't personally know."

Vic saw the change of expression on Hiram's face, and felt sure he knew what was coming next. "Victor, I know that I've no right to ask you a question like this, but how about telling me a little bit more about Laurel's folks. We thought that Marcus had just about settled on a girl here in Gainesville. Then after that hunting trip over there he started talking about Laurel. Then after the second trip over there he started writing her letters, and that's when Harriett started getting worried. I didn't think a whole lot about it myself, one reason being I always figured that it was every man's business to pick out the woman he wants, though I've come to realize that he's not always the one that does the picking. Then, from what little experience I've had with it, when a man and a woman take a notion for each other, there's not a whole lot you can do about it anyway. Then last Sunday evening after church, we were sitting at the kitchen table having a piece of cake and a glass of milk, and Marcus looked over at his Mother and said, "'Mama, I might as well tell you and Daddy that I'm going to ask Laurel to marry me.'" I thought there, for a minute or two, that she was going to faint. I'm not at all sure that she's reconciled herself to Marcus's surprise announcement because she hasn't mentioned it to me since and I'm usually the first one to hear about anything she's upset about."

"Well Hiram you know what it is to be brought up out in the country. Grace told me you and Harriet were both born and raised up in White County so you both know what that's like. It is true that Will makes a little liquor and sells a little liquor. But he makes it and sells it to folks like you and me, so that comes out about even, or at least I think it does. They put a lot of stock in their church and when there's an honest need in the community, Will and Carrie are always there. If Will McClure owes you a nickel that's a nickel you can count on being repaid, and he expects the same thing from everybody else -- me included. Laurel knows what it is to do housework and she knows what it is to work in the fields. When Ben was born, Ben is the youngest child, she had to raise that kid till Carrie could get back on her feet."

Vic stopped for a few seconds and chuckled to himself before he continued. "One other thing I'll tell you because sooner or later you're going to meet up with em. Laurel has two old maid Aunts who would do anything legal or illegal to keep her from marrying a Methodist."

Vic and Hiram both laughed at Vic's warning before Hiram continued, "Well I understand that and I guess you do too Vic."

"Hirrram!!! Hiram!!! Dinner's ready."

Hiram waved an acknowledgement from the front of the buggy shed. "Well Vic, are we goin to tap this little keg before we go?"

Vic rubbed his hands together and his face broke into a wide smile. "Damn right."

And so it was that out of the talk there in Hiram Taylor's buggy shed, and the drink of sweet mash corn whiskey from Will McClure's oak keg, a life-long friendship began and grew between the two men. A friendship that not only included their families, but soon included the family of Will and Carrie McClure. It was a friendship that one day would have a turning effect on the life of Ben Tyler McClure.

CHAPTER 20

The sun was hardly an hour high when Marcus and Laurel walked the half-mile from his parent's house and turned off the main road onto what appeared to be and old field road. Here he took Laurel by the hand, and led her up a short rise to a wooded area covered in white oak and hickory. Dogwood trees grew at random throughout the woods, their stunning white blossoms giving the place where Marcus and Laurel stopped an aura of reverence. Looking down a gentle slope and across a meadow of spring green grasses, they could see the slow moving water of the Chattahoochee River sparkling in the morning sun.

Laurel drew in a quick breath and slowly exhaled, "oooohhhhh Mark, it's the most beautiful place I have ever seen." Marcus, deeply moved by the beauty and expression of awe on Laurel's face could only say, "I know, I know it is … it is for me too."

Then everything happened very quickly, but not at all in the way Marcus had planned. Only as Marcus thought about it later, it was better. Just as Marcus reached for Laurel's hand, a cool breeze sent a shiver through Laurel and she tuned directly into Marcus's arms. She slipped her arms around Marcus's waist and leaned her head on his chest. Speechless they stood quietly in each other's arms for several moments. From somewhere Marcus remembered the line about time and the tides --- so Marcus waited no longer. "Laurel I want to ask you if ---- No ---- I want to tell you how much I enjoy being with you and how much you mean to me ---- and so I ---- Laurel ---- I love you----and I have for a long time now. Laurel this piece of land here is my wedding gift from Momma and Daddy, and the older I get the more it means to me. That's why I wanted to be sure I had the right girl when I brought her here."

"Laurel ---- will you marry me? ---"

"Mark, all my life I have known what it is to love and to be loved. Loved by my family, by Aunt Nora and Aunt Cora, by Grace and Dr.

Holden, but I always wondered what it would be like to love a man. Mark do you remember the night we went down to the river for Ben's all night fishing party, and coming back to the house, you kissed me for the first time---times.

"Then on Sunday you got Vic's buggy and took me to church and we went back to our house and had Sunday dinner, and then you had to leave for home. Mark, when I woke up on Monday morning I've never been so happy and so miserable at the same time in all my life. Well by Wednesday I had to talk to somebody, so when I saw Dr. Holden go by, on his way to make a house call, I went to see Grace. The kids were playing in the back yard, so we sat down on the back porch and I told her everything. How I felt about you, and how wonderful I feel when I'm with you, and how awful I feel after you leave. Mark I really wasn't sure whether or not you would come back.

"When I finally hushed, Grace put her arm around me and said, "Laurel honey, the only thing that's wrong with you is the same thing that happens to every woman who falls in love with a man. It makes us feel wonderful and awful, but we wouldn't want life without it, would we? Vic says that's what life is all about anyway, and I guess he's probably right.

"Mark I guess I've loved you ever since I've known you, so marrying you and making you a good wife will be the answer to all my prayers. Since that night and that weekend you're all I've wanted or ever will want."

They stood quietly for a while; Laurel still folded in Marcus' arms, her arms around his waist, her head still lying on Marcus' breast. After several moments Marcus released her and they stepped apart.

"Laurel, let's go find Grace so we can tell her first."

"All right, but why do you want to tell Grace first? Why not your mother and father?"

"Because she's the one who told me about you."

They walked out of the woods where their home would soon be built, and back up the road to the Taylor house. Arm in arm they walked in the early morning Sunday sunshine.

END OF PART 1

God-Fearing Criminals

Part 2

CHAPTER 1

The first part of Ben McClure's teenage years were, for the most part, a very pleasant time. Ben was four years old when James cut him a cane pole and gave him his first piece of line and two old rusty fishhooks. He already knew how and where to dig grubs and worms and James pointed out the best grasshoppers and lizards. From that early beginning, Ben developed a great love to fish and became an expert fisherman. Ben was good enough that Dr. Vic Holden sought him out to fish with, even before he was a teenager.

It was on a Saturday morning that Vic and his son Franklin came to go fishing with Ben, only to find that Ben had left at daybreak for a day of fishing on the Amicalola River. Will gave them instructions where they would probably find him. Vic shaded his eyes with his hands and looked far out across the cornfields in the direction that Will pointed.

"That boy loves to fish don't he?"

Will turned to Franklin and grinned as he replied.

"If Ben couldn't find any other place to fish, I believe he would fish out of a gallon bucket. Even if he had to fill it up."

Ben was not as skilled at hunting as he was at fishing. While he usually made his kill on their annual deer hunt, he was just as thrilled at the beauty of a herd in full flight. He hunted small game for the table and trapped only "to keep the varmints from eatin us alive." Ben did not hunt bear. There was a violent nature about bears that created a fear in Ben. Neither did he care for the taste of bear meat. As far as Ben was concerned, it was not fit to eat.

While Ben did not enjoy the long days of hoeing and plowing the terraced hillsides and bottom land fields that lay along the Amicalola River, he did experience a certain satisfaction from watching a crop of cotton and corn grow out of the ground and mature, ready to be harvested. Always subject to the whims of nature, some years were too dry to produce a good crop, an occasional summer of excessive rainfall occurred when everybody's crop was --- "Just astanding there while the ragweed and crabgrass grow up around it."--- But there were more years than not, when even the most cynical of farmers had to admit that the condition of his crop was ---"looks as if there might be a fair chance of one if we can just keep it cleaned out and get it in the barn"---

But irregardless of the quality or the quantity, the harvest of the crop was of the utmost importance. If a good crop was "brought in" it was indeed a reason for Thanksgiving. If a crop that was not sufficient to winter the family and their livestock was harvested, measures were immediately taken to see the family through the winter and into the next crop year. The appearance of failure was as much to be avoided as failure itself.

The McClure farm as well as the Perry farm and numerous other farms that lay along either side of the Amicalola River and contained large fields that ran right up to the banks of the river, were known as river bottom farms. A river bottom farm is always in great demand, not only because the soil is generally very fertile but also because crop failures on a river bottom farm are rare, even though weather conditions during the growing season may have been unfavorable.

As always, there is an exception to every rule, and that is certain when the weather is involved. For those who experienced it, the year of 1925 became forever known as the dry year. During the late winter and spring of that year, there was little more than scattered showers of rain that fell across the area south of the great Smokey Mountains and extended as far west as Texas and Oklahoma. For the farmers whose land lay around and in the foothills of the North Georgia Mountains, mid May is the accepted end of planting season with the exception of a cotton crop. Depending on the weather, and the speed of a farmer's team of mules, his cotton crop was often not in the ground until the last of the month of May. There was always competition between each other and the weather, and there were two expressions of warning that they admonished one another with. "Boys, if you ain't got your watermelons planted by the 10th of May, you ain't goin to make many watermelons." Or "There'll always be a cool spell during the light nights in May."

In 1925, the planting season started early and was completed early, due to the favorable weather conditions. Conditions that were favorable because with the exception of a late afternoon shower, there was no rain. The dry weather continued on into June and with the beginning of summer, the searing heat came. The cotton crop, always planted in the upland fields, because it thrives in hot weather and requires less moisture, sprouted almost every seed out of the ground. But with the baking temperatures and no rain at all, many of the tender young sprouts began to wither and die. The huge fields of corn, usually dark green and growing so rapidly that growth is discernable everyday; stood with blades folded and twisted, having to bear the full force of the mid-afternoon sun and bone dry soil.

Then in July the hot and dry weather became dangerous. Word came from Lumpkin County that a sixty five year old man, trying to raise some moisture in his corn crop by running a plough though the middle of his corn rows, was found dead in the corn field. His arms stretched above his head, the plow handles having pulled out of his hands as he fell. So many people lined up on Dr. Holden's front porch with heat exhaustion and sun stroke that he couldn't see each patient or family individually. After the first few days he or Grace started coming out on the porch with a big bottle of aspirin and a bucket of water with a dipper in it. After the aspirin and water were taken, he gave the following instructions: "Start work at daylight and quit for the day no later than dinner*time. Drink water every hour and stay out of the afternoon sun. One 75 year-old farmer glared up at Vic from the bottom step of the front porch. "Now how in hell am I supposed to make a crop by workin barely a half a day at a time in it?" *see glossary.

Vic glared back at him. "Well, you better find out or somebody might have to haul you back here in a shape that I can't do nothing about."

All across the drought stricken area, cottage prayer meetings and church services began. Denominational lines were either forgotten or ignored as the community gathered together and interceded with God on behalf of their great need. They   realized that every family in the community was faced with the same disaster.

Raymond Baker was a deacon at Shoal Creek Baptist Church. It was at the home of Raymond and Lettie Baker where one of the first cottage prayer meetings was held. The meeting was scheduled for the last Saturday in June and set to begin with a singing. Planned at first to be held inside the house, it was moved outside under the huge oak trees in the front yard when a much larger than expected crowd began to assemble. Along with every available chair, a table was brought from the house, and soon it was piled high with pies and cakes of every size and flavor. Children ran and played in the front and back yards and the older boys crossed the pasture and raced all the way to the big branch where the cows stood cooling themselves in the less than half full stream.

Guitars, banjos, mandolins and fiddles were brought from the wagons and buggies and soon the familiar strains of – *I'll Fly Away, I Am Bound For the Promised Land, Angel Band* and *Amazing Grace* drifted out across the bone-dry fields of the Baker place. Then just at sundown Raymond Baker stood up and a hush fell across the crowd. They were ready to begin the service in which they would ask the Lord God in whom they placed their trust, and who they believed was the final source of power and authority, to send the rain that would end the drought that was destroying everything they possessed, and would in turn bring them to ruin if not destruction.

Raymond welcomed everyone to their home and the meeting. He thanked the ladies for preparing the refreshments and he expressed his appreciation to their pastor, Boyd Williams, for coming to lead the gathering in the prayer service. "If Brother Williams will spare me just a few minutes I would like to tell you of the experience I have had in the last two or three weeks. That experience is also the reason I wanted to have a prayer meeting here at our home."

Boyd nodded his approval. "Now you go right on Brother Raymond. I'm very much interested in your experience myself."

"Most of you know that I am a strong believer in signs. The best I know how, I go by the signs to plant my crops. I cut my winters supply of wood and I kill my hogs when the signs are right. I get all this information out of the Farmers Almanac and I know that many of you do the same."

"As most of you know, there's hardly a chapter in the Bible, especially the New Testament, that does not make some reference to signs and signs of the times. This is where I made a bad mistake. A few evenings ago, right after supper*, I brought my Bible and chair, and sat down under that oak tree right over there. As dusk came on and I could no longer see to read, I laid my Bible to one side and sat watching the lightin bugs and thinking on what I had just read. I must have fell sound asleep, because when I woke up, a full moon had rose just above the tree tops over there and it was very huge and red as blood. Well, as it rose further on up in the sky, I couldn't tell that it got any smaller and it stayed just as red as it was to start with. I came back out here for the next three nights, and while it rose a little later each evening, it seemed to me as if it got a little redder and a little dimmer each evening. Folks, I became firmly convinced that the moon was goin out and that was a sign that a biblical event was at hand, perhaps even the end of the world. Then, when Dr. Holden stopped by the house to bring Lettie's medicine, I asked him if he had noticed the condition of the moon lately?" His answer made me realize how wrong headed a man can get in his thinking. Here's what he told me."

"I sure have Raymond, and it's not a good sign as far as this spell of dry weather is concerned. It's dust. I read in the Atlanta paper where this drought has spread all the way out into Texas and Oklahoma. The winds out there are picking the topsoil off their dry fields and blowing it this way.

Not only are they having to contend with a drought, but they are losin their dirt too. It's not a good sign Raymond, not a good sign."

"So here we are sufferin through the worst drought we've ever had, and instead of praying for rain, I'm lookin up in the elements for a sign. That's why I wanted to have a prayer meeting here at mine and Lettie's home."

August brought record temperatures that soared well over 100 degrees, and word came from Texas of a tornado that killed over a hundred people. Heat lightening burned all night in the sky and then worst of all, wells began to dry up. The Amicalola and the Etowah Rivers dropped to alarmingly low levels. A mule team driver pulling a load of supplies out of Atlanta reported that "you can walk across the Etowah River almost anywhere you want to and never get your feet wet and the Chattahoochee ain't much better."

One evening during the first week in September Will told Carrie and Ben of the plans made by him and the other farmers in the community. "Durin the next two weeks we are goin to harvest everything that's worth savin, and after that we are goin to start turnin our stock out at night. Ben you'll have to help me every day for the next couple of weeks. We are goin to need every corn stalk and nubbin we can find. Carrie, I noticed the well water was getting dingy. Ben, first thing in the morning, help your Mama move her wash pots and tubs up to the spring head and then you build her a *'battling board' up there. Take a shovel and clean out the spring head, but be mighty careful with it. We don't want to do anything that might cause it to go underground. I'm sorta worried now that we might not get any rain 'til December. *see glossary.

And then it rained.

Far out in the Gulf of Mexico, that fickle and undependable spell of weather, known to people in the South as the "September gales" began to form and take shape. The September gales were labeled undependable because in most years they never appeared. In fact in most years, they were not needed nor wanted, because a spell of foul weather could do more damage than good to a crop of corn and cotton ready for harvest. But this year, as if in answer to a great outcry of need, it formed itself into a much wider and deeper than usual band of weather, sucking huge amounts of water out of the gulf as it headed for land. Making landfall all along the Gulf Coastline, it blew off toward the Northeast, soaking fields and answering prayers as it went.

Will came only half-awake as he felt and heard the surge of wind against the side of the old house. "It's that devilish wind again." Will said to himself, slowly shifting his legs about, in order to relieve his aching knee joints. He thought again of Vic's warning that the weather was not apt to change until the wind quit blowing steadily out of the West. The old house cracked again, as another surge of wind rattled windows and doors, and this time Will came fully awake. That wind's not out of the West, Will thought to himself, that wind's coming out of the South. As he lay quietly listening for the next rush of wind, he heard a gentle ---ssswwwisshh---- travel across the split white oak boards that covered the house. Will lay in shocked silence --- waiting---waiting---not willing to move until he could hear it again. It came again, only this time it was louder and it was soon followed by a soft drip from off the roof onto the ground.

Will carefully slipped sideways out from under the covers, turned the wooden latch and pulled the door open. He was met by a blast of water laced wind full in the face. "Well, it's a-rainin --- Carrie, it's a-rainin."

"Well I declare, it is a rainin ain't it? Get up Ben, it's a-rainin."

Carrie followed Will out onto the porch, but even in the darkness she knew he was not there. In a prolonged flash of lightening she saw him standing several yards from the porch steps. "Well help my time, that foolish man will catch his death of cold. He's a-standin out there in that rain in his drawer tail with nothin else on but his old hat." Then in an act completely out of character for her, Carrie walked down the steps, and out into the yard to stand by her husband. Will stood with his arms outstretched looking up towards the heavens, taking the full force of the rain on his face. But Carrie stood, as if in an act of submission, with face and eyes cast toward the ground.

CHAPTER 2

Ben's late teen and early twenties were neither as simple nor as uncomplicated as his earlier years had been. That is not to say that he did not find the transition from being a boy to becoming a man, as a time to be savored, because he did. But like every girl woman and boy man that has experienced the excitement and frenzy of maturing from a child into an adult, Ben began to want *things*. The simplest and easiest way to obtain anything, of course, is to purchase it with money but Ben did not have money. Another, and perhaps the best way is to barter or trade for it. Better, because if you are a skilled trader you might be able to trade your possession for something of a much greater value. So, without making a conscious decision to become a trader, Ben started to trade and after a few efforts where Ben later admitted to himself that --- "I got my ass burned off" --- he became known as one of the best and shrewdest in the art of trading.

Will knew about his son's involvement in the trading and bartering business and was quietly amused by it. He was also supportive of it. But it was Carrie who voiced her concern about it when she observed Ben driving two calves into the barn late on Saturday evening. "You're going to have to look into what that boy's doing Will. Who do those calves belong to?"

"They must belong to Ben, he's the one that had the rope on em, and he put em in the barn."

"What I mean is where did he get them? You know as well as I do that he's got no money to buy two calves with."

"He traded for em' Carrie. I wish I had sense enough to start out with a few old Barlow knives and wind up with two calves. Maybe I ought to watch what he's doin. They say it's never too late to learn. I might learn how to do something besides make liquor and use a mule's ass for a compass, yet." Will sat grinning at his wife's back while she kept peering out the kitchen window toward the barn.

Either she did not hear Will's sarcasm, or she chose to ignore it altogether as she continued, "Well help my time, what will that boy think of to do next?"

With no hesitation Will replied. "I'll tell you what he says he's goin to do next. He says he's goin to rebuild that old two horse wagon out there in the barn and trade it for a T-model Ford truck."

"Whaaaaaaaaat?"

"That's what he said Carrie, and he wants me to help him with it and when he gets it, it'll be half mine. Just think Carrie, we could go all the way to Dawsonville and get back home before dark."

"I never thought I'd live long enough to see something like this come to pass. I suppose, without asking, that I know what your part in this foolish scheme is?"

"Well I guess you do Carrie, but just so you'll not have any doubts about it, my part is a brand new ten gallon white oak keg filled with sweet mash corn liquor."

"The Lord help us, both of you are going to wind up in the penitentiary. Why in the world you crave one of those devilish contraptions, I can't understand. The gasoline to make one of the things run, costs more than coal oil does, and the tires have to be blowed up with air. You heard Dr. Holden telling about the man up in Dahlonega that got both arms broke trying to crank the motor up in one of the things, didn't you? Then he told of another man that started down a hill and let it get away from him and he wound up-upside down in a ditch. It's a thousand wonders it didn't kill him. You've got no idea Will McClure how to start one of the things and if you did you wouldn't know how to stop it. You're not going to get me in one of the crazy lookin things. The day I get too good to ride on a wagon seat, I'll stay at home."

Will sat with no further comment, rolling and smoking one cigarette after another, with an occasional shake of his head.

CHAPTER 3

Will did not get to help his son rebuild the old wagon. Ben did trade for a used Model A Ford pickup truck, but it took him two years to do it, and he did not get to share the ownership of it with his father. The great labor of love in Will McClure's life was farming, notwithstanding the long days of sunup to sundown work and exposure to the heat and humidity of summer in the South.

Will believed that soil preparation was just as important in the making of a good crop as was getting the seed planted at the right time. To do this he used a fourteen-inch Oliver turning plow, and when he deemed the soil conditions to be right, Will plowed from sunup to sundown. Once started, except for water and dinner breaks, Will followed this routine until the plowing was finished or falling weather forced him from the fields. Will would not turn his ground if it was too wet. He contended that plowing ground, especially bottomland that was too wet, made it break up in clods that dry out too fast. That left the soil hard to cultivate and would not produce as good of a crop, as it should or could have.

In the year of 1926, after the dry year of 1925, Will planted a larger than usual crop of corn. It was a wise decision that paid Will a handsome profit, and he made plans for another large crop of corn in 1927. Blessed with good weather, Will began plowing in mid March and by the first of April he was over half finished. Carrie knew that Will was driving himself too hard, but she knew it would be useless to speak to him about slowing down. Ben offered to relieve him during the afternoon but Will refused and said, "Ben, if you'll get the smoothing harrows ready, you can start harrowing part of the time next week. Depending on the weather, we should be able to plant some corn in two weeks."

But it was not to be. The McClure family was about to suffer the loss of its first member. On Friday afternoon Carrie always prepared a huge meal. The reason for that being, that by adding a bowl or two of canned fruit or

J.M. Burt

vegetables, to the food that was already prepared, she did not have to cook on Saturday and unless company was expected, neither on Sunday.

The following Friday, Carrie was still in the midst of preparing the large meal, when she glanced out the kitchen window and saw Will lead his team of mules into the hall of the barn. Even though the sun was still an hour high, Carrie was not concerned by Will's unusual quitting time, until she saw the slow and unsteady manner in which he removed the harness and turned the mules into the lot behind the barn. She knew that something was seriously wrong when he held to the hitch rails in the hall of the barn, and stopped twice before he got to the back porch and sat down.

Carrie brought a glass of water and sat down beside Will. "Will, what's the matter? Have you turned sick? You're as white as a sheet."

Will took one small swallow of water and sat the glass beside him on the porch. "Well I don't exactly know Carrie. All of a sudden, I just got so tired I had to quit. I thought I would never in this world get the mules back to the barn and turned into the lot. Comin on to the house, I didn't feel like I could get one foot in front of the other."

Carrie noticed that Will kept rubbing his face. "Maybe you got too hot and forgot to drink any water. Let me help you into the house and you can lay down till I get supper ready."

Will got slowly to his feet, using the porch corner post to pull himself up, with Carrie to steady himself on. He put an arm around her shoulders, while she supported him with both arms around his waist. They walked unsteadily across the porch into their bedroom. She sat him on the edge of the bed while she unhooked his overalls and unbuttoned his shirt. She removed his shoes and socks, lifted his legs and let him turn and lay on his back, his head falling gently to the pillow. That was when Carrie noticed the tremor in his right arm and leg.

Completely unaware of the events that had just taken place; Ben was almost finished with the harrow and plows that would be needed for the planting season. He was in the process of attaching the double and single-trees to the harrow, when Carrie came hurrying through the door of the shop. "Ben, you must fetch Dr. Holden as quick as you can. I'm afraid your Daddy's bad sick. He barely made it to the house and I had to help him get to the bed."

Ben started toward the barn, wiping the dirt and grease from his hands with a piece of burlap. "All right Mama, I'll make all haste that I can." Carrie followed her son part of the way toward the barn. "Ben if he's not there you'll have to go on and find him. Tell him that I'm terribly worried for Will."

Ben was in luck; Vic was sitting on his back porch taking a drink of water when Ben arrived. He had just returned from making house calls, so his rig was still hitched and standing in the back yard. When Ben relayed his mother's message, Vic stepped from the porch, hurried across the yard and into his buggy.

"Ben, tell Grace, and come on quick as you can."

Carrie and Ben had brought chairs from the kitchen and were sitting on the back porch when Vic came from the bedroom, holding his stethoscope in one hand and a towel in the other. "Carrie, it's a stroke and I'm afraid it's a bad one. He's already paralyzed on his right side and his heart has not stabilized as yet." Vic stood for a moment looking from Carrie to Ben, slowly wiping his hands on the towel, a look of helplessness on Vic's face. "Well, let me get back to him. You all be praying for Will. Maybe, I can get him stabilized, and he'll pick up a little strength."

Ten minutes later Vic was back. "Carrie you and Ben come on in. I think he's had another stroke. He's sinking fast and there's not a thing I can do to help him. Both of you talk to him, he can hear you and that will help him."

Carrie came to the bed and took Will's hand. "Will, can you hear me Will? I'm right here by your side, where I've always been." Ben came to the other side of the bed and took his fathers other hand. "Daddy, don't worry about Mama. I'll take care of her and I'll look after our place."

*　　　*　　　*

The funeral service for William Tate McClure was held at Shoal Creek Baptist Church on Monday, April 10 at 11:00 o'clock a.m. Due to the hour set for the service, the men of the community arrived early in order that Will's grave would be finished before the service started at the church. But when the grave was finished and the other men left to attend the service at the church Raymond Baker remained at the gravesite.

From his tools Raymond selected a wide bladed hoe that had been straightened at the crook and was freshly sharpened. Beginning at the top, Raymond carefully shaved all four sides of the grave and resquared the corners. He did the same for the box receptacle in the bottom of the grave then removed all of the dirt that had fallen to the bottom as he shaved the sides. Then he spent several moments making sure that the bottom was perfectly smooth. When the grave was finished to his satisfaction Raymond and the undertaker's helper set the wooden box in the bottom of the grave, unrolled the artificial grass under the canvas awning, seat out the chairs and aligned the casket lowering support over the grave.

Then just as the service at the church was ending and the pallbearers began to form on the front of the church; Raymond walked diagonally across the cemetery and knelt beside the headstone of a small grave. Engraved at the top of the white marble marker was --- Mary Lettie Baker ---. Below the name and in letters and numbers of the same size was --- Born April 10, 1894 --- died September 14, 1898. Then, as he always did when he visited the grave of his and Lettie's first born child, he put a work hardened finger on the first line of the verse cut in small letters at the bottom of the headstone and read aloud.

"There on the Shepherd's bosom,
White as the drifted snow
Lay the little lamb
We missed one morn,
From the household flock below."

CHAPTER 4

Even before they were schoolboys at the first through seventh grade at, Amicalola Elementary School, Wesley Cochran and Ben McClure were buddies. As teenagers they became close friends who remained boyhood buddies, so it was only natural that, after Ben's father died, they became partners in almost everything they did. They helped each other during the planting and harvesting season, loaned or shared their tools and equipment, and they hunted and fished together. They were at the same parties and picnics and sometimes, but not always, they dated the girls together.

It was therefore, because of their friendship and the mutual understanding that neither would do anything, of any consequence, without first telling the other. So Ben was shocked and hurt when Welsey and Nellie Crawford announced their engagement in the midst of their circle of friends one Sunday morning before church. "Come on Ben," Wesley implored his friend later that afternoon. "That's the way she wanted to do it, and she made me promise that I wouldn't tell anybody until we could tell everybody, except for our folks of course. You know how girls are."

"No Wes," came Ben's dour reply, "I don't know how girls, are. But if this is what I can expect from my friends, I'll take it as a damn good lesson about how they are." But Ben did not stay angry, nor did he try to be stubborn, especially when Nellie threatened to postpone the wedding plans if he would not agree to be Wesley's best man.

The following Sunday afternoon Wesley and Nellie sat holding hands and slowly swinging back and forth in the big swing on the front porch of the Crawford home. "Have you seen Ben this week," Nellie inquired.

"Oh yeah," Wesley answered smiling at Nellie but thinking about his friend. "We worked together on Monday and Tuesday and then we went over to Gobblers Knob yesterday. There's a bunch of folks that get together up there and trade on Saturday afternoon."

"What do they trade Wes?"

"Whatever they've got and whatever's there. Zeke Turner brought a coon dog up there yesterday, made three trades and took the same dog back home."

Laughingly Nellie asked, "Well he didn't do much good with his tradin did he?"

"Oh, I forgot to mention that he carried two more dogs home with him."

Nellie broke into peals of laughter, "Wesley Cochran, you're crazy as a loon."

Wesley continued on a more serious note. "But you were askin about Ben. Ben's okay. Ben's not mad at me, nor upset with you, but Ben has got to realize that we won't be runnin around together as much as we used to."

Nellie snuggled against Wesley's shoulder, "You can bet on that sweetie. In a little less than a month now, I'm goin to start takin care of your runnin around." After a short pause, Nellie continued. "As a matter of fact, since I'm the one that's takin you out of circulation, I just might be the one who takes care of Ben's, running around by himself, problem also."

"Well now, what's this young lady? Is there something goin on here that I don't know about?"

Nellie feigned a mischievous smile. "Oh no, nothing like that, it's just that you haven't met my bridesmaid yet --- and neither has Ben."

"Oh boy, I think I'm beginning to understand, and the plot sounds familiar. Ben's not been educated about the wiles of women, but he can be a cagey cuss if he thinks somebody's trying to corner him. Tell me about her, you've already got my curiosity up."

"Well, she's my first cousin and her name is Martha Barnett. She's from Forsyth County and they own a big farm on Settendown Creek between Coal Mountain and Cumming. Mama said that even her Daddy has tried to get her to settle down and pick somebody, but she won't or she hadn't last time I heard. You know what my Daddy calls her Wes? He calls her a high stepper, but Mama just says that the higher they fly, the farther they fall and the harder they hit the ground. I cant' wait for Ben to meet her."

Wesley chuckled as he thought about Ben's continual search for the prettiest faces as well as the fullest of figures. "Well she certainly sounds like somebody that would get ole' Ben's attention. I'd like to see him get blindsided by your high steppin bridesmaid Nell. A fall off that lofty perch he's on just might do him some good. If nothin else maybe it would deflate that ego a few sizes.

And fall he did, but lucky for Ben he didn't fall by himself.

The wedding rehearsal was set to begin Friday evening at 6:00 o'clock with the wedding to be the next day at 2 p.m. Nellie had been expecting Martha all afternoon, but when she left for the rehearsal, Martha had not arrived. Then at fifteen minutes before 6:00, a green and black 1929 Model A Ford Roadster pulled up to the side entrance to the church. "Well finally," Nellie said, obviously much relieved.

Martha came hurrying up the steps and into the church, followed by a dark blonde-headed youngster who was at least six feet tall. But, it was Martha who drew all the attention. "Nellie, I'm so sorry to be late. I had to help Mother get their things ready before I could leave, and then we had to stop and ask for directions twice. I have never been to Amicalola Church before; I was so afraid that we were going to be late. This is my brother David-he's younger than I am though you'd never know it by his size. They won't let me learn to drive so I have to depend on David if I'm to go anywhere that Mother and Daddy are not going. Now Nellie, if you'll introduce me to everyone, we'll rehearse your wedding."

Ever so lightly Wesley pushed an elbow into his friend's ribs. "Well now, what do you think about her Ben? Will she measure up?"

Just as quietly, Ben answered, "ummm-ummm, tell me about it. Wes, I can't believe you haven't told me about her."

"Ben, this is the first time I've ever laid eyes on her. How could I?"

Nellie arrived with Martha in tow.

"Martha this is Wesley and this is Wesley's best man, Ben McClure."

Martha's manner was refreshing and gentle.

"Wesley, I've heard so much about you that I feel as if we had already met. I'm happy to make your acquaintance Ben. I do hope we can get better acquainted while we are here. I understand we are going to stay for church and Sunday dinner before we start back." During the introductions and ensuing conversation, Ben did not release Martha's hand until she turned for another introduction and gently pulled it away.

Immediately after the wedding Wesley and Nellie left for a honeymoon trip to Chattanooga and Lookout Mountain, Tennessee. Knowing that Martha was somewhat at loose-ends for the next day, Ben extended and Martha accepted an invitation to escort her to church the next day. And, by way of Martha's discreet suggesting to Mrs. Crawford, Ben received an invitation to Sunday dinner with the Crawford family.

When Ben was learning the art of being a trader, one lesson that he learned the hard way was that if you missed out on a good deal, rarely ever did you get a second chance. Ben soon realized that, with the opportunity having presented itself, he should pursue an acquaintance with Martha

Barnett. He did not want to take a chance on making a mistake that he would look back on as being crucial in his life, a mistake where there would certainly be no second chance. Shortly after a delicious Sunday dinner and while preparations were being made for the Barnett family to depart for home, Martha and Ben were sitting in the big swing on the front porch, the swing barely moving. Ben knew that if he wanted to further his acquaintance with Martha, now was the time.

"Martha, before everybody gets in the midst of saying goodbye, I want to tell you how much I have enjoyed gettin to know you, and then how much I have enjoyed being with you."

Ben heard a short intake of breath before she answered.

"Why Ben, how nice of you to say that. Getting to know you and Miss Carrie and Wesley, of course, has made my weekend all the more pleasant. Nell and I have been girlfriends as well as kinfolks since we were children. We have always visited each other for a weekend in the summer and sometimes at Christmas. Now that she is married, I'm going to tell her that I refuse to let being married interfere with our summer visits. But, she'll probably be too busy, being a good married wife, to even remember."

"Nobody could be that busy, and I don't see how anybody could forget about spending" – Ben's ears and neck colored a fiery red – "I'm sorry I didn't mean for it to come out that way."

Martha smiled up at Ben and laid a hand on his arm. "It's okay, I'll take that as a nice compliment regardless of how it came out." Martha paused for a moment and then continued. "I've an idea Ben, and maybe I can return the hospitality for a wonderful time this weekend. There's going to be a square dance at Matt School house a week from Saturday. Why don't you come for the dance and stay for church on Sunday? Besides, that will teach those honeymooners to go off and leave us, won't it?"

*   *   *

There was, in addition to a swing on either end of the wide front porch of the Barnett house, a third swing suspended from a low limb of a huge sycamore tree standing in the front yard about half way from the house to the road. Upon their return from the square dance Martha chose the swing under the spreading and falling limbs of the sycamore tree. "There's one thing you can say for the Barnett family – if you happen to be in a swinging mood, you've come the right place. Mama had Daddy put this one out here because it's much cooler on a real hot evening, and sometimes she comes out here in the morning and feeds the birds."

Then for awhile they sat together in the swing, it hardly moving, as they talked about the dance. Martha confided that the fiddle player, who was a favorite cousin, had offered to give her lessons for free, but her mother had vetoed the plan and made Martha refuse the offer. "Whoever heard tell of a girl playing a fiddle for a square dance? You'd be the talk of the whole settlement."

They talked and laughed some more about the wedding and how they wished Wesley and Nellie were here tonight. "I've only seen Wes twice since they got back; I don't have any idea what they could be doing." – Two stifled gasps of laughter – "Hush Ben, Wesley is your very best friend – I'd be ashamed."

The night sounds became more pronounced as everything settled into its place for the dark hours. A whip-o-will sounded its presence from a bush beside the barn, and from a hardwood thicket along the banks of Settendown Creek a hoot owl questioned in the night. Ben felt a shiver where Martha's shoulder touched his arm. He reached for her hand and laced their fingers together. Martha spoke quietly as she squeezed Ben's hand. "I've always heard that it was bad luck for a whip-o-will to fly into your front yard and start calling."

"Well if it is, I'm in for a world of bad luck. I think that about half the whip-o-wills in the world live around the Amicalola Falls."

Martha continued, "Mama said the night that her old Aunt Tek died, whip-o-wills were calling from all four sides of the house, and she died just before daybreak."

Ben did not answer, but he slowly lifted Martha's hand to his lips and held it there. Then just as Martha laid her head on Ben's shoulder, a dimly lighted lamp was placed on the hall table.

"Oh my, Ben, that means that I have 15 minutes to be on my way up the stairs to my bedroom with the lamp. It is getting late Ben and Mama insists on the whole family getting to church in time for Sunday school. If David snores too loud just goose him in the ribs. That usually works or it used to when we were kids. Goodnight Ben – I enjoyed the dance." Then to Ben's breath-catching delight, Martha turned, placed her hands on his shoulders and lightly touched Ben's lips with her own. Martha tiptoed quickly up the steps, across the wide front porch and through the door.

During the long hot days of that summer of 1929, Martha and Ben fell in love. During that delicious and delirious fall, they shared experiences that even years later evoked memories that were to Ben a little outlandish. As they were with Martha, but she was a woman in love, and for her it was all part of the unstoppable and unrestrained experience of loving a man for the first time.

Martha and her brother David paid Nellie and Wesley a visit on the first Sunday in May. During the dinner hour Martha announced that David was teaching her how to drive. Her announcement brought a stunned look to her brothers' face. "I'm not doin no such a thing. I let her try it through Thompson bottoms and she almost ran the car off the road twice. I thought she was goin to tear the transmission out of it trying to get started, and when I told her to stop she turned off the switch and stomped on the brake. She couldn't even mash on the clutch and work the gear shifter at the same time."

Martha had already given Ben an impish grin and a long slow wink. "Oh come on David, it wasn't that bad, and besides, you're an excellent teacher."

During an after dinner walk in the woods; Martha invited Ben to attend May Meeting with the family on the third Sunday in May.

"Come on Saturday Ben and we'll go wadin in Settendown Creek and make ice cream after supper." Ben, of course, accepted. On Friday, before his weekend visit with the Barnett family, Ben spent the afternoon washing and cleaning his 1928 Model A Ford pick up, while Carrie washed and pressed enough clothes for the weekend.

Ben completed his barn chores, picked up his bucket of warm fresh milk, and started out of the barnyard toward the house. The footpath that led from the barn to the house passed under two huge old red oak trees. Ben could not remember, even as a boy, playing in their shade when they did not seem huge and old. Almost always, if time permitted, he stopped under the trees, looked down the gentle slope and across the pasture and corn fields that reached the growth of trees that lined the Amicalola River. If you were standing in the right place at just the right time you could see the sun reflect off a small patch of water that sparkled through the trees.

Just as Ben saw the silvery white sparkle from the water, he was shaken by an overpowering desire to see Martha. Surprised and feeling a little foolish, he shook the emotion off and proceeded on to the house for supper with his mother. After a supper of steamed, fried cabbage, Irish potatoes boiled in their skin, green beans cooked down in a black cast iron pot with chunks of hog jowl, corn bread and big glasses of spring cold buttermilk, Carrie set to washing and drying dishes.

Ben prepared two tubs full of hot water, one to wash in and one to rinse off in. He took a bar of cut lye soap, and beginning with the top of his head and finishing up on the bottom of his feet, took a hard scrub bath. Then after making sure that everything necessary for an early morning departure was in order, Ben looked in on his mother and went to bed. With few exceptions when Ben went to bed he went almost immediately to sleep. But on this Friday night, anticipating a wonderful weekend with

Martha, he was not able to do so. Then after what seemed hours of tossing and turning on a restless bed, and just as he began falling through the first silky layers of sleep, he came full awake; overtaken again for the second time today by a powerful desire to see Martha.

"Get a hold on yourself boy," Ben admonished himself, "You're goin to see her tomorrow, quit makin a fool of yourself."

But sleep would not come, and presently the emotional desire to see her struck again, worse this time if possible, and it did not subside. Like most folks of his day Ben was somewhat superstitions. He believed that dreams had meaning, took mental warnings seriously, and believed that some things were to be accepted as preordained. Was something wrong with Martha? Was she in danger – danger that she was not aware of? He knew that she was thinking about him and their weekend together, but did she need him, and if so did she need him sooner than later? Ben's bed became a bed of coals.

Finding no answer for his unusual feelings or a peaceful settlement in his mind, Ben pushed his bedcovers aside, sat up on the edge of his bed, lit his lamp and began dressing himself. He knew that he had to tell Carrie he was about to leave, but before he did so; she came from her bedroom adjusting the wick on her lamp as she came.

"Son, what in the name of common peace are you a doin?"

"I'm fixin to leave Mama. I'm goin to go on down there tonight."

"You're what?"

"I'm goin on down there to see Martha tonight." Ben could not understand his unusual desire to see Martha.

"Well help my time, I've never heard of no such a thing in my life. Her daddy is liable to take a stick to you and put you in the road. That's what I'd do if it was me."

"Well he may do it Mama, but I'm going just the same. You go on back to bed Mama and don't worry about me. I'll be back home late Sunday evening."

*   *   *

It was shortly after midnight when Ben pulled his truck to the side of the road and stopped under the overhanging branches of a walnut tree. He was parked about 500 feet from the driveway that led to the Barnett house. He knew better than to expect an invitation to get out and come in if he drove his truck in the driveway at this time of night. Actually, Ben expected it might not be an invitation at all, since he and Henry Barnett had little more than greeted each other since he had started calling on

Martha. However, neither Henry nor any of the family had ever made him feel unwelcome. A waning half moon gave plenty of light as Ben walked up the driveway and stopped under Martha's open and screened window.

As was the case with most boys as they grew up, Ben was an accurate rock thrower. He selected a small round stone from a flowerbed and gave it a slow underhanded toss. The little stone hit almost exactly in the center of Martha's window screen and fell to the porch roof with a small klunk. Almost immediately Martha appeared in the window. Through the screen Ben saw her lips form a silent --- "Oh Ben" --- and she disappeared. Seconds later the front door opened just enough for her to slip thru and she flew bare footed and in her night gown down the porch steps and into Ben's arms.

"Oh Ben, how wonderful, you did come. All day long I knew you were thinking about me. I've never felt so completely alive in my life --- and I wanted to see you so bad --- hold me Ben --- come let's sit in the sycamore swing. They won't be able to hear us from there."

Henry Barnett always milked his cows in the morning while his wife Dora prepared breakfast for the family. They were two beautiful Jersey cows, always seasoned so that one was giving her full amount of milk for the family, while the other was sharing hers with a new calf. This Saturday morning was no different from hundreds of other mornings as he crossed the backyard with his two shiny milk buckets. But as he took the footpath to the barn he noticed that the swing under the sycamore tree was occupied.

Never, since he had hung the swing there for his wife years ago, had he seen anyone in it at this time of day. Sitting the milk buckets on the ground he started across the front yard until he recognized who was sitting in the swing. Henry stopped immediately in his tracks, turned and walked back across the yard, onto the back porch and into the kitchen.

"Did you know they were sittin out there in the swing in the front yard?"

Dora turned from her long wooden dough-mixing bowl to her husband standing in the kitchen door, "who is?"

"It looks to me like it's Martha and Ben."

"Whaaaaat?"

"Well, go out there and see for yourself-that's what I did."

After a long moment of peeping through the front window, Dora returned with an incredulous look on her face. "They're sitting out there in that swing together, and she ain't got nothin on but her night gown."

"That's the way it looks to me."

"Outside of that flimsy night gown, she ain't got a thing on her bosoms."

"Dora what in the hell are you a talkin about?"

"Henry, you're goin to have to put a stop to this."

"I ain't goin to put a stop to nothin. You know as good and well as I do, that it's too late to try to put a stop to it."

"Well, what are you goin to do about it?"

"I'm goin out there and wake em' up and tell em' to come on in the house. That you've about got breakfast ready."

Ben waited on the front porch while Martha disappeared up the stairs, and in a matter of moments reappeared; brightly dressed in a skirt and blouse. Her hair fairly sparked from a vicious brushing. Taking Ben by the hand she pulled him into the kitchen where breakfast was just going on the table. "Mama – Daddy, look who came to see me and got here in time for breakfast. Oh! Mama, everything smells wonderful."

Henry ushered Ben to the back porch wash basin. "You've just about got time to wash Ben, and we'll be ready to set down."

Presently David came from his room into the kitchen. "Why hello Ben, I didn't know you was here. You must've got here pretty late."

Ben saw Martha and her mother exchange a passing glance.

"Well David, I don't know if you would call it pretty late or mighty early, but I do know I sure am glad to be here."

Breakfast became something of a festive occasion that Saturday morning in May. It was during that weekend, and especially during the times when they were all together, that Henry and Dora became aware of how much their daughter had changed. Not only were they astonished by how much she had changed but also, by the fact that for the most part, it had gone unnoticed before their own eyes.

CHAPTER 5

Years later, even after Josh was born, Ben still referred to their July 4th weekend as --- "the damndest stunt we ever pulled," but Martha called it their --- "stolen weekend ---." And for the rest of her life, whenever she saw a beautiful sunrise, she always thought back to that moment. When, after spending over an hour climbing to the top of Amicalola Falls, they arrived just as the sun threw its first brilliant rays over the horizon and directly into their faces. She remembered how Ben had taken her hands and turned her so that she stood facing him, her back to the rising sun. "Look Martha, we've turned into gold. Your hair looks as if you have a golden crown." She remembered that for the first time she took Ben into her arms and kissed his lips, his nose, and his forehead and again on the lips, this time harder and longer.

They had discussed the July 4th weekend and Ben knew that he was supposed to arrive at Martha's house that Saturday morning as early as possible. Which he did, just after 9 a.m., and sitting in the bed of his truck was his new leather hand grip* packed with his clothes for the weekend. As Ben pulled up the driveway and stopped, he saw Martha's suitcase and hatbox sitting on the porch. Ben had no doubt that the misunderstanding was his, but on the spur of the moment, he could find no plausible excuse for his wrongheadiness. So, unable to see a way out of his dilemma, Ben took what was for him the prudent way out, he did nothing.

He sat with the Barnett family for awhile on the front porch and gave Dora the flower seed sent by his mother. Then sensing that Martha was ready to go, packed her luggage on top of his hand grip, helped Martha into his truck and they left. As they came through the Matt community, Ben decided that if Martha did not notice he was not going to tell her.

Regardless of whether Ben needed gas, they usually always stopped at Wills General Merchandise Store in Silver City. They were Martha's kinfolks and Ben, being a trader himself, liked to walk around the store, amazed and amused at what Calvin Wills kept in his store. "Well, I try to keep a little of everything, so we usually wind up with a lot of stuff we can't sell. So if you need something you can't find anywhere else, just ask me. I've probably got it, and you might be surprised at what I'll take for it." Ben knew a good salesman when he saw one.

Another product that Calvin Wills kept in his store was ice cold Coca-Cola. Most stores and service stations kept a variety of sodas, but not many places as yet kept their soft drinks on ice or in electrically refrigerated cooling boxes. Not so with Calvin, his were kept cold in the largest upright Frigidaire refrigerator he could find, and the temperature control was turned down as low as it would go. When a customer asked Calvin if he kept cold drinks, his answer was always the same. "Shore do, go in there and look in the Frigidaire."

Martha, however, did not share Ben's unquenchable thirst for Coca-Cola. "No Ben, those things cause my face to break out, get me a Nehi grape soda please." As they started to leave, Martha looked over into the bed of the truck to check on her luggage and she saw Ben's hand grip and the cloth bag that held his dress shoes. Instantly she realized what had happened.

"Ben, I'm so sorry, why didn't you say something. I would have been happy for you to spend the weekend with us. Surely you know that. As a matter of fact Mama and Daddy wanted us to go with them to the all day gospel singin on the square in Cumming. Why don't we still do that? I'll tell them that I was the one that changed my mind. They won't think a thing about it. Daddy says I change my mind about every five minutes, anyway."

After a moments thought Ben suggested a compromise and Martha agreed. "Let's go to the picnic up there. You can spend the night with Wes and Nellie, and then we'll go to the singing in Cumming tomorrow afternoon."

Just after they crossed the Etowah River and started through the long stretch of Thompson Bottoms, Ben glanced at Martha and saw the impish smile on her face. A moment later she slid across the seat and put her hand on Ben's arm. "Ben, do you know that nobody knows where we are? Your mother thinks you are at my house, and Mama and Daddy think I'm at your house for the weekend. Ben lets do what we want to do this weekend, and nobody will ever know but you and I. I dare you!"

"My God Martha, what if something happened and they sent for you. You know what everyone of them would think, whether it was true or not. I'd never be allowed within hollerin distance of your house again.

I'll guarantee you it would be a lot worse than us sittin in your swing all night long."

"Oh Ben, nothing's going to happen. Quit bein a fraidy cat. We're not running away, and we're not sneakin' off somewhere. If they find out I'll tell them it was my idea, and if they put me out I'll show up on your front porch, and then you'll have to take me in."

"Somehow or other I've wound up on the wrong side of this argument. I ought to be the one wantin to be alone with you for the whole weekend --- which I am. So tell me, where shall we go and what would you like to do first. This A-model Ford chariot is at your disposal Mam."

"First, I would like to go to Gainesville. You have told me so much about Laurel and Marcus, I want to meet them. You did promise that we would go sometime --- remember. We'll have to stop somewhere and get your two nephews some candy and a Roman candle each. Then I'd like to go to Dahlonega and go to the Gold Museum, and I'd like to see North Georgia Military College. I've never been to Dahlonega --- I've never been anywhere Ben!"

"You've been to Stone Mountain, and that's one of the wonders of the world." Rankled by Ben's pointed reminder, Martha decided to try him with some of his own medicine.

"Well tell me, Mr. Smarty Pants, just how many wonders of the world are there?'

Ben knew that he was cornered. He grinned across at Martha and repeated the phrase so often used to describe Stone Mountain. "Well Miss Smarty Pants, I have no idea how many there are, but Stone Mountain has got to be one hellacious rock to get to be one of them."

Ben loved to hear Martha laugh. He felt that the thrill of her laughter contained all of the sounds of joy and song. Today she did something more, she placed her arm around Ben's shoulders and spoke just loud enough for him to hear and then laid her head on his shoulder. "That's okay Ben. I have no idea how many wonderful things there are in the world. I'm sure there are hundreds of them, but you are wonderful enough for me."

They arrived at Mark and Laurel's house just as Laurel was setting their noon meal on the table. Two additional places were quickly added, with Ben and his two nephews, Jacob sitting on one side, and Jordan sitting on the other, occupying the bench. Laurel, remembering the bench from her childhood days, insisted on one for her boys, and Ben the trader had supplied one from an old farmhouse sale.

Needless to say, Ben was idolized by his two nephews. They lived in anticipation of their next visits to the farm in Dawson County, where their Uncle Ben was a giant, and their Grandma was the best cook in the world – she knew how to make sawmill gravy and syrup candy – and the Amicalola was mightier than the Chattahoochee. So Jordan and Jacob and Mark and Ben laughed and talked about their favorite stories from the farm as they shared lunch together.

Not so with Laurel and Martha, since it was generally accepted that at some future date they would become sisters-in-law, they were engaged in the friendly, yet dead serious process of getting to know each other. But they soon realized that the polite inquiries and personal revelations about their likes and dislikes were altogether unnecessary. They saw in each other what Ben saw in each of them. That day, they became friends and in time, came to admire each other. They became the only members of the McClure family that wrote letters to each other on a continuing basis.

Their meal finished, they sat together for a short time on the screened back porch that looked down a gentle slope and across a pasture to the gray brown water of the Chattahoochee.

"Well, little sister, I sure have enjoyed my dinner, and I hate for us to eat and run, but we are on our way to Dahlonega. Martha has never been there and I have promised her a visit, so we are headed in that direction." Then turning to his nephews, he addressed them seemingly to the exclusion of everyone else. "Now then, Jordan let's see here, when is it that you and Jacob are coming to spend a couple of weeks with me and your grandma at the farm?"

But it was their mother that answered, "It's for only one week, Ben, and it's the first week in August. We'll bring them over on Saturday and spend Saturday night at the farm. I want to see Grace and Dr. Holden and I must get by and see Aunt Nora and Aunt Cora."

Ben circled the courthouse in Dahlonega and continued north on the road toward Suches Gap for about three miles. Turning left on a narrow and bumpy road, with only a single set of tire tracks, they soon came to the parking area for Caine Creek Falls. The water tumbled down a rocky face into a huge pool at the bottom, where a large crowd of people, mostly families on a Saturday afternoon picnic, were swimming and wading in the water, warmed by the sunshine of the hot July day. After removing their shoes and socks and leaving them in the bed of Ben's truck, Ben took Martha's hand and they waded around the shallow waters edge to a large rock were they sat for almost an hour laughing and splashing and talking the nonsensical small talk that only young lovers know how to talk. Presently, they retraced their steps, and made their way back to Dahlonega.

Ben parked his truck on a side street just off the square, and from there they walked around the square. They stopped in at Lipscomb's Drug Store where Ben bought two double cones of ice cream – Martha had one dip of vanilla and one of chocolate – after which they took in the Gold Museum and Courthouse. Martha looked at every picture and examined each piece of mined ore and mining equipment on display. In the upstairs courtroom, she sat in the judge's high-backed chair and rapped on the judge's stand with his huge wooden gavel.

They walked across the campus of North Georgia Military College and onto the parade ground where they sat down on the concrete steps that led up to the drill and running track on the far side. "Ben, I'm worn out, I can't go any farther right now. Let's rest here for a few minutes, okay?"

Ben smiled down at Martha as she laid her head on his shoulder.

"Tell you what let's do. You sit here and rest for a while, and I'll go back and get the truck. Then you meet me right up yonder where the road from the track here runs into the Dawsonville Highway. I'll meet you at that stop sign there. See it?"

"All right, are we going to Dawsonville, Ben?"

"Yes ma'am and we are going to the movies."

"Movies – I didn't know there was a movie show in Dawsonville."

"There ain't, but that traveling tent show is, and accordin to the paper, they are havin a Bob Steele double feature tonight. Want to go?"

"I'm game if you are. What time does it start?"

"Just as soon as it gets dark enough."

The double feature movie lasted almost three hours, and unless you brought your own pillow, the seating was a worn smooth wooden plank. Martha observed that almost everyone leaving the tent was rubbing and massaging either their back or backside to relieve the numbing cramps brought on by sitting for so long on the wooden seating.

"Well, where next Sir Galahad, but if we have to go on a horse, you'll have to leave me behind. I'm afraid that riding a horse might be as bad as sitting on those wooden planks and I don't think I can take any more of that."

"As my mama calls my truck, we are goin to be ridin in that contraption parked right over there, and we are goin to the Amicalola Falls. When we get there, my dear, we are goin to eat supper, which I took the liberty of buying when I went back to get the truck."

"Glory be, I was about to suggest that we raid somebody's apple orchard or watermelon patch. I know it's considered uncouth to mention it in mixed company, but my belly's beginning to growl."

Midnight was less than an hour away when Ben parked his truck near the bottom of the Amicalola Falls. A first quarter moon provided a pale glow through the trees, and Ben lit his hunting lantern and placed it in the bed of his truck. He lowered the tailgate, covered it with brown paper bags and together they set their midnight supper out and hungrily began to eat. Their meal consisted of a loaf of unsliced bread, hoop cheese, cucumber pickles, two chocolate Bon Bons, a Nehi grape soda and a Coca-Cola. Ben however, was drinking from a dark brown bottle that foamed over the top when he jerked the bottlecap off with the opener on his pocketknife.

"Ben is that beer that you're drinking?"

"No, it's homebrew. I got me a couple of bottles from the feller I was talking to standing outside the tent."

"Can I taste it?"

"Sure, but it's got a little alcohol in it-about the same as beer."

Martha took a small sip, tasted it, made a grimacing face, and spat it out in the ditch. "Oh my Lord, Ben, that's the awfulest stuff I've ever tasted in my life. How can you stand to drink that stuff?" Ben chuckled as he took another sip from the bottle." It's better than a Nehi soft drink and it'll make you feel better than a Coca-Cola."

"Well, better you than me. If it was left up to me, the homebrew makers would starve to death."

Martha repacked the leftovers and they sat holding hands, swinging their feet back and forth on the tailgate of Ben's truck. They watched as layers of damp mist, caused by the water falling on the rocks at the foot of the falls, came floating down the narrow valley. The tiny droplets of water, glowing in the pale moonlight, gave the whole area an ethereal presence.

"What a beautiful place this is. I feel as if we were in some faraway place, all by ourselves. Do you feel that way Ben?"

"Well, it is a beautiful place Martha, and the Indians must have thought this was a beautiful place also. The word Amicalola is Cherokee and it means "tumbling water." Somewhere I read that the falls are seven hundred-twenty nine feet high, and that it is the highest waterfall east of the Mississippi River."

"Why Ben, I'm impressed. But tell me, does it mean anything that you have carried me to see two waterfalls today?"

Martha's question and the manner in which she asked it, seemed to Ben as if she expected a certain answer. Ben was unsure how to answer Martha's question. So, for the second time today, Ben took what was for him the only way out. He made no reply to Martha's question.

"We used to walk and come here when we were kids. A lot of families and churches have their Fourth of July picnics here. As a matter of fact this is where Shoal Creek Church had their picnic today. We just got here about twelve hours too late."

"Shame on us, when I tell Mama you took me to the Amicalola Falls I'll forget to tell her that it was almost midnight when we got here. Speaking of midnight, it has got to be way past it, and I'm beginning to get cold. Let's get in the truck and roll up the glasses."

But this time, sitting alone in the cab of Ben's truck, they soon realized that something was different. They had spent the day and now most of the night together. During that time they had laughed and talked and touched and, whenever possible, shared increasingly heady kisses. Now, alone in the night and locked tightly in each others arms, they experienced the gripping desire and loss of reason that led them, eagerly and demanding, head long into the searing flames of lust.

Within moments they were both pulling at buttons and snaps as they removed each others shirt and blouse. Ben pulled the straps on Martha's bra off her shoulders and down on her arms, but she pushed him away and turned her back to him. "Unhook it and take it off darling --- now lets press our breasts together --- Oh Ben, it's wonderful --- hold me close --- closer --- Oh Ben ---."

Ben's kiss quickly moved from Martha's lips, down the graceful curve of her throat to the creamy softness of her breasts. With no hesitation he took a hard and enlarged nipple in his mouth and began to caress it with his tongue. Never in her life had Martha permitted a man to remove her bra, much less kiss and fondle her breasts. Now, having encouraged it to happen, and, as Ben continued with their intimacy, Martha experienced feelings that left her shaken and consumed. She felt faint' and then completely powerless, her arms and legs watery and useless. Then almost instantly, and over her entire body, she broke out in shivering goosebumps.

She felt Ben's hand moving on and up her legs, pushing her dress and petticoat aside, until he reached her most intimate under garment. Martha had no desire to resist. She felt suspended, with no will power of her own. She moved her body and legs to assist Ben as he pulled her panties over her thighs and slid them down her legs and over her feet. Reaching for the undergarment that Ben had just removed, she saw in the dim moonlight that her panties were entangled on the knob of the gear shift lever of the truck.

The sudden realization of how ridiculous they must look, along with the shock of knowing that she was sitting with Ben in the cab of his truck, bare breasted and her clothes in a state of complete disarray, brought Martha to her senses. She bolted upright on the seat of Ben's truck, retrieved her undergarments that had been removed and with a deftness that surprised Ben, put them on and slid across the seat, her back to the door.

"No Ben, we mustn't. I'm sorry, we --- I didn't mean to let things get so out of hand. I should never have taken my --- it's my fault --- Oh God, what have I done --- I'm so sorry --- please forgive me ---."

Ben was sitting with his head leaned against the back of the cab his eyelids tightly closed. "No it's not your fault Martha. I'm the one that started it, and then neither one of us wanted to stop. If you hadn't stopped us, I wouldn't have and you know it. We --- men don't have any stopping sense about some things, and I guess that's one of them."

"I never want to do anything that would hurt you. Martha, I want to tell you something. I have this dream, and it's always the same. In this dream, I have come to see you, and you're gone. Even though I'm searching everywhere I can think of for you, I already know the reason I can't find you. It's because you have changed your mind, and you don't want me any longer – and then I always wake up. I lay there wide awake with this empty feeling, and sometimes even after I wake up, I'm still afraid that you --- Martha will you ---"

"No Ben --- please don't ask me that tonight. Don't you see Ben, that's what I wanted you to do --- ask me to marry you tonight. When I decided you weren't going to ask me, I decided to use myself to make you want me enough to ask me. Trouble is it worked so well that I got caught in the same trap that I set for you. Maybe that's why Mama tells me that I haven't learned how to use my female senses yet."

Ben sat quietly for a moment before he continued. "I don't know anything about female senses. I just know that ever since the night of Wesley and Nellie's wedding rehearsal I've wanted you to be my girl, and I'd ask you again right now if ---." Martha slid back across the seat and put a hand over Ben's mouth.

"There'll be another time darling, and if it's the right time we'll know it, and we'll be glad we waited." Then with a hand on each shoulder and looking directly into his eyes she continued. "By the way darling, just so you'll know, I am a virgin even if I do act a little crazy sometimes. Besides, you're the first man I've ever thrown myself at, and it looks like I missed."

Ben's laughter was barely audible as he took Martha in his arms, "looks to me like I had my chance, and dropped it." They laughed then and held each other and without intending to do so, fell asleep, their heads resting on each other's shoulder.

They woke to a cool damp dawn, climbed out of Ben's truck and stood looking up at the stream of water as it came crashing down the mountainside.

"Ben did you say you had climbed to the top of the falls? Let's climb it, you want to?"

"Martha it's not an easy climb, besides you've got a dress on."

"I know how to climb, and I have a pair of slacks in my suitcase. Please Ben, let's climb to the top and see the sunrise together.

They reached the top of the falls just as the sun threw its first rays of sunlight across the top of the Blue Ridge Mountains, and bathed them in early morning sunshine. Ben stood Martha between himself and the horizontal beams of sunlight and said, "Martha, you're wearing a golden crown --- I wish you could see how pretty it makes you look."

Martha took Ben in her arms and with tenderness that completely caught Ben offguard, kissed him and then laid her head on his chest. "Ben, do you know how long it will take me to remember and think about everything that has happened to us this weekend?"

Ben folded Martha in his arms and they stood quietly for a long moment. "Well, it does seem like a lot has happened since I left home yesterday morning, and we've still got today to see what else we can find to do."

Martha did not seem to mind that Ben spoke lightly about their weekend. "It will take me all the rest of my life, and when I do, I'll always think of it, as our stolen weekend."

*   *   *

Ben waited until he was sure that Carrie had left for church, when he drove his truck into the back yard, out of view from the road. He heated water and carried it to the guest bedroom where Martha washed and changed clothes. Ben shaved and washed up on the back porch and changed clothes in his bedroom. He carried Martha's suitcase back to his truck, and stored it in the truck bed.

In the warming closet of Carrie's stove, they found biscuits, fried fat back and a big bowl of gravy, still warm from her breakfast. Ben often teased his mother that she didn't know how to make a small bowl of gravy, and in return she chided him that he always had too many cats and dogs for her to make a small bowl of gravy. They consumed every piece of fatback and used every biscuit to soak up the last spoonful of gravy. Then as Martha washed the dishes, Ben took a pencil and paper and left Carrie a note.

Dear Mama,

I have carried Martha to see the Amicalola Falls. I believe that she liked them better than the Cane Creek Falls, which we saw yesterday. We came back by here but I guess you are eating dinner with Aunt Nora and Aunt Cora. We had the rest of your breakfast for dinner and it sure was good. I'll try to be home by dark but if not, don't worry.

Ben

Martha teased Ben that he had created more questions than he had given answers with his note. Then she added a note of her own at the bottom.

Dear Carrie

The biscuits and gravy were wonderful. We owe you a big favor.

I love you

Martha

Several years later as the family was going through Carrie's personal things after her funeral, they found the note, along with many dried flowers from weddings and funerals, pieces of ribbon, poems and clippings from magazines and newspapers, pressed between the pages of her bible.

*   *   *

They arrived in Cumming just before two o'clock and found Martha's mother and father sitting on a quilt in the shade of a huge oak tree on the courthouse lawn. The singing was still goin strong and would for another two hours. Dora made room for them on the quilt and poured two glasses of lemonade from a thermos jug. "How was the picnic? I believe you said it was going to be at the Amicalola Falls didn't you Ben?"

"Yes mam, it was held up at the Falls."

Martha interrupted and finished answering her mother's question. "It was a wonderful picnic Mama, and it wasn't nearly this hot at the Amicalola Falls, was it Ben?"

Henry was fanning himself with a hand held fan from Ingram Funeral Home and before Ben could answer he said, "Well, that's where they should have had this singing. I'll be danged if I ain't about to burn up. I've been trying to get your Mama to leave here and go home for the last hour."

"Martha, I think we are going to leave and go through the Matt community and see your Aunt Lula Belle for a little while before we go home. You and Ben stay as long as you want. Ben, will you stay and eat supper with us?"

"No mam, much obliged for the invitation, but I promised Mama, I would try to be home before dark."

Henry and Dora were barely out of Cumming before Martha looked at Ben with imploring eyes. "Ben will you carry me home please before I do something very unladylike."

Ben smiled as he answered "I sure will, but what unladylike thing would you do?"

"Stretch out here on this quilt and start snoring."

The sun was still an hour high when Henry and Dora arrived back at their house. Henry let his wife out at the front porch and proceeded to park his car under the car shed he had built on to the side of the smoke house. When he entered the house through the back door, he saw Dora standing at the foot of the stairs with a startled look on her face. Henry did not ask for he knew that an explanation was forthcoming. "I don't believe that girl has one iota of common sense, and I believe this caps the stack."

Henry answered in a mild voice, wanting to calm his wife's upset condition. "What are you talking about Dora? What caps the stack?"

Dora pointed toward the dining room. "Her suitcase and shoes are setting in there on the dining room table, the clothes she was wearing are scattered all over her bedroom floor, and she's in her bed sound asleep with nothing on but her brassiere and her bloomers.

"And I suppose you woke her up and made her put on her sleepin gown."

"I couldn't get her to wake up."

"Dora, she's in her room, and I guess she had her door closed. She's in her bed and I guess she was under some cover. She probably stayed up half the night talkin to Nellie and she's probably wore out. Besides that it really ain't none of your business if she's in her bed buck-naked. Why don't you leave her alone?"

Dora's startled expression changed to one of pure shock. "Well help my time. I've never heard the like of that kind of talk in my life. Henry Barnett, you ought to be ashamed of yourself."

CHAPTER 6

Then, just as every wind of good fortune seemed to blow in Ben's direction; he encountered a spell of ill fortune that almost cost the McClure family its second fatality in less than three years. Yet, over the long term, it not only saved him but it saved every thing that he owned.

The last two weeks in October is usually a time of natural beauty in North Georgia. The leaf colors are varied and brilliant, and by then the nights have turned cool and the days are almost always cloudless and delightful. Martha invited Ben down for the last weekend in the month, and her plans for Saturday were to pack a picnic and do some hiking and fishing along the Etowah River. Also, that evening, they were invited to attend a corn shucking and candy pulling at her Uncle Joe and Aunt Doshia's house over in the community of Ducktown.

As the story is told, the community of Ducktown was given its name when a heavily traveled crossroad, located in the Southwest corner of the county, about eight or nine miles from Cumming, was chosen for a post office. When Howard Land, the new postmaster, was signing the necessary forms for the new post office to be located in his house, he was asked what name the post office would be given. Howard was known in his community for the large flock of ducks that he kept, and being unable to come up with a name that suited him any better, he named his new post office Ducktown. The post office officials offered no objection, and surprisingly his neighbors liked it. Soon their community became known as Ducktown community and then followed the Ducktown grocery store and so forth. One other distinction the folks of Ducktown claimed was that it was them who coined the expression of advice to each other and any visitor who came by --- "Remember to keep your ducks in a row."

That Saturday in October turned out to be not only the kind of day that Martha hoped for, but her plans for the day were just as enjoyable as she wanted them to be. Sunday, however, turned out to be an altogether different kind of day.

Ben heard the wind as it began to rustle its way through the trees. Softly at first, but by first light it was gusting against the side of the house strong enough to cause an occasional creak and moan. Ben eased out of the bed, using care not to wake David, and let himself out through the side door onto the back porch. He was surprised at how much the weather had changed in just a few hours. Last night when he and Martha returned from the party, there was a cloudless sky and no wind. Now with the wind blowing out of the east, the sky was overcast with a red tint in the clouds where the sun would soon rise. Ben knew that an East wind and lowering clouds in the morning sky, was not a good weather sign during the autumn months of the year.

During breakfast they discussed last night's party and corn shucking. Henry was interested in the, quality and amount of his Brother Joe's Hickory Cain variety, corn crop. Then Martha and David, who was there with a red headed girl and later told his friends that he caught it hot and heavy from his sister about her; talked and laughed about who else was there and with whom and the whispered tidbits of gossip, some in confidence, some overheard.

After breakfast Ben walked with Henry to the barn, and while Henry worked his morning chores, he walked to the top of a small rise behind the barn. Facing into the wind Ben caught the first smell of rain, cold and moist, and he knew that it would probably last well into Monday before it rained itself out. Ben knew he would be needed at home. No further decision was necessary. His grip stowed in the cab of his truck against the coming rain, he said his goodbyes to the family. Ben and Martha sat for a few moments alone in the parlor. Martha promised to write by midweek, and Ben promised to return in two weeks if at all possible. They stood and held each other and shared a long intimate kiss. Little did they know it would be Thanksgiving before they saw each other again, and it would be Christmas before Ben visited in the Barnett home again.

Ben was crossing the Thompson bottoms when he noticed the first small drops of rain on the windshield and by the time he reached Dawsonville it was a steady rain.

Since the road was covered with a thick layer of dust, the tire tracks soon became dangerously slick. But Ben was a careful driver, and with little traffic on the road, he soon passed through the covered bridge over Cochran's Creek within a few miles of home. He slowed to a crawl where the road narrowed and crossed over a small stream on a bridge of thick wooden planks. It was then that he saw the almost new Model A Ford sitting at a dangerous angle, its front end down the muddy embankment, almost in the watery ditch. Ben knew that this one was going to be trouble, but you just didn't pass up a man with car trouble, more especially one with women in it. Ben stopped in the road and rolled his glass down as the other driver pushed his door open and got out.

"Looks like she got away from you and took to the ditch."

"I was goin real slow but it must have hit a rock in that rut back there. The steering wheel jerked to the right and before I could get it turned back we were in the ditch."

Ben turned the ignition off, opened the door and stepped out into the middle of the muddy road. Thankfully the rain had temporarily subsided to a slow drizzle. The driver extended his hand and introduced himself. "I'm John Cooper and that's my wife Kate, and that's our daughter Geneva in the back. We're from over in Hall County, and we were spending the weekend with my wife's folks up in Gilmer County. I was afraid we were in bad trouble when it started in raining on us by the time we got to Johntown."

Ben touched his hat and nodded to the women in the car. "Well, I'm Ben McClure and I live right on up the road a piece. Maybe I can help you out some."

"Well I'd certainly be much obliged. I'll never be able to get this car out by myself. I do have a twenty five foot piece of chain and a shovel though.

"All right then, I'll pull my truck up a little and we'll hook them together with your chain and give it a try."

Ben was not surprised when that plan accomplished nothing but a great deal of wheel spinning and mud throwing. The Cooper car was too far over the edge of the road and the tires sunk too deep in the mud.

"Mr. Cooper, that's a waste of time and effort. If you'll shovel the mud from around your tires, while I go to the house and get my team of mules, I believe I can pull it out. I'll make all haste possible. I know it's gettin late, and you're still a good ways from home." By the time Ben drove on home, explained to Carrie what he was doing, pulled on his rain suit, installed the harness on his team of mules and returned to the Cooper's car, almost two hours had passed. John Cooper, now muddy to his knees, had finished shoveling the mud from the tires and shoveled two tire trenches from the rear tires to the shoulder of the road. Ben saw him as he came in sight of his car, anxiously pacing back and forth on the muddy road.

Ben used about ten feet of chain and secured the double tree to it. Then he hooked the singletree from the mule trace chains to the doubletree. He rechecked the gearing on each mule, and then took a firm girp on the reins.

"Now Mr. Cooper crank up your car and when I tell you, put it in reverse and ease down on the gas peddle just hard enough to help the mules when your car starts to move. Wait till I tell you though."

Ben turned his attention back to his team. He was confident they could pull the car out of the ditch because they were already experienced at it. Ben had to make sure that they started together and pulled together.

"Mag – Lou, step up to it, and see what you've got to do." The two mules moved against their harness together, but stopped and stepped back after feeling the load on the trace chains. Ben let them stand for a few seconds.

"Mr. Cooper, are you ready?"

Ben turned his head and saw John Cooper staring straight ahead, both hands gripping the steering wheel, his head nodding up and down without stopping.

"All right Mr. Cooper, ease back on her just a little." Then, just as he heard the engine load up, he spoke sharply to his team.

"All right Mag – Lou, git' up there – git' into it." All four trace chains snapped tight at the same instant. Their backs bowed and their hind quarters squatted against the load.

The Model A Ford came backing up the embankment, over the shoulder and up the road backward for another fifty feet before Ben stopped the team. There, the Cooper's Model A Ford sat, with the Cooper family sitting in it. The back and right hand side covered with chunks of mud thrown from the spinning tires of Ben's truck with water and mud dripping and plopping from underneath all four fenders and both running boards.

Ben turned John Cooper's offer to pay him aside and said, "Mr. Cooper, if you don't have anymore trouble, you'll be able to make it home before dark."

*   *   *

Ben drove his team of mules back to the barn, dropped the trace chains loose from both single trees, then removed and hung the harness from each of his mules in the hall of the barn. He rubbed each mule down with a burlap bag then gave them each an extra measure of feed. He worked the remainder of his evening chores, and walked slowly from the barn to the house cold, wet and exhausted. He ate supper with Carrie, his first food since breakfast with the Barnett family. Ben soon wished his mother a good night and went off to bed.

Ben awoke on Monday morning with a sore throat and tightness in his chest that seemed to get worse as the day wore on. In the afternoon he worked for a while in his shop, but after developing a throbbing headache, he gave that up and went back to the house. That evening during supper, when Ben again complained about the tightness in his chest and a headache that would not go away, Carrie grew concerned that he was suffering from something worse than a chest cold.

After the supper dishes were washed and put away, Carrie took two flour sacks, stitched them together and cut a hole in the top large enough for Ben's head to come through. Then using liberal amounts of mustard seed salve on the inside front and back, made Ben a mustard poultice. Warning Ben to close his eyes, "It's terrible if you get even the smallest amount in your eyes son," she slipped it on over his head and tied it tight at his waist. That done she rubbed his neck and throat with the salve, tied a wool sock around his throat, and sent him off to bed.

Carrie could tell that Ben was having some difficulty with his breathing. Twice during the night she heard the spell of coughing that told her he was trying to loosen and cough up the substance that was causing the restriction to his breathing. The condition that had Carrie so deeply concerned was a malady of that day known as 'membranous croup'. The reason membranous croup was so dreaded and so deadly was that once the sickness was contracted, phlegm built up on the membranes in the throat so rapidly that in many cases it actually choked or smothered the afflicted person to death.

Carrie came wide-awake in the predawn darkness to hear Ben's ragged breathing and hoarse cough. She rose from her bed, lit her bedside lamp, pulled on her housecoat against the morning chill and went immediately to Ben's bedside. "Ben, are you worse? That cough doesn't sound to me as if you're any better."

"I'm having trouble breathing Mama. I guess you might better send after Dr. Holden when you see somebody on the road goin in that direction."

"Ben, I'm going after Dr. Holden myself. There might not be anybody on the road for another two or three hours."

When Ben offered no objection she knew he was aware that his condition was rapidly getting worse. Minutes later and just prior to her leaving, Carrie looked in on her son. He motioned her closer and asked, "Mama, will you ask Dr. Holden to send Franklin on to get Aunt Nora and Aunt Cora?"

As Carrie started out the door, she reached for Will's walking stick standing in the corner by the front door where he had left it after using it the last time. Then walking slowly but at a steady pace, Dr. Holden's house came in sight just over an hour later.

Sitting in his usual place by the window, having his last cup of morning coffee, Dr. Victor Holden saw the lone figure come into view. While it was not at all unusual to see people traveling on foot, Vic felt sure there was something familiar about the walk and appearance of the approaching figure, but it was not until she was almost to the driveway that he recognized who it was. Vic shoved away from the table and went hurrying toward the front door.

"Good Lord Grace, it's Carrie, coming up the driveway and she's a foot."

"Oh, Lord Victor, something must be terribly wrong at their house. Surely it's not Ben, he's never been sick a day in his life."

Both Victor and Grace met Carrie on the front porch. "What's wrong Carrie? Surely you haven't walked all the way from your house have you?"

"It's Ben, Dr. Holden. I'm afraid he's got that bad croup. He's already having trouble breathing, and I'm fairly certain he's getting worse. I need to set down and rest for a minute before we start back."

"Set down right here Carrie while I get the car. Get my bag Grace, and I'll be right back."

Carrie noticed that Franklin was standing just inside the screen door and motioned for him to come out onto the porch. "Franklin will you go and tell Cora and Nora that Ben is bad sick with the croup and he wants them to come?"

"Yes Mam, I sure will Aunt Carrie. Just let me get my cap and tell Mama."

As Vic turned out of the driveway onto the road he turned to Carrie and said. "Now Carrie, tell me everything that's happened. I need to know."

Fifteen minutes later Vic pulled his Model A Ford to a stop in front of Carrie's house, hoisted the scarred old doctor's bag that had belonged to his father, and went immediately to Ben's room. When Vic saw Ben's condition, and heard his labored and ragged breathing, he knew without further examination that his friend was in a critical condition. He also knew from past experience with this sickness, that with the buildup of phlegm in Ben's throat and chest this far advanced, the remedies and treatments were limited.

"Carrie, get a pan of water boiling hot. I want him to breathe in all the hot steam he can stand."

Vic turned his attention back to Ben.

"Now Ben as soon as Carrie brings the boiling water, I'm going to help you sit up on the side of the bed, and while you breathe in the hot steam, I'm going to make you cough by pounding around on your back and chest."

The little black buggy with the red spokes turned off the main road and came hurrying up the driveway. "Whoa babe, stop right there please," Nora Perry admonished the little bay mare, and handed the reins to her sister Cora. "Sister unhitch Babe and find an empty stable for her. I'll take one of the ragbags and go on in. I've go to see how Ben's a-doin."

Nora came through the front door just as Carrie came from the kitchen with another pan of boiling water. "Nora I'm afraid that he's worse. Maybe you can think of something else to do. I'm beginning to fear for my son's life."

Nora went directly to Ben's bedroom and took her place on the opposite side of the bed from Vic. " Dr. Holden I'll be glad to do whatever you tell me to do. Do you think there's any improvement?"

"Well not so far as I can tell Miss Nora. I have gotten him to cough some, and a little phlegm has come up, but not enough to give him any relief. Do you have any suggestions?"

"Could we get Carrie to take the pan of water back to the stove and melt a can of Vicks salve in it?"

"Yes, would you do that for us Carrie, it could help to open his breathing passage some?"

Nora took Ben's hand and leaned close to his face, listening as well as observing. Fear griped at the pit of her stomach at what she heard. "Ben honey, this is your Aunt Nora. We are going to do everything we know how to do to get that devilish stuff in your chest to turn loose."

Nora noticed that the white of Ben's fingernails was beginning to turn blue. She saw that his rib cages were dilating from the difficulty with his breathing. She looked up at Vic with a silent plea to do something. Vic gave a quick shake of his head, and turned his palms up.

Never in his life had Victor heard Nora pray aloud, but he was not at all surprised when she leaned across the bed, placed her hands on the pillow, one on either side of Ben's head, and began to pray in a quiet but firm voice.

"Dear God in Heaven, you know that I stood by this man's bed while he was still an unborn baby. You know that I was ready and willing to let him die if that's what it took to save his mother's life. That day, Oh God, you showed me that you were the giver of life, and I had no part in it. That day Lord, you saw fit, not only to spare her life, but you spared his too. Now Dear Lord, here we are again, the same ones that was in his room that night nearly twenty five years ago, and if you don't help us or show us what to do-that baby you saved that night is about to die. Dear God I pray in Jesus name." ------

Then almost as if it had happened yesterday, the memory of that Saturday afternoon fishing trip on the Amicalola River came flooding back into Nora's mind. She saw again the tow headed boy and his three friends standing at the back porch, holding their fishing poles and worm bucket. She remembered the knowing smile between herself and sister Cora. It was not that they needed someone to show them how to fish, because they were all expert pole fishermen. It was that she and Cora were the best, "cornbread-hushpuppy and pan fried, corn meal rolled, catfish over an open fire," cooks in Dawson County, if not North Georgia.

Nora's aching back from her bent over position brought her back to reality. She took Ben's hands in hers and part way straightened up. There seemed to be a slight improvement in his breathing with his arms held in a straight up position.

But the memory of that long ago fish fry continued to unfold in Nora's mind, until finally she realized it was the eggs she needed to remember. It was after the fish fry and while they were sitting around the dying coals of the cook fire that Wesley Cochran noticed the left over eggs, and challenged his fishing buddies to a raw egg sucking contest. Wesley and the two Turner boys actually enjoyed tapping a hole in either end of an egg and sucking the contents down, but not Ben. Before the first swallow reached his stomach, it came gushing back up, soon followed by his fish supper, leaving Ben retching and gagging and so sick that he had to be taken home.

"Dr. Holden, hold Ben's arms up like this, I'll be right back."

Nora furiously beat the eggs together in a bowl with a fork, handed the fork to Cora and hurried back to Ben's bedside.

"Ben honey, open up your mouth now. I want you to drink this. I know it's hard for you to swallow, but it will go down easy."

With obvious difficulty Ben opened his mouth a short distance, and quickly Nora took hold of his nose and poured a portion of the raw egg mixture down his throat.

"It's raw eggs Ben," Nora spoke loudly in his ear.

AAAAAAARRRRRRGGGGGGG!!!!

Great gobs of raw eggs came spewing out of Ben's mouth, reaching almost to the ceiling. The room was galvanized into immediate action. Vic grabbed Ben by the shoulder and rolled him over so that his head hung over the edge of the bed. "Hold his head while I get his tongue out Miss Nora. We mustn't let him get strangled."

Cora yanked the rag bag open and scattered rags on the floor for Ben to vomit on. Nora spoke again in Ben's ear. "Ben honey, I recollected that drinkin raw eggs used to make you deathly sick, and that's why I poured them down your throat before you knew it. Now don't try to hold it back, you've still got to get that devilish stuff to break loose and come up. "Ben retched and struggled for a deep breath. Then from the bottom of his stomach, everything came up including strips and chunks of greenish yellow phlegm. After each spasm of vomit Carrie washed her son's face and Cora changed the vomit filled rags on the floor.

Finally when Ben was doing nothing but gagging and retching, Vic eased him back on the bed. "I believe that's got the most of it."

Ben searched the room with his eyes until he found the face of his Aunt Nora, and then after taking several deep breaths said, "I can breathe again," twice. He relaxed on his pillow and immediately fell asleep.

Following Dr. Holden's orders Carrie and the Perry sisters woke Ben late that evening and coaxed him into drinking a cup of sassafras tea along with a bowl of chicken broth soup. They managed to get the same treatment down him again at midnight, but he revolted at breakfast. "That stuff is dangerous for a well man to take, and it's liable to kill a sick man. How about fixin us all some breakfast?"

Gladly they hurried off to the kitchen, and prepared a meal much more to everyone's liking. Fried ham along with a bowl of ham gravy and eggs scrambled in the pan where the ham was fried, two pans of hot biscuits, a large bowl of fresh butter, sorghum syrup, pear preserves along with a half-gallon of coffee poured from a blue and white spatter ware coffeepot that narrowed at the top.

Ben came to the table on wobbly legs and a queasy stomach, but after consuming a large meal of solid food for the first time in two days, he was much improved, physically as well as mentally. Ben sat quietly in his chair, listening as the three women recounted the events of yesterday and Carrie retold the story of the Cooper family's misadventure and Ben's involvement in it. During a lapse in the conversation, he began speaking, as if remembering.

"Well I knew I was mighty sick and I could tell I was getting' worse instead of better. I knew that Doc Holden would do everything that he knew how to do, but I felt like if everything else failed, Aunt Nora would come up with something, even if she had to stick her hand down my throat." Ben paused here for almost a minute before he continued. "I don't know why it kept coming to mind, but I remembered one time that Aunt Nora showed me in a book where President Washington died of a sickness sorta like I had. I knew that if his doctor couldn't do anything to save his life, I had my doubts that Doc Holden could do anything to save mine."

All during the conversation Cora had said very little, but Ben's referral to the book regained her attention. "Ben, that book you were speakin of was given to us by old Dr. Holden --- that's Victor's father ---, and he gave it to us --- to sister and me --- to read up on sicknesses like diphtheria, scarlet fever, quinsy and the like. I know that we all remember the flu epidemic in 1918. Dr. Holden said that it was a worldwide epidemic that killed more people than the war. He said that it killed so many babies and children that we almost lost a whole generation of people."

Cora sat quietly for a moment before she continued. "I don't think that anything could be anymore pitiful than holding a baby on your lap and watching the breath go out of it."

Cora stopped again, but when no one else spoke, she went on. "Sister and I have seen so much suffering. I've wished a few times that Ma had not trained us to be midwives. We've talked about this wish we have --- that sister and I have. Wouldn't it be wonderful if somebody could invent a medicine that would prevent so much sickness and suffering before it happened? Wouldn't that be a miracle? It would be a miracle medicine."

CHAPTER 7

Ben received a letter from Martha that Thursday afternoon, and that evening after supper he took his stationery and pen (a Christmas gift from Laurel, both imprinted with his initials, and the envelopes with his name and address) to the dining table, and wrote her a rather lengthy letter in reply.

In his letter Ben gave a detailed account of his experience with the Cooper family and a brief account of his bout with membranous croup. Martha was both concerned and frustrated when Ben dismissed the subject by saying that Dr. Holden felt like he was doing much better --- Ben was never sick, and here was the doctor saying he was doing better. Ben asked or invited, she could not decide which, Martha to come for Thanksgiving dinner and then stay for the weekend. He mentioned that she could stay with him and Carrie, but Martha knew that some of the McClure family always came for Thanksgiving. She also knew that on Friday after Thanksgiving, every male, old enough to carry and shoot a shotgun, went rabbit hunting. For supper on Friday evening and breakfast on Saturday morning … they ate fried rabbit, biscuits and gravy.

This must have come to Ben's mind for later in his letter, he mentioned that she might want to stay with Wesley and Nellie. Martha had no idea what Ben's plans for the weekend were, so that evening after supper she wrote Nellie a letter and Nellie's answer came by return mail. Martha was shocked and then gripped by a cold fear as she read of Ben's near death sickness and also of his seemingly miraculous cure.

Martha reread both letters, Ben's first and then Nellie's answer to her letter, but she was still unable to rid herself of the worry and concern over Ben's sickness. She decided to write Ben another letter, making a further inquiry about his illness and why, if it was not serious, was Dr. Holden involved. But after several attempts, and the realization that he would surely know about her letter to Nellie, Martha put the whole undertaking aside and made preparations for bed. Even though she retired later than usual, Martha did not sleep well and that in itself was unusual. She laid the cause for it, of course, to the worry and frustration over Ben's illness, and now the excitement of spending Thanksgiving with Ben and seeing her now pregnant cousin Nellie. The luminous face of her small bedside alarm clock read one o'clock when Martha slipped quietly from her bed, crossed the floor to her bedroom window, and pushed the curtains aside. A filling moon in a clear autumn sky, shed a golden light strong enough that trees and buildings cast a dim shadow, and little noticed objects seemed to stand out in greater detail.

As she looked out on the familiar landscape that encompassed the view to the front and both sides of her window, as far as she could see, Martha realized with a sudden poignancy, how much a part of her this place had become. She had lived here all of her life, and here she had grown from childhood into a mature woman. Here her world was safe and her place in it was secure because she was part of the family of Henry and Dora Barnett. While that kinship would never change, Martha knew that her life was about to change. Regardless of her love for her family, her home, her things, and irregardless of the love that her family had for her, Martha knew that the time had come for her to make her own way.

Martha returned to what she was afraid would be a sleepless bed. But she immediately fell into a peaceful sleep, and awoke at the first light of morning, glad in spirit, her body fairly tingling with the happiest of female emotions --- anticipation. Later that morning Martha wrote Ben a note, accepting his invitation to Thanksgiving dinner and the weekend visit. In a separate note to Carrie she thanked her for the invitation to spend the nights with them, but since she had seen so little of Nellie since her wedding, she had accepted an invitation to stay with her and Wesley.

*   *   *

Thanksgiving dinner at the McClure house was not, just a large meal served at 12 o'clock high noon, as might be expected. It was, if a better description is wanted, Thanksgiving—Supper*, and it was served as close to 3 o'clock p.m. as possible. Possible being as close to 3 o'clock as the women can get it ready, and get as much of it as possible on the table. There was no set menu, but rather, beside the meat dishes, every vegetable, bread and dessert imaginable. The meats were either baked chickens or turkeys, always baked ham and usually venison, but rarely ever beef. (Hogs killed during the first cold spell provided most of the meat for winter consumption.)

There was always, located at either end of the table, a large platter of Carrie's cornbread dressing. (Never to be confused with or referred to as stuffing). To drink there was of course coffee, milk and tea. (Tea was still a luxury not served except on a few special occasions, Thanksgiving being one of them). Following the custom of his father, Ben kept a two-gallon jug of sweet mash corn liquor in a burlap bag conveniently located in the corncrib. Beginning before noon there was a growing number of trips to the barn by the men, supposedly to relieve themselves in a barn stall but also to pay a visit to Ben's corncrib.

Needless to say, beginning with the Thanksgiving meal, food and drink, in bountiful supply, were available as long and as late as there was an appetite for it.

CHAPTER 8

Martha arrived just before noon. She came by way of Wesley and Nellie's house where she left her suitcase and two hatboxes. She changed clothes, freshened up and made preparations to go. Nellie followed her out to the car, holding the door as Martha climbed in. "Go on up there and knock their eyeballs out, especially ole' Ben. He's still a little bit puny from his sick spell, but when he sees you; his juices will start running again. You act a little up tight or something. Are you on a mission of some kind that you're not telling me about?"

Martha laughed as she started the car and moved the shift lever into reverse. "No Nellie, I'm not. I haven't seen Ben in over three weeks, and I am a little anxious to see him you know. Then, of the rest of the family, I only know Carrie and Laurel and Mark and their boys, and I've met James and Eunice, so I'm a little nervous about that also. Don't wait up. I'll see you in the morning and we'll talk all day. Where did that pretty round belly come from?"

"I must have swallowed a seed of some kind, and it's sprouted and started to grow."

"Well you might ought to see a doctor. I want to hear all about it tomorrow. By the way, this is the first time I've driven the car on a trip by myself. I really got the once over when I came through Dawsonville."

Martha arrived at the McClure family Thanksgiving Reunion to a rousing welcome. So much so that Ben received nothing more than a neck hug and a brush of velvet lips on his cheek before Laurel and Eunice carried her away on a round of introductions. Then just as quickly, one of Carrie's ruffled and ironed apron's was tied on her waist and pinned on at her shoulders, and Martha soon found herself drawn into the quickening pace of food preparation.

After an hour Ben started through the kitchen door, but immediately found Laurel blocking his intended pathway toward Martha. "Hey you, what are you lookin for, a job?"

"No, little sister, I'm trying to ---

"Don't little sister me big boy, I cooked supper the night you were born. I know what you're doing, but she's busy. As soon as dinner's over with, she's yours for the rest of the day. Now git', or I will give you a job --- like washing pots and pans. I think every pan and bowl in the house is dirty." As Ben turned toward the door to leave, he saw Martha holding a large platter overhead, waving it at him.

Consuming the huge Thanksgiving dinner-supper, or as much of it as anyone could possibly want, required well over an hour. True to her word, as the table was vacated and the women began to clear the table and wash the huge stacks of dirty tableware, Laurel shooed Ben and Martha out of the house. "All right you love birds, make yourselves scarce, and don't let me see you coming back before dark."

Already knowing where he was going, Ben opened the gate beside the barn, then closed it as they passed through. Taking Martha by the hand they walked across the pasture, through the back gate, along an old field road, and entering the woods they took a footpath, coming out under a huge water oak that stood a dozen yards from the edge of the Amicalola River. The late evening sun shining through the overhanging branches of the water oak left a leafy green and yellow pattern on the slow moving surface of the water.

"Oh Ben, it's absolutely beautiful. Is this on your farm?"

"This side of it is. We could come down here and have a picnic anytime we wanted to."

Martha resisted a pulling temptation to look at Ben and succeeded. They stood quietly for awhile, watching the curling motion toward the middle of the stream, listening to the gentle lapping sound of the water as it came flowing by on its way toward the rocky shoals farther downstream.

When Martha thought about it later, she had no remembrance of the length of time they stood there, side by side and hand in hand. But when Ben released her hand, and took her in his arms she remembered that she came eagerly into his arms and folded herself completely against Ben's body.

"Ben, why didn't you send for me? Nellie said you almost died."

"I wanted to see you so bad Martha, and I didn't know what to do. I thought when Dr. Holden got there I would be all right. Then, when I heard him tell Aunt Nora we had waited too long before we called him, I realized I was about to die, and I knew it was too late to send for you."

"Ben, I'm not trying to make you feel sorry for me, but do you know what would have happened to me if Wesley or James had come and told me you had died. Not even knowing you were sick, and then being told you were dead. Don't you see that everything I do, or say, or even think, is always with you in mind and how it relates to you and me. In my mind I'm Martha that belongs to Ben -- Martha who wants to be where Ben is -- Martha who wants to take care of Ben. If you were gone I would simply be Martha without that part of her, called Ben.

"Do you think of me that way Ben? Have I become so much a part of you, that if I were gone you would be Ben who no longer has the part of him called Martha?"

They stood there for a while, Martha's head lying on and against Ben's chest. Then gently Ben began to stroke and pat Martha's hair, face, then down her back and on her arms. "Martha, let's not talk about what would happen, if one of us were gone. I don't even want to think about it. Let's enjoy today Martha, Thanksgiving Day of 1930. I'm standing here on what I think is one of the most beautiful spots on God's green earth and, I'm holding what I think is the loveliest breathing thing God ever created, in my arms.

"Martha, do you remember that night at Amicalola Falls when you said that when the time came we would know it. Martha, if this is not it; I won't know it when it does come. I don't want to wait any longer. I don't want to take a chance on something happening to either one of us. Martha I want to marry you. Do you want to marry me? I mean, what I'm trying to say or ask is, will you marry me Martha? I have loved you ever since that night you came to practice for Wes and Nellie's wedding."

Her head still lying on Ben's chest, Martha did not move nor answer Ben's proposal for so long, that he decided she either did not understand, or that she was about to refuse him. Then quietly and slowly she answered. "Oh Ben, yes I'll marry you tonight or tomorrow or anytime you say, I'll marry you.

"I would not be truthful Ben if I didn't say I was hoping this weekend would be the time when we knew --- both of us knew --- that it was the right time. That there was no future for us unless it was as man and wife.

"These last weeks have been filled with so much stress and worry and even anger that I was overwhelmed with doubt and fear. When we came out of the woods to stand here close together and close to the river, I thought of the twenty-third Psalm. You know where it says, '*He leadeth me – us – beside the still waters,*' and then the rest is for me, '*He restoreth my soul.*' "Being here in this beautiful place, and finally knowing without any doubt, that you want me for your wife, has restored my soul, has healed me, has made me whole again."

Suddenly, with absolutely no warning that she had experienced a complete change of emotion, Martha bolted out of Ben's arms, took him by the hand and started hurrying back along the path toward the house. "Oh Lord Ben, come on, let's get back to the house. I've got to tell somebody. Let's both tell Carrie, and then I want to tell Grace and Laurel and Eunice. Then I'm going to go wake up Nellie and tell her even though I said I wouldn't ... wake her up I mean."

CHAPTER 9

So it was that on a, beautiful blue sky and spring green, Saturday afternoon in early May of 1931, Martha Jean Barnett and Ben Tyler McClure were married in Mount Zion Baptist Church, filled to overflowing with family, relatives and friends of the bride and groom. Then, as soon as the wedding party arrived at the Barnett place, Dora and Henry served bar-b-que and Brunswick stew until as Henry put it "everybody got their bellies full and the women folks got caught up on all the gossip."

All things considered, Martha and Ben's wedding day was a day to remember. During the remainder of that spring and summer, at Communion and May Day services, revivals and even funerals, it was not uncommon to hear some part of "Martha's wedding day" discussed, and no church wedding was planned without some part of "Martha's wedding ceremony" being used. There was one anticipated incident or experience that did not happen on Martha and Ben's wedding day, and that was, much to Ben's disappointment. The marriage was not consummated!

First of all when they excused themselves and went up the stairs to Martha's bedroom the hour was already well past ten and Ben noticed that Martha's face was visibly pale from exhaustion. Then when Ben closed the bedroom door, Martha went directly to her bed and collapsed backward across it. Immediately from underneath the bed came the clapping, jangling, rattle of cowbells. Martha laughed but barely moved. "That's from that brother of mine. I'll get even if it's the last thing I ever do." As Ben slid under the bed and retrieved the bells from the middle of the bed springs he said with a chuckle in his voice, "And if he's rigged up this bed so that it falls, I'll get evener' than that."

Martha straightened herself on the bed and looked up at Ben with a doleful expression on her face. "Ben darling we can't, everything that has happened today has been so wonderful, and I don't want this part of it to be a disappointment for either of us. I want to enjoy it too you know. Can you understand that Ben?"

"Sure I can honey, and I do. To tell the truth I'm sort of bushed myself-it's all right. I want you to enjoy it too, if you didn't, I don't think I would either. If these bedsprings started squeaking everybody in the house would hear them. Or like I said a minute ago, what if the bed should fall? Wouldn't that be hard to explain in the mornin at the breakfast table. Visualizing that thought they began laughing and fell into each others arms.

"It would be --- it would be awkward Ben darling, that's what it would be." Still laughing, they undressed for bed, put out the light, and keeping their passion in control, kissed and held each other for a moment as they fell into a light sleep. So on the first night of their married life Mr. and Mrs. Ben and Martha McClure did not get to *know* each other.

CHAPTER 10

It was still two months before the wedding when Ben asked Martha where she would like to go on their honeymoon trip. After several moments of contemplation she replied, "I would like to go anywhere just as long as I can see the ocean and go wading in it. All my life I have wanted to see the ocean."

Even though Ben had hoped that Martha would want to go to Nashville and see the Grand Ole' Opry, he agreed that a trip to the seashore would be fun. He suggested, and Martha happily agreed, on Savannah. She was even more thrilled when Ben suggested going on the train and getting a place to stay as close to the ocean shore as possible. The more Ben thought about a trip to the ocean the better he liked it. Not only would he have Martha all to himself, but also he might be able to fulfill a dream that had enticed him since he had become an accomplished fisherman in the lakes, and streams of North Georgia. He might be able to come up with a plan to go deep-sea fishing.

END OF PART 2

God-Fearing Criminals

Part 3

CHAPTER 1

A married man now, with a wife growing heavy with child, Ben's standing as an honest and dependable man in his community continued to grow. It was taken for granted that Ben would be, because of his family, but as always the final proof of that standing was judged by the actions of Ben himself. In almost every case, it was the man of the house who was judged as being honest or dishonest in his dealings, and his word dependable. Only on the rarest of occasions was fault ever laid to the wife. Usually it was she who was in sympathy given the benefit of, "That poor woman has had a lot to put up with."

Mountain people were and are, for the most part, a somewhat cynical, yet wholeheartedly forgiving and supportive people. Even the men who, through their own "Downright sorriness," gained the title of "Not being worth the powder and lead to blow their brains out, " and then, "Made a change" and started "Stayin at home and takin care of their families," were forgiven as having taken "a little longer than some of the rest to get over fool's hill."

The generally accepted custom of the southern family of that day was that the child who remained with the parents, and helped provide for their care and keep during their failing and final years, received the first and most valuable part of the family estate. In most cases that was the home place. Not necessarily because of its value, especially when anything received for a property would be divided among each family member, it was in the eye of the beholder and his or her desire for it.

The two hundred forty acre, river bottom farm, of Will and Carrie McClure that lay along the Eastern side of the Amicalola River was known as the McClure place. The child that remained with Will and Carrie and accepted the roll of head of household upon his father's death was Ben, and to Ben the value of the McClure farm could not be measured by the size of rubies or the weight of gold. It was a love that transcended natural values.

In the year of his father's death, Ben saw to every liability that Will and Carrie had been accountable for, both public and private. He consulted with his mother to make sure she was able to, "Pay the church what you usually pay," for the rest of the year. He participated in every community work project that Will was involved in, even the public road repair which Will had annually organized and helped with.

As long as Carrie lived, Ben saw to her every reasonable need, once complaining to Dr. Vic Holden that, "Seems like the older she gets the more set in her ways she gets," and Carrie confided to the Perry sister's that, "Ben has always been a good boy. Now that's not to say he don't kick out of the traces every once and a while, but it don't usually last too long."

Until she died, even after Ben and Martha were married, they referred to the house as "Your house" because they could see that it pleased her, and Ben was continually carrying out some repair or change that Carrie felt was needed. "This place is goin to be yours one of these days Ben, and I think you'll be glad you did that."

The weather and the condition of the roads permitting, on the third Sunday of every month, Ben and Carrie arrived at Shoal Creek Baptist Church for "Meetin day." Carrie never became comfortable riding in an automobile even though the few miles to and from Shoal Creek Church constituted the major part of her trips in an automobile, she constantly admonished Ben that, "I'm fearful of this contraption son, what if it should tip over in a ditch with both of us pinned under it, what would we do? We might have to lay in such a condition all night."

To which Ben would grin and answer to his mother, "Mama if you weren't at home or at Shoal Creek Church, the whole settlement would be out lookin for you. Don't worry about it."

When the stock market crashed in 1929, and dire predictions of disastrous times at hand appeared in magazines and newspapers across the country, there was a cloud of apprehension and fear that spread rapidly across the land. There was also a large segment of the population, especially those living in areas of the country already grappling with living conditions that bordered on starvation. Those predictions were answered with a cynical invitation to "Join the crowd, we've been living in hard times for so long we didn't know there was anything else."

Will and Carrie McClure's family and thousands of families in like condition were born into and lived their lives in the meager years following the Civil War. Like most families they worked and sacrificed for what they had, worked for what they had to eat, for what they had to wear, to pay their debts, their taxes and finally the wherewithal to bury themselves with.

Calamity struck with maiming accidents, terminal illness, and acts of God such as the dry year of 1925, or deadly tornadoes and storms that devastated land, crops and houses alike. They did not blame nor accuse God, but accepted and submitted to it as just punishment for sins of omission and commission. Did not the Lord God use flood and famine to punish his chosen people, the Israelites, when they sinned against him?

"Pray for mercy, church," the Reverend Boyd Williams preached in his last sermon as pastor of Shoal Creek Baptist Church, "If he gave us justice, we'd all burn in hell."

However hard the times, Ben McClure's family, like most other families that lived in the Southern foothills of the Blue Ridge Mountains, did not live in nor suffer from starvation. For the same set of reasons that affect the condition of human existence, that benefit was the result of actions taken, intentionally and unintentionally, by previous generations, desperate to survive the intended annihilation of their homeland during the last days of the Civil War. Even the so called Yankee carpetbaggers helped when labor and materials were required to construct and operate their business of federally granted privilege.

Across the South when Confederate money was deemed worthless, and there were few means by which the average Southerner could earn the 'new federal dollars,' a system of barter and trade was initiated that was in some ways better than money itself. For regardless of what the barter or trade concerned, whether animals, food, clothing, farm equipment, even labor, the goods were either there or immediately available for use when the trade was made.

Like Ben McClure, thousands of men and boys began trading and bartering. Beginning with what few possessions they had, they grew their enterprise into a profitable business -- a business that performed a necessary service for a great number of people immobilized by their location and condition.

Wesley was not a good trader. He did not possess that keen insight that enabled him to recognize the value of his possession in relation to the desire of another trader to own it. One Saturday evening after a brisk morning of barter and exchange at a trading ground near Burtsboro, Ben surveyed the results of Wesley's trades for the day.

"Wes when you make a trade and you think you're tradin about even, try to get something to boot. You never can tell when you might need a little something to make a real good trade. You let that feller from Auraria burn your britches off when he traded you out of that double tree and two single trees."

"I thought I did all right."

"For a wheel barrow? Everybody's got a wheel barrow; on top of that it's got a wooden wheel on it."

"I know it but I was planning on tradin you out of that metal wheel hangin in your shop." Ben grinned at his friend as they finished loading their trades in the back of Ben's truck.

"I'll have to admit one thing though Wes. If you keep makin trades like that, you may not make any money, but you'll draw a damn good following for us."

None of them, Ben included, became a captain of industry, and certainly none of them earned a great fortune. Some did establish places for their business, and became influential men in their community. As the South struggled to free itself of economic bondage, every small town and community grew up around a large mercantile business that bought, sold, bartered and traded everything from anklets to automobiles. They were all part of that huge culture of people who either knowingly or unknowingly, helped start the painfully slow movement that nudged the South out of its era of helplessness.

In August of 1931, Wesley and Nellie Cochran became the parents of a baby girl. They named her Elizabeth Marie after a number of ancestors on both sides of the two families.

In November of 1932, Ben and Martha McClure became the parents of a baby boy. They named him Joshua Tarpley and no one on either side of either family had any recollection of ancestors with either of those names. When Cora Perry first heard the names given to Ben's child she stood for a full minute drying her hands on her apron. "Well help my time. So far as I can recollect I've never heard tell of anybody named Tarpley, let alone any of Will and Carrie's folks."

It was on an 'after the Thanksgiving deer hunt' with Ben and Wesley that Dr. Vic Holden chided his two young friends. "I hope there ain't any danger of you two young bucks gettin in a race with this baby business. I know that both of you are full of piss and vinegar, but I can tell you from personal experience, when you wind up with one in the shop and one in the crib and one crawlin around on the floor, it puts a strain on everybody. Take your time, it aint' goin nowhere, and if you do, it'll be there when you get back."

In the year of 1932, Dr. Holden and the Perry sisters delivered seventeen babies. Of that number two were stillborn and three more died within three months of birth. Thankfully they lost none of the mothers, but their recovery required a much longer than usual period of time. After one particularly hard delivery that required all afternoon, Vic and Grace sat on the back porch discussing the delivery. "It was her first baby and I had to help her have it."

"Well that's not uncommon for a first baby is it?"

"Well no, I reckon not, but she was wore out when it was over. The baby was so weak it was barely whimperin."

"They are not getting enough to eat Victor. Is there not any help available?"

"Well, they are beginning to bring in more of those government commodities. The hell of it is that a lot of the people won't take them when they are offered."

"Well Dr. Holden, that's where you come in. You can start with the babies and order them to use the powered milk and flour. Write them out a prescription if that's what it takes."

"Oh hell Grace, what are you trying to do, make me a commodity distribution representative for Dawson County?"

"If that's what it takes I am. I'll help you and I know Cora and Nora will too. Besides that, my beloved physician, didn't I read somewhere that you swore to help heal the sick?"

CHAPTER 2

"Wes, this whole thing is happening just about the way Doc Holden said it would when the stock market in New York crashed," Ben said as they left the trading grounds in his truck. "We didn't have much of any way to make money to start with and since that happened seems like it's been gettin worse all the time. Doc Holden says he's afraid it may get worse before it gets any better.

"Just like today. I guess I've made a dozen trades, and I've come out with less than two dollars. Time was I could come out with eight or ten dollars without even trying. How about you Wes? Did you make any money today?"

"Not a dime Ben, fact is if I would have had a few dollars, I could have made a couple of real good deals myself."

The time was mid-September of 1932 and Ben and Wesley were discussing the results from their day of trading on their way home from a farmer's market and trading ground near Dawsonville.

"I'm just about out of money Wes, and I sure didn't want that to happen right now. It's only about 2 months 'til the baby's due, and then there's Christmas comin right after that."

"Well, I didn't either Ben, but we've been runnin pretty close ourselves. Seems like everytime I would get a few dollars ahead, something always comes along and I have to spend it. I have been thinkin about cuttin a few loads of logs and haulin then to the mill. We can work together on it if you want to. You've got some real good poplar trees up your spring branch back there."

"Well, all right Wes. Let's look into that and see what our chances are." Ben fell silent for a long moment before he continued, "What I had in mind, and what I think we could do to make some money, is to make some liquor. We still have my Daddy's still, and there's rarely a week goes by that I don't hear from one of Daddy's old customers, especially this time of year. What do you think Wes? Want to try it?"

CHAPTER 3

Wesley looked thoughtfully across the cab of the truck at his life long friend. He soon realized that what Ben was suggesting would require a change in the direction of their lives. Perhaps out of necessity, because he knew that Ben McClure was not a man who accepted adversity without a remedy, but a change nonetheless.

Wesley remembered it was just this morning, while they were still at the market, that he noticed Ben standing by the door of a new 1933 V8 Ford, rumored to be so fast that the engine was already being used in stock cars and also installed in some open wheel racers.

Wesley noticed that as he approached the car, the man sitting inside stopped talking and nodded in his direction. Ben motioned Wesley closer and made the introductions. "Wes, this is Frank Kirby. Frank and my Daddy were good friends. Frank, this is Wesley Cochran. Wes and Nellie live over on Johntown Road, not far from Cochran Creek." Frank leaned back in the seat and extended his hand out the window. "Wes, I'm glad to meet you. I probably know a lot of your folks, and I've heard Ben mention your name several times." As Wesley shook the offered hand he leaned forward to get a better look at Frank's face, and also a look at the inside of the car. But the thing that caught Wesley's eye was the No. 8 brown paper bag sitting upright on the seat next to Frank. The bag was filled to the top with rolls of money. Wesley had no way of knowing how much money each tightly rolled and securely wrapped with a rubber band roll contained, but he did know that the bag contained more money than he had seen at one time in his whole life.

"Well, I'm glad to meet you, Frank. Yeah, Ben and I work together quite a bit, especially when a strong back and weak mind is needed."

"Well, two heads are always better than one. Ben, let me know what you decide. I'll be glad to help anyway I can. Fellers, I need to go. I'll see you boys later, okay?"

As Frank's car crossed the shallow ditch that was crisscrossed with deep rutted wagon tracks in order to get to the road, Wesley noticed there was no spring or sway to the rear end of the car. Both men knew it was an indication that additional springs, heavy duty shock absorbers and six ply tires had been installed on the car in order to support an extra twelve to fourteen hundred pounds of weight, and still look normal on the road.

"Probably built to support about two hundred gallons," Ben said as much to himself as Wesley. "He's one of the Kirby's from over there around Yellow Creek, Wes. His folks still live there and I guess he does too. He's been tripping liquor to give to politicians, sheriffs and police, and he sold that cheap liquor, that he and his brothers made, to bootleggers in Vine City and Buttermilk Bottoms. But he pays every man every dime that he owes him, and that goes a long way. They tell me that between owning a part in the still and hauling all of the liquor from it, he's made enough money to burn wet dogs with."

Ben knew that Wesley had never been directly involved in the liquor business, but like most people in Dawson and the surrounding counties, he knew some of the men involved in the making, hauling, and selling of it.

Ben knew that his friend was, "No more than what was normal," afraid of neither the risks nor the dangers involved. There were some of both, but not out of the ordinary. He knew that Wesley was not afraid of the work involved and there was plenty of that. Ben also knew that financially, Wesley was in bad shape, but as his Daddy told him several years before he died, "Don't expect a Cochran to complain. That's one thing they don't do much of."

When Wesley answered Ben's question, it was not a yes or no, but rather with a question of his own. "Ben, what are you going to tell your wife? Because whatever you tell Martha is what I'm going to tell Nellie."

"Wes, I'm sure you know that's what me and Frank Kirby was talkin about this mornin. He's promised to take every gallon of liquor we can make between now and Christmas. He wants us to double the sweet and sour mash and use nothing but corn meal and corn malt. He wants to use that for his Christmas presents. After that, we don't have to double it and we can use some sugar if we want to.

"Wes, Martha knows and I'm sure Nellie knows that we're runnin short in the money department this year. I'm goin to tell her that one of Daddy's old customers has offered us a good price to make him a few rounds on my Daddy's still. I estimate that if we have good luck, we ought to make between two and three hundred dollars apiece by Christmas."

"Well, I guess that's about enough said. What do you want me to do first?"

"Wes, I want you to get started cuttin those logs first thing Monday morning. Just so you don't arouse any suspicion, go ahead and cut as many loads of poplar and pine as you want. I want enough poplar to build eighteen-four x four boxes, four feet high. We'll only build eight or nine to start with but we'll have the rest of the lumber on hand.

In the meantime, I'll see to the corn meal and the corn malt. I'll check the Copper Still and the Condenser out and make sure they are all right to use. Let me know how you're comin along with the lumber for the boxes, and we'll get together right away and pick us out a place. We'll be 'cooking in' the mash just as soon as we can get everything together."

CHAPTER 4

Ben and Wesley did not profit from their first attempt at making liquor as much as they had hoped for. The reason, however, was not the result of any failure on their part; actually for a first effort they were quite successful. It was just that they underestimated the amount of time required to put the whole undertaking together, and then put it into operation.

While Ben knew the basics, they still had to learn by trial the best way to operate a copper still. They also taught themselves the proper method of "cookin in" and "breakin up" and mixing the ingredients into a mash that worked itself into still beer with the highest possible content of alcohol.

They soon discovered one more ingredient required in the "moonshine liquor" making trade - Elbow grease.

"Ben, this is the hardest work I've ever done in my life, and we're havin to do it at night on top of that."

"Well, it will help you to stay on your side of the bed a little better, Wes. You remember what Doc Holden said, don't you?"

Not only did Frank Kirby keep his promise to take all the liquor that Ben and Wesley produced for the rest of that year, but just before Christmas, he made them another offer.

"Ben, if you and Wes are interested, I'll go in with you and we'll put up another still in January. You and Wes can keep runnin yours and we'll get a couple of still hands to run the other one. I'll get the cans out of Atlanta and bring them in, and you boys can get everything else from Rabb Turner. I'll take all the liquor from both stills and pay seventy five cents a gallon for it. We ought to be able to make liquor 'til you boys want to quit and make a crop. What do you think? Want to give it a try?"

Ben looked at Wesley for a moment before he answered. "Well, that's something to think about, Frank. Give us a day or two to talk and we'll let you know, how's that?"

"That's fair enough. Just let me know."

Later that afternoon as they were cutting wood to heat the still, Ben asked Wesley what he thought of Frank's proposal for a second still?

Wesley continued cutting and trimming with his long handled, double bladed axe for a couple of minutes before he leaned the axe against a tree and sat down on a stump.

"Ben, how long are you plannin on staying in the liquor business, or had you even thought about it?"

"Yeah, I have thought about it Wes, and I was goin to mention it to you. Martha's not too happy about it and neither is Mama."

Ben stopped for a moment and grinned at Wesley as he continued. "Mama said I was headed for the penitentiary at Maxwell Field, Alabama, just as fast as I can go. How in the hell she knows there's a penitentiary at Maxwell Field, Alabama, I'll never know Wes. Anyway, they know how bad things are right now, so they will just have to understand.

"But to answer your question, Wes, I haven't decided yet. We've got a pretty good thing goin, and if we don't have any bad luck, we ought to do all right by the time we quit in the spring. But if you want to quit when we stop for Christmas, it's all right Wes. Don't do it if you're not satisfied about it."

"Well, Nellie's not too happy about it either, but she's well aware of the shape we were in before we started. Besides, it looks like she may be in the family way again, or at least she thinks she is."

"Well, I'll be damned Wes. I can see I might as well go and get Doc Holden on your ass -- You recollect what he said about havin one baby after another?"

"Well, all right then. But I'll have to remind him, that brood of his is pretty well bunched together when he starts remindin me about his fatherly advice."

The two men grinned at each other, enjoying their friendly exchange.

"Ben, you know what Nellie said about us workin at our still all night long? She said when she heard me come in early in the mornin she didn't know whether to take off her shimmy or get up and start fixin breakfast." That evoked a good belly laugh from both men.

"Tell you what Ben, if you're all right with it, let's go in with Frank on another still and when we quit in the spring, I'll know for sure whether or not I want to stay in or get out."

"Good enough, Wes, good enough. Let's try to get Zeke Turner to run the other still, and if he ain't doin nothin right now, we might get Red Spencer to help him.

And so with that loosely termed agreement, the two men embarked on a venture in which the goal of the legal system of their country was to take from them their freedom, yet all the while condoning the same activity by another, provided they held a tax-paid permit. However, they understood and accepted that risk.

As a result of that risk they became both the hunted and the hunter, which in turn, required them, not only to conceal their illicit liquor making operation from the Federal, State, and local officials, but to operate it in complete secrecy. They profited as a result of the misery from a deep depression in their country, and justified it with the knowledge that they sold their remedy a lot cheaper than the government allowed its remedy to be sold for.

Their wives lived in constant dread and fear of tragedy that could, and oftentimes did, strike at any time. They accepted the loss of a liquor still in operation, and the capture of themselves or their stillhands as a cost of doing business.

Ben and Wesley were well rewarded, money wise, from their years of involvement in the moonshine or white liquor business. But they were far from being immune to the trials and tribulations that accompany being part of an illegal trade. As a result, neither Ben nor Wesley, nor any other man that involved himself in the illicit liquor business for any length of time, ever considered himself to be a successful business man.

In their discussions with each other, and in their private reflections, they recalled their failures, their mistakes and their losses. Losses mostly of time, money and material, but on occasion the heart-breaking knowledge that they were responsible for the loss of a man's life.

CHAPTER 5

The making of liquor requires a few basic ingredients, such as sugar (brown or white), corn and/or rye meal, corn malt or bakers' yeast (to speed up the fermentation process) and a plenteous supply of good water, preferably spring water. All of this, in addition to an available supply of containers to put it in. Needless to say, the bigger the size of the operation, requires a proportionally larger amount of supplies. Likewise, just as important as having a demand for the finished product, and a means to deliver it, is having a convenient place to procure the necessary supplies, and a means to deliver them to the still owner without being seen enough times to give away the location of the still.

Such a man in the Amicalola community of Dawson County was Rabb Turner.

Rabb and Annie Turner and their three children lived north of the Amicalola Falls to Dahlonega Road. Their three hundred and twenty-acre farm lying along the southern edge of the Chattahoochee National Forest.

Rabb kept on hand most everything necessary to make liquor and what he didn't have he knew where to get it. There was another dividend besides convenience, if you were a trusted customer of Rabb's. Since the Turner Farm bordered on the Chattachoochee Game Reserve, a deer hunt always provided game, and a fishing trip rarely failed to produce a full stringer, if you were lucky enough to be asked to go on one of their hunting or fishing trips. Needless to say, Ben and Wesley became trusted and valued customers, and because Dr. Holden was their friend as well as their doctor, he was included in their hunting and fishing trips that sometimes carried them far into the federal forestland.

The eldest of the three Turner children was Newton, or Newt. Newt's ambition was to be a farmer and his dream was to be a cattle farmer. With the help of Rabb and his mother, Newt owned a one hundred fifty acre farm adjoining the Turner farm and a small herd of some eighteen head of white faced Hereford beef cattle. While Newt helped his father when and how he was needed, he had no interest in getting further involved in the moonshine liquor business.

Not so with his younger brother, Clyde Ezekial, better known as Zeke by everyone except his mother. Zeke had no intention of being involved in anything other than the liquor business. In order to show his father just how serious he was, and to prove to his friends that he could do it, before his tenth birthday, he built a ten gallon still, worked off two ten gallon buckets of mash, and made a half gallon of liquor.

Zeke proudly presented his jug of liquor to his father, who immediately took a small taste and rendered a verdict. "Well, son, considerin how you made it, it's not half bad. I'll tell you one thing though; I've had a hell of a lot worse."

Coming from his father, for Zeke, that was high praise.

Zeke Turner had another talent, which every man or boy that competed against him was at first amazed and then envious of. He was such a swift runner that not one of them could catch him, let alone, outrun him. "They ain't no revenue officer can catch me. I can run just as damn fast as I want to," Zeke bragged to his schoolmates, which was one of the reasons, that by the time he was eighteen; Zeke was much sought after as a still hand.

CHAPTER 6

Neither Rabb nor Annie were very handsome people. Rabb was a big rawboned man with a long face and a wide mouth filled with big gapped teeth. Annie was a short, dumpy woman with a round face above a short neck and sloping round shoulders. Annie's redeeming characteristic was a warm smile, usually on display, and a sunny disposition. Their two sons were passable in looks, and Newton was easy to know and friendly. Zeke was not even tempered. Therefore, there was nothing on either side of Rabb nor Annie's family, past nor present, that could account for nor explain the exquisite beauty of their third child, a girl whom they named Clara Mae.

When Dr. Holden returned from making the delivery of Annie's baby, he told Grace that, "I've delivered a lot of them, but I believe that's the prettiest baby I've ever seen." To which Grace replied, "Well, she surely must be something. All I've ever heard you say about a newborn baby is that they are red all over, and usually screaming at the top of their lungs."

When Dr. Holden let Rabb and the two boys in to see the new baby, Rabb stood for a long moment in amazement before he said, "Dang Miss Annie, she's about the purtiest little thing I've ever laid eyes on. I don't hardly see how she could belong to you and me, do you?"

Surprisingly soon, Clara Mae recognized and responded to her brothers with kicks and squeals, which they returned with a double measure of attention and adoration. Annie looked on the beauty of her child with a troubled mind. She knew that a beautiful girl was looked upon with suspicion and jealousy, and even worse a beautiful woman was both envied and criticized. Also because of their self-vanity, they either, got or took if necessary, their hearts desire, with no regard to who was hurt or what was damaged. Perhaps just as bad as vanity, a beautiful woman was thought of as being proud, or one who is filled with pride.

Clara Mae Turner did mature into a beautiful woman, and for the most part, she handled it quite well, but pride was a controlling attribute in her life, and it became one which she did not handle well at all. Clara Mae was not only pride filled, she was motivated by it. She took pride in herself, what she did and what she had. Pride helped Clara rise above her personal circumstances but kept her from being ashamed of what they were. And so it was some years later, when someone she loved was taken from her, it was her pride that almost destroyed her. But through it all and at a most crucial time, it was the abiding love and steadfast friendship of Elizabeth Marie Cochran that saved her, and restored her.

CHAPTER 7

Harley Gayton was a sawmiller. Harley was not a part time sawmiller, but working at sawmills was Harley's lifelong avocation, and he was good at it. Harley's job at a sawmill was running the log yard or log pile. This entailed keeping the logs separated as to kind, such as pine, oak or poplar, and keeping the large and small logs separated as some sawers required. Also, if and as needed, he helped the sawyer load the mill carriage, so it was not uncommon for Harley to follow a sawmill as it moved from one location to another, in order to keep his log yard job. Sometimes moving into an adjoining county prevented Harley from coming home, except during a spell of unusually bad weather or on weekends when the owner would shut the mill down both Saturday and Sunday for necessary repairs.

Harley owned twenty-five acres of land where he and his wife Sara lived in a square four room house with a shed porch on the front and back. There was a front and back door to the outside, but it had door openings without the doors to pass from one room to the next on the inside.

The Gayton place was located about four miles from the McClure Farm, but it lay on the western side of the Amicalola River. The two families knew each other but since they lived on opposite sides of the river and a road crossing was some distance downstream, there was little in the way of social contact.

Harley and Sara had been married less than a year when he came walking up Doctor Holden's driveway late on a Sunday afternoon and asked to see the doctor.

"Doctor Holden, my wife Sara is in the family way and she thinks the baby is goin to be born tonight. She wants you and Miss Cora and Miss Nora to come and help her. I can pay you cash money now if you'd ruther."

"Well Harley, I never have made anybody pay in advance and I'm not going to start with you. We'll settle up after the baby gets here, if that's all right with you."

"That's all right by me Doctor Holden."

"Harley, you go by Cora and Nora's house and tell them, for me, to go on to your place and get everything ready. Then you make all haste and get home to your wife. Tell Miss Sara that I'll be there directly."

After ten long hours of hard and determined labor, and with some help from Victor's forceps, Sara delivered a small, purplish red baby that he felt sure was dead. Cora tied the umbilical cord and Victor cut it, made sure the air passage was open and still seeing no sign of life, handed the baby to Nora. Victor turned his attention back to Sara, motioning to Cora at the same time. "Quick, Miss Cora, we must hurry." Cora had already replenished the stack of clothes from their now famous rag bag, and they began again the ageless battle for life against time and free flowing blood.

Long minutes later, more than an hour actually, they looked at each other, nodded, and lifted their blood-soaked hands from Sara's body, satisfied that they had stemmed the flow of blood and stabilized her breathing and blood pressure. They turned to find Nora with a small whimpering and squirming form clasped to her breast, great silver tears running into her mouth, which was stretched wide with a beaming smile. "Dr. Holden, did you think there was something wrong with this little ol' boy? Seems to me like he's doin just fine. He's already started smackin his lips and stickin his tongue out. What this boy needs is a titty full of milk to suck on."

On his birth certificate, Sara requested their son be named Luther Harley Gayton. "There's not every man whose son is named after him." Harley said, obviously touched by Sara's request. He was however, never known as or called by anything other than Luke, his mother included.

Neither Sara nor Harley ever attended a day of schooling in their lives. So when Amicalola Elementary School started in the year of Luke's sixth birthday, Sara and Luke walked the five miles to the Amicalola School House where she proudly enrolled her son in the first grade.

With Harley gone most of the time, on occasion coming home only on weekends, Sara and Luke formed a near perfect mother and son relationship. Soon realizing that his mother was not a strong woman, Luke gradually took over all outside work, and with Sara's encouragement offered his ideas on problems that arose and decisions that had to be made in his father's absence.

Luke was ten and in fourth grade when the idea of a part time job shoveling sawdust and doing other odd jobs for a nearby sawmill owner's operation first came to mind. With Christmas holidays at hand, he would discuss his idea with his father, whom he felt sure would be home for a few days for Christmas.

As it turned out, Luke's wish came true. A spell of cold rainy weather took hold at the start of Christmas week and the mill owner, where Harley worked, shut the sawmill down, paid his hands and sent them home for Christmas.

For the rest of his life, when Luke thought of Christmas, he always remembered that Christmas when he was ten years old.

When Harley drove his Model A Ford Truck up the muddy driveway and stopped beside the back porch, he unloaded several bags of groceries and a burlap bag from which he removed a stalk of ripe bananas and hung them from a cord over the kitchen table. "Eat all of them that you want, Luke, just so there's enough left for Sarrie to make us a great big banana puddin for Christmas Day."

Luke had cut a six-foot cedar that he found growing along the pasture fence and nailed a crude stand to the bottom end of it. While Sara was preparing their supper on Sunday evening, Luke and his Daddy erected the tree in the corner of the living room as far from the open fireplace as possible. "We don't want to take no chances on it catchin fire, Luke. It'll git' purty dried out before you take it down after New Year's," Harley reminded his son.

Then on that cold and rainy Sunday evening, as daylight suddenly turned into darkness, they ate a huge meal of boiled backbones from one of Harley's recently killed fattening hogs, along with fried kraut, baked sweet potatoes and cracklin corn bread. After supper, they decorated their tree with some old red and green roping along with popcorn strung on red and black thread from Sara's sewing machine. Then, as ice formed on the mud puddles and rain froze into icicles on limbs and branches, they sat admiring their handiwork drinking from steaming cups of Luzianne coffee and chicory and eating Sara's fried apple pies.

Christmas morning broke to clearing skies and a cold wind blowing out of the northwest. When Luke awoke, he saw that a roaring fire was burning in the fireplace, and he heard the familiar kitchen sounds that meant breakfast was being prepared. He dressed quickly in the cold room and hurried through the curtained doorway to the Christmas tree. There was the new pair of winter workshoes, a red and black flannel shirt and a pair of high-backed Carhartt overalls. There was, for everyone's enjoyment, a box of mixed apples and oranges and two boxes of stick candy, one peppermint and one of mixed flavors.

Luke saw the two red and yellow boxes first, sitting on the floor behind a shoebox, and as he bent over for a closer look, he saw the shotgun, behind some of the branches, leaning against the wall.

"Oh, I cain't believe it. Is it for me, Mama and Daddy? Is it really for me?"

"Yeah, it's yours, Luke," Harley grinned at his son, "it's yours just as long as you are careful with it and take care of it. Your mama and me and ol' Santa Claus got it for you along with them two boxes of shells. It's a Fox 20-gauge double barrel. If you'll look on the side of the barrel, there you'll see a fox with a big, bushy tail engraved in the metal."

"I will Daddy, I'll always take care of it and keep it cleaned and oiled. Can we go huntin while you're still off for Christmas?"

"Sure we can, son. We might go tomorrow if this wind lays. I've been cravin some squirrel dumplings ever since cold weather got here.

CHAPTER 8

Irregardless, of her near death experience that resulted from her first pregnancy, Sara's dream and desire was for another pregnancy from which she would give birth to a girl baby. It was for her then, a joyous occasion when in February, after Harley's week off for Christmas, that Dr. Holden confirmed that she was pregnant. Sara had no doubt that her prayer of many years was about to be answered.

Along with the usual dosage of calcium and iron tablets, Victor warned Sara to be especially careful during the first three months of her pregnancy. "Sara, I hope I don't come by your house on wash day and see you using a battlin stick."

Sara followed Dr. Holden's advice about using a battling stick, but she did something else that was just as bad for a pregnant woman to do. She exchanged the battlin stick for a rubboard and hand scrubbed every pair of Harley and Luke's work clothes. The next morning, she saw a red stain on her underclothes and vowed to be more careful about doing too much strenuous work. Sara did spend the remainder of the day patching and mending clothes, but tomorrow was ironing day and that had to be done.

Sara always heated her irons on the stovetop while she prepared breakfast, and by the time she finished washing the breakfast dishes, she was ready to start ironing. Sara ironed without stopping until the noon hour, letting one iron reheat on the stovetop while she ironed with the other. She ate a cold biscuit and left over gravy for her dinner, and finished ironing just as Luke arrived home from school. Then while Luke was milking their cow, Sara started preparing their evening meal, stopping when Luke brought the evening milking in to be strained, poured up in a clay pitcher and with a heavy cloth tied over the top, sent it to the spring house by Luke where he set it handle deep in the cold water of their boiling spring.

After supper, while Luke went back to the barn to stable and feed the mule, Sara washed the dishes and put her ironing away. With first dark coming on, she lit the lamp and looked out the back door for Luke. It was while she was standing in the door that the first pain came. Almost as hard as a birthing pain, it did not completely go away until another one came, along with a feeling of being extremely tired. Sara knew that she had to lie down.

"What's the matter, Mama, have you turned sick?" Luke asked from the doorway to his mother's room.

"Well I guess I've just over done it a little the last couple of days, son. Bring me a glass of water and then you work on your lessons until bedtime. Don't forget to blow out the lamp when you start to bed."

Still feeling very tired and weary, Sara dozed for an hour and awoke with a pressing backache and she sensed that her underclothes were wet. She knew that it was blood, and she also knew that she was probably still bleeding. She made an effort to get out of bed to change her clothes, but she could not. It was then that Sara realized that she was about to miscarry her baby.

Luke came to her bedside after being called only once.

"Mama, are you worse?"

"I'm afraid I am, son. Would you be afraid to light the lantern and go after Dr. Holden for me?"

"Why no Mama, I'll go right now."

"Alright son, but don't try to run all the way now, or you'll be give out before you get there."

"I won't, Mama, but I'll make all haste that I can."

When Luke stepped out on the back porch he saw the half moon almost overhead and realized that he did not need a lantern. He pulled on his old and worn shoes because they were the lightest, walked down the driveway to the road, and started a ground-covering jog that would take him to Dr. Holden's place in the shortest amount of time.

Well over two hours had passed when Dr. Holden turned into the driveway and stopped with the driver's side of his car beside the front porch steps. Luke hurriedly pushed his door open and started to get out.

"Dr. Holden, I'll go in and light the lamp and see how Mama is."

"Luke, I have a flashlight here, so let me go in first and light the lamp. Luke, I want you to sit down there on the front porch while I go in and see about your Mama. Will you do that for me, Luke? That's what I'm supposed to do, you know."

"Alright, I'll do that Dr. Holden. I'll just set here on the edge of the porch 'til you call me. The lamp and the matches are on the kitchen table."

Victor sat his bag on the table and lit the lamp. He replaced the globe and adjusted the wick. Leaving his bag on the table, he picked up the lamp and walked into the bedroom where he found what he both feared, and expected to find.

Sara's sightless eyes staring out of a lifeless face, her body relaxed in the quiet repose of death. Victor lifted the quilt and saw the large bloodstain on the bed sheet that covered her body. He established an approximate time of death and closed Sara's eyes. He pulled the quilt over Sara's body, stepped back from the bed and stood for a moment of quiet reflection. Victor returned the lamp to the kitchen table, picked up his bag and walked back out on the front porch where he sat down on the steps and put his arm around Luke's shoulders. But he did not have to tell Luke what had happened.

"Mama's dead, ain't she Dr. Holden?"

"Yes, she is Luke, and there's not a thing either one of us could have done about it. It was too late when she sent you to get me."

They sat there for several minutes, Victor feeling an occasional sob and shiver in Luke's shoulders before he said, "I was afraid that she was, Dr. Holden. Mama was in the bed when I got back from the barn after supper. That's the first time in my life I ever remember seein Mama in the bed, while I was still up."

The sawmill where Harley worked was located about ten miles from his home, and for the next two months after Sara's death, he drove home every evening after work. The mill owner, sympathetic to Harley's plight, encouraged him to leave work each evening in time to get home before dark. But then, as they were in the process of sawing out and making preparations to move the mill to the next set, he asked Harley if he would be available after the move, which was to Lumpkin County, about twenty miles away.

"Well, Mr. Wright, I've worked for you off and on for better'n five year now. So if you've got a job for me, I think I'll go with you. Luke has been wantin a job doodlin sawdust, so I'll just bring him along with me if that's alright."

"Well, it's not much of a life for a kid of a boy, but if that's what you want to do, it's alright with me."

But it was not all right with Luke.

"No, Daddy, I don't want to do that. I want to stay here and go to school. I promised Mama I wouldn't quit school 'til I finished all the grades at Amicalola School. I'll take care of our mule and I've been milkin our cow for almost a year. I'll be real careful and if I need anything, I'll go and see Miss Cora and Miss Nora. They said for me to. They knew that you would have to go with the sawmill when it moved. Mama wouldn't want us to leave our place. She didn't want me to see about that job at the sawmill until school was out and I promised her I wouldn't."

Harley realized that the only way he would get Luke to leave would be to force him to go, and he wasn't going to do that. "Alright, Luke, but it's against my better judgment. I'll mention it to Ben McClure also, so that if I'm needed here, he can come and get me."

Living alone was not as easy as Luke imagined it would be, and when Martha McClure found out that Luke was living alone, and her husband was aware of it, Ben found out just how uneasy it made his wife.

"Ben, you mean to tell me that you think it's all right for that child to live over there by himself, and nobody living any closer to him than we are?"

"Well Martha, I didn't say that I thought it was alright, but his Daddy said he couldn't get him to leave without forcing him, so I don't think he would leave if you or me wanted him to, Do you?"

"I don't know. But I think we ought to go over there and see about him."

"All right, Miss Martha, I'm ready to go when you are."

Luke was putting the mule in the barn when he saw Ben's truck turn in the driveway and stopped by the front porch. He started waving when he saw that Martha and Josh were with him. Josh jumped down from the truckbed and came running toward the barn. "Hello, Josh, I sure am glad to see you all. Let me feed this mule a bundle of fodder, and we'll go back to the house."

Josh, not yet five, admired Luke as if he were a grown man, even more so now that Luke owned a shotgun and hunted by himself.

"Luke, are you afraid to stay here at night by yourself?"

"Well, I was a little to start with, but ol' Boss and Lady sleep out there on the front porch and if anything comes around, they let me know. Last night, I woke up and Lady was growling. They don't usually do that, so I got up and slipped over there and looked out the window. There stood that dang mule out there in the front yard, so I just went back to bed and left him standing there. This morning, he was back down there in the hall of the barn. Daddy said not to worry about it, if something got me it would turn me loose soon as it come daylight."

Luke gave his young friend a playful slap on the back and continued, "He may be right, but I still keep a chair leaned under the door knobs just to be on the safe side, and I keep my shotgun leanin against the wall at the head of my bed."

Martha and Ben were removing pots and covered dishes from the truck as Luke and Josh walked up the footpath from the barn.

"Luke, I didn't think you would mind if I brought our supper over here and we ate with you."

"No, ma'am, I sure don't. Cornbread and milk get mighty old when you have it about every night. Miss Cora and Miss Nora have come and brought supper twice and Miz Holden has sent me something to eat by Dr. Holden a couple of times."

After supper, they all helped Martha wash the dishes and clean up the kitchen. The sun had just disappeared behind the ridgeline of trees to the West as they came out on the porch. Ben took an old rocker to sit in and Martha the swing, while Luke and Josh sat on the edge of the porch, their feet on the top step. Martha, using the tip of her shoe, pushed the swing just enough to start a slow swinging motion. Giving her husband a mischievous smile, she spoke to her son.

"Josh, do you know that swing in the front yard of your Grandma and Grandpa Barnett's house?"

"Uh-huh, I love to swing big in it."

"Well, I think that's where I caught your Daddy."

"Is that right, Daddy? Tell us what happened."

"That's right, Josh. Martha, I think you ought to tell them what happened and while you're at it, I think you ought to tell them what you had on."

"Hush, Ben, you didn't have to say that."

"Please, Mama, tell us what you had on. Tell us what happened."

Martha saw the expression of pained sadness on Luke's face.

"No, not now, Josh. Someday I'll tell you the whole story and you and Luke can have a good laugh about it. Luke, we are worried about you staying here by yourself. Wouldn't you like to stay at our house some, or stay some with Miss Cora and Miss Nora? They would love to have a man about the house. As a matter of fact, they really need someone since Miss Cora is having so much trouble with her rheumatism."

"No Mam, I have to stay here and see after our place and our things. I promised Mama I wouldn't quit school until I finished at Amicalola. Daddy comes home on Friday after work and he don't leave 'til Monday mornin. I'm goin to come by and help Miss Cora and Miss Nora some, and I'll come and see Josh and eat supper with you some, but I just cain't leave right now."

Martha's concerns' were relieved to some extent when she later heard that Zeke Turner was staying overnight with Luke if the weather was bad or if Luke needed some help with a job that he was not able to do alone.

Martha would not have been at all relieved had she known the result of Zeke Turner's friendship with Luke. After Ben figured it out, he made every effort he could think of to keep her from finding out.

Keeping Martha from finding out what Zeke and Luke were doing was only part of Ben's worry. He knew, in all probability, what was coming next, and he had to figure out how to handle it. Ben didn't have to wait long because Zeke stopped him on the road the following Monday morning.

"Ben, I guess you have figured out by now that me and Luke are makin some liquor together ain't' you?"

"Well Zeke, I had about decided that was the case. How come you got coupled up with Luke? He's a little on the young side to be workin at a still ain't he."

"Well, Mama cooked up a bunch of stuff and sent me over there with it. While we were eatin supper, it come up a bad cloud and he wanted me to spend the night with him, so I did. Next mornin when I started to leave he wanted me to come back and go squirrel huntin with him and I promised I would. So I went back the next week and went huntin with him. We was huntin along that creek that runs through their place when we come on this rocky faced bluff about twenty five or thirty feet back from the creek in a thicket of trees. Ben it was the best place to put up a still I've ever seen, so I just asked him about it. I told him I would pay him if he would let me put a still in there but he insists on helping me, so I guess I'll split with him."

"Well I've got a thirty five gallon copper still and four boxes in there and we have run it twice. We've got twenty five gallons of pretty good corn liquor and I was wonderin if you could sell it for us or we could sell it to you. Either way will suit me. We plan on runnin again next week."

It was what Ben expected, and since he was in a position to help, he saw no reason not to, albeit he was still concerned about Luke. "All right Zeke I'll handle it for you, and since your goin even up with Luke I won't take anything this time. Don't count on that in the future though. I'm not in this business to play Santa Claus and I expect you're not either.

"Now Zeke, if I'm goin to be able to help you, you've got to keep my name out of it. Nobody but Wesley and Frank Kirby will know about it from me, and you be damn sure that nobody but your daddy knows about it from you. Do you know what I'm sayin here?"

"I know what your sayin Ben, and I'm right with you."

"Good, I'll count on that Zeke. Now then, I expect that you'll have between forty five and fifty gallons after you finish your next run. Is that about right?"

"About right Ben, we'll just have two boxes ready, but we're getting' a pretty good turnout."

"That's good, I'm glad to hear that. On Thursday mornin, just about daylight, if nothin happens, Frank will be there. Have it stacked up on the back porch by the well curb, and you be there to help load it. Be ready because Frank don't waste any time. He thinks that as long as he's got his car on the road they cain't catch him.

"Now if anything goes wrong, let me know first hand and I'll do the same for you."

Ben paused and looked across at his young friend. Rabb had told him about the difference in his two sons. He was proud of both of them, but he worried a lot about Zeke. "He's got a pretty good head on his shoulders, but he's as wild as a jack rabbit. He'll go off sometimes and be gone for two or three days without lettin us know where he's at. It just about worries his Mama to death."

Ben knew that he had to give him a chance and in doing so he would find out how dependable he was. "All right Zeke, have you got everything straight?"

"I've got it Ben, and I'll be there. I appreciate the help Ben and I'll return the favor. Just let me know when and how and I'll return the favor.

"Well I'm glad to help when I can Zeke. Your daddy's helped me out several times and he'd expect me to do the same for you. One other thing Zeke, why don't you just let Luke sleep? You won't need him because Frank won't be there that long, and besides that he's got to go to school that day."

CHAPTER 9

"I declare Cora," Carrie said as they sat before the fire talking. "I've got to where I dread to see winter comin on worse every year. My hips and legs ache so bad during the cold rainy spells that I cain't hardly stand it. A lot of nights I'll heat both irons and put them in the bed and put my feet against them. It still takes forever for me to get the bed warm enough so I can get to sleep."

"Well I know it Carrie and it's about the same with me. Nora and I have been trying to get Elizabeth and Joshua's quilts finished, and on them cold and rainy days I cain't get my old fingers to hold a needle, let alone quilt with it. I reckon we're just about wore out Carrie. Then again, I suppose we ought not to complain. We've both lived past our allotted time and there's not many in our time that's been able to do that."

Carrie and Cora's longevity past their seventieth year was not long extended. Carrie's heart quit beating on a fine November evening in the fall of 1936. She did not suffer a stroke or a heart attack. As she lay sleeping her heartbeat began to slow, and continued to beat slower and slower until it stopped beating of its own accord.

Cora died some four months later on a cold blustery day in March of 1937 as a result of what she and Nora called "Neumony Fever." In February Cora came down with a case of influenza which deteriorated into pneumonia. Nora told friends that stayed with her both before and after the funeral that, "Cora tried her best to get better, but havin to contend with the flu and the "Neumony Fever" both, just got the upper hand of her."

*   *   *

After Nora passed her sixtieth birthday, with Cora being more than five years her senior, she began more and more to dread the thought that one-day soon she might have to live alone. One lonely day followed by another one, Nora feared that she would be thought of as just another old woman living alone and growing older.

After Cora's funeral a few of Nora's closer relatives remained for a few days to help with the usually first responsibility of, "going through Cora's things," cleaning the house and putting it back in order. Just having some family around for awhile, even though Nora appreciated the concern and care, she experienced a feeling of relief with the departure of the last of her kindred.

For over a week now the house had been overrun by friends and family and a horde of kids constantly eating away at the huge stacks of food that were replenished hourly it seemed to Nora. She had been hugged, patted and squeezed and waited, on until, as Nora said to herself. "I'm as grumpy and jumpy as an old sore ass'ed cat."

Nora knew that her grief and aloneness would come tomorrow, but she was so exhausted that she went to bed before sundown and slept soundly until sunup. As she ate her morning meal, alone for the first time that she could remember, Nora realized that she had reached a decision on one thing. She had no intention of retiring behind closed doors.

Nora lived well into her eighty's and years later, when she thought back over the years just after Cora's death, she was amazed at just how involved in the life of her community she became. Nora was one of the first to own a radio strong enough to pick up the Grand Ole' Opry without the sound continually fading into static. So she usually had company on Saturday nights, even some of the young couples in the community.

Along with Zeke Turner and Luke Gayton doing most of the work they planted Nora's river bottom fields in corn and did quite well from the proceeds. Nora experienced no reservations from the knowledge that most of the corn was converted into corn malt to satisfy the local demand.

On yet another occasion, Nora's two young partners in the corn crop project came to her with a plan to put a liquor still on her property and split the profits three ways. Nora's responsibility would be to do all the cooking and they would do all the still work. While Nora was considering the offer Zeke came by and told Nora they had to make a change in their plans for the present time.

While Nora missed that chance to get involved in the moonshine liquor business that time, there was another chance. This time she did get involved. It was however, not a good time.

*　　　　*　　　　*

While it is true that a federally licensed distillery was located in

Dawson County after the Civil War, it was not the only county in North Georgia to have received that distinction. While moonshine liquor was produced in almost every county in North Georgia, Dawson County was widely recognized, even acclaimed, as the moonshine capitol of Georgia. If you asked a dozen different people why this label was generally accepted as being true, you would in all probability, get a dozen different answers. One being, "How in the hell would I know. I guess it's because Dawson County is the hardest place in Georgia to get to. There aint' but three or four main roads comin into the county, and not the first damn one of them is paved."

During a September term of court in Dawsonville an enterprising young lawyer asked the sheriff for the name of all the men he had made a case against for operating a moonshine liquor still. To which the sheriff replied, "Cutting down liquor stills is not my responsibility. There are state and federal revenue agents whose job it is to find and destroy liquor stills and capture the operators. My job is to enforce the law and keep the peace."

The Dawson County representative to the state legislature in Atlanta answered a reporter's question from the Atlanta Constitution. "There's no more moonshine liquor made in Dawson County than there is in any other county in North Georgia. We just get the blame for it. Your newspaper thinks it has to find somebody to blame for everything. So you have made us responsible for all the moonshine liquor made in Georgia."

The reality was that there was a degree of truth in all of their conjecture. Dawson County was isolated and even worse had little political clout to help in dealing with that problem. It was well into the 1930's before roads into and out of the county were paved.

Local elected lawmen had little to do with destroying the liquor stills, and less than that with catching the operators. Doing that was a sure way to get voted out of office.

But it was the improvement of roads and the availability of faster and more dependable automobiles that provided an answer to the demand for huge amounts of cheap liquor for the poor white and black population of Atlanta.

Dawson County, located some sixty miles north of Atlanta along the southern edge of the Blue Ridge Mountains, was one of the isolated places that became a well-known source for its available supply of homemade liquor.

CHAPTER 10

Without making a decision to do so, Ben and Wesley became more and more involved in the moonshine liquor business. This was due in large part to the increasing demand for more liquor from Frank Kirby and his new partner, his son, Robert.

Rob Kirby was, in many ways, like Zeke Turner whom he had come to know as a result of his father's relationship with Ben and Wesley. Like Zeke, there was never any doubt that he would be involved in the liquor business. The only difference being, that while Zeke made it and sold it, Rob bought it, hauled it and sold it. Frank and Rob were trippers.*

Frank furnished moonshine liquor or "shine," as it was called around Atlanta, to two bootleggers. One was a white man called 'Lefty,' who ran a wood yard in a white section of Southside Atlanta known as 'Buttermilk Bottoms.' The other was a black woman who ran a bar-be-que stand on Ashby Street just south of Simpson Street. Her name was Kansady and she was known of course, as 'Sadie.' Her bar-be-que stand was known as 'Sadie's Place.'

Franks' connection with Lefty Cain was the result of an uncle from Hickory Flat in Cherokee County that sold wood to Lefty. When Lefty discovered the Frank's Uncle Jasper was from Cherokee County, he wanted Jasper to conceal onion sacks containing five one gallon tin cans of liquor in the wood and deliver them along with his load of wood. Having no interest or desire to get involved in the liquor business, Jasper sent for Frank and the connection was made.

Frank's connection with Sadie and the relationship that resulted, happened much differently, as much by chance as by anything else.

Frank's usual drop for Lefty's liquor was in a basement garage not far from his wood yard. He entered the garage – called a stash,*-- from the rear and stacked the onion sacks of five one-gallon tin cans of liquor against the front wall and covered them with a tarpaulin. A knock on the door at the top of the stairway landing was answered by an elderly woman with a, "Good Morning, Lefty said to give you this," and she would hand him a brown paper bag of money. The money was always in rolls of bills of various denominations that contained $100. The rolls of money were always securely wrapped with brown rubber bands.

Unless Lefty wanted him to come by the wood yard for some reason, Frank backed his car from the garage and using care to attract as little attention as possible, re-entered the street and quietly disappeared.

Frank's departure from Dawson County with a load of liquor did not provide an opportunity for a morning meal. If he had to return by way of the wood yard it was usually near midday when he started home. On those days Frank began stopping at a small eatery located on the corner of North Avenue and Marietta Street called the 'Yellow Jacket.' The popular choice on the menu at the Yellow Jacket was chili covered hot dogs on a toasted bun, and to Frank they were a culinary delight.

It was however, Frank's casual acquaintance with a black carhop called 'Apple' who worked at the Yellow Jacket that was responsible for the fortuitous series of events that affected the fortunes of Frank Kirby and his family for years to come.

"Mist' Frank, why it is you don't keep no back seat in yo' car?"

Apple was positioning the metal serving tray, laden with four chili dogs and a bottle of Pabst Blue Ribbon beer, to the driver's side door of Frank's 1935 2-door Ford Sedan, one of the two trip cars he was presently using. The other was a1936 2-door Chevrolet. The Chevrolet was a light green color and the Ford was black.

"Well Apple, ain't' nobody but me drives this car so I just leave the back seat out so I'll have plenty of room to haul something should I need it. Did you bring me plenty of mustard?"

"I brung you a full bottle. I spect' that ole' blanket back there is to keep them things wrapped up with."

Frank turned his head to one side and looked up at Apple. A grin barely touched the corners of his mouth.

"Whatever I need it for I've got it."

"Mist' Frank, I knows why you ain't' got no back seat in yo' car, and I knows what you use the blanket for too."

"Apple if you know so damn much, why are you askin me so many questions?"

Apple laid extra napkins on the tray and carefully uncapped the bottle of beer.

"Mist' Frank you needs to go see my Aunt Sadie."

"And what does your Aunt Sadie do Apple?"

"She run a baa-bee-que place out on Ashby Street,"

Frank didn't think he was trying to sell bar-be-que, but he had to be sure.

"Well, ain't nobody likes bar-b-que and Brunswick stew any better than I do, but that's a little out of my way so I guess I'll have to pass."

"Mist' Frank, Sadie need somebody she can buy shine from. She been gettin' some from up in Paullin County, but they ain't got all she need. Whyn't you go see her? She strait and I spec' you be strait too."

*   *   *

"Wes, there's no way we can furnish Frank with the amount of liquor he's wantin from us."

"How much liquor is he wantin Ben?"

"Well, as you know, he's been gettin' one load a week. When he picked up his load Tuesday mornin he wanted to know how soon we could start havin him a load on Thursday mornin."

"I told him that we just didn't have any way to do that right now but we would talk it over. Frank said that his boy Robert was goin to start haulin a load or two a week. Course, Frank and his brother Cliff are makin part of what they need."

"Ben, what in the hell is he goin to do with seven hundred to eight hundred gallons of liquor every week?"

"Well, he said he had a white man on the south side that was wantin two loads a week. He had a black woman on the westside that, when he asked her if she could take a load at the time, she just looked at him and said – shit --. Frank said that she runs a bar-be-que place in an old grocery store on Ashby Street. He said that she sits on a big stool with an old cash register on the counter in front of her and the only way out is the door by the cash register. He said that she wore a man's black hat, a set of big gold ear rings and half a dozen gold bracelets on each wrist, and she told Frank that, "I wants a load of lik'kuh on Thusdy, and I wants a load` of lik'kuh on Friday.

"So you can see Wes, that old Frank has stumbled on a gold mine if he can get the juice down there to them."

"Well, what do you think we ought to do Ben?"

"Well, I'll tell you what I think we ought to do Wes. I think we ought to go to Chattanooga, Tennessee, buy us a brand new upright boiler and put us up a still with eighteen boxes and start makin enough liquor to keep Frank supplied. We've got two good still hands in Zeke and Luke. They've

163

been wantin to run a boiler, so let's go get them one and put em' to work. What do you say?"

"Well, yeah I guess that's what we need to do. If Frank is wantin more liquor, and they are wantin us to put em' up a still big enough to make more liquor with, why should we look a gift horse in the mouth? You know of a place where we can put a boiler and eighteen boxes?"

"Wes, do you remember Zeke tellin us about the place him and Luke found on Miss Nora's spring branch?"

"Yeah, I remember that Ben. Do you think that she'll let us use it?"

"Well, I think so, but let me handle it. I'll tell her that we want to rent it, and we want her to board and feed two work hands. Miss Nora ain't nobody's fool and I know that she's been runnin a little close this year."

"All right Ben, you want to go and look at the place?"

"Naw, if Zeke likes it, it's okay with me."

"Then you are goin to see Miss Nora, and I will see Zeke and Luke and tell them to get the boxes ready to move; right?"

"Right, and on Monday Wes, we are goin to Chattanooga and buy us a brand new boiler."

Ben and Wesley got their first liquor still using steam from a coke fired upright boiler in operation in the fall of 1937.

The advantage of making liquor using steam from an upright boiler to extract alcohol from a fast and super fermented still beer is of course time and money. Super fermented by adding corn or rye meal and baker's yeast to a still box full of heavily sugared water that is then heated with steam from the boiler. The mixture will start the fermentation process within one to two hours and furiously work itself into a still beer having a high content of alcohol in approximately twenty five to thirty hours.

Stillers call the fermentation or working off process, "hog guttin," because the mixture rolls on top as it ferments, and "blued off " when the fermentation process is completed and the mixture is ready to be run through the still. The disadvantages are that a larger operation requires more traffic, more people involved and a location that is much harder to conceal. In addition, and perhaps worst of all is that a large operation that concentrates on increasing the amount of liquor produced, ends up making a poor quality liquor. They accept and justify the fact that they are makin and sellin cheap liquor, by knowing that their cheap liquor is being sold at a cheap price to the black and poor white population of Atlanta. The producers know it and the consumers know it. Both producer and consumer accept the trade-off as being acceptable and worthwhile. The producer, produces more and sells for less while the consumer, consumes more and pays less.

CHAPTER 11

Ben and Wesley knew that in Zeke and Luke they had two of the best still hands available at the time. Zeke, the oldest and the most experienced, enjoyed operating a still and Luke wanted to learn and was willing to do his share of the hard work and more. Not only did they work well together, but they liked each other. It was their lack of experience in the operation of an upright boiler that concerned Ben.

When a boiler is being operated under pressure and making steam, the amount of water inside the boiler is shown on a glass tube mounted on the front of the boiler at approximate mid-point. The amount of steam inside the boiler is shown as pounds of pressure on a steam gauge mounted at the top of the boiler.

Water is injected into the water chamber of a boiler that is under pressure by means of a device called an injector. The injector is mounted on the side of the boiler and uses steam pressure from the top of the boiler to force or carry water into the boiler. That was the reason for Ben's concern for his two still hands. If, during a time of intense activity they were to forget about keeping water in the boiler, disaster would almost certainly be the result.

"Now boys, if there's any one thing I want the both of you to pay attention to when the boiler is under pressure and makin steam, it's the water glass and the steam gauge. Never, and I do mean never, let the water in the water glass get below a quarter full. If the pressure on the steam gauge gets too high, just open all the valves in the steam lines and the pressure will drop right straight. But, if you let the water get too low and the steam pressure too high, then you could have a bad problem. The injector may not work. If that should happen open the valves, on both the water and steam line to the injector, and give the injector a few light taps with a hammer."

"If we do all of that and, it still won't work, what do we do then?" Luke asked. Ben saw that he had their complete attention.

"Well the boiler's got a pop-off valve on it if the steam pressure gets too high, but it can still get hot enough to melt the flues without any water in it. So when you decide it ain't goin to take water, one of you open the door to the fire box and draw the fire while the other'n opens all the valves, then both of you haul ass away from there. If it was to blow up and you were within a hundred yards of it, it could still scald the hide off of you. Of course, if both of you 'assel' around and let mine and Wes' new boiler get messed up, I'll take some skin off your asses anyway." Ben was grinning at the two young stillers as he said, "Best thing to do is to be damn sure it don't happen in the first place."

CHAPTER 12

They were all there, all four of them Ben, Wesley, Zeke and Luke, early on that Monday morning in late September of 1938. They had decided in advance that in order to have Frank a load of liquor on Friday morning they would have to put the sweet mash (first) round one in six boxes, of their newly assembled distillery on, on Monday morning. Six more boxes would be mashed in tonight and the remaining six boxes on Tuesday night. The six boxes of mash that they were putting on this morning should be worked off and ready to run through the still on Thursday night. On Friday night the second set of six barrels would be run and the first set of six barrels would be put back on as the sourmash or second round.

Out of this beginning then, a rotation in which six boxes of still beer would be run through the still each night and six boxes would be put back on or mashed in for the next round, each night.

Wesley watched as Zeke, wielding a heavy mash stick, worked the ingredients of corn meal, brown sugar and water into a mash. The cakes of bakers yeast would be hand crumbled on top of the mash and the box of mash heated with a steam line from the boiler.

Zeke was known as a top still hand, and the measure or standard of a top stiller was one who consistently produced fifteen gallons of 90 proof liquor from a one hundred pound sack of sugar. With Zeke running their distillery, Ben and Wesley expected a yield of one hundred-eighty to two hundred gallons of liquor from six boxes of still beer … A modest nights run on their newly assembled distillery of eighteen boxes.

Rabb told Ben and Wesley of a recent occurrence that made them realize just how skilled Zeke had become as a top still hand.

A still owner from Lumpkin County who was buying his supplies from Rabb asked him if he had any idea what could be causing the turnout from his still to keep dropping. He told Rabb his turnout was down to less than ten gallons to a sack of sugar. Rabb replied to his customer that he had no idea what was wrong, that it had been years since he had been around a still. But if he wanted, he would get his son to go with him and take a look. Understandably harboring some concern but wanting to help, Zeke accompanied his father's customer along an old field road and down a wagon trail to a small branch flowing from a nearby spring. The still was across the stream under some popular trees. As Zeke stepped across the stream, he stopped and sniffed the smell coming off the still boxes.

"We'll go take a look at what you've got but I can tell you what's wrong with your still."

"The hell you say. What is it?"

"Your pottail is soured."

"The hell you say. How can you tell?"

"Well if you cain't smell it, then taste it."

"What do I do? Put more sugar in when I put the mash back on?"

"Puttin more sugar in won't help. Your pottail is still soured. It will work for a while and then quit. It'll just get worse."

"What do you reckon went wrong?"

"If I was to say, I'd say that your pottail was too hot when you put the sourmash back on."

"Well what do you recommend that I do?"

"Pour it out and start over."

"The hell you say. We just have got started. We cain't do that!"

"Suit yourself, it belongs to you. But like I said, it'll only get worse."

Rabb interrupted his story and chuckled as much to himself as he did to his two friends. "I'll tell you what fellers. That boy is goin to be a damn good stiller, if he ain't already one."

"Well, did he pour everything out and start over like Zeke told him to" Wesley inquired?

"Not before he tried another round, he didn't, and it was just like Zeke told him it would be, only worse. I think he got about five gallons to the sack on that last one."

"Well I'll be damned," Ben said, "All that, and he still had to start over. That's tough luck, ain't it?"

"And that ain't all," Rabb continued, "let me tell you the rest of it. When Carl was pourin all that pottail out, he noticed that the corn meal had settled to the bottom of the boxes. Carl got him a bucket and started dippin the meal up and feedin it to his four fattening hogs. Well, he said that they ate every bucket of that fermented corn meal that he fed them, but he said that on the fourth day he noticed that when they finished eatin,' they just stood there with their snouts restin on the bottom of the feed trough. Then the next mornin, he said that all four hogs were layin stretched out in the pen and he couldn't get them to wake up let alone stand up. They slept for two days without eatin or drinkin a thing and when they finally woke up on the third day it took them 'til the next day before they could stand up. Well we had a good laugh about it, but I think it had Carl right worried about his hogs. He said, "Rabb it was the damn'dest thing I've ever heard tell of. I'd say that every one of them hogs lost twenty five pounds apiece. If I had lost any of them, it would have been the first time I ever heard tell of anything or anybody that got drunk and slept itself to death."

"Mix it up good Zeke," Wesley encouraged as he pumped water into the still box, "Frank says he wants three loads of liquor every week, and we need to be the ones to make it for him. I don't know about Ben, but payin for half of the boiler over there just about cleaned my pocket book out."

Zeke leaned his mash stick in the corner of the box he was working on and grinned at Wesley as he rolled a cigarette.

"Wes, if Ben can get Luke trained up on how to manipulate that steam engine over there; I'll boil enough liquor out of these beer boxes here to keep old Frank on the road day and night."

Ben nodded his head toward Zeke and said, "Luke, do you hear all that talk about our boiler goin on over there. Well, what we're doin right now is puttin the temper in her. You can see that we've got the pointer on the steam gauge in the red. Well, we want to keep it there for a couple of hours at least, and we want to keep the boiler full of water. Luke we want to burn this boiler in so good, that when you and Zeke need a whole lot of steam real fast, you can swing the door to that firebox open, and the pointer on that steam gauge will gain twenty pounds."

All four men saw the movement at the edge of the woods at the same time, but only Zeke reacted. He bolted between the two rows of still boxes and was about to enter the woods when he heard Wesley say. "Well, Miss Nora, we wasn't expectin you. You have sort of given us a scare, but it's all right. I shure do hope that you've got what I think you've got in them two buckets."

"Well now Wesley, if you was hopin for something to eat, then you're right. It's after dinnertime, so I just fixed a gallon of soup along with a pone of corn bread and a pot of coffee. I thought you might like to have a little something sweet, so I put a dried apple fried pie in for each one of you. Zeke, did I scare you hon? I hate that I done that to you. Come on over here and sit down while your Aunt Nora fixes out our dinner. I'm goin to eat with you'all if it'll be all right."

Nora carefully surveyed the still site, paying close attention to the boiler, the stills and the still boxes.

"Well help my time. I've heard about corn liquor stills all my life, but this is the first time I've seen one this close up, and I'm over seventy years old.

"Now Luke I want you to do something for me. When you get some liquor made I want you to bring me a gallon. I've got several boxes of camphor ice, which I bought from the Watkins man. I'll make us all some camphor. Everybody ought to keep a bottle of camphor in the house."

Ben's face broke out in a smile as he chided his Aunt Nora.

"Aunt Nora you think that Luke ought to bring you another gallon to sip on."

Nora looked up at Ben from where she was setting their meal out on a sheet.

"Well, since you mention it Mr. Ben Tyler, I am gittin a little low from that last you brought me. Temper me a gallon of sweet mash liquor with water from that springhead up there to ninety proof. Will you do that for your Aunt Nora?"

"I will Miss Nora, and I'll have it for you next week."

CHAPTER 13

Without missing more than two nights of run, Zeke and Luke ran Ben and Wesley's distillery until Christmas. At which time they ran out and took Christmas week off to rest and refresh themselves. Then during the first week of the New Year, they poured the used and smelly pottail in the branch, washed everything down and started again with a new round of sweet mash.

With only a partial refreshment of their pottail during Easter week, they ran the still until the end of June and ran it out. This time as they ran out, they pumped the pottail in the branch and filled the barrels and still boxes full of water to keep them from drying out and leaking.

During the summer months of July and August, the demand for raw white liquor decreased substantially. Ben and Wesley always took the opportunity to shut down for the summer, and this time nobody was more in agreement with that decision that Zeke and Luke. What could possibly be any better than to have two months of summer vacation and a brown paper sack full of money.

In mid September Zeke and Luke went back in to the still site and began making preparations to put the shack (distillery) back into operation. They spent two days pouring out, cleaning up and washing down everything about the still and beer boxes.

Between the four of them, they had kept a close watch over the location of their still during the two months they were out of production. They felt reasonably sure, the still had not been found, and just as important they found nothing missing from their still.

This time it was only Zeke and Luke who came early on the following Monday morning, fired the now well used, boiler and began mashing in a new round of sweet mash.

"Well Luke, what and all did you do while we were off," Zeke asked as he whipped the mash stick through the box he was working on.

"Well I loafered around a lot. I stayed part of the time with Aunt Nora and we went to several revival meetings together. We went fishin a couple of times. We carried Josh and Elizabeth with us. We all had a real good time together, and then we all went swimmin, all of us but Aunt Nora. She just waded around the edges. Aunt Nora don't git' around as good as she used to.

"Zeke is that girl I saw you with at Cox's tent show your sweetheart?"

"Nah, she's just a girl I run around with some."

"I wisht I had me a girlfriend that purty. What is her name?"

"It's Ruth Weaver; you want me to get you a date with one of her friends?"

"Naw, I guess not, I wouldn't know how to act."

"How to act, Luke what in the hell are you talkin about. You don't act anyway. You just sit around and talk a while, and then you try to git your arms around her and kiss her. Luke, you want me to tell you what Ruth said I was the other night."

"What did she?"

"She said I must be a foreigner."

"A foreigner, what did she mean by that?"

"She said I had Roman hands and Russian fingers."

"What did she – Oh yeah, I know what she meant."

"You're catchin on fast Luke. Tell you what Luke; while we're off at Christmas, I want you to go with me to see her. I guarantee you a good time. Okay?"

"Well, okay Zeke, I'll give her a try if you think Ruth won't mind."

"It's a deal, we'll take'em to the Big Bear Drive-in to eat and then we'll go to the movies. Then we'll go to a place I know and park, and then guess what happens next Luke?"

"I don't know Zeke, what?"

"What happens next is up to you old buddy. Best thing I can tell you to do is just let nature take its course."

Zeke slapped his friend on the back, and then they laughed and teased each other as they thought about the possibilities of what could happen between a boy and girl parked in a car on a dark night in a secluded place.

Luke finished filling the boiler with water, opened all the valves in the steam lines and started a fire in the firebox. He walked over to where Zeke was working in a still box with his mash stick.

"Zeke, you want me to tell you a tale?"

"A tale, you mean tell me a joke, a dirty joke."

"No, it's not exactly a dirty joke, but it does have some dirty words in it. You want to hear it?"

Zeke leaned his mash stick in the corner of the still box, took out his tin box of half-and-half tobacco along with his cigarette papers and began rolling a cigarette. He grinned at Luke as he fired a kitchen match with his thumbnail and drew smoke from the burning cigarette into his mouth and lungs. Luke watched as he exhaled a huge pall of blue gray smoke out of his mouth and nostrils.

"Sure Luke, go ahead, tell me a tale."

"Okay, well once upon a time"—

"Luke, are you tellin me a dirty tale or a fairy tale?"

"It ain't no fairy tale Zeke. My daddy told me this tale one Saturday last summer when he was at home from the sawmill. I ain't never heard him tell no fairy tales."

"I was just pullin your leg a little Luke. Go ahead on now; I won't butt in no more."

"Well this feller from Georgia went in a bar in Atlanter and ordered a glass of beer. While he was sittin there drinkin it, this guy wearin a ten gallon hat and a black patch over his left eye, came in and set down by the boy from Georgia and ordered him a beer."

"Howdy young feller," he says, "Are you from Georgia?"

"Yessir I am," the boy from Georgia said, "where are you from?"

"Well son, I'm from Texas. I figured you could see that."

"No sir, I couldn't, not unless everybody from Texas wears one of them big old hats."

"Well it's purty obvious to me that you're a mighty smart feller. I'd like to propose a toast to you and the great state of Georgia. Will you let me do that?"

"Yessir, I shure will, and I thank you sir."

"The guy from Texas raised his glass and made this toast."

"Here's to the eagle, she's a grand and noble bird. She flapped her wings over Texas, and over Georgia she shit a turd."

"He set his glass on the bar and asked the boy from Georgia what he thought of his toast."

"Well sir, that was a mighty fine toast, mighty fine, and if you'll let me, I'd like to make a toast to you and the great state of Texas."

"Why I shure will young feller, and I appreciate it."

'The boy from Georgia raised his glass and made this toast.'

"Here's to the great state of Georgia, with her soil so fine and rich. We need no turd from your noble bird you one eyed son-of-a-bitch."

As Luke finished telling his story, his face broke into a smile that wreathed his entire face. Zeke's face almost immediately changed from an expression of surprise to a good leg slapping belly laugh.

"Luke, that's a good one. I'll have to remember that one. That's the best one I've heard lately."

CHAPTER 14

Ben and Wesley's hope, of course, was that they could duplicate the success of the first year's operation of their distillery, with a second year of mostly trouble free operation. Zeke and Luke, now skilled operators of a steam driven liquor still, were confident that the second year would be far more productive than the first.

They were well on the way to doing that, when as the result of an unexpected shortage of containers, Rabb had to make an unplanned trip to Atlanta to supply the immediate need of Ben and Wesley's still.

The result of that unscheduled trip was a disaster, a disaster not only for Ben and Wesley, but also for Rabb and Luke. But not for the swift of foot Zeke, although it did result in a temporary loss of employment, Zeke's name and fame spread, especially among still hands and still owners. Even before the Federal and State revenue agents assigned to work that area of North Georgia learned his name, they heard about and talked about that still hand from Dawson County who bragged that he could run just as damn fast as he wanted to.

A state revenue agent recognized Rabb's truck on Highway 5 North of Canton and although the solid sides of the body were covered with a tarpaulin, which indicated a loaded truck, he did not follow. Instead, he contacted the Federal agents in the area and gave them a description of Rabb's truck. "My guess is that he'll come on to Jasper on Hwy 5 and then turn right on the road across Burnt Mountain. If you want to find out where he's going, be there at the intersection of Burnt Mountain Road and the Amicalola Falls Highway. Give him at least two hours and make sure he can't see you. He might lead you into something big, but you'll have to be careful. Sometimes, I wonder if these guys cain't smell us."

*   *   *

They heard the truck coming for several minutes before the headlights finally came into view. Their vehicle concealed in a thick stand of alder bushes, the Federal Revenue agents watched as Rabb's tarpaulin covered 1936 ton and a half Ford truck stopped at the intersection with the Amicalola Falls Highway and switched his motor and lights off.

"Bingo," agent Earl Simpson whispered.

"Be quiet, he's going to get out and listen for a while," Clay Willard, the senior agent warned. "I hope there ain't enough moonlight to reflect off the chrome headlights."

Five minutes later Rabb cranked his truck, turned on his headlights and turned his truck in the direction of the McClure place.

From there it was easy for the revenue officers to follow Rabb's truck with their lights off, until suddenly the lights on Rabb's truck went out, quickly followed by a turn into Ben's driveway.

When the lights on Rabb's truck went off, the Revenue agents immediately stopped their car. When the truck turned in at Ben's driveway they put their car in reverse and backed up until they located a place to pull off the road and for the second time that evening, hide their vehicle.

Lee Hasty, the last of the three agents in the car, pulled on his hat and coat against the evening chill and took hold of the door handle.

"I'm going to try to get close enough to that truck to see if I can tell what's on it. If I'm close enough to see what's on it, maybe I can hear them talkin about what's supposed to happen later on tonight. Anyway, you boys sit tight and be quiet. You know how sound carries at night.

"I'll be back as soon as that truck leaves and maybe we'll know a lot more about what their plans are. Like Keller said when he first saw him over there on Hwy 5, it might be something big or it might be Rabb lookin for a place to stash a load of something."

With that Lee Hasty carefully opened the car door to which all the interior light switches were taped over, stepped out on the ground and disappeared.

Ben knew that it was Rabb's truck even before he saw it turn up his driveway with the lights out. Ben picked up his flashlight and started across the yard as Rabb pulled his truck under the big oaks in the back yard, shut off the engine and stepped out on the ground.

"Well Rabb, looks like you made it there and back in purty good time."

"Yeah, we done fair I reckon, but I'll guarantee you one damn thang. My ass has chewed a hole in that seat cushion. That trip across Burnt Mountain has wore me and the brake linings on that truck slap ka-dab out."

"Well did you see anything out of the ordinary?"

"No we didn't Ben; we didn't see a thang. We stopped on top of the mountain, and set there for a while with the lights out, and then we stopped up yonder at the Burnt Mountain intersection and listened for a little bit. We didn't see or hear a thang."

Rabb nodded his head toward the young boy sitting in the cab of the truck.

"Ben, this is Doyle Edwards. He lives near us on the reservation. He'll be helpin me some. He's alright."

"Is this the boy that Zeke mentioned the other day?"

"Yeah, that's him."

"How you doin Doyle?

Ben could see enough to tell that Doyle's long billed cap never turned to look at him.

"Howdy."

"If you're alright with Rabb and Zeke, you're alright with me, Doyle."

"Well, let's get to it Rabb. Back her up to the hall of the barn back there. You're goin to leave me five hundred, is that right?"

"That's right, Ben. Stand back there with your flashlight and show me where to stop."

Less than an hour later, with Rabb in the truck bed and Ben and Doyle stacking them in an unused stable, they had unloaded one hundred onion sacks, each sack containing five tin cans. Each can contained a partially installed cork stopper and the inside of the can was treated with a protective coat of hot paraffin.

"Doyle, tie that canvas down back there on the tailgate while I talk to Ben for a minute."

"Ben, are them boys runnin tonight?"

"Yeah, they are runnin right now. They had enough cans to last for a while, so they went ahead and started. Zeke is supposed to be here about midnight to get enough cans to finish tonight's run."

"Good enough. Now when Doyle leaves fifty bags of sugar in Wes' smokehouse later on tonight, that should be enough to finish out the week. Is that right?"

"That's right, Rabb. I'll be by there on Tuesday to settle up with you."

"Good enough. We've got to go, Ben, I'll see you on Tuesday."

Rabb was a quarter of a mile up the road when he turned his lights on, and after relieving himself at the edge of the yard, Ben went inside and took his seat in his rocking chair by the window. Intending to watch and wait for Zeke, it was only a short time until Ben had drifted into a completely relaxed spell of unknowing sleep.

What neither Rabb nor Ben saw was the lanky figure of Lee Hasty as he slipped into the stable where they had so recently stacked the cans. Then some fifteen minutes later, having counted the entire lot, he stepped out of the stable, walked behind the barn, and staying in the shadow of trees, he strode rapidly back toward the car where the other Federal Revenue Agents waited for his return.

Using care against making any unnecessary noise, Lee eased himself onto the rear seat and closed the door with a barely audible click.

"Well, boys, looks like we're in luck this time. Not only have these guys got a liquor still, they've got it in operation right now."

"How big is it, and where is it?" inquired Earl Simpson.

Lee thought for a moment before he answered. "I cain't give you a definite answer to either question, but that truck left five hundred cans there and I heard Ben tell the one named Rabb that Zeke was comin about midnight to get the rest of the cans they needed to finish tonight's run. And Rabb told Ben that the boy called Doyle would deliver fifty bags of sugar to Wes' smokehouse later on tonight. So it's your call to make Clay. Do we go after it tonight, or do we stake it out and watch it for a day or two?"

Clay Willard sat for several minutes, not only considering his options, but trying to decide what his options were.

Presently, he began, "Now men, help me to look at both ends of this thing as we go. There are several things involved here, some of it you know and some of it you may not know. If Zeke is comin at midnight, that gives us about an hour to decide. We've had an unbelievable streak of good luck so far tonight, and we sure do need to get the rest of it right. But as you said Lee, it's my responsibility to make the call, and so whatever happens, I take full responsibility for it." Clay continued, "We have known for some time in the district office that Rabb Turner was a sugar supply man, as well as most anything else these moonshiners need to make liquor with. We could have indicted him for selling supplies or aiding in the manufacture of non taxpaid liquor and already have a good case against him. But we've been holdin off, hopin for something a little better to come along."

"Better, what would be better than what we already have?" Earl Simpson asked.

"What would be better?" Clay answered, "Conspiracy would be better, and if we can finish the job here tonight, I think we might have enough evidence on enough people to get a charge of conspiracy through a grand jury." Clay turned to Lee and said, "Now, Lee, I want you to go back to McClure's barn and wait for Zeke to get there. Try to get close enough to see him and see what kind of truck he's driving. If Ben comes out to help him, do your best to hear everything that's said. My guess is that the still is not too far from here, but we don't know that. I'm hopin that we are just before findin out. So here's what we do next. That truck will probably be comin from the still to get the rest of the cans needed to finish tonight's run. If so, it will go back the same way. So, Lee, if it does come from this direction, and does go back the same way, we'll follow it with our lights out until we see it turn off this road. If that is what happens, Lee, you start walking in this direction and we'll be back for you just as soon as we can. Now, if it comes up the road from the other direction and goes back the same way, get down to the road after he leaves and Ben has gone back in the house. Give us one flash with your light and we'll pick you up. We have got to be damn careful here. We don't want Ben to see nor hear anything, but we musnt let Zeke get far enough ahead, to chance losing him. I look for him to turn off on an old field road, or a sawmill road, or if they are payin somebody, he might go right through their front and back yard. I think, though, we might have the advantage on Zeke. He will be in a hurry, and if they have been working that still since dark they are bound to be gettin tired."

"Alright, Lee, go when you're ready. We'll be watching for your light if he's goin your way. Let's give it a try and see what happens."

The time was almost 12:30am when Zeke backed the 1936 Chevrolet half-ton pickup truck into the hallway of Ben's barn and killed the engine.

Wesley had bought the truck at a small used car lot in Buford. He counted out the sale price in cash and had the dealer make out the bill of sale to "Bill Bailey." Wes signed the bill of sale "B. Bailey" with his left hand, and drove their *shack truck to Highway 20 and headed toward Cumming. On Highway 19, north of Cumming, he stopped at a junk yard and bought four used, oversized 6-ply tires and a variety of spring leafs, spring hangers, and U clamps.

Ben and Wesley put the truck in Bens shop and spent a day installing extra spring leafs in the rear springs, and the 6-ply tires on all four wheels. They already knew that the straight six engine would travel slow and quiet in the two lowest gears.

Within a week after they turned the truck over to a delighted Zeke, he had dubbed it 'Lopin' Lena.' When asked why he had given it a name like Lopin Lena, he replied with a grin that, "She can haul anything that you can get on her, and she will go anywhere you want her to go."

Zeke was already stacking sacks of tin cans in the bed of the truck when Ben got to the barn.

"I was about to get worried about you, Zeke. Is everything alright?"

"Everything is okay, Ben. Luke don't like to blow pottail by himself, so I helped him draw and put back on before I left. Comin after these cans is goin to cause us to run a little late, but we should be done by daylight."

"One other thing, Zeke, Doyle is goin to put fifty sacks of sugar in Wes' smoke house sometime before daylight."

"Okay, that's enough cans, Ben, and we'll go by and git what sugar we need when we go in tomorrow night."

In one fluid motion, Zeke pulled the truck door open, slid onto the seat as he pushed in on the clutch and started the engine. The truck, already in reverse, started to move back as he released the clutch.

"I'll see you later, Ben. What's behind me?"

"Come on back as far as you want to."

Lee watched as Zeke switched on his lights and turned left down the road.

He watched Ben as he stepped up on his back porch and, without stopping for a moment to look and listen, as was his usual custom, went inside.

As soon as Lee heard Ben's back door close, he crossed the pasture between the barn and road and carefully crawled under the barbed wire fence. Then, using his body as a shield from Ben's house, he flashed his light in the direction of the two Federal Revenue agents, watching and waiting beside the road.

When Clay backed the car into the road and started in Lee's direction, he drove very slowly and with no headlights.

"Ben may be in the bed, but I'll bet you a wooden nickel that he's not asleep yet."

After a day and now part of a night that was more than eighteen hours long, Ben was in a state of near exhaustion. As soon as he stretched out on his bed, he immediately began falling through those silent and mind-relaxing layers of rest that resulted in a deep and restoring sleep.

Ben did hear the passing of an automobile on the road past his house, but his only thought was of who would be on the road at this time of night. He was unaware that, the car was not using its headlights, nor did he notice that the car stopped for a few seconds and then started on again.

The left rear door was open when Clay stopped the car and Lee quickly got in.

"I hope we ain't lost him. He was goin purty fast when he went over this hill here, and then I lost the sound of him."

They topped the hill and started down a long, gentle slope in the road.

"I don't see a thing. He must be stopped somewhere. I cain't believe that his headlights could be completely out of sight this quick," Clay said in a barely audible voice.

"Stop, stop right here. Let me git out and listen," Lee said, already pushing the car door open.

Lee stood for several seconds beside the car, letting his eyes and ears adjust to the sigh and sounds of darkness. He was on the verge of getting back in the car when he saw the sliver of light flash through the slats of an old barn, standing a hundred yards back on the left hand side of the road, a half mile away.

"I see him," Lee whispered. "He's goin through the hall of that old barn. He has probably stopped to put the bars back up on this end of the barn. He'll be comin out the other end in a minute."

As Lee predicted, in a matter of minutes, they saw the dark shape of the truck appear out of the back end of the barn and disappear into the woods following an old field road.

"Well, boys, there we are," Clay said to the other two officers, "All we have to do now is follow that field road and I'm purty sure we'll find us a moonshine liquor still, and I think it will be a purty good sized one to boot."

"Well we cain't drive this car in there. What are we going to do with it?" Earl asked.

"That's right Earl, we cain't drive the car in there, so we are goin to drive it in the hall of the barn and leave it there."

"Good idea, Clay," Lee said, "I was thinking the same thing. That will put a stop to anybody trying to get away in a vehicle."

Clay turned the car off the road and after Lee and Earl took the bars down at the front of the old barn, drove all the way to the back of the hallway so that the car could not be seen from the road.

After they had followed the field road for about half a mile, Clay stopped and spoke to the other two officers in a low voice.

"Now Lee, you and Earl wait here. I'm goin to see if I can get close enough to look the situation over. I need to see if there are more than two men workin the still, and figure out the best way to go in on them. I should not be gone more than an hour at the most."

After Clay had been gone for about ten minutes, Earl said in a quiet voice, "Lee, did you get a good look at the guy they called Zeke?"

"No, not much. They had a lantern sittin in the hall of the barn, but I couldn't tell much about them. Why do you ask?"

"Well, I'm purty sure he's the one that said there wasn't a revenue officer that could catch him. He said that he could run just as damn fast as he wanted to."

"Well now, is that right? What did you say his name was?"

"Zeke, Zeke Turner. He's Rabb's boy. You know, the sugar man. He ain't ever been caught, and you can bet that Clay is fixin to put you on him."

"Well now, Earl, that is interesting. If you was to check my record, you would find that I ran track at Valdosta State, and I've never been caught either. I broke every track record when I went to school there in '36 and '37."

Earl chuckled as he said, "Well, we may be about to have the damndest foot race that ever happened in Dawson County. Maybe I'll at least get to see the start of it."

CHAPTER 15

First light was breaking through the trees as Zeke and Luke finished running the last still full of beer, from the night's run.

"Blow the pottail and draw the fire, Luke, while I proof and can this last batch. We'll throw this stuff on old Lopin' Lena and we'll be gone here purty soon. We've made one hundred ninety gallons of liquor and had to go after cans and we're still only runnin' a little over an hour later than usual."

*   *   *

When Clay returned from his inspection of the still site, he described the layout to the other two officers. He assigned an officer on each side of the still with himself coming in from the rear. And just as Earl had thought, he stationed Lee on the side of the still that he felt sure Zeke would run toward.

"I think Earl and I can handle the boy named Luke. He's firing the boiler and workin the injector. They are just about finished with tonight's run, so Zeke will be over on your side Lee, proofing and canning up the last batch of liquor from tonight's run.

"Now Lee, Zeke is the one we want. He's Rabb's boy and he'll make a conspiracy charge all the more convincing. Besides that, he has done a little too much braggin to suit me. I sure would like to see his little ass took down a notch or two.

"Alright then, let's go. Remember, I'll show myself first. I'm hopin that Luke will see me first and run toward you, Earl. If he does I'm purty sure that Zeke will come your way, Lee."

The raid did not happen as Clay had hoped, but the initial reaction of the two still hands occurred just as he had predicted.

Just as Clay came in from the back side of the still, Zeke stood up to get a sack of empty cans and immediately saw him.

"Run, Luke, it's the law."

"Halt, you're both under arrest by Federal Revenue Agents."

Luke turned and ran almost directly into the arms of Officer Earl Simpson.

With his second step, Zeke was in full flight. Astonished at Zeke's quickness, Lee made his first mistake. He showed himself too soon, and set himself in a wide stance to take on Zeke's blazing rush to escape.

Seeing his pathway blocked, Zeke reacted with instant clarity. He used the corner post of a still box for a handstand, and with the gliding motion of a deer in flight, landed on the other side of the still boxes and disappeared into the woods. Unfazed by his mistake Lee recovered and with fluid motion came flying into the woods. He spotted Zeke immediately some thirty yards ahead and the chase was on.

In full daylight now, there was no danger from hitting a tree or getting caught in a patch of undergrowth. They were running about fifty feet from the stream through a stand of oak and poplar. The footing here was fairly good, but Zeke knew that was about to change.

The chase entered a thick stand of pines and here, the footing was a bit more treacherous due to the slippery smooth carpet of pine needles. Seconds later, they crossed the old field road and entered an open field where a growth of alders, blackberry vines, and thorny brier bushes made a hedge row through which the stream, by the still, flowed along on its way to join up with the Amicalola River.

Despite the boasting and bragging about his ability to run as fast as he wanted to, Zeke knew that if he was up against a good runner this morning, he was in bad trouble. He did not sleep well in the daytime, and after getting a scant four hours of sleep yesterday and working the extra long night just completed, he was already feeling the effect of tired legs.

The pace quickened as they raced along beside the hedgerow and Zeke quickly realized the spring and power in his knees and thighs was almost gone. He began looking for a break in the hedgerow to cut through and throw his pursuer off long enough to gain an advantage by a sudden change of direction.

Zeke saw the break just in time to make the cut into it, but not soon enough to see that he had made a mistake. As he leapt the stream, he ran headlong into a thicket of honeysuckle and thorny briers that brought him to a complete stop.

Lee caught onto a small hickory sapling and did a wrenching, twisting turn - only a momentary delay and no loss of distance.

Zeke jerked himself free of the entanglement and stumbled backwards across the stream. Glancing back up the stream, the inside of the hedgerow formed into what seemed to be an open tunnel. Supposing that the revenue officer would be coming into the opening, Zeke started running up the inside of the hedge row and immediately realized that he had made his second dangerous mistake in the short span off thirty seconds. If Lee had chased Zeke up the inside of the hedgerow, he would almost certainly have had him caught. Not fifty feet up the stream on the inside of the hedgerow, the tunnel ended in a mass of undergrowth.

But amazingly, Lee did not follow Zeke into the opening in the hedgerow. He ran back up along the outside of the hedgerow and started hollering at Zeke.

"Alright, boy, come on out of there. I've got your gangling ass caught now. I know who you are, Zeke, so come on out and give yourself up."

Zeke was not fooled nor alarmed by Lee's threats and the fact that Lee had called his name. Both men were aware that the – "If you cain't catch him, you cain't charge him" – rule was accepted and abided by in these cases. And besides that while Lee was running back and forth hollering at him, Zeke was resting.

He was, however, very much aware of the precariousness of his situation. He had not been able to elude his pursuer. He was tired but Lee's mistake had provided him with an opportunity to catch a breather. His clothes and shoes were, for the most part, dry and looking back down the hedgerow tunnel, he picked out the best places to step when he made his break for the opening. He must not stumble and he must go through the hedgerow opening at all possible speed.

Time to move - and he did.

He caught Lee moving the wrong way and beat him out of the opening by three full steps. They waged an all out burst of speed as they continued along the hedgerow. Twice, Zeke felt Lee's hand on his shoulder, but on both attempts, threw it off with a slight feint.

The stream in the hedgerow joined up with a small creek before they flowed into the Amicalola. It was toward the juncture of those two streams that the chase was coming at a furious pace.

Zeke knew there was an old three-strand barbed wire fence running along the edge of the creek and he adjusted his stride in order to begin his jump at just the right instant to clear it. With all the agility of a high jumper, he sailed across the fence, and before his jump ran out of distance, he reached out with both hands and caught on to the upper part of a tall hickory sapling, vaulted all the way across the stream and landed in the freshly ploughed ground on the other side.

Lee realized that Zeke was going to try to jump the creek, and it was then that he saw the barbed wire fence. "He cain't jump all the way across the creek and the undergrowth on both sides, but he's hopin it will help him to lose me. I'm goin to do my best to land right on top of that bastard then, even if it hurts both of us, I'll have his ass caught."

Lee cleared the fence and caught hold of the hickory sapling intending to ride it across the creek just as Zeke had. Too late and irreversible, Lee realized that he had made his most grievous mistake of the day as soon as he grabbed onto the treetop. The motion of the springy hickory sapling was coming back toward him from Zeke's jump. Lee came crashing and cursing down into the creek. It was however a mostly soft landing, due to being entangled in a mass of muscadine grapevine.

Lee was turned in the right direction to see Zeke disappear into the tree line along the Amicalola River, and then he heard his voice as it drifted back across the open field.

"So long you gangling ass son-of-a-biiiiiiitch."

*   *   *

Even though the chase had lasted less than thirty minutes, it was over an hour before Lee returned to the still site. Earl was in the process of using an axe he had found at the still to knock the sides out of the still boxes and let the fermenting mixture pour out onto the ground. Some of it was now beginning to reach the stream, turning the fresh water in the stream to a smelly brown color as it flowed away.

Luke was sitting in the cab of the shack truck with one arm handcuffed to the steering wheel.

"I knowed you wasn't fast enough to catch him. He run off and left your big ass in a cloud of dust didn't he?"

Earl grinned as he looked his, disheveled and limping, fellow officer over.

"Well, Lee, from lookin at you, I cain't tell if you was the chaser or the chasee. Unless you've got him hid out somewhere, he must have outrun you.

Lee leaned wearily against a tree and slid down into a sitting position.

"Let it go Earl. I don't need to listen to any bullshit from you or anybody else right now.

"Where's Clay?"

"He's gone to this Cochran guy's house to see if he can find that fifty sacks of sugar that you said was goin to be stashed there. Then he's comin back here with the camera to take pictures and some dynamite to blow the boiler with. By the way, there's one hundred ninety gallons of moonshine liquor stacked up right over there if you need a little drink. They say it's good for what ails you, and you look like you could use a little help."

"Earl, that little son-of-a-bitch jumped a three-strand barbed wire fence and used a hickory sapling to pole vault into a plowed field. It was as good as anything I've ever seen."

* * *

Ben was still asleep after yesterday's long day and night when someone started knocking on the back door. Martha, in the midst of preparing their morning meal, opened the door to find Wesley in a highly nervous state and with a frightened look on his face.

"Martha, get Ben up. I'm afraid they are cuttin our still."

Ben was already standing in the kitchen doorway.

"Ben, they are cuttin our still. They must have followed Zeke in last night. Their car is sittin in the hallway of the old barn."

"Well, that's bad luck Wes, mighty bad luck. I heard a car go by not long after Zeke left, but I didn't think too much about it. Looks like I should have, but I didn't."

"Ben, Doyle has already put that sugar in my smokehouse. Ain't no way I can get fifty sacks of sugar moved in a hurry if they start searching."

"And I've got about sixty sacks of cans out yonder in my back stable. At least we don't have to worry about them findin no liquor in Miss Nora's barn. Rob got all that was there yesterday."

After a moment of thought, Ben continued.

"Wes, go on back home and go about your business just like nothin has happened. There's not a thing we can do, 'til we find out what they have done and what they know."

If Ben had followed the advice that he gave Wesley, the confrontation that occurred later that morning might have been avoided and the events that followed might not have been so rancorous.

Martha admonished her husband, "Ben, how many times are you going to walk from the house to the barn and back?"

"Well, I'm worried about Zeke and Luke."

Brrummp – the low rumble came from the direction of the still.

"Ben, what was that?" Martha asked.

"That was that damn bunch of revenue, and they just blew up the boiler."

Still furious from the realization that their whole operation was now destroyed, Ben climbed the steps to the front porch and sat down in a chair pushed all the way against the wall of the house. He knew there was a good chance they would come out in this direction as they made their way toward Dawsonville and on to Gainesville.

What Ben did not think about was that when they came in sight, their car was followed close behind by their shack truck,* and it was piled full of various parts of the still and samples of supplies to be used as evidence of the size and the potential for the amount of production from the still.

The forlorn face of Luke peering out the window of the Federal Revenue agent's car was the last straw. "There you go, you sonzabitches," Ben bellowed at the top of his lungs from where he was sitting on the porch.

"Ben, what are you trying to do, get yourself arrested?" Martha gasped, from where she was standing just inside the screen door.

"Oh Lord, Ben, they are stopping."

The car and truck pulled over on the shoulder of the road and stopped.

Ben recognized the officer and knew his name to be Clay as he got out of the car and came walking across the yard to stand at the edge of the porch, looking directly up into Ben's face.

"Mr. McClure, do you know whose liquor still that is down yonder on the back side of your pasture?"

Ben returned the look with a cold stare of his own.

"It looks to me like it belongs to the damn guvermint. They've took it over."

"We know more about who it belongs to than you think we do, and we're goin to get to the bottom of the rest of it."

"Well, while you're gittin, you can get the hell off of this place. By God, this ain't Russia yet."

"What I stopped by here to tell you was that we caught Luke workin at that still, and we are taking him to Gainesville to make a case against him. If you will, let his folks know where he is, and we'll turn him loose as soon as somebody comes over there to go on his bond."

Ben let the toughness go out of his reply.

"Alright, I'll do that. Tell Luke I expect there'll be somebody over there to make his bond sometime this evening."

Without further comment, Clay turned and walked back across the yard, got back in the car, and within minutes, they were gone.

For several minutes, Ben did not speak, even though Martha continued to stand inside the screen door. When he did it was obvious that he was speaking as much to himself as he was to Martha.

"Well they didn't get Zeke, but they sure as hell cleaned us out."

After they had passed through Dawsonville, and with Luke asleep on the back seat, Lee turned to Clay and said, "He looked like he was talking pretty tough. Was he?"

"Yeah, well he was, but you cain't blame him for being madder than hell. We have just destroyed a liquor makin operation that had to be makin some good money.

"We poured out one hundred ninety gallons of liquor and knocked down eighteen boxes of still beer there this morning. I don't know what moonshine liquor sells for at the still, but I would say that we have destroyed over a thousand dollars worth of stuff this morning alone."

"Are you goin back for that sugar in Cochran's smokehouse?" Lee asked.

"Well, I have seen it myself, and you can testify to what you heard said about the sugar that was goin to be delivered to Cochran's smokehouse at McClure's barn last night. I'll leave that up to the boss though. If he wants me to do it, I'll get a search warrant and go back over there and let them know that we know, and we know where it was goin to be used."

As they passed the crossroads at Lumpkin Campground Community, Lee asked Clay his opinion about the case and who they would go after?

"Clay, if they go after Turner, McClure, and Cochran, do you think they will try to get them for conspiracy?"

"I think they will, Lee, and they are the ones they'll go after. The department had been wanting a chance to go after some of the owners and suppliers. They know that the only way to make a dent in the moonshine liquor business is to put a stop to the money. We can cut stills and catch still hands 'til hell freezes over, and all that will do is put still hands on probation and make our performance records look good.

"This time we are giving them a chance to see what they can do. We're giving them three solid citizens who are property owners, and all three of them live in the same community. We can give direct testimony of their collusion to erect a distillery with the intention to supply, make and sell illicit non taxpaid liquor together.

"I believe with the evidence we have, and if that evidence is presented to a jury in the right way, by a prosecuting attorney that's worth a damn, we can get a conspiracy conviction against them. If we can get a conspiracy conviction against all three of them, the government will go after them for tax evasion."

Lee looked at Clay and shook his head. "Do you reckon the poor bastards have any idea what they are in for?"

Clay looked across at Lee with a grin on his face.

"I don't know, but I would like to be the one that serves the papers on Ben McClure, informing him that if he doesn't pay the taxes on all that liquor he has made, the federal government is going to sell his property at the courthouse door. I didn't much care for his sarcasm when I went up there to tell him to send somebody over here to make Luke's bond. And I damn sure didn't like being ordered off his property, whether he had the right to do it or not."

CHAPTER 16

On Wednesday of the second week after Ben and Wesley's still had been destroyed by the Federal Revenue agents, Ben received a letter from his sister, Laurel. In her letter, Laurel apologized for the lateness of her letter, but due to a matter that her husband, Marcus needed to talk about with Ben, they would be coming for an overnight visit on the following Saturday morning.

Ben reread the letter twice, but he could find no indication of why Mark, who was now a full partner in his father's Gainesville law firm, would have a need to see him. It had to be, Ben decided, something concerning or in connection with the loss of their distillery. Ben's concern here was that as far as he knew, Mark and Laurel knew nothing of his involvement with the still.

As he had already done on several occasions, Ben rethought the incidents that occurred during the night the still was cut and the next day when the Federal Agent came to his house to tell him that Luke had been caught at the still and would need someone to come to Gainesville and make his bond.

That same afternoon, Ben had Rabb send his other son Newton to carry Raymond Baker to the county jail in Gainesville and go on Luke's bond. They returned with Luke, relieved and happy to be home.

"I shure was glad to see Newt and Mr. Baker come and get me out of jail. I was afraid I was goin to have to spend the night in jail."

"We wouldn't do that Luke. Not if there was any way around it. Luke, did you hear any of the Revenue Agents mention mine, or Wes, or Rabb's name?"

"Well, I went sound asleep in the car, and when I woke up they was talkin about the evidence they had on our shack truck* but I guess I went back to sleep. I shure was tired, still am, as far as that's concerned."

Ben could not rid himself of the feeling that something unforeseen lay in wait. The revenue agent named Clay had threatened that they knew more than they were telling. Was he bluffing? If so, why was he bluffing?

At just after ten on Saturday morning the black Pontiac Chieftain turned up the driveway and stopped in the shade of the huge oaks in the back yard of Ben and Martha's house. All four doors opened at practically the same instant and soon it was a melee of kids and adults talking and hugging and shaking hands.

Laurel never returned to the place of her birth without experiencing the mixed emotion of gladness and sadness. Even though she was aware of the reason for their visit this weekend, Laurel was glad in knowing that her sons had come to love the Blue Ridge Mountain Country of North Georgia and Dawson County. This was not only her place of birth, but here was where she had come to know the importance of having a sense of place. Having and knowing a sense of place was a trait that Laurel coveted for her sons.

Soon after the two families completed the noon meal that Martha already had prepared, Ben and Mark had picked Wesley up at his house, and now all four men were seated together on Rabb Tuners back porch.

Mark had insisted on talking to all three men at the same time. First of all he simply did not want to have to go over what he had to tell them three different times. Secondly, he wanted to be absolutely sure that they heard exactly the same thing from him and thirdly he wanted them to ask any questions they had about the charges in each other's presence and then they had to decide how they wanted to proceed. If they wanted his help they had to agree with each other on how they wanted to proceed, and they had to agree to let him handle all charges made against them.

Ben asked the first question and with it launched the three men into what would become the three most trying months of their lives.

"I'm not goin to tell you where I got this information because none of you would know him if I told you nor would you understand the circumstances by which I came by it. I can tell you that I think its straight or I wouldn't be out here telling you something I wasn't pretty sure of. I sure don't want to worry you anymore than you have already been."

"Well Mark this sounds sorta like its purty bad. I didn't know you knew anything about us gittin our shack cut."

Mark had, in fact, come by the information about the federal revenue agents destroying a huge moonshine still in Dawson County by the slightest of chance.

He was having lunch with a friend from the University of Georgia Law School, who was now an Assistant District Attorney General in the Gainesville office when he started telling Mark about the Feds destroying a huge moonshine liquor still in Dawson County. They had lucked into getting one of their agents close enough to hear the owners making plans to supply it and operate it. They had destroyed the still, caught one of the still hands, and unbeknownst to the owners they were about to go after them before a Federal Grand Jury.

"Sounds pretty wild Howard, do you remember any of their names?"

"Well as a matter of fact I do Mark. One of them is a guy named Rabb Turner. He's the sugar supplier and they have known about him for awhile. Wesley Cochran seems to be the guy that does most of the legwork, and a guy by the name of Ben McClure is the one they think is the kingpin. I helped with some of the background paper work. They have a whole bunch of evidence on a built up Chevy truck and, with the talk their agent overheard, they think they've got the dead wood on the whole bunch of them."

"You have any idea what they are goin to ask the Grand Jury for Howard," Mark had asked, wanting to get as much information as possible.

"Conspiracy, and if they can get a jury conviction on conspiracy they are going after them for tax evasion.

"I'm afraid it is serious Ben, and that's why I wanted to talk to all three of you at the same time. Let me tell you the rest of what I know and then I'll answer any questions if I can."

*   *   *

"Rabb, they have known for some time now that you were a sugar and supply man, and the night you brought that load of containers to Ben's barn they followed you till they saw you turn in at Ben's driveway. Then one of the agents came up behind the barn and saw and heard everything you said and did. He did the same thing when that worker came and got that load of containers and then they followed him in. You know the rest except that the agent named Clay Willard went to your smokehouse and saw that fifty bags of sugar stacked in there, Wesley."

"Wasn't that son-of-a-bitch trespassing on my property," Wesley asked?

"They'll say they had information it was there and they were just checking it out," Mark answered.

"Well Marcus, it sure as hell sounds bad," Rabb began, "Do you have any idea what they are fixin to do to us, or try to do to us."

"My information is that they are goin to take their evidence before the

Grand Jury which meets in two weeks and they are goin after all three of you."

"What are they goin to ask the Grand Jury to charge us with?"

"Conspiracy!"

"Oh hell boys" Rabb said, "That is bad news."

CHAPTER 17

During the May meeting of the Grand Jury of the Ninth District, U.S. Federal Court, held in Gainesville, Georgia, the last week in the month of May of 1940, the Grand Jury returned a true bill of indictment against Mr. Rabb Turner, Mr. Wesley Cochran and Mr. Ben T. McClure.

The Grand Jury charged the three men of conspiring together to operate an illegal distillery, without a license, for the purpose of making and selling illicit spirituous grain alcohol and that they further conspired together to evade the taxes levied against the making and selling of said spirituous grain alcohol.

At their arraignment, held a month later the law firm of Taylor & Taylor was certified as the attorneys of record to represent the accused.

When the bill of indictment, with its description of charges was read, and the Judge asked each of the accused to enter a plea of guilty or not guilty as to the charges read, Mark answered that with the court's permission, since he was the legal representative for each of the accused he would enter their plea. Knowing that Mark wanted no mix-up of words at this time, he nodded his head in agreement. Mark entered a plea of not guilty.

The Federal case charging Ben, Wesley and Rabb with conspiracy and tax evasion was forwarded to the Clerk of Court's office where it was added to the docket of cases to be tried during the September term of Federal Court. The September term of Federal Court was set to convene at 10 am on Monday the 2nd day of September of 1940 at the Federal Court House in Gainesville, Georgia.

The accused, their legal representative and witnesses were notified to be there at the proper time.

When they received a copy of the court docket, and Mark pointed out to his father that they had been placed Number 1 on the docket, Hiram Taylor looked up at his son with and ironic smile on his face.

"Well Mark, you are not too much surprised at that are you?"

Mark stepped on into his father's office and closed the door.

"Dad they have everything against them. They've got the evidence against them and they have sworn testimony against them. Right now I don't have a whole lot going for them. I'm really worried about it."

"Well you ought to be worried about it, that's your job."

"You know what they want don't you?"

"Hell yes, I know what they want. They want to take everything those three men have and then put them in a Federal Penitentiary if they can."

Hiram Taylor's bushy eyebrows pulled down and together.

"Now listen here son. I'll help you, but you might as well dig in on this one. Start out by rounding up every character witness you can find. Get their preachers; better yet get all three of their preachers, to come. Get those two old maids, who came to your wedding, to come if you can."

"One of them is dead."

"Well bring the other one."

This time it was Mark's turn to smile.

"Dad she was boarding and feeding the work hands from the still."

"The hell you say. Was everybody in Dawson County involved in that moonshine operation?"

"Aunt Nora loves Ben McClure more than his mother did if that's possible. Laurel told me about it. I'll have to tell you the story sometime."

"Mark you have got to question and contend with every witness they put up. Argue every point, find something they did that was illegal, that wasn't done right – ask for a mistrial. If you ain't got much to start with then start something.

"One other thing, I'll find out who the lead prosecutor is going to be and see if there is any interest in doing some plea bargaining. Probably not, but it won't hurt to find out. Does it tell there what judge is going to be presiding?"

"Yeah, it says here Judge Arthur Douglas presiding."

"Well, he's tough, but I have always found him to be fair. He comes from up in Towns County, so he knows what apple brandy tastes like."

Hiram stood up, walked around his desk and laid his hand on his son's shoulder.

"Mark you have heard me say this before, but I'm going to say it again. Sometimes I wonder if God all mighty himself knows what is going to happen when a bailiff locks twelve men up together in a jury room."

CHAPTER 18

During that period of time when courts convened for a term or session, they were normally in session for a week, whether there was sufficient plea entering, settling out of court and trial work to be done or not.

Perhaps as good as any description that could be used to describe the activity that occurs in a courtroom during the hour before the gavel falls; calling the court to order is controlled pandemonium. It was into this beehive of activity that Mark led Ben, Wesley and Rabb that Monday morning.

Luke Gayton was not among the group that Mark led up the marble steps and into the Federal Courthouse to face a trial by jury. During Luke's arraignment, Mark had taken Luke before the Judge and had him to enter a guilty plea to the lessor charge of making spirituous grain alcohol. Luke was sentenced to serve two years in a Federal Penitentiary, but since this was his first offense, Luke's sentence was probated and he was assigned to a probation officer.

"Now listen," Mark admonished the three men as they crossed the lobby and started up the stairs to the court rooms, "Pay no attention to all these folks running around here shaking hands and playing grab ass with each other. Half of them are jackleg lawyers. They ain't here for nothing but to see and be seen."

Mark found seats in the courtroom for the three men and immediately disappeared. Promptly at 10 am, Judge Arthur Douglas gaveled the September term of Federal Court in Gainesville, Georgia to order and the court system of deciding the guilt or innocence of its accused citizens was set in motion.

The carnal use of a woman's body for profit may be the oldest profession, but since the incidence of deciding the guilt or innocence of an accused person with a panel of his peers, the ability to be involved in the choosing and refusing of who sits on that panel has surely generated a parallel in the use of time, the investment of money, and, if not the same amount of emotion, the craftiness.

From the day that Mark received a jury list, not a day passed that he did not spend some amount of time with his Father examining and discussing every name on the list. Since their case was still posted as number one on the court calendar, they started with juror number one on panel number one. Some of the names received a check mark, some an x mark, and some a question mark, but when they were finished, they had a good idea of who they wanted, from his performance on other juries.

Hiram Taylor was regarded as a skilled and wily craftsman at the business of jury selection. So it came as no surprise to anyone that he was sitting at his son's side when Judge Douglas issued the familiar instruction to, "Call the first panel."

For the next two hours Mark and Harrison Davis, the attorneys out of the district office chosen to prosecute the conspiracy charge against Ben, Wesley and Rabb worked their way through almost three panels of the jury list. With one last check of the names on his list, Hiram leaned close to his son's ear and said, "That's about as good as you're going to do."

With a nod of his head Davis signaled his agreement and Judge Douglas swore and set the jury.

"The first four jurors from panel number four will serve as alternates," the Judge added, "You will be called and sworn if needed."

"Mr. Davis, proceed with your opening statement," which was followed immediately by Mark's opening statement for the defense.

At 5:30 p.m. the Judge instructed the court and the jury that court would convene at 9 a.m. on Tuesday and the impaneled jury would come directly into the jury box.

The first day of court was dismissed.

*   *   *

On Tuesday morning while Judge Douglas was instructing the jurors about the duties of serving on a jury, a tall middle aged man dressed in starched and ironed khaki work clothes, sitting on the back row of the jury box stood and partially raised his hand about shoulder high.

"Yes sir is there something I can help you with," Judge Douglas asked?

"Yes sir, there is Your Honor."

"State you name and tell me what it is please sir."

"Your honor my name is Edward Palmer and I'm from down in Oakwood. I was on the Grand Jury when this case came before us."

"Mr. Palmer, are you sure about that?"

"Yes sir, I am. I'm sure because this is the first moonshine liquor case that I have ever been on."

The Judge turned to the clerk who had been rapidly flipping back and forth through several jury lists.

"Have you checked it out Winston?"

"Yes sir, I have -- looks like he's right. I have no idea how it could have happened."

"Very well Mr. Palmer, step down out of the jury box. You have the court's apology. You will be paid for the day and you are dismissed from this case."

"Call the first alternate."

"G.F. Cooper"

"Will G.F. Cooper come to the jury box?"

To a stunned courtroom, Judge Arthur Douglas included, a slim dark haired woman, wearing a beige sweater buttoned at the neck, walked down the aisle, through the barrier gate and took the just vacated seat in the jury box.

Still holding his gavel some 6 inches high the Judge asked, "Are you G.F. Cooper?"

"Yes sir, I am. I'm Geneva Cooper and I'm the third grade school teacher at Flowery Branch Elementary School."

"Your honor, can I approach ---."

"Sit down Mr. Taylor. I'm going to seat her. You're out of strikes anyway. Raise your right hand to be sworn Miz Cooper."

Mark slowly sank back down in his chair as he silently cursed this unbelievable turn of events.

"Two weeks of work trying to get a jury I can work on, and now it's shot to hell."

Harrison Davis concealed his smile behind a manila folder as he thought to himself. "There are still times when manna from heaven does yet fall."

CHAPTER 19

Beginning with his longer than necessary list of character witnesses, Mark used every opportunity, not only to exemplify their character, but also to make a statement about their value to the community.

"Since my sister died I have to depend on Ben for everything from seein about my place here to carryin me to church. Not a day goes by that some of them don't come by to see that I'm all right," Nora Perry said, sitting on the very edge of the witness chair, walking cane and handkerchief in hand.

"It was Ben's daddy that started the men in the community getting together and doin a lot of road repair work. Since he died Ben and Welsey have sort of taken that over. We have very few paved roads in Dawson County and since I'm a doctor it sure is good to have somebody you can depend on to see about a bad mud hole or a washed out bridge," this coming from Dr. Victor Holden.

Through the rest of the morning and into the afternoon Mark continued with his parade of character witnesses. It was however, Dr. Holden's testimony about road building and Ben McClure that caught Geneva Cooper's attention.

That evening during their supper meal, Geneva steered the conversation back to that, years ago, Sunday afternoon incident and asked, "Dad, do you remember that man's name that used his team of mules and pulled us out of the ditch that time?"

"I sure do," John Cooper immediately replied, "His name was Ben McClure."

When Geneva returned to the jury box on Wednesday morning she said nothing. Now on the jury, by a judge's decree, she was not willing to again call the courts attention in her direction. One woman on a jury in a Federal Court in Gainesville, Georgia in 1940, Geneva knew had to be the most minor seat that a minority ever found to sit on. Geneva was satisfied that this Ben McClure was the same man who had taken the time to walk a team of mules through a cold and wet Sunday afternoon in order to help her family out of what was to her, at that time, a perilous and impossible situation. Then, when they were safely back on the road, she remembered that he had waved them on their way. When she turned and looked out the back, he was standing in the road, wet and muddy with one hand on his mule's back.

Geneva abhorred the thought that any man would involve himself in the business of making and selling liquor. Now due to a series of events that even Geneva found hard to believe-she found herself in a position where she was going to be required to judge and decide on the guilt or innocence of one of the few men who she believed to be above reproach. Geneva believed that the use of alcohol was damning to perdition the lives and soul of the people that consumed it.

When Harrison Davis began his prosecution of the government's conspiracy case against Ben, Wesley and Rabb, he left no doubt about his intentions. He was, of course, aware that the burden of proof was his to prove. Harrison was confident of his ability to do that.

There was however, another requirement involved in prosecuting and proving a conspiracy case. That requirement was that not only did each person involved in the crime have to be proven guilty, but also that each person was guilty of conspiring together to commit the crime. Little wonder that not many district attorneys undertook prosecuting conspiracy cases, let alone assistant district attorney's.

Hiram angled his way across the lobby of the courthouse and intercepted District Attorney Adam Kasay as he was leaving that Wednesday evening. The two men, always cordial toward each other except when they were faced off in front of a jury, shook hands and walked down the courthouse steps together, "Well Hiram, Harrison tells me that he and your son are having a pretty good tussle so far."

"So I hear Adam. I haven't been there a whole lot, but word keeps coming across."

As they reached the sidewalk, Hiram stepped close beside the DA and made his offer.

"Adam, we will plead guilty to owning, making and selling. We'll take three months in the penitentiary and three years of probation for each of them if you will drop conspiracy and tax evasion."

The DA shook his head and gave Hiram an implacable answer to his offer.

"No deal Hiram, not this time and no counter either. I'm tired of seeing still hands get two years of probation or six months in the penitentiary, while the liquor keeps flowing and the money keeps coming right back to the owners and sellers pockets."

Hiram put out his only bait.

"Well Adam, he ain't proved conspiracy yet."

"Well Hiram, we ain't done yet."

Both men wheeled and stalked away in opposite directions.

With the approval of Judge Douglas the last thing that prosecuting Attorney Davis did on Wednesday evening before the jury was dismissed for the day was to conduct the jury en masse down to the lowest level of the courthouse where the evidence from the distillery, still loaded on the shack truck, was located.

Reminding the jury that Federal Agent Hasty was still under oath Harrison led Lee through a complete testimony of who and what he had seen and overheard that night at Ben McClure's barn.

Then, while the jury looked at the pictures of the still taken before the boiler was dynamited, he questioned Agent Clay Willard about the still and its location. Clay also testified that he had personally seen the fifty bags of sugar in Wesley Cochran's smokehouse. On both occasions when Harrison offered the witness for cross-examination, Mark replied, "No questions."

Then, on Thursday morning, just as Judge Douglas was about to call for closing statements, Mark rose and made a motion asking for the bench to declare a mistrial.

"On what grounds Mr. Taylor?"

"Your honor, I expected that every aspect of the government's evidence in this case would be examined here in open court, and the hearing of the testimony pertinent to that examination would be given in this court room, as designated on the article of indictment."

"I was informed by the prosecution that this trial would be moved out of this courtroom and into a room in the basement of this building after court was reconvened after the noon recess yesterday. What time I had was spent preparing my clients for what was about to happen and where it was going to happen. I had no opportunity to prepare a defense of testimony given under those circumstances or conditions. With due respect given to the bench for approving that change, I request that you consider that the defense of my clients is at least impaired if not put in jeopardy. I request that you declare a mistrial of the Federal Government's charges against my three clients."

The District Attorney was already standing when Judge Douglas asked, "Well Mr. Davis what do you say about his motion for a mistrial?"

"Your honor, the defense has neither grounds nor precedent on which to make such a motion. He's grabbing ---."

Judge Douglas glared down at the District Attorney as he interrupted.

"Mr. Davis I asked for your answer to Mr. Taylor's request and his reason for making it. I'll make the ruling whether or not his request for a mistrial has grounds or precedent or merit. You may continue."

"Your honor I apologize to the bench and to the court. Mr. Taylor has had as much opportunity as I have to look at the evidence before the trial started. Surly he knows that bringing a vehicle, which is part of the evidence, into the courtroom is not possible. I called only two witnesses for testimony with the evidence available for the jury's inspection. In both, instances he was given the opportunity to question the witness. Your honor knows and the jury knows that at both opportunities he answered, "No questions."

Taking no chance of making any further comment that might raise the judge's ire, Harrison sat down, and for almost a minute an unusual hush fell over the courtroom.

Mark had a feeling for what was coming, but he had hoped that raising a question about the District Attorney's procedure might find some judicial sympathy. Outside of Harrison putting his foot in his mouth, and getting his butt kicked, it didn't work.

"Mr. Taylor as you noted in your motion for a mistrial, the prosecution asked for and I granted their request for the jury to see the evidence taken from Mr. McClure's barn and the site of the distillery. I am sure that you are fully aware that a jury has every right to hear and see any and all evidence available that will or can help them to establish the guilt or innocence of an accused. Your motion for the bench to declare a mistrial in this case is denied.

"Gentlemen, prepare your closing statements. It's Thursday."

CHAPTER 20

The Seth Thomas clock on the wall of the jury room read 5 minutes past 1 o'clock p.m. when bailiff Lester Brooks lead the eleven men and one woman into the room. He laid a copy of the charges, the stack of pictures taken at the still site and a sheet of paper containing the names of the twelve jurors on the table.

"Lady and Gentlemen if you will be seated I have a couple of things to tell you before you start your deliberation," Lester began. "I am Lester Brooks and I am your bailiff. While you are here in this jury room, if you need something, knock on the door and I'll get it for you. If you need more information, let me know and I'll carry your request to the Judge. As Judge Douglas told you, you must elect a Jury Foreman to be your spokesman. Here is the form for the Foreman to fill out and sign when you have reached a verdict. There is the men's room and Miz Cooper, Judge Douglas has told me that I am to let you go to the Ladies room at your request. I'll be outside this door as long as you are in session."

They elected Walter Blake as the jury foreman. Walter owned and operated a feed, seed and hardware store in the Milltown section of Gainesville known as New Holland. As a business owner he was known throughout much of Hall County, but more important to most of the jurors for this trial, he had served before, on both Grand Juries and Traverse juries.

"Well folks, I'll do the best I know how as your foreman, and I think the best thing we can do to start with is get acquainted with each other. I'll start it and let's go around the room, stand up and give our name and where we are from. Then I would like to ask Reverend Lewis to lead us in a word of prayer and then we'll get to work."

At 3 o'clock the jury foreman stood and addressed the jury.

"We have spent about two hours now getting acquainted with each other and discussing our thoughts on the testimony that we have heard. If there is no objection, I would like to take a ballot in order to get some idea of where we stand. While this is not a secret ballot, I would like for you to write your decision on a piece of paper. I will read each ballot and then lay it on the table for all to see. If at this time you have not reached a decision, then you should write 'no decision' on your ballot."

When the twelve ballots were counted, seven were for conviction, three were noted 'not guilty,' and two were noted 'no decision.'

At 5 o'clock bailiff Lester Brooks knocked on the door and informed the jury that Judge Douglas was adjourning court for the day and wanted to know what the jury's plans were.

Walter Blake, the jury foreman answered, "Tell Judge Douglas that I am about to call for the second ballot and then, if there is no decision, I will ask the jury if they want to continue or quit for the day.

"Folks I am going to ask you to write your decision on a piece of paper one more time, but if there is not a unanimous verdict reached, we will begin voting by a show of hands until we reach a verdict."

As the other jurors were filling out their ballot, Geneva Cooper stood and spoke to the jury foreman.

"Mr. Blake may I ask a question?"

"Yes Mam, you certainly may."

"As I understand from the charges, if we find these men guilty of making illegal whiskey, we are also finding them guilty of conspiring together to avoid paying the taxes on that whiskey to the United States Government, is that right?"

"Yes Mam, that is correct."

"A guilty verdict will give the government the authority to seize and sell their homes and property, is that right?"

"Yes Mam, if they can't collect it any other way, they can seize and sell their property."

"Thank you Mr. Blake."

When the twelve ballots were counted, six were marked 'guilty'; four were marked 'not guilty,' and on two was written 'no decision' again.

*　　　*　　　*

When the twelve jurors were assembled in the jury room on Friday morning, Walter Blake stood and waited until he had their attention.

"Folks, Judge Douglas called me into his chambers early this morning and gave me this message for the jury. He said for me to tell you that he would like to have a verdict today. He said if we don't get a verdict today, he's going to bring us back tomorrow and keep us until we do get one."

"That sounds a little strong to me Mr. Blake. Sounds to me like he's trying to pressure us into a verdict," said Jack Haynes. Jack was a produce farmer from Lumpkin County. His farm was located north of Murrayville on the Gainesville to Dahlonega Highway.

Jasper Duncan was a dairy farmer from Barrow County. His dairy was located near a crossroads country store called Hog Mountain. Being a dairy farmer, that processed and sold his own milk by delivering it on a milk route in Winder, Jasper and his two sons had already finished the morning milking and delivery before he left that morning for jury duty.

Jasper was normally a mild mannered man, but he bristled at the thought of having to sit on a jury on a Saturday. He had no intention of letting that happen.

"The first thing that we have got to do is get these no decision folks to make up their minds. We have been told what these men are charged with, and we have heard the testimony from both sides. Our responsibility is to make a decision – to reach a verdict. I think it's high time for us to get busy and do what we are supposed to do. Let's decide on what we want to do with these folks. Mr. Blake I make a motion that you take another vote. I vote guilty just like I have on every ballot that has already been taken."

Surprised and taken aback by Jasper's outburst, the remaining juror's sat speechless, waiting to see how the jury foreman would reply to the disgruntled juror. But, before Walter could answer Jasper's demands, Geneva Cooper stood again but this time she directed her words toward Jasper Duncan.

"Mr. Duncan I would like to apologize to you and to the other jurors, as well, for I am one of the two jurors who have been marking their ballots no decision. If it was just a matter of convicting these three men guilty of making and selling whiskey, I would have been in favor of finding them guilty on the first ballot, because I think they are.

"Mr. Blake has just told us that if we find these men guilty of making and selling whiskey, and that they conspired to defraud the government by not paying the taxes due on that whiskey, the government can take action against them to collect those taxes. According to Mr. Blake the government can collect the taxes even if it means selling everything they own, and that includes their homes and farms. Punishing a man for breaking the law, even sending him to prison if the offense calls for it, is one thing, but taking his home and place for breaking the same law is something altogether different and I'll tell you why.

"If we find these men guilty and then the government sells their property to collect the taxes on their illegal liquor, we will be punishing the wife and children of these men. We will be voting to let the Federal

Government punish innocent people. I can remember my Grandma telling about when Grandpa got home from the war. His right arm and shoulder was shot up so bad he couldn't even hold them up let alone work with them. Grandma said that after a year he got to where he could feed the stock and keep plows and tools repaired. He would hold them between his knees, keep them propped in place with his right arm and work with his left hand. He changed from being right handed to being left handed for the rest of his life.

"Then about that time they started sending out notices that if we didn't pay our property taxes within a certain time, they were going to start selling our property at the courthouse door. Well Grandpa didn't have any money, and didn't have much of any way to get any, especially the new Federal money and that's what they had to have. My old Granny would laugh and say that it didn't take them long to realize that the best way to get some of the new money was to sell or trade with the people that had it, and that's exactly what they did. Grandpa's two brothers from up in Gilmer County came down and spent the winter with them. They put up a liquor still and made moonshine whiskey and hauled it and sold it to the Yankee soldiers that were camped around Marietta. Well that's the way I feel and that's why I feel that way, and I just wanted you to know why I feel that way. I hope--- I didn't mean ----."

Geneva fell silent, stood for a few seconds, suddenly awkward and embarrassed, then quickly dropped down on her chair.

Judge Arthur Douglas had gone to his chambers and remained there since he had called the court to order at 9 o'clock in the morning, and then almost immediately he put the court in recess to wait for a verdict from the one jury that was deliberating on the one case that he had heard during the whole week. Judge Douglas was furious, furious with the District Attorney and his assistants, furious with the courthouse politics and disgusted with himself.

"Never," he mused to himself, "have I presided over a term of court, that I couldn't get it to go in one direction or the other. I have looked and acted like a damned jackleg all week, and all week long if it ain't been old Adam Casey, it's been that damn Taylor boy kicking my ass back and forth like it was a flat football. Enough is a damn nuff and I have had enough."

Judge Douglas had made up his mind to terminate any further business of the court and then dismiss the court when the one jury returned with a verdict. "Maybe that will bring them out and remind them that I still have a little say so about what goes on around here."

There came three light taps on his chamber doors.

"Yes, who is it?"

"It's Lester Brooks, Judge Douglas.

The jury is ready to come out."

"Lester, the jury doesn't have to come back to the court room before they go to lunch. Tell them to go on."

"That's not it Judge Douglas. They have got a verdict."

The Judge bolted out of his chair and jerked the door open.

"The hell you say. When did this happen?"

"Just about five minutes ago. Mr. Blake opened the door and said for me to inform you that the jury had reached a verdict."

"Well I will just be damned and I had just about decided that I had a hung jury. Lester, send the other bailiff out to spread the word that I will be calling the court to order in thirty minutes. Then you go back and hold the jury in the jury room until I call for them."

Before 11:30 arrived every seat in the courtroom was taken and every office and stair and hallway in Hall County Federal Courthouse was empty.

Hiram Taylor had put his coat on and started out his office door when he turned, walked back into his office, and hung his coat back in the closet. Hiram crossed the floor to his office window and pushed the drapes all the way to either side. Spread before him and to either side were the perfectly maintained rectangular city blocks on which stood the plain yet stately buildings of the County and Federal courthouses. The bright sunshine of midday seemed to accentuate the sloping rooflines and bring out in sharp detail the cut and curve of windows and doors down the side of both buildings.

Hiram was suddenly seized with astonishment. How long had it been since he had looked out of this window and surveyed the scene where so much of his life had been spent and experienced and used. Again, the awareness came that the events that defined who he was and what he was, had taken place in these two buildings. And even now, standing here looking across at the Federal Courthouse, he knew that his son was, this day, facing what would be one of the defining events of his life. Was he tough enough? If he lost today, was he big enough to see where he had failed and learn from it?

He looked down and saw Laurel's car circle the block, looking in vain for a parking place. He smiled in admiration when she pulled in at the service station on the corner, handed her keys to the attendant and pointed to the grease pack. She turned and hurried off toward the courthouse. Hiram turned from the window, crossed to his desk and sat down. He picked up a cup sitting on his desk and carefully turned it around to read the words imprinted on each side. On one side was printed, THERE IS

NO BETTER FRIEND THAN A FATHER, and on the other side, THERE IS NO BETTER FATHER THAN YOU. The cup was filled with brilliantly multicolored small stones gathered from the riverbed of the Amicalola River where it flowed by the McClure farm in Dawson County -- The place where Laurel was born and raised.

CHAPTER 21

Judge Authur Douglas came hurrying through the double doors into a standing courtroom and took his place behind the bench. The clerk seated the overflow crowd and called the court to order. Judge Douglas surveyed the size of the crowd and wondered why there was such a sudden interest in a Friday afternoon verdict against three men charged with making moonshine whiskey.

"Folks you can stand in the back and along the sides but the area around the door and the aisles must be kept clear. Bailiff perform that duty and close the door. Bailiff will you escort Mrs. Taylor down front and make room for her on the front row."

Laurel blushed pink and red. "Good Lord, I didn't even know that he knew me."

Mark turned from looking at his wife and bowed toward the bench.

"Mr. Kasay, are you and Mr. Harrison ready?"

"Yes, we are Judge Douglas."

"Are you ready Mr. Taylor?"

"Yes sir, we are."

"Very well, Mr. Brooks let the jury come in please."

"Yes sir."

Within thirty seconds the jury began filing into the jury box.

A murmur rippled across the crowd. A few that were seated stood for a better view.

"Ladies and Gentlemen let there be order in the courtroom."

Robert Blake, the jury foreman, was the last juror in the jury box. He carried in his right hand a folded form of paper. Lester Brooks, the bailiff came last and closed the door. He laid on the jury box rail the copy of charges and various other forms and manuals used by the jury.

With the exception of the ticking of the Seth Thomas clock above Judge Douglas' chair there was not a sound in the courtroom.

"Mr. Blake, you are the jury foreman I believe?"

"Yes sir, I am Judge Douglas."

"Mr. Blake, has the jury reached a verdict?"

"Yes sir, we have Judge Douglas."

"May I see the verdict please?"

Robert handed the form to the bailiff who in turn passed it to Judge Douglas.

Judge Douglas spent some seconds looking at the form.

"I find the verdict to be in proper form and execution."

He folded the form and passed it back to the jury foreman.

"Let the defendants stand."

Wesley, Ben and Rabb rose slowly to their feet.

Mark stood with them and when Ben turned to look at Laurel, he saw that she was standing also.

"Mr. Blake will you read the verdict?"

"We the jury find the defendant ---"

Robert, realizing there was more than one defendant, stopped and started over.

"We the jury find the three defendants not guilty of all charges."

The silence in the courtroom continued for about two more seconds. Then a tidal wave of human sound went crashing through and out of the top floor of the Hall county Federal Courthouse. Judge Douglas heard the pent up bitterness in "the son-of-a-bitch," but let it pass. He knew where it came from and would render a measure of justice at a later date. He dismissed the jury and adjourned the court and quickly left the courtroom.

Laurel rushed through the gate separating the seating from the floor of the court and threw herself into Mark's arms. "Oh Mark, I'm so proud of you, we all are. Harriet said your Dad had hardly slept for the last two nights."

Then as Harrison Davis came over to offer his congratulations Laurel held and kissed on the cheeks of her brother and his two friends.

"Ben, don't you see, it's like a clean slate. You, Wes and Rabb are all three free and clear. I wonder if you know how happy it would make us – your wives and me -- to have you stay that way – free and clear I mean."

The courtroom was now almost empty, yet the three men were still standing near the table and chairs where they had just a short time ago received the words of their deliverance. Finally Ben pushed his chair under the table and made ready to leave.

"Well boys, Laurel said we're free and clear. I hope that means what it says. What do you think?"

Rabb, who was looking across at the empty jury box said, "I think we ought not to take any chances and get the hell out of here. It will do them no good to tell me they have made a mistake and I'm not free and clear. They will have to find me before they can catch me, both ends of which will take a little doing."

Wesley chuckled as they walked out of the courtroom into the hallway.

"Well Rabb it's not anything left over from this time that they will be looking at. But startin about Monday morning it's what they will be watching for that we will have to worry about."

As they reached the bottom of the stairs and started across the lobby, Ben was met and stopped by the woman who had just served as a juror on their case. She shook hands with all three of the men, but spoke only to Ben.

"Mr. McClure, I am Geneva Cooper. My father is John Cooper and we live at Flowery Branch. My father and mother are well, I'll tell them that I saw you, and you seemed to be in good health."

With that she turned and walked out of the courthouse. Some moments later when they came out of the courthouse and were walking down the steps to the street level, Ben saw her get in the back seat of a car, with a couple which he felt sure were her parents. She did not turn nor look in his direction again.

They had passed through the Lumpkin Campground crossing when Ben came suddenly awake. He had climbed in the back seat of Wesley's car and had fallen asleep before they passed through the city limits of Gainesville.

"What did Geneva say her last name was?

Wesley turned and answered over his shoulder.

"Her name was Cooper, Geneva Cooper. Said her daddy's name was John Cooper. Did you know him?"

Ben did not answer but continued to sit quietly on the back seat of Wesley's car. Then just as they were coming into Dawsonville, they heard him say to himself several times again and again, "well I will just be damned." Then he said one other thing, which at the time did not seem connected to what he had said first. Since Ben had not answered Wesley's first question, they did not ask about this one.

"If that's her, and that's it, then she has saved me. Saved me and everything I own. Some how and some way she went in that jury room and saved every one of us."

Neither Ben, Wesley nor Rabb were surprised to find that the good news of their being found not guilty had already been delivered to their wives. By the end of the day, word that Ben, Wesley and Rabb had beaten the conspiracy charge would be known in every house where there was a deeper and more vital interest in knowing.

The deliverers and spreaders of the good news were Newt Turner and Luke Gayton. After the families were told, Luke and Newt went next to Dr. Holden's house, and then to the house of Aunt Nora Perry. The news about Ben left Aunt Nora in high spirits. She insisted that Luke and Newt stay for supper. After Luke chopped the head from one of her spring roosters, they scalded, picked and singed every feather and quill from the fat yellow carcass. When they gave Nora the chicken dressed and drawn, she laid it on the washstand, drew a razor sharp butcher knife out of her knife drawer and cut up the whole chicken into a black iron pot. Some two hours later and after a cup of whiskey poured from Nora's charred oak keg, they sat down and devoured a huge meal of Nora's chicken and dumplings.

After they had cleared away the dishes, they moved closer to the stove because of the chill in the September night air. Then as they sat smoking and listening, Nora told Luke and Newt about the night that Ben was born. Nora told the story this time in great detail. So much so in fact that Luke and Newt felt as if she were actually reliving the experience as she retold it this time. This was not the first time that they had heard the story of Ben's birth, and how close she and Cora had been to being guilty of his death even before he was born. It was however, the last.

On the following Wednesday, Nora suffered a stroke so severe that on his first check of her vital life signs and responses, Dr. Holden advised Ben and Martha to make her as comfortable as possible. Nora died on Thursday morning and Ben, knowing of her personal desire for her funeral service to be held in Shoal Creek Baptist Church on a Sunday afternoon, delayed her customary burying time by one day and granted his beloved Aunt Nora a last and final fulfillment to a simple and meaningless request.

"It was something that mattered to her, so it ought to matter to me." Ben said to Laurel as they stood by the hand-crested mound of fresh dirt.

"God only knows how hard it has been, for two women, who spent their lives working and waiting on others, from the time they were old enough to wash bloody rags until the day they laid down and died themselves."

CHAPTER 22

The day and days that followed, Ben, Wesley and Rabb, being found not guilty of all charges brought against them, were days spent in thankful relief. They knew, and their families knew, that a tragedy that would have affected them for generations had been avoided. Only Ben knew how close and how personal the danger had come. He saw no reason to make it known.

Upon his return home that Friday evening, Ben had found Martha in their bedroom sitting in Carrie's rocking chair. Will and Carrie's picture album was laying open on their bed. A new album, which had been a Christmas present from Laurel, Mark, Jordan and Jacob, was open on her lap. She had been pasting pictures and post cards in the album. She looked up and tried to smile when she saw Ben standing in the bedroom door. Ben saw that she had been crying. Her attempt at a smile turned into a red-eyed grimace. She looked very tired, and sitting in Carrie's high backed rocker, she appeared to be small and fragile.

"My God" Ben admonished himself, "is this what I have done to my wife. Surely she's not bad sick. I knew it had been rough, but I never thought about this."

"I was afraid they were not going to let you come home Ben. Newt said things didn't look too good, and then last night and this morning you seemed so worried. But now you're home and everything's all right. It is all right isn't it Ben? Today has been the longest day, or it was, until Luke and Newt came by and told us you were all free and clear. Josh has gone to tell James and Eunice and when he gets back I'll fix us all some supper."

Ben walked across the room, picked Martha up out of Carrie's rocking chair and sat down on their bed with her on his lap. She leaned her head on Ben's shoulder, her hands folded in her lap. Ben spoke quietly as he gently stroked her hair, face and arms.

"Yes, my Martha, it's all right, I promise, and, I promise it's over. There's one other thing I promise, as of today I've quit the liquor business."

When Josh returned and looked in his mother and father's bedroom, he found them sitting on the bedroom floor, pasting pictures in their new picture album.

Hannah Belle McClure was born nine months and two weeks later at ten minutes past 3 a.m. on what would be a beautiful spring day in June.

Joe Thomas Cochran was born ten months and five days later at fifteen minutes past 11 p.m. on what had been a hot day in July.

"Why in hell is it that women cain't have their babies in the middle of the day instead of the middle of the night," Dr. Vic Holden grumbled, but the corners of his mouth were turned up in a wide grin.

END OF PART THREE

God-Fearing Criminals

Part 4

CHAPTER 1

Then the war years came. With the war came the implementation of the most dreaded of wartime events, especially so for a mother with a grown son. It was the necessary practice of drafting young men into one of the branches of military service. Waging war requires a great number of trained men and women to fight when needed. The draft is the first and most noticeable of all changes and it is the change that affects the most people.

There were other changes of course. The appearance of an ever-increasing number of men in uniform, army convoys passing through the countryside and the construction of military bases and supply depots.

From down in Cobb County came the best news of all. Between Marietta and Smyrna a huge aircraft plant and airfield were to be constructed. A giant 4-engine bomber named the B29 Superfortress was going to be built there by the Bell Aircraft Company.

There was also another change that started slowly at first, and gained some momentum as the war years continued on toward the mid-forties. There was across the South a noticeable improvement in the living conditions for a majority of the people.

With the exception of the creation of, the draft board and the rationing board, there was little increase in the number of jobs available in Dawson County. There was however a greater demand and a better price for the goods and services that the people of Dawson and surrounding counties had always produced and provided.

The one product, for which Dawson County received a great deal of notoriety, was for the production of moonshine liquor. Like every other product that was illegal or black-marketed the demand for mountain made liquor doubled and tripled until the demand completely outstripped the supply.

The main reason for the shortage in the supply of moonshine liquor was due to the shortage of the ingredients required to make it. Mainly a shortage of the one ingredient most necessary to make still beer ferment ... **sugar.**

Ben, Wesley and Rabb had not been involved in the business of making and selling liquor since their nearly disastrous brush with the Federal Revenue Officers some years before. Rabb however, did not quit the sugar and container supply business, although the hauling and delivery was done much differently and Rabb was no longer directly involved.

The three old friends and their wives did visit. Usually on a Sunday after church and that always resulted in a large meal being prepared by the wives while the men sat outside under the trees and talked. Do not think the wives felt that they were being put upon, or that they resented having to prepare a large meal in a hot kitchen on a hot Sunday afternoon. It was what they did, and it was what they expected to do, and it was always done well.

The conversation was informative, and because women had to know what was happening in their community, it was gossipy, funny, intimate and very necessary. Even Clara, Elizabeth and Josh, unwanted and unneeded, were sent to the front porch to watch over Hannah and Thomas. But their time would come later, after the Sunday dinner was over. Josh however did not mind. He was in the company of the two most beautiful girls-women he had ever seen, and today it seemed he was the object of their undivided attention. Today was the first time that Josh felt the attraction and desire that the touch, feel and smell of a woman awoke and aroused the senses in his mind and body.

CHAPTER 2

Ben sat with his chair leaned back against the trunk of a huge oak tree that spread shade over a large area in Rabb Turner's backyard.

"Well Rabb, has the sugar shortage slowed things down much?"

"No, not that I can tell Ben. Hell you know how this business is. When there's as much demand for liquor as there is right now, they'll get sugar from somewhere. There was a man come to me last week who was in a tight for a ton of sugar. Well I sent one car to Gainesville and Buford and I sent another car to Canton and Cartersville. I told the drivers to stop at every country store they came by, and buy all the sugar they could get without a ration book. It took us two days but we got him a little over a ton of sugar. That's getting it the hard way, but it shows that there is always some around."

"How about the molasses that some of the big stillers are using?"

"Yeah, well they are all right Wes, and they say that molasses will make still beer work real good. Some stillers say they can get a better turn out using molasses than they can get from sugar, though I doubt that. The still hands hate having to use molasses. Can you imagine getting them heavy containers of molasses to a still house in the middle of the night, and then having to dip or pour them into a still box and then mix them with the boxes of still beer? One still hand told me that when he got ready to go to bed his britches were so stiff from working with molasses all night that he just slid them off and stood them up in a corner."

They all three got a chuckle out of that one.

"Are you hauling and selling molasses Rabb," Ben asked?

"No, it's a little bit more of a job than I want to get mixed up with right now. Most of it has to be hauled out of New Orleans, and I would have to get a bigger truck to do any good with it. I'll just stick with selling a little sugar and hauling a few loads of tin cans for the time being."

"Well what about you boys? I don't want nor need to know anything about any definite plans, but both of you have been out of the business for a pretty good spell now."

Rabb's question went unanswered for a long moment. Both Ben and Wesley seemingly were waiting on the other to speak. Finally, it was Ben who spoke first. "Well Rabb, I have always tried to be careful about saying never, but I guess I'm thru."

Wesley's answer was neither straightforward nor definite, "I'll have to think on that for a while. I wouldn't want to tell you boys one thing and then go and do something else."

Annie Turner walked to the edge of the back porch.

"Rabb, dinner's ready, y'all come on and get washed up."

"Now boys that's what we've been waiting to hear. Let's get to it."

CHAPTER 3

Ben had already told Wesley of his decision to quit the liquor business prior to their Sunday afternoon dinner at Rabb and Annie's place. If Ben had experienced any doubts or temptation about his plans for the future, the birth of Hannah dispelled them all. Having made his decision, Ben urged Wesley to make his own future plans based on what was best for him and his family.

"Now Wes, we have always worked together in this business, fact is, it was me that talked you into it to start with. But if I can help it I don't plan on having anything else to do with it. If I can help you any way without getting involved, you know I will Wes, but I would just as soon not know anything about your business when I don't need to."

"Well Ben, I appreciate the offer, you know I do. I don't know right now whether I'll get back in the business anytime soon or not. I have thought about it, and I have talked about it with some other folks. I would like to get in one more good lick before I quit myself."

"One other thing Wes, all the copper and valves and hoses are yours. You know where they are, so just get them if and when you need them. That boiler can be fixed, if you'll get a good welder to work on it. You might have to get a few flues for it but it can be fixed and it's a good one too. Do you remember when we went to Chattanooga and bought it new Wes? I was as proud of that boiler as I would have been with a brand new pickup truck."

CHAPTER 4

Ben knew, when Wesley admitted that he had talked with some folks about giving the liquor business another try, that he had already decided or was very close to it. He knew his old friend too well. He was also fairly certain that the folks he was referring to were Zeke Turner and Luke Gayton. Ben was not at all surprised when a few days later he saw Luke and Doyle Edwards pass his house together in Luke's car.

Ben was not exactly right in his thinking about Wesley, Zeke and Luke, but as usual he was not altogether wrong. Wesley and Zeke had done little more than talk about a partnership in a liquor making operation. The reason that their plans had not progressed past the talking stage was simple enough. They had been unable to find a safe place to locate a distillery. Unlike any other place, the location of a still in the woods and the means of a secure access to it, is of the utmost importance.

Beginning in the latter war years, as if the men who erected stills in the woods were not already working under enough of a liability, they began having to deal with another one. The Federal Revenue Officers began using small spotter planes to locate stills on the streams in the North Georgia Mountain woodlands. Then on a Saturday morning as Wesley and Zeke were talking after a chance meeting at the small gas and grocery store near Wesley's house, the opportunity they had been looking for presented itself. Raeford Grant came out of the store and walked over to where Wesley and Zeke were standing. Wesley and Raeford shook hands.

"Well Wes, it's been a while. How have you been?"

"Been doing all right Rafe. It's good to see you. You just moved out of the settlement and left us, didn't you?"

"Yeah, well after our spell of bad luck, I thought it might be the best for everybody concerned if I just got out of the way for a while."

"Somebody told me you moved over in Pickens County, Dug Road I think, is that right?"

"That's right Wes; we live in the right good sized community of Pea Ridge."

Wesley turned to Zeke. "Zeke this is Rafe Grant, Rafe this is Zeke Turner, he's Rabb's boy."

The two men shook hands. "Zeke, I'm glad to meet you. I've heard a lot about you, and I have known your daddy for a long time."

"Zeke, Rafe owned the barn that we went through to get to the still that you and Luke ran for me and Ben."

"Well I'll be damned. I never did know that," Zeke replied. "I always wondered whose barn that was." After a moment Rafe turned to Wesley and said, "I have kept up with you and Ben thru a feller that we all know."

"That right, who would that be?"

"Frank Kirby"

"Why sure, I should have known that."

"Fact of the matter is, Frank suggested that I look you and Ben up."

Wesley realized that Rafe was here for something more than to pay a visit to his old friends.

"Rafe, have you heard that Ben has quit the business?"

Rafe chuckled and then continued.

"Frank said he had heard that, but didn't believe a damn word of it."

"Well I had my doubts about it too to start with, but so far he's stuck with it."

"What about you Wes? You haven't quit too, have you?"

"Well, no, at least I haven't made any promises one way or the other yet."

"Not that it's any of my business, but do you and Zeke have any plans?"

"We have done more looking and talking than anything else Rafe. Why, did you have something in mind?"

"Well I might have, if the right kind of deal came along."

"And Frank sent you to see us," Wesley inquired.

"Frank thought it would be you and Ben, but if Ben has quit, you and Zeke are all right with me."

"You mentioned the right kind of a deal. What did you have in mind Rafe?"

"A full share."

"Well, I'm sure we can work that out. What about Frank, what does Frank want?"

"Hellfire Wes, you know what Frank wants. He wants liquor, and a lot of it. He said to tell you and Ben that he would take every gallon of liquor you can make between now and the end of this year."

"Liquor business in Atlanta must be pretty good."

"Well it must be. Rob has moved to Atlanta, and he's taking care of that end of the business from down there."

"Who is tripping* their liquor for them Rafe," Wesley asked?

"Zeke, do you know Bradford Parks?"

"Yeah I know Brad, came from up around Jasper, I think. Last I heard he was driving a stock car for the folks that run Cherokee Motors there on Spring Street. They race mostly at Lakewood and up at that track in Gainesville, I think."

"Yeah he's the one. Well Frank told me that Rob went out there and made a deal with him to haul liquor for them. Rob told him that all he was going to get from driving a stock car was his neck broke because he wasn't going to make any money at it. Rob told him that he still might get his neck broke, but at least he would be making some money."

Rob bought a 1946 Ford Coupe from Cherokee Motors and had the engine builder at Spring Street Garage build a motor for it. Frank said that every law car between Ellijay and Atlanta had chased him and nobody had caught him yet, and him with a loaded car. The Sheriff in Forsyth County sent Brad word that the next time he got after him; he was going to shoot his tires down. Brad sent him word back that he doubted that because he didn't have a gun that would shoot that far."

"That sounds like Brad," Zeke chuckled, "He was always pretty good at letting his mouth get him in trouble."

Rafe grinned as he said; "They always told me that it wasn't bragging if you could do it."

Wesley interceded in the conversation. "Getting back to our end of the business Rafe, if you want us to come down and take a look at what you've got in mind, we'll do it."

"All right Wes, that's what I had in mind. Just let me know when I can expect you, so I can be sure to be at the house when you come."

What Rafe had in mind was a distillery using an upright boiler for steam and twenty-four boxes to ferment the still beer in. When in full operation the still would produce about two-hundred fifty gallons of ninety proof liquor every day. Very much like the still that Ben and Wesley had owned together, except, that still had eighteen boxes and this one would have twenty-four boxes. Access to the distillery would be the road between Rafe's two large chicken houses. Each of the two houses contained five thousand chickens and both were in continual operation.

The still site that Rafe had selected was located at the base of a rocky faced bluff with a fair sized stream of water flowing out of two spring heads a few hundred yards upstream. The still site and the quarter mile long access road from the chicken houses would both be located in a thick stand of field pines making them all but impossible to be seen from the air. Supplies for the still would be carried from the chicken house storage room to the still and the liquor brought from the still back to the storage room by a mule drawn rubber tired wagon.

As Rafe, was showing Wesley and Zeke the access road and still site he pointed out one other condition that could work to their advantage. "The chicken houses are on my property, but the still site would not be on my property. The folks that own the property, where the still would be located, live in Jasper and I have agreed to keep a watch over it for them. I guess the law would make a case against me if the still were to be found, but that would be my end of the bargain."

Two days later, as Wesley was checking out the road coming in and leaving Raeford's place, he stopped by.

"Well Rafe, everything I have seen looks good to me. Zeke says that he likes the looks of it too. First thing I have got to get fixed is the boiler. It will have to be re-flued and new boilerplate welded on the side that was blown out. Zeke will have made sure that our two still hands are going to be available when we want them, and check with Rabb to make sure that he can keep us supplied with sugar and cans when we get ready for them."

"Rafe we will be back here on Saturday to make sure that nobody has changed their mind and that everybody understands their part of the deal. Is that agreeable with you Rafe?"

"That's good by me Wes. I'll be looking to see you on Saturday."

"In the meantime Rafe, if you see Frank, tell him that if everything works for us we should have something for him in two or three weeks."

CHAPTER 5

Zeke shifted the one and a half ton International truck into a lower gear, and just as he came even with Rafe Grant's first chicken house, he switched the headlights off and swung the truck into the narrow entrance road. He drove the truck between the two chicken houses and braked to a quick stop at the far end. He switched the engine off, jumped down from the cab and ran back to the road where he stood listening for several minutes. Finally, satisfied that he had not been followed he walked back to the truck where Luke Gayton and Doyle Crowder were already in the process of removing the canvas cover from the stake body truck bed. With the canvas removed, Zeke removed the pins from the tailgate hasps and swung the tailgates open.

"Well I'll be damned," Luke said as he looked at the contents of the truck bed."

"You mean we are going to use them barrels instead of boxes to mix the beer in," Doyle asked?

Stacked in the bed of the truck were twelve large barrels with the head removed from one end. They reeked from the strong smell of red wine.

Zeke chuckled as he told the two still hands about the wide ended barrels. "That's right boys, they are called hogsets and they are used to ship wine over here from Europe. They hold 240 gallons each, about the same as a 4x 4 still box. They are built out of thick oak staves and wide metal bands. They will last a long time if we keep them full of beer and the damn law don't knock them down."

After a moment Zeke continued. "Did Wes bring the boiler in?"

"Yeah he did, brought it in yesterday. He drove his truck down to the shack* place and we set it up on the base right off the back of his truck," Luke explained.

"Then when you get these barrels in there, you'll have everything you need to get started with, is that right?"

This time Doyle answered. "That's right Zeke. Soon as we get them down there, we are going to put eight barrels on and we'll be in business."

"All right, sounds good, let's get the truck unloaded so you boys can get to work. I'll be back here tomorrow night about this same time with the other twelve barrels."

*   *   *

The following Thursday morning just after daybreak, Brad Parks turned the light blue 1946 Ford Coupe off the road and drove between the two chicken houses to the storage room located at the far end of the three hundred fifty foot long building. The powerful engine throbbed in the early morning quiet. Brad did not shut the engine down.

Rafe stood concealed between two trees at the edge of the yard, listening and looking for sound or movement in every direction.

The door to the storage room opened and in a matter of minutes, two hundred gallons of liquor in onion sacks holding five, one-gallon tin cans were loaded into the car. With the rear seat cushion removed, one hundred twenty five gallons was loaded in the front, and seventy five gallons was loaded in the trunk. Brad closed and locked the trunk and the passenger side door.

"Doyle, I'll be here about an hour later in the morning. I don't want to be seen on any of the roads around here at the same time from now on. That all right with you?"

"All right with me Brad. I'll have it ready whenever you say."

Brad slid behind the wheel, closed and locked the door and pulled the shifter into gear in almost the same motion. He turned south, toward Atlanta, out of the driveway and picked up to a speed that would not be noticed on the dirt roads of North Georgia.

Just under two hours later, Brad turned left off of Simpson Street onto a quiet tree lined side street on the west side of Atlanta. He saw that the garage door to the fourth house on the right was standing open. As he pulled the car into the garage, the garage door was closed and he heard a car pull into the driveway behind him.

This was another one of Kansady Miller's stashes* and over the next two years Brad would unload several thousand gallons of liquor into it. Unfortunately, however, not all of it would come from the illicit moonshine distillery of Wesley Cochran and Zeke Turner.

CHAPTER 6

For the remainder of 1946, Wesley and Zeke's still was operated with nothing more troubling than a broken part or a round of still beer not ready to be run. They also seemed to have located their still in an area that was not covered by either the Federal or State Revenue Officers.

But whatever the reason being, it was to the advantage and benefit of Rafe, Zeke, Wesley, Luke, and Doyle and they were all aware of it. They were also aware that there was little chance that their run of good luck would continue indefinitely. They did however decide to press forward for just a short while longer.

Making that decision was a bad mistake. Not only did their luck turn bad, but this time, it went terribly wrong. When a crime is committed, the solution of that crime usually depends on information given to the local officials by someone that either witnessed or has first hand knowledge about the crime. Depending on the severity of the crime and whether or not life was lost, the person given credit for helping solve the crime and capture the perpetrator gains a certain amount of notoriety in their community. Even after the person who commits the crime has been tried and sentenced, his indictment is still that "they ought to lock the son-of-a-bitch up and throw away the key."

There is an altogether different kind of notoriety reserved for the person who contacts a Federal or State Revenue officer and gives the location of a liquor still and the names of the people who own it and operate it. They are known as "a Reporter" and they are called "a reporting son-of-a-bitch." They are however not always men.

Such a man was Troy Pierce. Troy worked in the quarry at the Georgia Marble Company until one of the huge blocks of marble, being lifted on to a railroad flat car, shifted just enough to break both of his legs just below the knees. The company paid Troy's hospital bill and salary. Then, after three months of recuperation, they offered him a job loading gravel with a front-end loader. Troy refused and sued the company and lost. Angry at the company, Troy quit his job and lost his salary. That's how, at forty years of age, Troy became a loafing deadbeat.

Troy found that supporting a wife and three children, beside himself, required more of his time than he was willing to give. That's when he discovered the Georgia Farmers Market Bulletin. There were two categories of materials listed in the market bulletin that were of interest to Troy. One of these categories was the section on poultry and fowl. Troy's interest here was in game chickens because he raised, trained and sold fighting gamecocks. The other category and the one that was of the most interest to Troy was the section on herbs. Listed in this section he found the names of three different people who wanted to buy the roots of two plants known as bitter root and yellow root.

For several months Troy had been looking for someone who needed a supply of the two plants that are used in the making of liquid herb medicine and powdered herb mixtures as well as several other home remedies. Troy was able to become a supplier of herbs due to an accidental find while he was engaged in another of his money-making endeavors. He was looking for spring lizards along the spring fed stream that ran through the heavily wooded valley a half-mile from Pea Ridge Road. It was here that he found several large patches of yellow root and bitter root plants growing along the stream banks.

The following Monday morning, Troy turned his truck off of Pea Ridge Road and followed an old field road until he was stopped by trees fallen across the tracks. Taking two large burlap bags, the roots were not overly heavy, but required more space; he proceeded on down the hillside to the stream and soon located the patches of yellow root and bitter root plants. Then using his short handled mattock and hunting knife he soon filled one bag with the roots of the bitter root plants and the other from the roots of yellow root plants. After tying the filled bags he set them under a poplar tree and started walking up the stream. Troy had decided to go back to a waterfall and pool of water that he had found on the stream during his previous visit. It was a cool shady place to rest and a fine spot to get a drink of water.

Troy was kneeling beside the pool of water, dipping and drinking from his cupped hand when he noticed the discoloration in the water. The murky white color curled around and gathered in the backwater. When Troy worked the white colored water aside he saw that the bottom was covered with a fine layer of white sediment. Troy was satisfied that an illegal liquor still was causing the murky color and sediment in the stream. He also knew that he had to find the still and then get away without being seen.

Moving with the utmost caution, against being seen or heard, Troy walked upstream for almost and hour before he found the still*. He was shocked at the size of it, and he stood, for several minutes, admiring the location and setup of the largest moonshine liquor still that he had ever seen. Having located the still, Troy knew that if he was going to be able to use his new found knowledge for the most financial gain, it was of the utmost importance that he get out of the area without being seen or recognized. He retraced his steps back downstream to the two burlap bags of roots. Taking a breather in the shade of the popular tree he listened for any indication that he might have been seen or heard. Then tying the two bags together, he slung them over his shoulder, one in front and the other in back, and made his way up the hillside to the field road where he had left his truck.

The sun was no more than an hour high over the western horizon when Troy turned his truck out of the field road onto Pea Ridge Road. Making sure that there was not another vehicle in sight, he stopped his truck, and using a pine top he hurriedly brushed out his tire tracks into the field road. Thirty minutes later he was going thru Marble Hill on his way home. As Troy drove his truck along by the Marble Quarrys carved into hillsides on the road from Marble Hill to Tate, he was already thinking about who best to contact that would pay him the most up front cash money for the information and location of the huge liquor still he had found today. This information would provide an unexpected cash dividend for him. But the same information would initiate a shattering disaster for the owners and operaters of the illegal liquor still located near the Raeford Grant place.

CHAPTER 7

Lee Hasty pulled his car off the steep and winding road across Burnt Mountain and parked it at the edge of the overlook. Parked some twenty five yards away sat a 1932 Model B Ford pickup truck with the hood raised. A middle-aged man wearing overalls and a cap was leaning against the left front fender. Lee walked over to the truck and put his left foot on the front bumper. "Howdy, my name is Lee Hasty. I have a letter here from a Troy Pierce. Would that be you?"

"Yeah, I'm Troy Pierce and I wrote the letter, but I didn't know whose name to put on it."

"Well I'm the supervisor of the Federal Revenue Officers out of the office located in the Federal Courthouse in Gainesville. You said in your letter that you knew the location of a big still in Pickens County. Is that right?"

"That's right and it's a big one."

"How many boxes?"

"It ain't got boxes. It's got big barrels."

"Uh huh, well how many barrels?"

"Twenty four"

"Twenty four, are you sure?"

"Hell yes I'm sure, I counted them twice. also it's got an upright boiler that's taller than I am, and that's all I'm saying."

"Well that sounds like a right good sized one. We usually pay Twenty-five dollars but if this one is like you say we'll give you Thirty dollars to show me where it is."

"Well it's like I say and it's the biggest still I've ever seen, but it's going to cost you Fifty dollars."

"We are not authorized to pay over Thirty dollars, but I'll add Five dollars out of my own pocket and make it Thirty Five dollars."

An hour later the price was still Fifty dollars and Lee paid it.

$*$ $*$ $*$

The following morning Lee turned off of Hwy 53 onto Pea Ridge Road at Dug Road Store. Seated in the front with Lee was Dan Plummer the youngest officer assigned to the Federal Revenue office located in Gainesville. To keep from being seen, Troy was part sitting and part lying on the back seat.

"Dan, follow the old field road until you find the trees fell across the road and then follow my instructions. You'll find the still, I'll guarantee it," Troy said from the back.

"After you have found the still, scout out the whole operation," Lee instructed.

"Find out how they are waiting on the still and where they are getting on and off this road. Okay here's the field road, be careful Dan, I'll pick you up here at five o'clock this evening."

Lee slowed the car to a crawl and Dan stepped out on the road and quickly disappeared into the woods. Lee looked up into the rear view mirror but Troy was lying down completely out of sight.

"Troy I'm going to let you out at the same place where I picked you up this morning. Now you be damn sure you tell no one about the still until after we have raided it, not even your wife. Can I depend on that?"

"You sure can Mr. Hasty. I might want to do business with you again some day."

When Clay Willard retired in the early 1940's, Lee Hasty was promoted to fill his position. Under Lee's supervision it was not long until Lee and his crew of field officers began making a name for themselves. Rarely did they raid a still without catching the still hands and on most occasions they timed their raids to coincide with the arrival of a loaded supply truck. They referred to it as cleaning house if the driver of the supply truck turned out to be the still owner.

There were five Federal Revenue Officers gathered in Lee Hasty's office on Saturday morning, three days after Dan Plummer had made his way up the spring branch and found the still. Besides Lee and Dan there were Earl Simpson, Wayne Whiteworth and Carl Potts. Potts was the only officer on his crew that Lee was concerned about. Carl was a heavy drinker and although he made every effort not to show it, his habit was common knowledge among the other officers.

Lee spoke first.

"Dan has made two trips to the still site so I'm going to let him tell you what he has found and then I'll tell you what I've got in mind."

"Well men it's the biggest operation I have ever seen, and they have the best plan to operate it that you can imagine."

For the next thirty minutes Dan described the location and operation of the still to the other officers in the room. Then Lee took over again.

"All right men, here's the plan as Dan and I see it right now. If necessary we can change it as we go along. The supply truck runs on Monday, Wednesday and Saturday morning sometime between one and two o'clock. The still hands fire the boiler about nine thirty and put the first still full of beer on about ten p.m. We think the trip car runs at different times so he won't be seen on the road at the same time.

"I want to raid this still next Wednesday morning at one o'clock a.m. Whit you will drive the car and let us off a half mile past the chicken houses. Carl and I will take the still and Dan and Earl will take the supply truck when it pulls between the chicken houses to unload. If our timing is right we will have the truck out of sight and be waiting on the trip car when it gets there. I will send Carl up to the chicken houses to help with the supply truck and driver soon as we get the still hands caught and handcuffed together. We'll go over our plan another time or two, but unless we come up with something we haven't thought of, that's about it. I'll see you men on Monday, get rested up, we are probably going to have our hands full next week.

*   *   *

The moon was about two hours high when Whitworth stopped the car in the road and dropped the four officers at the predetermined spot. They quickly moved about one hundred yards into the woods before they stopped to regroup. The moon shed just enough light to permit the men to walk through the woods without danger of colliding with trees or with each other, but not enough to see or be seen for more than seventy or eighty yards.

In a hushed voice Dan spoke to the three Officers. "The still road is about three or four hundred yards further in that direction, follow me."

Using care to make as little sound as possible they arrived at the still road some fifteen minutes later.

This time Lee spoke to the officers. "All right men, this is where we split up. Dan, you and Earl go up to the chicken house and get set up. Carl and I are going to the still and get our plan worked out. I am still planning to go in at one o'clock. Use care and good luck."

Lee left Carl about two hundred yards from the still site and carefully made his way to within fifty yards of where Luke and Doyle were working.

Standing behind an oak tree he observed the two men as they operated the still. He smiled to himself when he recognized Luke as one of the still hands. Then with his plan in mind he walked back up the road to the place where Carl waited. The time on Lee's watch read 12:35 a.m.

"Carl, if we work this job right, I don't think we will have any trouble. I want you to work your way around on the right hand side and stay hidden out in the woods a way's back. I am going to stay hidden right back here. I think they are just about ready to blow the old pottail* out of the stills and put a fresh round of beer back on. When that is completed they each have a job of their own to do. The boy over on the right hand side, his name is Luke, proofs and tempers the liquor to ninety proof and then cans it. The other man, I don't know his name, puts water in the boiler and fires it. Now while they are working their jobs their backs are toward us, and that's when we get them. I'm going to duckwalk down to the front row of barrels and when I straighten up, you go after your man, who is Luke, and I'll go after mine."

Lee's plan worked to perfection. After duckwalking to the front row of barrels he stood up and glanced to his right. He saw Carl walk behind Luke and take hold of his overall shoulder strap just as he reached out and took Doyle by the collar.

"We are Federal Revenue Officers and you two men are under arrest. Both of you stand over here. I am going to handcuff you to this sapling. Don't try to resist and there will be no trouble.

Lee grinned at Luke and continued, "Well Luke how are you doing? I thought you promised us that you were going to quit the liquor business if we would put you on probation. Looks like we'll have to ship your ass over to Maxwell Field, Alabama for a few years. What do you think about that?"

"Well Mr. Hasty, I think you know that I built every day of my probation just like I promised I would. Outside of that, I don't remember that I promised you a damn thing. As far as how I am doing is concerned, I'm doing just fine, but if you don't let me or Doyle put some water in that boiler, all of us are going to wind up with the skin scalded off our ass."

Luke saw what happened next, but he was so surprised by it that he stood speechless as it happened. As Lee was removing Doyle's handcuffs and walking him down to the boiler, Carl walked over to the condenser snout, picked up Luke's proofing vial, caught if full of liquor and drank it down in four swallows. Since the condenser had just started running liquor from the previous change over, the liquor coming out of the condenser snout was over one hundred fifty proof. It is called hi-shots liquor, or running gold dust since the proof is so high that it appears to have little specks of gold in it.

Lee made an additional request of Doyle, "Doyle open the boiler door and draw the fire. It will take a couple of hours for it to cool off now."

Luke watched for a second time as Carl filled the proofing vial and drank it down. Then from his back pocket he removed a small bottle, filled it with the hi-shots liquor and returned it without being seen by Lee. Luke marveled that the officer was not falling down drunk, but he seemed to be showing little effect from it.

When Lee walked Doyle back to the place where Luke was handcuffed to the small tree, he released Luke and then handcuffed the two men together. "All right boys, just sit down there and make yourselves as comfortable as possible. I don't like to do this Luke, but I have got to carry you boys in and I cain't take any chances. I don't think you boys would take to the bushes, but if you did I would have one hell of a time explaining that."

Lee turned to Carl and said, "All right Carl, go on up to the chicken houses and help Earl and Dan wherever they need you. I sure would like to get the supply truck and the trip car too. That would be a real haul, what I would call a real house cleaning.

*　　　　　*　　　　　*

It is not an easy thing to comprehend or believe, but absolute coincidences do happen. On how many occasions when tragedy has struck, would a one-minute segment of time have averted the disaster? Was it ordained or predestined to happen, or was it that all the elements of death and destruction were present and it just happened? When Federal Revenue Officer Carl Potts reached the end of Raeford Grants two chicken houses, he knew from experience that he was very intoxicated. As usual the first assumption of a drunk is that regardless of his condition, he is still very much in control. He saw Earl and Dan standing on the backside of the number two chicken house at the end, next to the road. He saw their hand signals, but thought they were giving him a wave of recognition, when in fact they were motioning for him to come in their direction. He returned the wave and moved closer on the road between the two chicken houses.

Dan dropped his arms and turned to Earl. "Where did he go?"

"I don't know, but I hope he went in the chicken house and hid. I don't think he's coming down here."

Ten minutes later.

"Earl I hear a truck coming."

"That's probably him, now remember when the truck goes between the chicken houses, we follow close behind and when the truck stops we go after him. One on either side."

When Zeke saw no headlights in his rear view mirror, nor any on the road before him, he turned his own head lights off and turned the loaded supply truck off the road and into the drive between the two chicken houses. Zeke did not brake the truck until he came to the supply room door, and that left Earl and Dan just coming around the end of the chicken house when he opened the cab door and stepped out on the running board. He did not see the two officers coming from behind, and he thought the man standing a ways in front of the truck was Doyle who had come to help him unload and carry a load of supplies back to the still.

"Hey Doyle, is that you? Where is your jackass mule and wagon? I've got a full load on this big sucker, so we need to get started. Doyle - -"

Carl realized he had been seen but not yet recognized. Not knowing the whereabouts of Earl and Dan he decided that he had to make a move.

"I'm a Federal Revenue Officer and you are under arrest. Don't try to run. I know who you are."

Zeke bolted into immediate action. As he dove back into the cab of the truck, he glanced in the rear view mirror and saw the two men coming from the rear. Then Zeke made a deadly mistake. He had only to slide across the seat to open the passenger side door and leave. The fleet of foot Zeke could have disappeared into the night leaving a drunken Revenue Officer wondering where he went, but he didn't and with deadly consequences. Zeke hit the starter and the engine immediately restarted. He kicked the clutch and yanked the transmission into reverse gear in almost the same motion. Then just as the loaded truck began to move backward, Carl took a half dozen running steps and swung onto the driver's side running board.

"I told you to halt, you are under arrest. Stop this truck and give yourself up."

"Get off my truck or you are going to get hurt."

Zeke pushed the accelerator pedal to the floorboard and the two officers coming from behind had to flatten themselves against the sides of the chicken houses to avoid being hit by the stake body truck. Earl, who had jumped to the left side as the truck came by, was astonished to see that Carl was holding his service revolver in his right hand.

Zeke saw the end of the chicken house on his left come by and spun the steering wheel hard to the left. The rear end of the truck turned left in front of the chicken house and even after Zeke locked the brakes on the loaded truck, the rear end crashed into a large brush pile on the far side of the chicken house. Zeke had already smelled the acrid aroma of raw alcohol on Carl's breath and he knew what that meant. The sudden stop of the truck threw Carl against the truck body, but the now enraged officer still managed to hold on. Zeke kicked the clutch in and jerked the transmission into low gear. He let the clutch out and pushed the accelerator to the floorboard in the same motion. The engine and transmission together gave a high-pitched grinding squall and the front end of the truck came several inches off the ground as it lurched forward.

"I told you to get off my truck you drunk son-of-a-bitch. Now I 'm going to put you off."

"God damn you, I told you to halt for the last time."

KAPOW!

The sharp blast from the muzzle of Carl's pistol reverberated over a wide area, swiftly carried on the cool clear night air. It was an ominous sound to everyone who heard it, coming as it did, at such an unexpected late night hour.

Zeke did not hear the sound as being the sound of a gunshot. He was sure that the Revenue Officer had struck him a hard blow on the left side of his head. Zeke's immediate intention was to knock the officer off his truck and then make his getaway. But it was then that the ringing started in his ears. He noticed that the truck was stopped and in order to make his escape he had to get it started. He was sure it was all due to the red skim floating down over his eyesight. Then the ringing in his ears changed to a loud roar and there was this strange light –

When Carl felt the kick from the discharge of his pistol, he partly fell and partly jumped off the running board of the truck. It was when he grabbed the door handle and pulled himself back onto the running board that he saw the small blue black hole behind Zeke's left ear. A few drops of blood had run out of the bullet hole and dripped down on his collar.

Carl realized that he was holding his service revolver in his right hand, and that it had just been fired. In that instant, Carl realized what he had done. He looked into the cab of the truck where Zeke was sitting; his upper body slumped forward, laying on the steering wheel. "I asked you to halt, but you wouldn't do it. I didn't have any choice." But Zeke was not there to hear Carl's last order. The light of life had quietly disappeared out of the breached body of Clyde Zeke Turner. Zeke was dead.

The other two Revenue Officers, Dan and Earl, rounded the corner of the chicken house just as Carl fired the lethal bullet into Zeke's head. They came to a dead stop and stood for a few seconds in stunned disbelief. Then Earl grabbed Dan by the arm and practically whispered in his ear. "Go get

Lee. Tell him that Carl has gone crazy. Tell him that Carl has shot the guy driving the supply truck. Tell him to hurry."

When Lee heard the shot, he knew that something had gone bad wrong. He looked at Luke and Doyle, but said nothing.

It was Luke who spoke up.

"Mr. Hasty, that feller called Carl was sneaking around drinking that hi-shots liquor while you and Doyle was down at the boiler."

"My God Luke, why didn't you tell me?"

"Well, you was hi-assing it around here telling me what you was goin' to do to me, so I just decided I'd let you find out on your own."

Lee took out his key and unlocked the handcuffs from Luke and Doyle's wrists.

"Luke will you and Doyle promise me to come in and make bond when I send for you?"

"I do," said Luke.

"I will," said Doyle.

That was the last time that either Luke or Doyle ever heard from Lee about being charged, or to come in and make bond on a charge of making illicit spirituous grain alcohol (moonshine liquor) without a license.

*   *   *

Lee stepped up onto the running board of the supply truck and looked inside the cab. Zeke's head was turned just enough to permit Lee to see the face and recognize who it was. Recognition came as a stunning blow. Lee stood seized by the memory of this vivacious young man with whom he had waged an all out foot and mind race through the woods and fields of Dawson county a few years ago. Although he had lost the race that day, he had come to admire this brash young man, who he had never met and now he never would.

Lee stepped down off the running boards and turned to face Carl. "Carl, can you tell me what has happened here? I sent you up here to help Earl and Dan and the next thing I know you have shot and killed a man."

"I ordered him to halt. I ordered him to halt three times but he wouldn't do it."

"So you shot him?"

"I didn't think I had a choice Lee. I had already told him that he was under arrest."

"What did you put him under arrest for."

"I put him under arrest for bringing that truck load of supplies in here to operate that still with."

"Carl with a dead man that you shot laying in the cab of that truck, shot because he wouldn't stop the truck, would you swear to what's on that truck?"

"No I wouldn't, because I haven't seen what's on it."

"Luke said you were drinking liquor from the still. Is that right Carl?"

"I took a drink, well two drinks, but that's all."

"Carl don't you know ---?" Lee stopped unable to continue. Filled with anger and disgust, Lee knew that if he continued he could lose what little control he had left. He could only imagine the mountain of patience that would be required of him during the next twenty four hours.

Lee saw Whitworth pull into the driveway and park their car. He nodded his head toward Carl.

"Earl, I want you to take him with you and go to Jasper. Find the sheriff and tell him what has happened here. Tell him that Lee Hasty is here and that I would like for him to get the coroner and an ambulance and bring them over here as soon as possible. Tell the sheriff that I would like for him to call the sheriff in Dawson County and ask him to come over here also. I will need him to go with me to see Zeke's folks.

"After that Earl, get him to Gainesville as soon as you can. I'm sure the boss will be in the office, so tell him what has happened. He'll know what to do. I'll be here until the coroner releases the body and they leave with it.

"Earl, get back here with the car as soon as possible. I want every Federal Revenue Officer out of Dawson and Pickens County **before dark this evening.**"

CHAPTER 8

The first light of daybreak was flowing out of the eastern sky when Raeford Grant turned his truck up Ben McClure's driveway and stopped in the backyard. Rafe and Wesley Cochran got out of the truck, walked across the yard and stepped up on the back porch. Wesley rapped lightly on the back door and called Ben's name in a low voice.

"Ben, it's Wesley. Can we come in?"

"Come on it Wes, the door's not locked. Well hello Rafe, I didn't know you was out there. You boys come on in and sit down."

At that moment Martha walked into the room. She had hurriedly dressed when she heard Ben speak Wesley's name. She had experienced a sense of foreboding. Martha returned their greeting with a smile and a "Good Morning."

Ben also sensed trouble and did not wait.

"Wes is something wrong?"

"Bad wrong Ben, Bad wrong. It's Zeke. The Federal Revenue raided the still early this morning and when Zeke tried to back the truck out and get away with it, one of the officers jumped on the running board and ordered Zeke to stop. When Zeke tried to sling him off the truck, he pulled his pistol and shot him. Zeke is dead."

Ben sagged against a chair. He took hold of the chair back for support. His face and neck turned a sickly shade of gray. Martha reached for her husband's arm but he quickly recovered.

"You mean to tell me that damn bunch has shot and killed Rabb and Annie's boy."

"They have Ben and it's as bad as anything I've ever seen," Rafe answered and continued, "one of them came up to the house and wanted to buy a sheet. I gave him one and watched as he took it down there and they covered him up with it. He was still in the cab of the truck."

242

"Luke told us the officer that caught him was drinking liquor that he caught right out of the end of the condenser," Wesley added.

"Did they catch Luke and Doyle both?"

"Yeah, they got both of them."

"Where are they?"

"They turned them loose on their promise to come in and make bond when called. Rafe brought them to the house where Luke left his car. I told them to go home and stay there for the time being."

Ben looked from Wesley to Raeford before he spoke. "Well this time I'm afraid they have gone too far. Unless something happens to change it, I think there's fixing to be a war in the woods."

Martha broke into the discussion and reminded them of what their first responsibility was.

"Ben, go change your clothes and get the car out while I get ready. I must get to Annie and Clara Mae. I'm afraid of what this might do to Annie. You know that she's been sickly for several months now."

*   *   *

When Ben and Martha turned into the driveway at Rabb and Annie Turner's house, and saw the sheriff's car, they knew, with little doubt, the reason for its being there.

"Oh Lord Ben, this is what I was afraid of, the sheriff is already here to tell them about Zeke. Do you think the sheriff has come alone? I cain't think of anyone who could be with him."

"Well, we'll know soon enough Martha." Ben did not tell his wife, but he had an idea who was with the sheriff and, of course, the reason why he was along.

Ben and Martha were met on the front porch by Newton, Rabb and Annie's oldest son, who led them through the hall and into the large front room on the left-hand side of the house.

Seated on the sofa were Rabb and Annie and their daughter Clara Mae. Clara Mae's arm was around her mother's shoulders and Annie's head was laying in the curve of Clara's neck. Annie was sobbing into a large white handkerchief that covered her whole face.

Rabb was staring at Lee Hasty. His stricken face set with an expression of stunned disbelief.

"Ben, this Revenue Officer has just told us that last night, when one of his men tried to put Zeke under arrest, and Zeke made a run for it in the still truck, he shot him. This officer is telling us that our boy is dead Ben. Do you know if that is right?"

243

"I'm afraid it is Rabb. We come on just as soon as we heard it from Wes this morning."

Ben turned a hard face and angry eyes toward Lee Hasty. "Mr. Hasty, since when has it become a killing offense for a man to run from a still to keep from getting caught? I'm nearly forty years old and this is the first time I have ever heard tell of it."

Before Lee could answer, Martha addressed both men with a sharp tone in her voice. "Ben, if you and Mr. Hasty have something you need to discuss, I believe you should do that some place besides here. This family has just been told that they have lost a son and brother and it has left them in a state of shock and grief."

Lee answered Martha's request with a note of regret in his voice. "Mrs. McClure, I apologize to you and to Mr. and Mrs. Turner. Rabb, let me just say, there will be a complete investigation into this matter, and you and Mrs. Turner will be given an explanation of what conclusions are reached. Ben, could I speak to you for a moment on the outside please."

The two men walked across the back yard and stopped in the shade of a huge old oak tree. "Ben, I don't think I have to tell you how much I hate that this thing has happened. How sorry I am for Rabb and his family and then you cain't imagine what a problem this mess is about to be for me. It got out of hand and I wasn't there to stop it. I hope you know me well enough to believe that."

Lee stopped long enough to give Ben a chance to answer, but he made no comment.

"Ben, you know that the real danger here is that one of these hotheads is going to retaliate or at least try to. I don't blame the still hands for being mad. I guess I'd be mad myself, but it won't work Ben, and I think you know it. Think about it Ben, if somebody shoots a Federal Revenue Officer down, it will be out of our hands. The FBI will take it over and for everybody in the business things will go from bad to worse. Can I depend on you to warn them about the FBI Ben?"

"Why no Lee, I'll not lift one damn finger to help you. One of your drunk Revenue Officers shoots a man down for trying to run and you want me to warn them not to shoot back. You know what the agreement has always been, and not only have you broke it, you have killed a man to boot. I would say that it's a damn good bet that somebody is going to retaliate. I probably couldn't do anything about it if I wanted to, which I don't."

"Come on Ben, you're still not thinking straight and the hell of it is that I cain't blame you. But if you and I cain't get something done, this thing could get out of hand."

Ben stood for a full minute before he replied.

"All right Lee, I'll listen, but since your side started it, what have you got in mind to stop it?"

"Well first of all it's going to take both sides to stop it, if it's going to be stopped. So let me say this to start with. I'll bring no charges against anyone involved in this operation. I'll see that Zeke's record is cleared of everything, past and present, and I'll destroy the file of evidence that we have on Rabb. Now Ben I'll make one other offer and it's one I don't have any authority to make, so tell no one I made it. Just tell the people who need to know about it. They will know what to do with it. There will be no Federal Officers in the woods in Dawson, Lumpkin nor Pickens counties for thirty days. For that I'll expect you, Wesley and Grant, to help get the word out that if a Federal Officer is shot, the FBI will be here with a reward and they won't leave until the shooter is captured and that includes the officer that shot Zeke."

As Ben stood, looking across the yard, thinking about what Lee had just offered to do, in order to prevent further bloodshed, he realized that he was looking at Zeke's spotlessly clean, black 1940 Deluxe Ford Opry Coupe. Ben knew that it was now time to deal or there would be no deal. "All right Lee, I'll agree to what you have offered to do, and to what you have asked for in return with one exception."

"What's that Ben?"

"Carl Potts will have to pay, but we won't kill him."

CHAPTER 9

The news of Zeke Turner's death, and the manner in which it happened, ran like a wall of wildfire through Dawson and Pickens and surrounding counties in a matter of hours. While death is the accepted and expected end of life for the old and the almost old, death is thought of as an unexpected invasion of life when it happens to the young. When the old die it is said that they have gone to meet their maker or gone to receive their reward, yet when the young die they are always taken from us. A further reminder that in the living of life, death does not always wait to come for the old.

There was an immediate outpouring of anger against Federal and State Revenue Officers after Zeke's death, but there were no acts of revenge against local law officials. The most outspoken of the men calling for immediate retaliation knew that it would be senseless to commit an act of retaliation against a local law officer. For under no set of circumstances would a local law officer shoot a man for working at or running from a still.

Local lawmen were also well aware that, if there was no immediate reaction to a tragedy of this magnitude, it did not bode well for whatever act of retaliation that would almost surely be taken in the future. The reaction then would not only be taken in retaliation for Zeke's murder, but also a reaction in which they felt that they were defending themselves.

CHAPTER 10

The funeral for Clyde Ezekial Turner was held on a cloudless Sunday afternoon in April of 1947. Since shortly after the noon hour a large crowd of people, made even larger because it was on a Sunday afternoon, began gathering at Shoal Creek Baptist Church. Many of those who came were distant relatives and friends of the Turner family, but just as many were curious onlookers who came to see who was there, and to hear what the preachers would say about Zeke in their sermon.

Long before the appointed hour of two o'clock, with the exception of the benches reserved for the family and immediate relatives, the church was filled to overflowing capacity. There were two preachers asked to conduct Zeke's burial service, the Reverend Boyd Williams, now in his eighties, was recognized and respected as the senior of ministers who served in churches throughout the northern part of Dawson County. The Reverend James Raymond McClure, Jr. the grandson of Raymond and Lettie Baker and Will and Carrie McClure, both now deceased, was now the minister of the Shoal Creek Baptist Church.

When Zeke was attending school at Dawson County High School, he was not a good student. Not because he was not intelligent enough, but simply because he was not interested. There was however, one course of study and one organization, that Zeke enjoyed. The course was vocational agriculture, and that was because the whole class went on field trips and attended local fairs together. Clara Mae asked the Future Farmers of America Quartet (FFA) to sing at Zeke's funeral. They came wearing their traditional blue corduroy jackets, embroidered with their names and the FFA emblem in gold.

Needless to say Zeke's funeral service was conducted by the two preachers, one young and one old but both his friends, in an eloquent yet plain and personal way. At one place in his sermon Boyd Williams said,

"This lovely young man has outrun this ancient old preacher back to the Father's House. Why could it not have been the other way around?"

There had not been and there was no direct mention made of the violent end of Zeke's life. But during an emotional part of James' sermon he quoted verbatim from the King James account of David's eulogy at the reburial of Saul and Jonathan.

"How are the mighty fallen in the midst of the battle! O Jonathan, thou wast slain in thine high places. I am distressed for thee, my brother Jonathan: very pleasant hast thou been unto me: thy love to me was wonderful, passing the love of woman. How are the mighty fallen, and the weapons of war perished!" (II Samuel 1:25,26, 27)

Then, at the last, the undertakers laid aside the blanket of deep red roses and opened the casket. Boyd and James took their place behind and one at either end of the casket. The FFA Quartet and their Accompanist were the first to view the body after which they went directly to the piano and began to sing one of the songs requested by the family.

*"We read of a place that's called Heaven, *1*
It's made for the pure and the free;
These truths in God's word he hath given,
How beautiful Heaven must be.

Next came the pallbearers, and then beginning with the people standing on the outside of the church and continuing with those on the inside, they filed by the casket and viewed the body of Zeke for the last time.

Perhaps the most unpretentious and unassuming person of all those who passed by Zeke's casket that day was Luke Gayton. Luke came with the people who were standing on the outside of the church. He looked at Zeke's body and passed out the side door. With the exception of Zeke's family, and without making an outward claim as such, Luke knew Zeke personally and more intimately, than anyone else in the great number of people in attendance that day.

Last of all came the grief stricken family to bid their son and brother a tear filled and lengthy farewell, and then it was over. The undertakers closed the casket and made it ready for the pallbearers to carry it out of the church and across the road into the cemetery.

During all of the time required to view the body, the FFA Quartet continued to sing. As the undertakers placed the blanket of roses back on top of the casket, the quartet came to the final verse of the last song requested by the family.

*I'm ready to go to that golden shore *2*
I want to meet mother and saints of yore
In heaven the home of the soul.

He'll hold to my hand – hold to my hand
As over death's river I go;
Then safe I'll be – safe I shall be
In beautiful Heaven I know.

*1 From an old gospel hymn entitled, "How Beautiful Heaven Must Be"

*2 From an old gospel hymn entitled, "When I've Traveled the Last Mile"

*   *   *

Some two months later when Zeke's tombstone was erected, the epitaph engraved at the bottom read: *Just in the morning of his love and life, he died.*

*   *   *

There were several of Annie's friends, Dr. Victor Holden and his wife Grace included, who were afraid that she would be so devastated by Zeke's death and the circumstances of it that she would be unable to survive the effects from the lasting ordeal. They were all pleasantly surprised when Annie came to Memorial Day service in May. She had regained her strength and seemed to be very much at peace with herself. During the afternoon visit to Zeke's grave she spoke lovingly about her son. To Annie he was always Clyde; she never called him Zeke.

"Clyde was always a good boy. He was never mean nor lazy. He was always good to help me and his daddy about the place. There was one time I even thought he might make a preacher.

As he got older he was gone more and more of the time. I couldn't help but worry about him. But now I don't have to worry about him any more. I know he's safe now. Nobody can hurt him anymore."

*   *   *

When Rabb looked upon the lifeless face of his son, he experienced the smothering grief of a parent for a dead child. Making his grief even more devastating, Rabb accepted full responsibility for his son's death. Rabb also admitted to himself that the Federal Revenue Agency, which he had always successfully eluded and evaded, had now, with one vicious strike defeated him … whether intentional or unintentional made no difference … At the end he was defeated. They had won.

249

*　　　*　　　*

Perhaps the most mortal of wounds was inflicted on the youngest of Zeke's family. As a child Clara Mae worshipped her older brother. As she grew older it was Zeke that she could talk to, that she could confide in, that she trusted and loved. When she was told that Zeke was dead, she did not believe it, and when she saw him, she fled to her room and would not come out. Later that day when the Wesley Cochran family came to pay their respects, Clara sent for Elizabeth, but then would allow no one else into her bedroom.

What Elizabeth found was not the lovely face and comely personality of her close friend, but an almost stranger with a face contorted with grief and eyes that burned with bitterness and hate. "Elizabeth they took him from me. I have always been afraid that something awful would happen to him. They couldn't get him any other way so they killed him. That Federal Officer that came here said that he never wanted anyone to get hurt or killed, but he was lying. They shot him; they didn't shoot him accidentally they intentionally shot him. They couldn't catch him so they shot him. I'll hate the lying sons-of-bitches until the day I take my last breath."

Elizabeth took Clara in her arms and held her for a long moment. Then taking a small brush from her coat pocket she began brushing and smoothing her hair.

"Clara please don't say that. You mustn't hate like that. The Bible says we mustn't. I know you aren't at yourself, so I'm going to take care of you. Clara when have you eaten anything?"

"I don't know, the thought of food makes me sick."

"I'm going out to the dining room and fix us both a plate of food, and after we have eaten you are going to lie down and take a long nap."

When Clara awoke she lay quiet and still for a time as the memory and grief of the days events came flooding back into her mind. She had no idea how long she had slept. The house was quiet and still with a dim light shed by the lamp on her bedside table. Elizabeth was gone from the chair where she had been sitting when Clara had closed her eyes. She must have immediately fallen into an exhausted sleep.

Clara sat on the side of her bed and slipped her feet into her house shoes. She opened her bedroom door and stepped out into the hallway. She heard muted sounds of movement and conversation coming from the front porch. She heard the quiet voices of women coming from her mother's room. She walked up the hall to the door of the front sitting room where Zeke's open casket stood. A shaded light standing at either end of the casket illuminated it. Elizabeth was standing beside the casket, bent at the waist until her face was very close to Zeke's face. Her right hand was tenderly caressing the features of his face. Clara saw the slight shake of her shoulders and heard the muffled sound of sobs that came from the handkerchief pressed to her mouth.

Clara stepped into the room.

"Elizabeth"

Elizabeth straightened; keeping her back turned toward Clara, trying to regain her composure. But she could not, sobs continued to rack her thin body until she turned into Clara's open arms.

"I have always loved him Clara. Ever since I was old enough to know what love is, I have loved him. I have tried to keep it hid from everybody, but I think he knew it. I was so thrilled to think that my love was also our secret. We have held hands before but tonight is the first time I have ever put my hand on his face. I have dreamed about it, but this is the first time I have ever done it. Clara, I would have run away with him if he had only asked. Now I wish to God I had asked him."

Clara stood stunned and overwhelmed by the revelation of what this girl-woman had just entrusted her with. Then she knew, and she understood that it was all true. All doubt was swept away. "Oh my God Elizabeth, what have I done to you. I have let you break yourself apart with my simpering self-pity. How can I ask you to forgive me?"

In the days and weeks following Zeke's death, and burdened with Elizabeth's confession, Clara finally admitted to herself the devastating toll of her vain hypocrisy on her family and friends and on herself. As a result Clara and Elizabeth became closer and deeper friends than ever. There were however, two women, each suffering a personal travail of her own.

*   *   *

There is an old axiom that states that time heals all wounds: In the case of Clara and Elizabeth that old standard proved to be true. There is another more divinely established truth as contained in the book of Ecclesiastes and located in Chapter 3, verse 1: *To everything there is a season, and a time to every purpose under the heaven.*

Since Clara and Elizabeth were both young, comely and gracious young women, one exceedingly lovely and one most exceedingly desirable in all her ways, then it is, as we shall in due time find, that their time had not yet come.

And o' the joy ---

CHAPTER 11

They dug his grave in the yard of the church,

And the clay was red like the blood of men.

They rolled his coffin down the aisle of the church,

Where he came with his boyhood friends.

As the scarred old organ with its worn out cloths

Swelled forth with his burial hymn,

They came down the aisle and passed by his coffin

to have their last look at him.

As each minds eye recognized death,

and passed on by,

They said it isn't him,

but it is the clay of him.

END OF PART 4

God-Fearing Criminals

Part 5

CHAPTER 1

Within days of Zeke's untimely death, Ben realized that there was growing unrest among the people who were currently involved in the mountain liquor business. Ben was somewhat irritated that for some reason he was immediately regarded as the leader of the people who wanted revenge against the Federal Revenue Officer whom they felt had intentionally killed their friend and fellow still hand. No amount of asking from Ben, could persuade any one of them to change their minds.

"Ben if something's not done about Zeke's killing, we might as well, all of us, come out of the woods and you know it. You know what needs to be done and how to do it. Let us know how much money you need and we'll get it together."

Early on Saturday morning, two weeks after Zeke's funeral, Ben was washing up for breakfast on the back porch when Luke pulled his truck into the backyard and stepped out on the ground.

"Light and see where you're at Luke. I believe breakfast is about ready. You're welcome to it if you're willing to eat sawmill grub."

Luke grinned as he answered, "Miss Martha's sawmill grub is a whole lot better than breakfast at the Dixie Hunt Hotel."

Luke leaned in the kitchen door, "Morning Miss Martha. I did get here in time for breakfast didn't I?"

"Why good morning Luke. You did indeed get here in time for breakfast. Go get washed up, biscuits are in the oven."

Ten minutes later Martha brought a large pan of biscuits to the table covered with a towel to keep them warm.

Sitting in the middle of the table was a large bowl of milk gravy, made in the pan where she had just fried the sausage. While Luke was washing up on the back porch Martha had beaten one-fourth cup of milk into the eggs, and quickly scrambled them in a hot greased skillet, leaving them steaming hot yet moist and soft. Ben followed Martha into the dining room carrying the large platter containing the eggs and sausage.

Luke was sitting on the bench, located on the backside of the table, against the wall. Josh and Hannah were sitting one on either side of Luke. Ben and Martha sat at their usual place, one at either end of the table, Martha at the end nearest the kitchen.

Ben motioned to Luke as he said, "Now Luke, let's take out and eat while everything is good and hot. We'll talk some after we get done eating."

Martha saw to the needs of the table, and made light conversation, as she ate her own meal. She did so with a troubled mind. She did not have to be told that Luke had come to tell them that he was getting ready to go back in the woods to work at another still. Since his mother's death, Luke wanted Ben and Martha to know he was gone and approximately when he would return. Had Martha known the real reason for Luke's visit this morning, she would not only have been shocked, but also terrified.

Their breakfast meal completed they sat and talked at the table for a while before Ben and Luke expressed their appreciation for the meal and moved out of the house to sit under the huge old oaks in the backyard. The early morning breeze, moving through the branches of the trees, made the shade a comfortable place to sit and talk.

"So you're going back to work, is that right Luke?"

"That's right Ben."

"I thought you might stay out long enough to see how this thing works itself out. I hope it don't happen Luke, but I'm sure you've heard the talk just like I have."

"Well I've had this offer from some folks up in Lumpkin County, so I guess I'll take them up on it. That is except for one thing ..."

Ben looked at Luke with a puzzled expression on his face. "What's that Luke?"

"Ben, outside of my mama and daddy and you and Miss Martha, Zeke was the best friend I ever had. I know that a lot of folks think that I'm not very smart, but Zeke didn't. Zeke liked me Ben, I know he did, and I loved him like he was my brother.

"Ben, you're right, I know what they are saying. But if you'll help me find out where he's at, I'll do the same thing to him that he did to Zeke, and I'll do it by myself. Nobody else will know when or how, but I'll promise you that it will happen."

Ben did not answer for some time because he knew that Luke was dead serious. He soon realized that now he needed to encourage Luke to go back in the woods to work. He saw, that if he was going to dissuade Luke from avenging Zeke's death, he had to choose his words carefully.

"Luke, listen here. It won't do. My fear is that if somebody shoots him and they don't catch them at it, you and Doyle Edwards are going to be the first one's they come after. Listen Luke, Lee Hasty warned me about this and I think he's right. He said that if it happens and the FBI comes in, they won't leave until they get the ones that done it. In the meantime there will be all hell to pay. Nobody will be able to do anything. Now Luke, you go on to work and I'll keep you up to date on what happens, if anything."

The two men stood and, after a brief moment, Luke turned to Ben and gave a nod of his head.

"Ben let me go and say goodbye to Miss Martha and I'll have to go."

"All right Luke. I know how to get in touch with you, if need be."

Luke grinned as he said, "Well I figured you did."

CHAPTER 2

Ben now regretted the threat he had made to Lee Hasty that day outside of Rabb and Annie's house, when Lee asked him to warn the still owners and still hands against taking revenge against a Federal Revenue Officer.

Having warned Lee that Carl Potts would have to pay, but not with his life, had made Ben the man to see, for the people who wanted retaliation for Zeke's death. Likewise Ben was the contact for the Federal Revenue Officers who wanted Ben to warn everyone concerned of the consequences that would result if anyone retaliated against them. Ben had already acted on their promise not to prosecute those affected, and the well-received promise to stay out of the woods for thirty days.

As much as anyone, Ben was angry and frustrated with himself. He had unwittingly let others put him in a position that he had no intention of getting involved in. "I'll be damned if I can believe it," Ben accused himself, "I have stood here like a jackass in a hailstorm, and let it happen."

Ben had about decided to see if the demand for retaliation against Zeke's killers would just die out and fade away. He knew that Potts had been transferred. He had expected that, but his new location was proving to be harder than expected to find. Moreover and just as important Rabb and Annie had asked for an end to the bloodshed. Rabb had brought the message from Annie.

"Retaliation would just bring about more killing, and some boy would end up in the electric chair or spend the rest of his life in jail."

Rabb spent over two hours with Ben. They talked and laughed about the past and their experiences together. Mostly about the liquor business and how it had changed over the years. With the exception of Annie's message, they did not talk about Zeke.

He told Ben that Doyle Edwards would be running the sugar and barrel business and would completely take it over before long. As for himself, he was going to be working with Newt in his cattle business. They were going to sow more pastureland in Kentucky 31 fescue and orchard grass. Their intention was to double the size of their herd as soon as possible.

When Rabb started to leave, Ben noticed that he moved a little slower and the air of confidence was not there as it had been only a few weeks ago. But Ben was already aware that the wound had been near to mortal, and that his old friend would never completely recover.

Ben had no idea that Rabb was not speaking for all of his family about the tragedy that took his son's life. He was not surprised that Annie wanted no more bloodshed, nor was he much surprised when Rabb told him that he was not in favor of retaliating against the Revenue Officer responsible for Zeke's death. But he was both surprised and shocked by the harsh bitterness that he encountered from, Rabb and Annie's daughter, Clara Mae.

CHAPTER 3

It was about 10 days after Luke's breakfast visit that Ben came to the house for his noon meal after a morning of pasture fence repair. As he was washing up on the back porch, Martha brought a clean towel from the kitchen and spoke in a quiet voice. "Ben, will you come to the front room when you are finished? Clara Mae is here and she wants to talk to you. She is very upset Ben. I don't believe I have ever seen her like this before."

Ben knew, without asking, why she was here, but he wondered to himself if there was any connection between this visit and that of her father's visit just a few days ago. "All right Martha, but I would like for you to go back in there with me while we have our talk."

Martha sat beside Clara on the sofa while Ben sat in his ladder-back rocking chair beside the fireplace. Ben noticed that Clara's hair was not as carefully brushed and combed as she usually kept it, nor was she dressed as neatly and with as much care as was her usual custom when she was visiting or at church.

Ben inquired about Rabb and Annie even though he had seen Rabb at the hardware store last evening. Martha asked about Elizabeth and Clara answered that she had finished school and was helping at home for the summer.

Ben sat waiting for Clara's questions. He did not have long to wait.

"Ben has the Revenue Officer that shot Zeke been located yet?"

"Not that I know anything about Clara Mae. I talked with a man at the hardware store yesterday and he had not heard anything new."

"Ben do you know Ivan Grizzle?"

"Why yes, I know Ivan. I didn't know that you knew him though. You ought to be careful around him Clara Mae. He used to be a pretty tough customer."

"Oh, I don't know him like that Ben. Surely you know me better than that. Anyway, I overheard him tell Daddy and Doyle that Potts had been transferred out of the state. Do you think that could be true Ben?"

"Yeah, that could very well be true." Ben did not tell Clara, but he was also of the opinion that Carl Potts had been transferred to another state. The house where the family had lived in Gainesville was empty and so far his contacts had been unable to provide him with any further information.

Ben was sure that Clara knew how Rabb and Annie now felt about retaliating for Zeke's death. He felt that now was the time to find out how much, if any, her feelings had changed about her brother's death.

"Clara Mae, when we find Potts, and I still think we'll find him, what do you feel like we ought to do to him?"

Clara sat in deep thought for a long moment before she answered.

"Ben you said that he had no reason to kill Zeke. You said that the Revenue Officer that came to the house that morning admitted to you that it was a mistake and that it shouldn't have happened. I think they killed him because they thought that was the only way they could get him, or get rid of him. But that doesn't matter now, because they got him, and they killed him in cold blood, whatever that means.

"They killed one of the few people in this world that loved me and he knew that I loved him in return. He was my brother and I know that I shouldn't put him above the rest of my family, but God knows I did. I know that hate and murder are sins unto death, but if I could find him and if I had a gun, I would shoot him, even if I had to shoot him in the back."

CHAPTER 4

Since Josh now had his driver's license, he usually drove for Martha, especially when she made her shopping trips to Gainesville. Her trips normally included a visit to Mark and Laurel's house and on occasion Ben went along and stayed with Laurel and his two nephews, Jacob and Jordan.

Ben did not go with the rest of his family on this trip and Martha did not go by Mark and Laurel's house. It had been a busy trip and there had just not been enough time. As they sat, at a later than usual supper of warmed up leftovers, there was very little conversation around the table. The trip to Gainesville had been especially long and tiresome and they were all looking forward to an early bedtime.

"Josh did you tell your Daddy what Mr. Johnson said?" Martha asked her son.

"Oh yeah, I was about to forget. Daddy we saw Lamar Johnson in Gainesville today and he said to tell you to come and see him. He said to tell you that he knows where he's at."

Josh's news caught Ben unthinking and unawares.

"He knows where who is at?"

"Well I figure he was talking about Carl Potts."

"Well I'll be damned. Now how did he find out where Potts is at?"

"He didn't tell us that," was Martha's dry retort.

*   *   *

Lamar Johnson was born and raised in Dawson County near the crossroads farming community of Burtsboro. When the chicken business grew to be an industry of national importance, Lamar bought a three hundred acre farm in North Hall County, about five miles from the small town of Clermount. He borrowed every dollar that the Gainesville Bank would loan him, and built four chicken houses that would hold eighty thousand broiler size chickens. Lamar, his wife and three children all went to work. They were in the chicken business. They were doing well, and they were making money. That should have been good enough, but it wasn't. His farm was carrying a lot of debt and Lamar did not like to owe anyone, especially a bank.

Lamar selected the most isolated of his four chicken houses. Measured off fifty feet from the back end and built a false end in that house even down to two-eight foot doors that did not open. A month later and with the help of Rabb Turner and Ben McClure, Lamar had two still hands operating an upright boiler and eighteen boxes of still beer behind the false wall in his chicken house. They were producing about one hundred eighty gallons of liquor every day.

Lamar operated the still in his chicken house for nine months after which he took the still apart and stowed it in his barn. He took the false end out of his chicken house and let chickens back in the area where the still had been. Lamar paid off his loan and opened an account with the Gainesville Bank. As a result, the manager of the loan department at the bank considered Lamar to be a very successful poultry farmer and they gave him an excellent credit rating.

Lamar and his wife Helen were the parents of three children, a son and two daughters. After her graduation from high school, Katherine, the eldest of the daughters, applied for and was hired to work in the records department in the Federal courthouse in Gainesville. As the newest employee, Katy was assigned the responsibility of pulling and refiling the personal folders of the employees working in the Gainesville District for the United States Government.

When Lamar heard that Rabb's boy had been shot and killed by a Federal Revenue Officer, he felt sure that another still hand would soon retaliate for Zeke's death. He was disappointed when it did not happen until he realized that immediate retaliation would almost certainly have a serious repercussion in their lives.

Then word reached Lamar that Carl Potts and his family had moved and as yet their new location had not been found. There were some that felt he had been transferred out of the state. All of this information came to Lamar in piece meal form, yet he felt that it was reliable information. Lamar made no contact with anyone, because outside of Ben, he knew no one to contact, and as yet he had no reason to do so. He had no useful information to give as yet. But unlike the other searchers, Lamar felt that it was just a matter of time until he knew where Carl Potts had been moved.

Lamar was exactly right. The following Sunday afternoon Lamar found Katherine, sitting on the front porch, swinging and reading a book.

"Katy, I need to ask a favor."

"Why sure Daddy. What is it?"

"At work, have you come across the name Carl Potts?"

"Why yes, I have Daddy. Do you know him?"

"No Katy, I don't know him. He is a Federal Revenue Officer that has been transferred out of the Gainesville District. I need to know where he has been moved to?"

"Well Daddy, you know that we are not supposed to give out any information from a document that we have access to in the records room. Is it something that's important to you?"

"Yes it is Katy, if it wasn't I wouldn't ask."

"All right, I'll see what I can find out."

"Katy, just to be on the safe side, let's keep this between you and me, Okay?"

On Friday of the following week as Lamar was finishing up his barn chores he saw his daughter come into the hall of the barn. "Well hello Miss Katy. I suppose that Gainesville is just about empty when the courthouse crowd goes home ain't it?"

"Why no Daddy that's when the country crowd like you and Mama get to town and liven things up till closing time."

"Well then, I better go get your Mama and take off, shouldn't I?"

Lamar thought to himself how good it was to hear the sound of his daughter's laughter in his old barn.

"Daddy, you asked me to find out where Carl Potts was transferred to."

"Yes I did. Did you see something?"

"I had already looked for his folder and it was not there, but there was a check out card in its place. Well just before quitting time today the secretary from the ATF office brought some folders in to be refiled and his was one of them. So when I started to file it, I just accidentally let it fall open to the last page and there it was."

"There 'what was' Katy? What did it say?"

"Transferred to Huntington, West Virginia."

"Well I'll be damned. Just like some of us thought."

"Thought what Daddy?"

"They thought they would hide him, and when nobody could find him, we would forget about him and then after awhile even the people that were going to do something about Zeke's killing would just let it go.

"Your talking about the man that was killed at that liquor still in Dawson County aren't you? Did you know him Daddy?"

"Well I know his folks Katy. They helped me out one time so I felt like I ought to return the favor if I can. I am not going to get directly involved so don't start worrying about that. Now Katy, I want you to promise me that you'll put this whole thing out of your mind, okay?"

"All right, Daddy. But I would hate to hear, that what I have found out for you has caused more trouble for anyone, especially for Zeke's Mother and Daddy.

"Don't stay in the barn too much longer Daddy. Mama will have supper on the table before long. I am going on to the house to help her."

Lamar was not thinking about his daughter as he watched her hurrying up the barn path toward the house. He thought to himself. "Well, they may have been trying to out smart us by sending him out of the state, but they may have outsmarted themselves this time. If I'm not mistaken Helen's Uncle Walt Howell lives in a little place, not far from Huntington, called Dickerson."

CHAPTER 5

With Wesley driving and Ben giving directions, on the way to go, they drove north out of Gainesville on US 129 Highway. The gently rolling countryside that they were driving through lay just South and East of the Blue Ridge Mountain chain. The farmland was planted in fields of dark green corn or lush pastures sown in Kentucky 31 Fescue and a mixture of Ladino clover and orchard grass.

The war years of World War Two did much to bring life to the economy of a country trying to pull itself out of the depression era of the 1930's. Almost as important, in raising the standard of living for the still struggling Southern farm family, was the advent of the chicken industry-beginning in the early 1940's and continuing on into the 21st century. After the original cost for the construction of a chicken house and the equipment needed to operate it, plus the two to three months required to raise the First House of chickens to maturity, there is an immediate infusion of cash money into the family finances. Finances which, until the birth of the chicken industry in the South, consisted of barely enough money to feed and clothe the family.

Besides the cash money received for growing the chickens until they are ready to market, there is a by product from the chicken's that has a long term benefit to the farm and the farm family. When the chicken manure is removed from the chicken house and spread on the farmland, it will, in almost every instance, double the growth and yield of whatever crop it is applied to.

*   *   *

"Now turn here to the right on 52 Highway Wes. He told Josh it was about five miles out this road. The house is on the left-hand side of the road. Their name is on the mailbox." Wesley turned up the driveway that led to the white frame house located about two hundred yards from the road. He parked in the shade of some black walnut trees in the back yard. They saw Lamar coming up the footpath from the barn.

"Get out and see if you can tell where you're at."

"Well Lamar we have followed the directions you gave to Josh and we have wound up here in your back yard. I think that's pretty good for Wes and me."

The three men shook hands as Ben and Wesley were turning and looking at the house and outbuildings, especially the four chicken houses.

"I was sort of expecting you two boys this morning. I went ahead and asked my woman to fix a little extra for dinner today, but of course it you hadn't come it would have been just as good for supper."

Wesley grinned as he answered," We don't want to put anybody to any trouble, but I'm not going to fuss with you about it."

"Why no, we are glad to have you. Have you fellers ever had any hot house fried chicken to eat?"

"Well, I don't know if I have or not Lamar," Ben answered, "but if Miss Helen is doing the fixing, it wouldn't make any difference where it comes from, it would be as good as it gets."

"Anyway it'll be a little while before dinner is ready. Let's sit here on the back porch and I'll tell you what I have found out." Lamar took out his tobacco pouch and the folder of paper leaves that he used to roll a hand made cigarette, while Wesley lit a cigarette from his package of Camels. Ben had not used tobacco since Martha objected to the smell of chewing tobacco on his breath. At the time Ben had mused to himself, "There are a few things that are more important than a plug of tobacco to chew on."

For the next half-hour Lamar told how his daughter Katherine had discovered where Carl Potts had been relocated. They were as surprised as he had been when he told them where he was now located. When he told them, about Helen having an Uncle living nearby, Lamar could tell that both men started thinking about what their next move should be.

"Now then, if you want to pursue this thing, I have a plan in mind that I'll tell you about. But if you don't, right now is the time to drop it. There is no need to go any further, if you are not going to follow through with it."

Both men sat staring at Lamar for several seconds. After several weeks, of talking and thinking in terms of "if" and "when," Lamar had just challenged them with the reality of now. They knew he was right. If, when and what they were going to do, now was the time to make the decision.

"Well Ben, what do you think" Wesley asked?

It was then that Ben realized why those in the business had wanted him to be the front man to gather the information and make the decision on how and when to avenge Zeke's death.

Now faced with the necessity of making that decision, Ben did not hesitate. "Lamar, the morning that I talked with Lee Hasty standing in front of Rabb Turner's house, I told him they had needlessly killed a man for no other reason than he had tried to get away from a still. He admitted that they had made a mistake and we made a deal about dropping charges which Wes and Rabb know about. I agreed with him that it would be a bad move, on our part, for a Federal Revenue Officer to get killed, but I told him that while we would try to see that Carl Potts didn't get killed, he would have to pay. So if you have a plan in mind that will help us get that done, we would like to hear it."

"All right Ben. The first thing we have to do, of course, is go to Huntington and locate him. Then we need to know if he is still working as a Federal Revenue Officer and if so how many others there are working with him. We also need to know where he lives. Now Helen and I have never visited her Uncle Walt, so I think a visit may be in order. If we are going to get Walt to help us find Potts, there's no way we can keep what we're doing from him. I'll feel him out real good before I tell him anything else though. Now Ben I'll call you when we get back. If everything up there looks like it will work, we'll get together and make the rest of our plan."

"Lamar, dinner's ready," Helen called as she handed clean hand towels out the kitchen door to her husband.

"All right boys, that's what we've been waiting to hear. Let's wash up."

Lamar poured water into two wash pans and laid half a bar of Octagon soap by each pan. They washed and rinsed their hands and faces and dried on the towels.

"Now boys, I've got a fruit jar in there. If you want to wet your whistle I'll be glad to go and get it."

Wesley shook his head no and then Ben said, "We're much obliged Lamar, but I guess we better pass. With Wes driving and me giving directions, we might take a wrong road and end up in Strugglesville, Georgia, and it coming dark."

They sat down to a long platter of golden brown fried chicken, two bowls of gravy made in the iron skillet where the chicken was fried and a cloth covered pan of large biscuits made with buttermilk.

"Now let's take out and eat while everything is good and hot. We're glad to have you come up and see us. We ain't had a whole lot of visitors from Dawson County yet," Lamar said as he began passing the food around.

"I heard Lamar asking if y'all had eaten any hot-house fried chicken," Helen said as she refilled their iced tea glasses. "Some like it better than yard chicken and some don't. This woman from the church told me that if I wanted to make good fried chicken, I should kill my chickens the day before, cut them up and soak them in cold sweet milk-overnite in the refrigerator before frying them the next day."

"Well, Miss Helen, if that's the way this chicken was fixed, I'm going to tell Nellie as soon as we get home," Wesley said as he selected his second piece. "If I have ever had any fried chicken that was better than this I cain't recall it."

*   *   *

Two hours later as they turned onto 53 Highway out of Gainesville, Wesley turned to Ben and asked, "Did you know Lamar's wife before they got married?"

"Well I knew her folks Wes, she was a Grizzle. There were two or three girls and two or three boys. They mostly raised cotton. Hugh, that was their Daddy's name, drove a team for the folks that ran the store there at Burtsboro. The one I know the best is one of the boys. His name is Ivan. Ivan Grizzle. Him and Lamar made a good bit of liquor together. I know that's the way Lamar got up enough money to buy that farm over there in Hall County, and I guess that's the way that him and Helen got together."

CHAPTER 6

Almost two weeks later a post card came to Ben and Martha's house. Printed in uneven letters it read. "We will be over to see you and Martha on Sunday the 12th. Would like to see Wesley too. Lamar Johnson."

"Well Miss Martha, I guess you better get out your iron skillet and get it greased up. Looks like you are going to get a chance to show off your chicken frying abilities on Sunday."

"Oh no I won't Mr. McClure … I think we will have something besides fried chicken. I'll decide what the menu will be. You go and see if Nellie and Wesley can come for dinner on Sunday. I'll have it figured out by the time you get back."

Sunday morning of the 12th dawned with a gold sky in the east and summer blue overhead. Mid-day heat was a certainty. Wesley and Nellie arrived early. Nellie did not know what Martha was preparing for their meal, but it did not matter. She only knew that she would be needed and that she was happy to help. She came into the kitchen tying on her apron.

"All right honey, what are we having and what do you want me to do?"

"We are having chicken pie, green beans, fried corn, fried okra and deep dish sweet potato pie.*

*See end of chapter six for recipes.

"Oh Lord, help us, if I was going to make a list of the hardest things to fix, those would all be on it."

"Quit complaining and make the biscuits. I'm making a large pie, so it will take a whole pan of your dainty little biscuits.

Lamar and his wife arrived shortly after ten. They turned up the driveway and stopped beside Wesley's pickup truck.

"Park it right over there in the shade and let it cool off for a while. Y'all get out. We have been expecting you so come on in here. Miss Helen come on in here and let me introduce you to my wife and to Wesley's wife. You'll have to be careful through or they'll put you to work."

Ten minutes later Ben was back to find that Lamar and Wesley were already seated in the chairs under the oak trees out back. For several minutes they talked about the trip and how long it had taken to drive both ways, but soon the talk changed to what Lamar had learned about Carl Potts on the trip.

"Well he's there all right," Lamar told the two men. "Helen's uncle has seen him and heard a couple of things about him.

"Potts and his family moved to Huntington about two months ago, which would make the timing about right. Walt says that he's assigned to the District Attorney's office in the Federal Courthouse, but he works with Officers from the State Revenue Office.

"The reason that Walt knows these things is because Walt was in the liquor business during the war and he's on pretty good terms with one of the State Revenue Officers. The State Revenue Officers didn't know what a Federal Revenue Officer was doing working with them until Walt told them. They didn't like it one damn bit but their boss told them to keep their mouths shut and forget about it. Walt said he didn't know about keeping their mouths shut but he could guarantee they hadn't forgotten about it.

"Now, Ben and Wes, Walt is willing to help us, but he cain't afford to get too much involved. Whatever happens he will still be there when it's over. He said for us to finish our plan and then let him know who is coming and when. He recommends late September or October. He is going to find out what area Potts works the most, and then he is going to work on a decoy to help us. One other thing, he said to be sure that whoever we send knows Potts when he sees him."

"Well I'll be damned. I hadn't even thought about that." Wesley said.

"I have thought about it, but I still haven't decided who the best two men for that job would be," Ben said.

"Why do we need two men?" Wesley asked. "Looks to me like one would be enough."

"I think Ben's right Wes," Lamar said, "I think we will want to go after him in the woods. If so, we'll want to put a man on both sides of him."

After a moment Lamar continued, "Getting back to finding two men to do the job. I know one who wants to do it and he knows Potts when he sees him."

"Is he somebody we know?" Ben asked.

"He sure is Ben, you know him very well. He's Ivan Grizzle. Him and a guy named Hunt Willams worked for me for about three months a few years ago. I would recommend them both."

"Ivan sounds good, but I don't believe I know Williams," Ben answered.

"I'm surprised that you don't know him Ben. He knows who you and Wes are." Lamar said as he looked at Wesley.

"I don't think I know him either Lamar," Wesley answered.

"Well I may know him and just don't recall it. I'll look into it though," Ben replied.

"Ben --- Ben, dinner's ready. Y'all get washed up," Martha called from the kitchen door.

"All right boys, let's get to it. When that woman calls, it's ready to go on the table," Ben said as the three men stood.

"One other thing," Lamar said as they started toward the back porch. "If this thing happens like we want it to, I'm going to take Ivan and Hunt out of circulation for awhile, just as soon as they get back."

No explanation to Lamar's statement was needed, both men knew what he was referring to.

*   *   *

There were eight at the table for Martha's dinner. Martha's meal was complete and waiting to be placed on the table, but she had waited until she saw Josh's car turn up the driveway. In the car, besides Josh, was her daughter Hannah, and Wesley and Nellie's two children, Elizabeth and Joe Thomas. They had been to Sunday school at Shoal Creek Baptist Church.

Needless to say Martha's chicken pie was a culinary delight. Beginning with Joe Thomas who said, "Mom this is great stuff. Do you know how to make it?" Everyone complimented Martha on her meal except her husband. Later while he was eating a dish of sweet potato pie, he caught Martha's eye, grinned and gave her a quick nod of his head. Only Ben saw the faint blush that colored her face.

"I had an Uncle," Lamar said as he finished his dish of pie, "who always poured sweet milk over his pie. When he finished his pie he would pat his belly and say, "when I die, I hope I die, with a belly full of sweet potato pie."

After their meal was finished they made their way into the living room. After much encouragement and finally after a mild threat from Nellie, Elizabeth and Hannah went to the piano. With Elizabeth playing and both girls singing, they sang. '*I Saw The Light*,' '*I'll Meet You In The Morning*,' and for their last they sang, '*Corinna, Corinna*,' as everybody joined in.

At 3 o'clock Lamar and Helen made ready to leave for their trip home. As the ladies said their good-byes, the men had an opportunity to talk for a few final minutes.

"Lamar if Ben cain't make it, I'll be over in about a week to find out if everything is set with Ivan and Hunt," Wesley said.

"All right then, and I'm going to go ahead and get the car and get it ready," Ben said.

As soon as Lamar and Helen were gone Ben and Wesley returned to their seats under the oak trees. "Wes, I'm going to go and see Rabb and Annie after while. I think they ought to know that we have found Potts and let them know what the plan is."

"Well Ben, tell me, what is the plan? Are we going to send those two men up there to kill Carl Potts?"

"No Wes, we're not! Rabb and Annie don't want any more killing over Zeke, and I don't either. Are you all right with that Wes?"

"I am Ben. I'll always have to live with the knowledge that Zeke was working for me when—when we lost him. That's bad enough Ben let alone having somebody else get killed over it. I won't ever get over it."

"Don't fault yourself alone Wes. You know that if it had not been you, then it would have been somebody else. It was a good location and a good plan. I expect that somebody just happened up on it and reported it for what they could get out of it. They are the ones with bloody hands and bloody money in their pockets."

Ben sat for a long moment looking out across his pasture toward the tree line that concealed the Amicalola River. Placid and quiet in the late summer afternoon sun. "But that doesn't change what I told Lee Hasty the day that Zeke was killed. We were standing there in front of Rabb and Annie's house and he warned me not to retaliate against Carl Potts for killing Zeke. In return he made some promises, that I thought were worthwhile, and I agreed with them. The deal was that we wouldn't kill him, but Potts would still have to pay. That's why we are sending two men up there Wes. It's time for Carl Potts to pay for killing Zeke Turner."

"Well, that I agree with. What are you going to do to him?"

"I'm going to have him put out of commission, Permanently!"

Marie's Biscuit Topped Chicken Pot Pie*
Enough home made biscuits to cover top
1 whole chicken, cooked, skinned-deboned
4 Tablespoons butter
4 Tablespoons flour
2 cups chicken broth
½ teaspoon Worcestershire sauce (more if desired)

273

½ teaspoon salt or to taste
½ c evaporated milk
1 cup grated cheddar cheese
2 Tablespoons chopped onion
4 teaspoons hot dog mustard
1 can veg-all mixed vegetables or 1 pkg frozen, cooked
1 - 1 ½ cups, cubed cooked potatoes

Place deboned chicken and cooked vegetables in baking dish. Melt butter in saucepan. Add flour and mix. Add milk, broth and seasonings to make sauce. Let thicken, then add cheese. Pour sauce over chicken-vegetable mixture in deep 3-4 quart baking dish. Top with biscuits and bake at 425 degrees until biscuits are brown and done in center.

TIP: I like to pre-bake my biscuits (*maybe the day before and just until they are cooked through but not browned.*) then cool and refrigerate. (*can also be partially baked the same day and allowed to cool.*) Next get chicken-vegetable mixture hot and put biscuits on top and continue to cook until the biscuits are brown. (Serves at least 8 hungry people)

Marie's Sweet Potato Cobbler*
4 large sweet potatoes, peeled and sliced
2 cups sugar
2-3 Tablespoons plain flour, mix this with 1 cup sugar
1 ¼ sticks butter or margarine (salted)
1 teaspoon vanilla flavoring
½ teaspoon nutmeg
Pie crust for top and bottom (recipe of your choosing)

Peel potatoes and slice 1 inch thick. Place in pot and cover with water and ½ cup sugar. Cook until tender. Roll out a crust and place in deep baking dish. Place cooked potatoes over crust in pan. Then add all liquids from potatoes to the pan. Sprinkle with 1 cup sugar with flour mixture, ½ of butter (sliced), ½ teaspoon of vanilla and ½ teaspoon of nutmeg and stir lightly. Add remaining sugar, vanilla, and remaining butter on top. Place the top crust over potatoes. Bake at 400 degrees until crust is brown. (Makes about 8 to 10 servings.) Yummy!!!!

CHAPTER 7

Ben turned left off the Dahlonega Highway into Rabb and Annie Turner's driveway. The house sat back from the road about three hundred yards, almost completely hidden in a grove of oak trees, the barn and outbuildings behind the house were invisible from the road.

For years Rabb had conducted a profitable sugar and container (both one gallon tin cans, and one-half gallon glass jars) business out of these buildings. The barn was now used in Newt's growing cattle business. The outbuildings now stood empty and unused.

Ben pulled his truck into the side yard and stopped it beside a solid black 4 door Pontiac Chief with, full tire with white wall tires on it. The gleaming black of the car's body and the glowing white of the tires created a stark contrast sitting in the light of the late afternoon sun.

Rabb and Annie were sitting on the back porch waiting for the house to cool before going inside to prepare their evening meal. "Get out Ben and come in," Rabb called from the porch, "we're just sitting here resting. I'm worn out from doing nothing all day."

"Rabb have you been trading cars? That's a mightily fine looking machine sitting out there."

"Naw, it's not mine. I wouldn't have the slightest idea how to crank it, let alone how to drive it. He said it had an automatic transmission in it. Far as I know that's the first car I have ever seen with an automatic transmission in it."

"Well, I guess it is for me too, Rabb. Whose is it?"

"It belongs to Rob Kirby."

"Well I'll be danged. I didn't know that Rob was up this way. I haven't seen him in over a month. I'd like to see him. Is he here?"

Annie had said little since Ben's arrival, preferring to sit and listen to Ben and her husband talk. Now she thought to herself, "Poor Ben, he hasn't figured it out yet, but it won't be long now. I think I hear them coming back from the creek now."

Clara and Rob came around the corner of the barn, Rob sliding the bars to the barn lot open and then closing them as they passed through. Rob had wanted to see the old millpond in the creek that flowed across the backside of the Turner farm. Coming back they cut across the pasture and as usual several of Newt's Hereford calves frolicked and raced around them and then stood looking through the barn lot rails as Rob and Clara passed through on their way to the house.

However much Ben was surprised at learning of, Rob and Clara's newfound courtship, Annie could not tell. When she looked at Ben's face it was wreathed in a wide smile that told her how happy he was to see these two people together. Annie said quietly to Ben, as Rob and Clara came across the yard laughing and holding hands, "Ben I have never seen her so happy. I just hope and pray that nothing happens to hurt her."

They came up on the porch, Clara blushing as she hugged Ben's neck and kissed his cheek, Rob smiling and embarrassed as he shook Ben's hand.

"Ben I'm glad to see you. I asked Daddy the other day if he had seen you lately, but he said he had not been up this way in over a month."

"Well Robert, I'm glad to see you too. I'm also happy to see that, even though you have moved off to Atlanta, you know where to come back to, to find the best women in the state of Georgia. The best looking ones too."

"Well Ben, I know that too," and then to everyone's surprise Rob blushed.

Ben smiled knowingly and said to himself, "She's got you boy, and I know how crazy it makes you feel."

"Ben we went to see Elizabeth but there wasn't anyone at home."

"They were all at the house for Sunday dinner Clara. Did you not get to see her?"

"Oh yes we did. We met them in the road almost at the Amicalola River Bridge. Rob recognized Wesley's car so we all stopped on the bridge. Nellie let Elizabeth get in the car with us, so we turned around and followed them home."

"Well was Elizabeth surprised to see you and Rob together?"

"Yes I think so, at least to start with. Then she asked Rob if he was going to move back to Dawson County. When Rob said no she asked him why he was coming all the way to Dawson County to find a girl to go out with. You would know that my best friend would find some way to embarrass me."

That brought a laugh and a smile to everyone on the porch, even Annie.

As he was looking at Clara and listening to her talk, Ben suddenly realized something he had not noticed before; Clara was no longer just another pretty girl. In what was now just a matter of months Clara had matured into a stunningly attractive, desirable woman.

It was not that Ben forgot to tell Rabb and Annie that Carl Potts had been found and what their plan was for him. But as they sat there together on the back porch of their home, Ben decided that he had no desire to reopen their still raw wounds of grief. Rabb and Annie were obviously pleased to see that their daughter was happy with the newfound joy of first love. Clara was radiant with the joy that love brings into the life of the young, and Rob was overjoyed that a woman with Clara's beauty and maturity was attracted to him.

It was, all in all, a very pleasant day, and Ben was thankful that he was here to be part of it.

CHAPTER 8

Ben slowed his 1947 Ford pickup truck and turned off the road to his right. He followed an old field road out along the edge of the cornfield until he saw what he was looking for. The rays of the early morning sun sifted through the treetops leaving patterns of sparkling light on the wet grass. Ben had already noticed the fresh tire tracks on the ground, so he was not surprised to find that Ivan Grizzle and Hunt Williams were there before him. He found them; the car backed up under the trees, so they would be completely out of sight from the road. Both doors of the car were open. Both men slumped almost out of sight, both smoking one cigarette after the other. Ben pulled his truck in on the driver's side of the car and got out.

"Morning boys! Looks like you got up kind of early."

"Well Ben, if we would have been planning on an early start, we would already be in a hell of a mess. We have been here since daybreak, and the sun is now an hour high."

Ben walked around the 1939 Ford two-door Deluxe giving it a careful inspection, especially the tires. "Well, I didn't mean to hold you boys up, but I had a few arrangements to make myself and that took longer that I had figured on. Is the car all right?"

Ivan got out of the car and followed Ben around. "Seems like it's all right Ben. I got an extra tire and an extra fuel pump to take along. It would be mighty unhandy for this thing to quit running or to have a flat on us -- especially if it was in the middle of the night."

Ben nodded his head in agreement as he leaned back against the side of the car. "Now let's see, you boys are due in the woods in about two weeks, is that right?"

Both heads nodded but Hunt answered for both men.

"That's right Ben. It doesn't have to be exactly two weeks, but we do need to be there pretty close to it."

Ben looked carefully at both men. "Now Josh has been over this job with both of you enough times that you know what to do, is that right?"

"That's right Ben!"

"You know how to get there, you know who to see when you get there, you know what to do when you get there, and you know how you're going to get home when you're finished, is that right?"

"That's right Ben!" Ivan answered. "Josh has gone over every bit of it with us a half a dozen times, and we've been over it with each other three or four times. We know what we have got to do."

Ben took his hat off and scratched the back of his head and neck. He put his hands in his front pockets, leaned forward and spit on the ground. As he straightened up he leveled a hard stare at both men. "Now you hear me, and you hear me right. There'll be no killing. Do you understand me Ivan?" Ivan nodded his head in agreement.

"Do you understand me Hunt?" Hunt also nodded his head in agreement.

"They don't have any idea that we know where Potts is, and they have no idea that we are fixing to come after him. So when we go all the way up there and blow his legs out from under him, it will prove to them that we are not going to stand any more killing. They will know, if there's another shooting, there will be a war in the woods and some of them will have to be dragged out this time. Nobody, in their right mind, wants something like that to happen, especially after what has already happened.

"If we cut his legs out from under him, they will know what it's for and purty soon they will let the stink die down. But, if you go up there and kill him, they will stay after you till they get you, and then, one way or the other, they will get it out of you. I will promise you this though. If you were to get caught, we have a lawyer in Gainesville, and we'll fight them just as long and as far as it takes."

Ben reached in his pocket and pulled out two rolls of small denomination bills. "Here is a hundred dollars apiece for expense money. When you come out of the woods and settle up, you'll be paid the rest of what we owe you."

Ben shook hands with both men. "Whatever happens don't worry about getting word to me, I'll know about it soon enough. Just come on back and go to work. Both of you need to stay gone for at least three months, and then you don't need to be seen together for awhile."

"Well, I don't know when we'll be seeing each other again, so I hope you both have good luck all the way around."

Ivan got behind the wheel and pulled the door closed. "We'll get the job done Ben, and we'll see that it's done right."

Hunt crawled in on the passenger side, pulled the door closed and looked across the seat to where Ben was standing outside the car.

"We'll do'er Ben, and I hope we can stay gone longer than three months. The old lady is wanting a new settee and I'm wanting a new car."

Ivan started the engine and looked out the window at Ben. "I sure do like the starter button on the dash." He pulled the shifter into low gear, moved slowly along the field road, turned onto the main road, picked up speed and was soon gone out of hearing.

Ben opened the door to his truck but stood for several minutes watching four crows and a red tailed hawk, high above the cornfield, diving and turning in an aerial fight between winged warriors.

CHAPTER 9

"That's it Hunt," Ivan said as he pointed to the mailbox on the right hand side of the road. "That's Walt Howell's place, and it's just like Josh told us it would be."

Ivan turned and looked back through the rear window. "Nothing coming from behind us Hunt." Hunt slowed the car, turned right onto the dusty driveway and did not stop until the car was behind the house, out of sight from the road.

The back porch on Walter and Mildred Howell's house was built exactly like the front porch. However, unless you were paying close attention to detail, the sameness would go unnoticed. The porch front was five steps above ground level with a swing at either end. Two high backed rocking chairs sat about equal distance between the two swings. Hanging between the posts on either side of the steps were two large containers of petunias, their blooms a rainbow of colors and their growth hanging down halfway to the porch floor.

The back porch looked much different from the front porch. That was because of what was on it, and how it was used. The back porch was one step above ground level with a wisteria vine growing out of the ground and climbing lattices all the way to the porch roof. Clusters of purple blooms hung in abundance from the climbing vines and they tainted the still August air with their sweet perfumed fragrance. A door from the kitchen opened out onto the porch on the east side and here is where Mildred did her washing and ironing except during the coldest months of the year. A door from the hallway opened out on the porch in the center of the house and the other side of the porch was taken up with Walt's sitting, reading and oft times during the hottest nights of summer, his sleeping place. It was here that Walt was part sitting and part lying on an old sofa.

The 1939 Ford came quietly by the side of the house into the backyard and parked on the far side of Walt's 1940 Dodge pickup truck. The doors opened and the two men inside got out and stood by the car, stretching and looking toward the house.

Walt Howell picked his hat up from the porch floor and slowly settled it on his head. Concealed behind the dense wisteria vine, he stood quietly watching for several seconds before he pushed the screen door open and walked across the backyard toward the two men. "Well, have you boys come all the way from Georgia to pay us a visit?"

"Yessir we have," Ivan answered, "and this is the farthest I have ever come to visit anybody."

"Well then, let's hope you are going to enjoy the visit. Are you Ivan?"

"Yessir I am, and this is Hunt Williams."

"We'll I'm glad to meet both of you, I'm Walt Howell." Walt shook hands with his two visitors.

"Ivan, you and I are a right smart kin you know."

"Yes sir, I know it. I have heard stories about my Uncle Walt from Mama and Helen for as long as I can remember, so I'm glad to get to know you too. I've got some pictures out there in the car for you. Mostly pictures of everybody's kids but there are a few of Mama and Daddy, Helen and Lamar."

Walt's face softened into a pensive look as he asked, "How are Myrtie and Hugh?"

"They're doing okay. Helen bought Mama a clothes dryer for Christmas and Daddy said that was the damndest waste of electricity that he had ever heard tell of. I help Daddy with his crop when I'm there. Helen and Lamar bought a farm over in Hall County and they have gone into the chicken and cattle business. They are doing real good at it."

Hunt who had said little since their arrival added, "Not just good, but damn good. That's where we are going when we get back."

With that after remark, Walt immediately knew the rest of the plan.

*   *   *

"Mildred, this is Ivan Grizzle. He's Hugh and Myrtie's boy, and that's Hunt Williams. This is my wife Mildred and that's Hugh Junior over there. He's the youngest of our children. All the rest have already married and moved out. We named him after your Daddy Ivan, but we have always called him HJ."

Mildred smiled and gave the two men a friendly nod of her head from where she was busily carrying covered dishes of food from the stove to the table. The table was already set with tall ice filled glasses of sweet tea beside each plate.

"We were expecting y'all at almost any time so I just kept our dinner warm. Wash up out there on the porch and I'll have it ready by the time you are."

"Now boys, I don't want you to be seen by nobody other than the three of us, that you have just met here today, while you are here," Walt said to Ivan and Hunt, as they took turns washing their hands and faces in a small wash pan on the back porch. "After you have eaten, HJ will show you to your room. Get some sleep and I'll wake you up later on this evening. We'll talk some and then HJ and I are going to take you on a little trip."

CHAPTER 10

"All right boys, shake the cob webs out with a cup of coffee there on the stove and then sit down here at the table with HJ and me."

"I slept so hard that I'm still tired," Hunt said as he brought his coffee to the table and lit a cigarette.

"I believe it would help if I could get another eight or ten hours of sleep like that," Ivan said as he stirred sugar into his coffee and took a small sip to test the temperature.

"Well I think you'll get caught up tonight and tomorrow. Nothing's going to happen on Sunday, but we've got a pretty good idea that you'll get your chance early on Monday morning." Walt paused for almost a minute before he continued.

"Now Ivan you and Hunt listen to me. Along with what we already knew, and with what we have been able to find out, we are satisfied that we know where Carl Potts is going to be Monday morning between eight and nine o'clock. Before it gets too late this evening we are going to drive by there and HJ is going to show you the old field road where we think Royston Hill and Carl Potts will come walking along early Monday morning.

"Now the reason we think that Royston and Potts will come along that old field road Monday morning is because we have set up a sucker trap for them. Royston is a State Revenue Officer who has been stationed here for a long time. There is no Federal ATF Office in Huntington. They just loaned Potts to this state office in order to hide him out. That old field road used to be a public road until Beech Fork Lake covered part of it up. Now it's a walking trail into some property whose owners are known bootleggers. One reason that makes them so hard to catch is that they make their own liquor. HJ has hired a couple of the young boys to patch up one of their old hog stills,* fill it with water, and start making smoke as if they are making liquor every Monday. To sweeten the pot, so to speak, we have reported our own still to Royston. So early Monday morning they are going to build a fire under that big old vat full of water and then go home. Another reason why we think it will work is because it has already worked one time before."

*see glossary

"All right then, that's it, but before we go, HJ, you want to show them the shooters?"

HJ got up from the table and walked into what Ivan felt sure was his bedroom. When he returned he was carrying an old hammer type single shot 12 gauge shot gun in each hand. He handed a gun and a box of shells to each man.

Both Ivan and Hunt hefted their shotgun, sighted along the barrel at the small bead on the end of the barrel, then broke the gun down and looked through the barrel. Hunt picked up the box of shells and looked at the printed information on the side of the box.

"What the hell Walt, this is bird shot?"

Hunt was looking toward Walt, but it was HJ that answered.

"I didn't think that you wanted to kill him."

"We don't, but we want to do more that give him a limp. Ben said that he wanted us to put him out of action permanently," Hunt answered with an angry voice.

"Hunt, we know what Ben said, and we know what Lamar told you and Ivan," Walt said without any shortness in his voice.

HJ continued, with no anger in his voice, but it did hold a light note of impatience. "Well I don't guess you noticed it Hunt, but the barrels of these two old shotguns are full-choked. When and if the time comes on Monday morning, if you are standing where I am going to show you to stand, and if you shoot him where I tell you to shoot him, the only way he is going to walk for the rest of his life is with a pair of walking sticks."

Ivan interceded in the discussion here because he did not want their exchanges to become any more intense. "Hunt, it seems to me like HJ has this job planned out down to the last detail, and it sounds good to me."

Hunt realized that he had no reason to be questioning the plan that must have been approved by Ben and Lamar. "Sounds good to me too HJ, I didn't understand about the shot guns, so I shouldn't have been questioning you about them."

HJ nodded his head in acceptance of Hunt's apology. But it was Walt who reminded his son who had done most of the planning, and Ivan and Hunt who were here to carry out the plan, of the reality of what they were about to do.

"Why no Hunt, no offense taken at all. All of us want to get this thing done, and we want to get it done right. Right now our job is to remind this officer of the law that he is also supposed to obey the law. I know that what we are about to do is not exactly straight, but it's what we have agreed to do, and I hope it will put a stop to the killing that they started.

"The mortal fear of every man or woman is that they might have to bury a child. Rabb and Annie Turner have had to do that and they will suffer from it until the day they die. What we are about to do won't help them. Not one sleepless night will it help either one of them. But maybe it will remind some 'trigger happy son-of-a-bitch' that when you start messing with somebody else's life, sooner or later, one way or another, you are going to pay.

"Well, let's go, its beginning to get late. HJ will need a little time to show you where you need to be on Monday morning and then where he will meet you after the job is done."

CHAPTER 11

Ivan was dreaming that he and Hunt were sailing down a river on a dark and blustery day. It seemed strange to Ivan, that instead of the river growing wider as the wind blew them ever faster along on the choppy surface, the high riverbanks were rapidly closing in on both sides of the boat. Then just as the boat was about to crash into the narrow banks of the river, a door opened and Walt Howell said, "Ivan --- Hunt, its 4 o'clock. I'm making a pot of coffee. It's about time to get started."

HJ had told them last evening that they should be clean shaved and wearing clean work clothes. "The last thing you want to do is attract attention when you get on that bus. If somebody asks, tell them that you work in the shipyards at Newport News and both of you are going home for a few days."

Fifteen minutes later they came into the kitchen clean-shaven and dressed in khaki work clothes. HJ motioned them to the table as he poured steaming coffee into the cups. "Well boys, are you ready to go home today," Walt asked, already sitting at the table drinking coffee.

"I sure am ready to start in that direction," Hunt answered, stirring sugar and cream into his coffee cup.

HJ sat his cup on the table but he did not sit down. He took four shotgun shells from the box and handed two shells each to Ivan and Hunt.

"Put one shell into each of your front pockets. I don't think you will have time for a second shot, but you will have them just in case. When you get your shot off and he goes down, get the hell out of there. Don't stand there trying to see where or how much you got him, just go."

Fifteen minutes later they walked out the back door into the damp morning air and stood waiting for HJ to bring the car around. "Ivan you tell Ben and Lamar that I'm going to give the car to HJ. He has done everything just the way they wanted it done."

Ivan grinned as he looked fondly at Walt, "They put your name on the papers that are in that box with the pictures."

"I'll have that changed. He has already changed the tag on it, so don't worry about that." As the car came slowly and quietly toward them, Walt shook hands first with Hunt and then with Ivan.

"Hunt I'm glad I got acquainted with you and I hope we'll meet again. Ivan tell everybody I said hello. If we get along all right, Mildred and I are going to try our dead level best to get down that way, maybe in the spring."

Hunt opened the passenger side door but the interior lights did not come on. HJ had taped over the switches in the door jam.

"Put the guns on the floorboard behind the seat. Let's go – we cain't be late."

Walt watched as the car stopped at the end of the driveway and they looked both ways for oncoming cars. Seeing none HJ switched on the headlights, turned onto the highway, picked up speed and soon disappeared from sight and sound.

Walt stood quietly for several minutes before he walked to his big chair on the back porch and sat down.

Presently Mildred came out of the house and sat down in an old, mule eared, hand bottomed, chair. "I heard them leave," she said, as much to herself as to Walt.

"The Lord help us Mildred. Who in the world would have ever thought that something like this could have happened after we tried so hard to get completely away from it?"

The Seth Thomas wall clock in the hallway struck six times.

*   *   *

"All right guys, let's go over it one more time," HJ said, keeping close watch on the road behind. "If there is something still not clear, speak up. When I let you out, go to the place where I showed you to stand, one of you on either side of the road. They will drive out the old road until their car cannot be seen from the highway. They will have to stop about five hundred yards from where you are. No smoking at all, cigarette smoke can be smelled a long way in the woods

"Load your guns and pull the hammers back while the cars motor is still running. You must not make a sound after they start out the trail. You can be sure that they are looking and listening. I'm sure that Royston will be walking in front with Potts about twelve to fifteen feet behind.

"Ivan, you take the lead here, and Hunt from here on out you do exactly what Ivan does. When you are both ready, Ivan you give a hand signal and Hunt you answer it. Then crouch down and make sure you are out of sight from the trail.

"Now Ivan, when Potts goes by, be sure that you wait for a step or two before you stand up. It would be a hell of a note for you and Hunt to shoot each other trying to shoot him. Hunt you watch Ivan and be damn sure you stand when he stands. Both of you should shoot at the same time. As you stand up together count – one, two, three, shoot.

"Start back for the car immediately. Hurry but don't run. Stay off the trail until you are past their car. Royston will have to see about Potts, and call for help, so you will have enough time, but none to waste.

"Any questions?"

"No!"

"No!"

"All right, here we are. Hunt get the guns as you get out. Don't worry about me. I will be in hearing distance and I will be here when you get back here. Good luck, now go."

HJ looked at his watch. The dial face read 6:50. The first gray light of dawn had arrived. The full light from the morning sun was rushing in their direction.

*   *   *

Standing almost directly across the old road from Ivan, they exchanged their prearranged hand signals one last time. Hunt let the fast moving chain of events from last week run through his mind. He was glad that the waiting was over, and the time for them to deliver on their part of the job had arrived. There was a nervous tightening in his chest but it was nothing that would prevent him from carrying out his part in the debt of revenge on Carl Potts. Hunt could tell that Ivan was also feeling the effects of the same case of nerves that he was. Not very talkative to begin with, Hunt had already noticed this morning that Ivan was even quieter and more intense than normal.

Watching Ivan now from across the old road, standing there quiet and waiting, Hunt realized just how important the success of their mission was to the people who knew and had worked with Zeke during the last few years of his life. Both Hunt and Ivan were aware that when their job of revenge on Carl Potts was completed, for them the most dangerous part of the job was just beginning. On more than one occasion, Ben had warned them that they must take every precaution against their identity being discovered or even worse, to be captured.

"Don't even think that they cain't get everything they want to know out of you. They have people whose job is to get people to talk, and they are damn good at it."

Hunt saw Ivan's hand signal and heard the sound of the car engine at the same time. Ivan held up his shotgun and pulled the hammer back into the firing position. Hunt acknowledged with his hand signal and watched as Ivan crouched down completely hidden from the trail.

Hunt loaded his shotgun and snapped the barrel closed onto the trigger mechanism, then carefully pulled the hammer back into the firing position. He crouched down until he was hidden from the trail. He could now make out part of Ivan's lower body. He would have to watch for his hand. It was now full daylight but the sun had not as yet appeared.

Both men had experienced the same unnamed doubt that the two Revenue Officers would come here as HJ had planned. But now they were here, it was going to happen. For the rest of his life, whenever he thought back over the series of events that occurred during the next twenty minutes Hunt never again doubted the necessity of having a plan for a dangerous undertaking. Knowing the plan, and then following the plan through to its completion. Hunt was now ready; he had no doubt that Ivan was also ready.

Ivan heard the car doors close and then some voices that he could not understand. He figured that they were discussing what equipment to carry with them. The voices were soon followed by the sound of the car's trunk lid closing.

Ivan heard the sound of boots walking in the wet grass.

"Carl, keep a sharp lookout. I don't expect any trouble, but you never can be completely sure when you are out in the woods alone."

Ivan saw the tall figure of Royston Hill go by.

"I'd like to get there about the same time they are finishing up. We might get three of them if somebody has come to haul the liquor out."

Ivan recognized the shorter figure following about fifteen feet behind Royston.

Two steps past his hiding place Hunt saw that Carl was about to be clear of any growth by the side of the trail. If he saw Ivan's slashing hand signal it was too late to react. Ivan was rising to his feet.

"One," he saw Hunt coming up.

"Two,"

Ivan aimed his shotgun just above Potts knee. He caught a glimpse of Hunts shotgun coming level.

"Three"

Ka-Pow-Pow!

The sound of the two 12-guage shotguns fired toward each other at almost the same instant, shook the area with all the explosive force of an overhead clap of thunder.

Royston dove headlong under a patch of honeysuckle bushes. As the echo from the simultaneous shotgun blasts came rolling back through the trees, it took several seconds before he realized that the keening wail in his ears was coming from Carl Potts.

"EEEEEEEEEEEEEOOOOOOOOOOO God, they got me."

"EEEEEEEEEEEEEOOOOOOOOOOO God, they have killed me."

"EEEEEEEEEEEEEOOOOOOOOOOO God, they have shot my legs off and I'm going to die."

It seemed to Ivan that Carl's screams were not going to stop. He saw that Hunt was already moving. It was time to go.

No sooner had Royston hit the ground, and he heard Carl begin to scream, he knew with near certainty what had happened. As he stood up he saw the bushes still moving on both sides of the road. "My God, it was two shots. They meant to get him good while they were at it, and they must have done it."

Royston ran back to where Carl was lying on his back in the middle of the old road, still screaming. "Royston, they have shot both of my legs off. Don't let me lay here and bleed to death. Help me Royston."

Royston saw that both pant legs were almost blown away at the knees. He quickly opened his knife and ripped both of Carl's pant legs above his knees. He saw that both of Carl's knees were mangled with shot, but he was not mortally wounded.

"Shut up Carl, you are not going to die. All that damn hollering ain't going to do no good. The right knee is full of shot but it's not bleeding much. Your left knee is bleeding bad so I'm going to have to put a tourniquet on it."

As Royston tightened the tourniquet he said to Carl, "Hold the tourniquet while I call for an ambulance." Royston raised their office on his two-way radio transmitter. "I have an officer down here on the Old Lake Road. You know where we are? Get an ambulance down here immediately."

"What happened?"

"Potts has been shot."

"Who shot him?"

"I've got a Federal Revenue Agent laying out here on the ground with his legs shot out from under him. Get an ambulance out here and be quick about it!"

CHAPTER 12

Ivan and Hunt came back onto the old road a short distance behind the Revenue Officer's car. The smell of exploded gunpowder was still heavy in the air as they hurried along the trail toward the paved road and the pick-up point by HJ. Neither of the two men spoke - both of them left almost breathless by the events of the last ten minutes.

Just as they were about to reach the end of the old road, the black 1939 Ford turned off the paved road and came to a stop in the old roadbed. Both doors came open and HJ stepped out on the ground. He quickly walked to the back of the car and raised the trunk lid. "Let me have the guns, one of you in the front and the other in back, both of you lay down out of sight."

He put the two shotguns in a burlap bag and pushed them against the seat back and closed the trunk lid. He checked the road for cars, slid into the driver's seat, backed out onto the highway and within minutes they were headed back along the road that they had traveled less than two hours ago.

"Both of you must have got him good. I heard him start screaming just as soon as I heard the shots."

"It worked perfect HJ," Hunt said from where he was lying stretched out on the back seat.

Ivan did not speak for several minutes and when he did his voice was tight with anger and disgust. "He knew it was revenge for Zeke that got him. When he went down he started screaming, "They got me." I hope the son-of-a-bitch saw Zeke's face, while he was lying there on the ground, and I hope he thought he was going to bleed to death."

"HJ what is going to happen to the shotguns?" Hunt asked."

"I am going to drop them off close to the house, and Daddy is going to pick them up sometime after dark. Tomorrow he will fire his shop bellows with coke and two shotgun stocks. Tomorrow night the barrels will sink into a deep hole in the middle of the Big Sandy. We don't want to take any chances, and, we don't want to have to answer any questions."

In order to stay away from Huntington, HJ kept to the South side of Beech Fork Lake State Park, then turned North on the Eastern side of Beech Fork Lake State Park and close to an hour later he turned East on US Route 60 and headed for Charleston.

"Okay guys, you can sit up now."

HJ kept his speed well within the speed limit, taking no chance on being stopped by the state patrol or a county patrol cruiser. Two hours later he parked the car around the corner from the bus station. He reached into the glove compartment and handed Ivan an envelope.

"Here are your tickets to Charlotte. The bus that leaves here at 12 o'clock is supposed to get you to Charlotte at 9 o'clock tonight. After you get to Charlotte, check the schedule for a bus that will get you to Gainesville after 8 o'clock tomorrow night. I think that will be the best time. The rest you know, about catching a cab to the Big Bear Barbecue Drive-in, where you will be picked up by someone who knows you. Is that right?"

"That's the plan HJ and if we can make it work as well as your plan worked we'll be home free." Hunt answered.

"Ivan if I can get Mama and Daddy to come, I will bring them down, probably in the spring."

"Well I hope so HJ; you know how glad that would make them to see everybody that can come. I promise if you come, you and Hunt and I will do a little kicking around together. We know a few places."

"Now I'm going to hold you to that, and you too Hunt."

With that HJ shook hands with the other two men. They sat without speaking for a short time, each of the three men knowing what was going through the mind of the other two, and how they had shared it together. For the rest of their lives, today was the dividing point of their life.

Ivan broke the moment of reverie by opening the door and stepping out on the pavement. "Well I guess that's about enough said," Ivan said.

"I guess it is, good luck guys," HJ said.

Hunt climbed out of the back seat and looked in through the rolled down glass after he closed the door.

"Good bye HJ. Tell Walt and your mother we said good bye."

"I will Hunt, goodbye Hunt."

The two men turned the corner and disappeared from view.

HJ sat for a moment before he started his car and turned left at the corner.

He glanced to his right, but they were already gone inside the bus station.

*   *   *

Lee Hasty had just returned to his office in the Federal Courthouse in Gainesville, Georgia from his lunch hour when his phone rang. As he picked it up, he noted that the time was eight minutes past one o'clock p.m.

"Hello, is this Lee Hasty?" Lee was expecting a personal call.

"Yes, it is. Can I help you?"

"Well no, but I have some bad news for you."

"What do you mean?"

"They got your man this morning."

"What the hell are you talking about?"

"This is Royston Hill in the State Revenue Office here in Huntington, West Virginia.

Carl Potts, the Federal Officer on loan to us from your district, and I were checking out a report that a still was in operation near Beech Fork Lake this morning. As we were walking down an old field road, two men were concealed in the underbrush, and as we passed by they shot him down from both sides of the road."

There was a complete silence on Lee's end of the line for about ten seconds. When he spoke his voice was choked with rage. "The sons-of-bitches! They found out where he was, and they tracked him down, and then they shot him down like a dog. The sons-of-bitches!"

"Well 'they' is who he called them, but he never did say who 'they' were." Royston knew the whole story, but he made no further comment.

"Well I know who they are, and if I can get hold of those two shooters, I'll still have the last word with a bunch of people. Is Carl dead?"

"Oh no, Carl is not dead. He's lying up here in the Cabell County Hospital with his knees shot all to pieces."

"But he's going to be all right then?"

"Well yeah, he's going to be all right, but the only way he's ever going to walk again is with a pair of walking sticks.

CHAPTER 13

Lamar had just finished the midday inspection of the feeders and waters in his four chicken houses and walked in through the back door when he heard the phone ring. Mildred appeared in the porch screen door and said, "It's for you."

"Hello."

"Hello Lamar, it's HJ."

"Well HJ, I was hoping you would call."

"How is it going?"

"Everything is going good, except for Carl. He is in the hospital."

"Well I hadn't heard that. Was the operation a success?"

"From what I heard, it was a great success."

"Well that sounds mighty fine. I'll let the rest of the folks know. How about the visitors?"

"They left about an hour ago. They should be in about when they are expected"

"HJ, come and see us when you can."

"I'll do that, and let's keep in touch. Bye."

*   *   *

When Lee Hasty heard that Carl Potts had been shot and badly wounded, he knew with a blind certainty, that it was an act of revenge meant to avenge the killing of Zeke Turner. Neither was there any doubt about who was responsible for finding Carl and then deciding what his punishment would be. After all, Ben McClure had warned him that Carl would have to pay, and now in spite of everything that he had done to prevent it, Ben had carried out his threat.

Immediately, after Lee learned that Carl had been shot, he asked the Georgia State Patrol to issue a bulletin requesting that all patrol cars, patrolling along the Georgia border with Tennessee and North and South Carolina be on the lookout for two men driving a late 1930's or early 1940's Ford car with Georgia license plates. They were wanted for questioning about a shooting in West Virginia.

The clock on Lee's bedside table read 12:35 am, when he awoke to the cold realization that Ben McClure would not let his two shooters drive a car back to Georgia. He would almost certainly have them ride a bus, but where to and arriving when?

*   *   *

"I'll be damned if I don't believe that this bus has stopped at every crossroads in South Carolina," Hunt grumbled as they came to the Georgia State line.

"Well I was beginning to believe that we was lost myself," Ivan answered partly jesting and partly in truth.

Two hours later, after stops at Toccoa and Demorest, the home of Piedmont College, they crossed the Hall County line. A passenger up front asked the driver how much longer it would take for the bus to get to Gainesville.

"About an hour. We are about on time, maybe fifteen or twenty minutes late."

Ivan leaned closer and spoke to Hunt.

"Hunt, let's be on the lookout as we get off the bus in Gainesville."

"Are you expecting trouble Ivan?"

"Hunt, I always expect trouble when Lee Hasty is around. Now listen, I know Lee Hasty and he knows me. I'll get off the bus first and if a tall sandy haired man starts toward me, that's him. When he gets almost to me I'm going to run over him and knock him down. He will probably have another officer with him, so you take him down and run like hell. Stay on the back streets and in the woods. I'll meet you behind the Hall County Hospital as soon as you can get there. Don't let them get you Hunt; if you do they'll never let you go."

Waiting in a car parked across the street from the Gainesville Bus Station were Lee Hasty and two of his officers.Luckily for Hunt and Ivan they did not ride the bus until it reached the Gainesville bus station. Just inside the Gainesville city limits the Greyhound bus pulled over and stopped at what appeared to be a private entrance. Hunt read from a small sign standing near the entrance, 'Riverside Military Academy,' bus and taxi stop only."

The door to the bus came open and the bus driver said 'Riverside.' As two young men dressed in grey trimmed in black uniforms got off the bus, a Victory cab pulled up to the entrance gate and four more cadets climbed out and began anteing up for the fare.

Then just as the driver reached for the switch to close the door, Ivan stood up and said, "Hold it driver, this is close enough. Let's go Hunt.'" With Hunt following, Ivan climbed down off the bus and walked over to the taxi still parked near the entrance gate.

"How much to the Big Bear Barbecue Drive-In?"

"A buck apiece."

Ivan handed the driver two crumpled one dollar bills from his right front pocket. "Let's go."

CHAPTER 14

As the Greyhound bus that had started its run early this morning in Charlotte, North Carolina pulled into the passenger unloading area, Lee Hasty and his two officers crossed the street and stood unobserved under a metal canopy. They watched as each passenger stepped down and filed into the station. With the bus unloaded, and with no appearance of anyone he recognized, Lee walked over and spoke to the driver.

"I'm Lee Hasty from the Federal Revenue Office here in Gainesville. We are looking for two men traveling together who may have gotten on your bus this morning in Charlotte. Have you seen two men that fit that bill?"

"Well yes, as a matter of fact I have. Two men traveling together were the first two passengers on the bus this morning. They rode the bus all the way from Charlotte until we got to the stop at Riverside Military Academy. When a taxi pulled up and unloaded a load of cadets, one of the men said, "Hold it, this is close enough." They got off the bus, got in the taxi and they took off back in the direction which we had just come."

"Son-of-a-bitch, that was them. I had them figured right, but I didn't count on that stop at Riverside."

"Well you know, it's not really a stop for a through bus. We do it to help the kids out. Saves them a taxi charge sometime."

"What kind of a taxi was it?"

"It was a Victory Cab, and I think that is it sitting over there across the street."

Lee and the two officers sprinted across the street. Lee showed his badge. "Driver did you pick up two men at the Riverside bus stop about an hour ago?"

"Yes, I did officer. What about it?"

"Where did you take them?"

"I took them to the Big Bear Barbecue Drive-In. It's about a mile back out the road from the Riverside bus stop."

Twenty minutes later, Lee pulled his car into an open space behind the Big Bear Barbecue Drive-In and rolled down his window. A tall brown haired carhop wearing a red halter and tight pedal pushers hung her metal serving tray on the side of the car and plucked a short stub of a pencil out of her hair. "Hi Hon, I'm Carlene, what can I get for you guys?"

Lee laid his badge and 4 one-dollar bills on the tray and said. "I'm Lee Hasty from the Federal Revenue Office here in Gainesville. Did you see a Victory Cab drop two men off here at the drive-in about an hour ago?"

"I sure did officer. Did they do something wrong?"

"Are they inside?"

"No, they are all gone."

"What do you mean they are all gone? Were there more than two of them?"

"Yes, there was Officer. About two hours ago this guy pulled in that spot right over there. He ordered a barbecue and fries and when I brought them he paid me and told me that he was waiting on two guys that would be here before long. An hour and fifteen minutes later a Victory cab pulled up and two guys got out. They got in the car with the first guy and called me over. They ordered four barbecues, two fries and a six pack of cold cokes. When I brought their order they paid me and gave me a five dollar tip and left."

Carlene pushed Lee's badge toward him with a long red nailed finger and deftly folded the four ones into the pocket of her pedal pushers. "They have been gone thirty five minutes and that's all I know. Y'all come back, bye."

CHAPTER 15

"I had them Lou, I had them." Lee said, as he and his wife Louise were having coffee the next morning. "I had them figured to come back here on a bus and I had the right bus. But damn it all to hell and back, I forgot about that stop at Riverside when there are cadets on the bus. But we could still have gotten them if that damn taxi had not driven up just when it did. The whole thing was a run of bad luck, but it seems like we keep having it."

Louise looked across the table at her husband and said, "Lee don't let this thing get the best of you. How important is it for you to catch the men that shot Carl Potts? You said yourself that he never should have killed that boy. You said that it was a bad mistake, and I agree. Let it go Lee. If it was wrong, quit trying to make it right. Carl Potts let his craving for a drink of liquor ruin his life, but guess what, good old Uncle Sam is going to retire him to the front porch of his farm in Virginia and reward him for his exemplary service to the Federal Government with a monthly check.

"Get on with your life and your career Lee. As you have, on occasion reminded me sweet boy, we ain't got no dog in that fight."

*   *   *

A mile past Howsers Mill, Ben turned out on Old Sawmill Road and after a deep rutted quarter of a mile stopped behind a 1946 Chevrolet sitting in the road. As he was getting out of his truck he saw Lee Hasty standing beside an old hickory tree. The bright yellow leaves were shedding off the tree and blowing along on the cool morning breeze in late October.

"Morning Ben. I hope you didn't mind that I sent word by one of my men that I needed to see you? I'm glad that you saw fit to come."

"Well Lee, you are right that we need to talk. I was right smart surprised when I heard about what happened in Gainesville. What have you decided to do, keep the war that we already have going, or are you starting a new one?"

"Come on Ben, I think you know better than that. I know we have had some trouble, but I don't think anybody would call it a war. I just wanted ---------."

"You wouldn't? How about telling that to Rabb and Annie Turner! Better still, if you will get in the car with me, I'll carry you to the cemetery at Shoal Creek Baptist Church. There's a new tombstone there with Zeke Turner's name on it. What would you tell them Lee? Would you tell them that it was just an accident and it couldn't be helped?"

"You know what I told them Ben, and you know there was no intent, on our part, to hurt anybody. Things just got out of hand."

"Yeah right, things like a drunken Federal Revenue Officer. I promised you that we wouldn't kill him, but I told you that he would have to pay and what happens? When we keep our promise, you pull out all the stops to catch them."

"Shooting a Federal Revenue Officer is a federal crime."

"Well by God what kind of a crime is shooting and killing and innocent man?'

"All right Ben, you are right. Zeke getting killed was a bad mistake on our part, and I know it. But what I wanted to tell you is that as far as we are concerned it's now over. There will be no further effort on our part to find out who shot Carl. The investigation has been dropped. Can I depend on you to get the word around to the people that are concerned?"

Ben stood for several minutes trying to decide how he should answer Lee. By admitting that Zeke's death was a mistake on their part, and then promising that there would be no further effort to find the men who shot Carl Potts, Lee had put the burden of settling the dispute on his shoulders.

In the end the decision was not hard to make. Both men knew that it was time for the dispute to be over. If not settled now it could, at any time now, break out again with results even more deadly than the incident that started it.

"All right Lee, I'll do the best I can with it."

"Good Ben, I'm glad to hear it."

After a few seconds the two men shook hands. It was the first time that Ben had ever shaken a Federal Revenue Officer's hand.

END OF PART 5

God-Fearing Criminals

Part 6

CHAPTER 1

As we have seen, the making, hauling, and selling of moonshine (illicit, non-taxpaid, spirituous, malt) liquor is long hours of hard work done mostly at night (by the moonshine). The still hands rarely live at home. They live and work under the strain of knowing that their work and workplace is illegal and if caught working there by a State or Federal Revenue Officer, they could be sentenced to serve a number of years in prison.

Perhaps the most dangerous part of the moonshine or white liquor business is that of hauling or tripping the liquor from the mountain counties into the poor black and white areas of Atlanta, Marietta, and Decatur. If it is not the most dangerous of jobs, then at least, the men who drive 'trip cars,' are something of a breed of their own.

For the most part, the huge amount of liquor that is hauled into these cities every day is transported in one of two vastly different kind of cars. The first is a car, usually about two to ten years old but in very good mechanical condition. The rear seat is removed so that one hundred fifty to two hundred gallons of liquor can be stacked in the area behind the front seat and in the trunk. Six ply tires, heavy-duty shock absorbers and extra leafs are installed in the springs to make the transition complete. These cars are known, as 'Creepers' because once discovered, the heavily loaded cars are no match for a faster and more maneuverable patrol car.

Sometimes a smart driver who knows the back roads can outfox his pursuers and slip away and hide. They are the exception rather than the rule. Most men driving creepers may offer some bumper banging resistance but they are not able to outrun their pursuers and they usually end up making "bush bond" ... "Jump off the damn thing and run like hell." If the driver thinks fast enough he should take the ignition keys with him. That makes a long day or night even longer and tempers even shorter for the pursuing officers whose job it is to bring the vehicle and its captured contraband to the nearest county headquarters. "I'll catch that son-of-a-bitch if it takes me the rest of my life."

Beginning in the late 1940's, county and state patrol officers began patrolling the roads, driving hi-performance patrol cars. The reason given for buying this expensive equipment was to catch speeding drivers on the new interstate highways. But the game they really enjoyed was to lay in wait for 'Trip' cars coming out of the mountains, and run a block on them before the drivers even have a chance to make a run for it. To equalize their chances against the performance engines in the patrol cars, the best drivers and their owners turned to what many of them already knew.

Drivers at red dirt racetracks scattered across North Georgia had, for years, been racing late 1930 through early 1940 model Ford coupes. The cylinder holes in the engine block were bored to accommodate larger pistons. Double and triple carburetors with Offenhauser cylinder heads, Amber camshafts and crankshafts that increased the piston rod stoke and cylinder head compression were all part of the racing equipment installed in what was once of flathead V8 Ford engine.

Drivers like Brad Parks, who already had the experience, quickly adapted the technology into the larger engine blocks of the later model 1946 and up engines. The result was both amazing and dangerous. Even loaded with one hundred fifty gallons of moonshine liquor, the cars would accelerate thru 100 mph in seconds. The days and nights of high-speed chases along the backroads and on the highways of North Georgia ushered in a new era in the business of transporting the large amounts of moonshine liquor into the huge metropolitan Atlanta area. The men who drove these powerful machines were known and admired by the young men and boys and in several instances by the young women of Dawson and surrounding counties.

Some, like Brad Parks, were local boys who loved racing, were naturals at driving powerful cars, and were lucky enough to get hooked up with a good owner. There were some of them who died along the way. None of them wanted to make driving a trip car their life's vocation. They were known as the men who drove the 'Trip' cars with the 'Big motors.'

*   *   *

If Clara Mae Turner knew what loving a man was all about, she reckoned that she must be in love with Rob Kirby. She enjoyed being with him and she missed him, sometimes acutely, when she did not see nor hear from him for a week or more. On one occasion she was both surprised and a little irritated when she caught herself daydreaming about what Rob had said and how he had looked at her.

Then there was the night that she had let Rob unbutton her blouse, push her bra strap off her shoulder and caress her breast. The whole experience left Clara shaken and breathless. Some hours later she awoke in her bed, her body in a cold sweat, her stomach quivering and her nipples hard and aching. She threw the bed covers back and tossed her long gown aside in almost the same motion. She switched on the light and stood naked before her full length dressing mirror her hands covering her breasts. "My God Clara, if you are going to have a fit like that ever time a man touches one of your titties you are in a hellacious fix." But just as quickly as the spell came, it passed. Clara switched off the light, left her gown lying on the floor, and climbed back into her bed. Almost immediately she fell asleep and slept soundly until she was awakened by the gentle morning sun. That had been her first intimate experience with Rob and she was surprised at the excitement she felt when the memory of that evening together returned again and again.

One day, when Clara had walked the near quarter mile to the mailbox, she heard and then saw Rob's trip car coming. Thrilled to see Rob coming toward her in his trip car that she knew was loaded with liquor she began waving with both hands. But when he came by the mailbox where she was standing, he did not see her. He was sitting turned slightly to his right in the seat, both hands resting light but firm on the steering wheel. Clara saw that he was looking up into the rear view mirror almost as much as he was watching the road ahead. Clara realized that Rob was so engrossed in operating the powerful trip car and watching the road behind him that he did not see her. Still Clara was hurt and a little angry. He could have at least stopped by for a few minutes when he came up this morning.

On Friday evening when Rob's Pontiac turned in at their driveway and stopped by Rabb's truck, Clara's hurt and anger quickly melted away. Rob stepped out of his car and stood waiting as Clara came across the yard to where he was standing. He took her left hand in both of his as Clara leaned her head on his shoulder and kissed him on his neck. She felt a light shiver as it ran through his body. "Oh my, was that me, or was it the chill in the mountain air?"

Rob did not answer for a long moment. He slipped an arm around Clara's waist and pulled her closer to him. "You'll never know how much I have been looking forward to seeing you today. I knew if I didn't leave today, I would never be able to leave tomorrow. So this morning I told Brad that he and Hunt would have to handle the business because I was going to see you."

"Who is Hunt?" Clara asked.

Rob was unaware that Clara knew the names of the two men sent to West Virginia after Carl Potts. He decided not to evade Clara's question. "Hunt Williams, we have hired Hunt to drive a trip car for us. He knows every back road between here and Sandy Springs."

"Rob, isn't he one of the men---?"

Rob did not let her finish. "Clara let's not go there, okay? I didn't know you knew who they were. I shouldn't have --."

"Rob I want to talk to him."

Rob decided he did not want to be completely disagreeable about her request.

"All right Clara. I'll bring him by here one day soon."

"Clara bring Rob in to wash up, its time for supper," Annie called from the back porch.

Rob took Clara's hand and they started toward the house. "Clara next to seeing you, I have been looking forward to hearing those words."

*   *   *

Supper was a large and festive meal of thick slices of cured ham covered with red eye gravy, baked sweet potatoes, turnips and turnip greens boiled together in a black iron pot along with a huge ho-cake made of unbleached wheat flour.

After their meal Clara and Rob walked down to the barn to see Clara's two Black Angus calves. The two calves were now a month old and Clara was bucket training them together. As she walked around the barn lot swinging the buckets, the calves raced and pranced at her feet waiting to be fed. Clara walked to the fence where Rob was sitting on the top rail.

"Rob, they will only run and dance after me. Aren't they beautiful?"

"They are Clara. They are so black I'll bet you couldn't find them at night. What are you going to do with them?"

"Oh, I don't know. I'll probably sell them to Josh McClure in a month or two. We should go and see Josh's herd. Josh has gotten to be a pretty well known Black Angus breeder."

"Clara will you go with me tomorrow and meet my folks?"

"What?"

"I would like for you to meet my Mama and Daddy."

Clara dropped her buckets and the two calves hungrily went after the feed in the buckets.

"Oh my God Rob, why do you want me to do that?"

"Because I want you to marry me Clara. You are the only girl I have ever wanted; I love you Clara, will you? Marry me, I mean?"

"Oh my God Rob!"

*   *   *

Robert Kirby was being very truthful that Friday evening when he proposed to Clara and confessed to her that she was the only girl that he had ever wanted. Since Clara had first realized that she wanted to marry Rob, just the thought of how much her life would have to change was a worry she could not rid herself of.

The uneasiness that would not go away, did not mean that she did not love Rob, because she did. It did mean that once married, it was her duty to take his name and, to live with him wherever he lived and that was, as Rob had told her, in Atlanta. Even worse it meant that she would have to move out of the house of Rabb and Annie Turner. Clara had, of course, known that this day would one day arrive, and now that it had, leaving home and her family, tore at the fragile fabric of her being.

Clara had on more than one occasion visited Atlanta. Once, after a weekend in which she spent three nights with Rabb's sister's family in Atlanta, she returned home to tell Rabb and Annie that she had enjoyed the visit but, "I would probably smother to death if I had to live there all the time."

So standing there in the barn lot with her two Black Angus calves rolling the feed buckets around her feet, licking for the last grains of feed, Clara was bereft of an answer that she could give to assure Rob that she welcomed his proposal. She did what women of all ages have done or resorted to when they find themselves in such an untenable position that a simple yes or no does not give the answer they want to give.

Clara started crying.

Rob leapt down from the wooden rail and took her in his arms. He led her out of the barn lot to an old bench sitting against Rabb's corncrib.

"Clara, whatever I did or said to hurt you, I'm sorry. I will never ask you to do anything that you don't want to do. Just tell me and I'll--." Clara put her hand over Rob's lips. "Hush Rob, don't say that. Don't you see --- it's not you --- it's me. I always have to do everything wrong. Besides all of my crazy blabbering, this is the first time that anyone has ever asked me to marry him.

"I may not act like it Rob but I do love you and I have for a long time. I'll be happy to marry you Rob, and I'll go with you wherever you want me to go. But Rob I have never lived anywhere but here with Mama and

Daddy. I'll get used to living away from here and apart from them, but you'll have to help me Rob."

Rob did marry the only girl he ever wanted, but he had to wait, through the rest of a cold winter and a rainy spring with many foggy mornings, before he got her on a beautiful Saturday afternoon in early June.

When Clara, encouraged by her closest friends, informed Rob that she had decided on a June wedding he offered no objections.

Late winter and early spring are normally busy times in the moonshine liquor business around Atlanta. The fall, winter and spring season of 1950-1951 was a busy and profitable one for Frank and Rob Kirby, Brad Parks and Hunt Williams.

Clara, Annie and the rest of Clara's wedding party immediately found themselves involved in the midst of planning Clara's wedding from the ring bearers to the wedding cake.

Rob however found himself in the midst of an undertaking for which he had no idea on where to start looking nor what to do if he found what he was looking for. Rob had to find and buy a house to move his new wife into. Better said and more to the point as "a place to set up housekeeping.."

Having been born and raised in the Yellow Creek Community located in Pickens County. Rob could not accept the thought of living in a house with another house directly behind his. A house on either side was acceptable, but not one "in my own back yard."

Rob finally decided on Northwest Atlanta to look for a house simply because that's where his apartment was located. With the location decided upon, Rob started his search. Almost every evening, unless he had to watch Brad or Hunt into and out of a stash,* he began riding through the residential areas of Northwest Atlanta.

A few days over a week later Rob turned off of West Wesley onto a quiet side street, and there was the house that he was looking for. The house was setting safely back from Nancy Creek and the [FOR SALE] sign said it was a three bedroom with a full daylight basement.

As Rob was copying the phone number down from the 'For Sale' sign, he was thinking to himself, his face covered with just a touch of a smile. "Well sweetheart I have found us a house. Now all I have got to do is get you moved all the way from Dawson County to Atlanta to live in it with me."

As Rob continued to sit in his car looking at the house, sundown turned to twilight and the streetlights came on bringing light back to the quiet street. Rob watched as lights winked on in most of the other houses on the street. But the house that Rob had found remained quiet and dark.

He wondered about the family that had lived here and then moved away. There must have been children. There was an old wagon and tricycle in a fenced area out back. Was it a lost job, a family tragedy or a divorce? A dark feeling of melancholy descended on Rob as he sat slumped behind the wheel of his car.

A car came by and turned in at one of the driveways. Car doors opened and closed. There were the sounds of children playing at other houses along the street. Finally Rob roused himself and sat up in the seat of his car. He looked at his watch and shook his head.

"What in the hell is wrong with you feller?" Rob growled to himself. "Get your head out of your ass, and quit feeling sorry for yourself. You have found the house you were looking for, and if you want to make her happy, get the house ready for her to start being your wife when you bring Clara to her new home."

CHAPTER 2

Zion Hill Baptist Church was Annie Carnes Turner's old family church. The church was located close to the edge of the Chattahoochee National Forest, and during the 1920's and 1930's the church had not done well.

Attendance and membership had shrunk during these lean years when some of the older families had died out and others had moved away. Toward the end of the 1930's there were seven families making up the clerk's membership roll of the church. Five of these families were active, the other two being elderly and infirm. The Carnes family was one of the active families or at least part of them were.

This is not to say that these five families were the only people that attended Zion Hill Baptist Church. The second Sunday of each month was the regular preaching day at Zion Hill, and on those Sundays there were always as many relatives and friends in attendance as there were members. Zion Hill was one of the least, but it was far from being destitute.

Rabb and Annie were both members at Zion Hill, but they attended church at Shoal Creek as much as they did at Zion Hill. Some of the people at Zion Hill expected Rabb and Annie to move their membership to Shoal Creek where Zeke was buried and Clara was now a member, but they never did.

Clara's wedding plans were well on in the making when, on a cold and rainy Sunday evening in March, as they were sitting at the supper table along with Newt, his wife Sara and their three children, Clara calmly announced that she wanted her wedding to be held at Zion Hill Baptist Church. She quickly added that Rob had no objections.

With the exception of the three children, everyone at the table stopped eating and looked at Clara. After a long moment of silence it was Annie who spoke. "Why child, the church is in such bad shape that it's not hardly fit to have a wedding in."

"Mama, it's yours and Daddy's home church. I thought you would be happy that I want to get married there."

"Well it's not that honey, of course we would be, but there's not even a room for the women to get dressed in."

"We can all get dressed here at the house, and then come on to the church in our cars. I told Rob that he might have to get dressed in the woods behind the church. He just laughed and said that it wouldn't be the first time, although he didn't recall putting on a tuxedo in the woods. He said he doubted that Brad had ever put on a tuxedo before, so it wouldn't make any difference with him where he put it on."

The mental picture of two men getting dressed in the woods brought peals of laughter from the three children.

"Well let's wait up a minute now Annie," Rabb said speaking for the first time. "If that's where Clara has got her head set to get married, ain't that sorta our end of the bargain?"

The next morning Rabb and Annie paid a visit to Zion Hill Baptist Church after which they realized that there was indeed much that needed to be repaired both inside and outside of the church.

Rabb Turner learned long ago, that if you wanted to get something done, make sure everyone involved understood what you wanted done and what you were willing to do to get it done.

Rabb met with the five deacons of Zion Hill Baptist Church the following Tuesday evening. Two of the deacons were older men (70's), two were middle aged (50's) and one was in his (40's).

While it in no way made the slightest difference in his respect for them as church deacons, Rabb had done a considerable amount of business with two of the men in their earlier years. One was known for his ability to make the best doubled and twisted pure corn liquor in Dawson and Gilmer County. The other of the two men was known for his skill in the making of pure peach or apple brandy. His peach brandy was made from nothing but peaches. His apple brandy was made from nothing but apples. They were men whom Rabb Turner respected.

Charlie Latimer was the eldest of the five deacons and therefore was recognized as the chairman of the board of deacons. Charlie never exerted any control over the other men on the board of deacons, unless there was a vote to be taken, or a discussion was about to turn into a disagreement.

After the usual round of handshakes, the inquiries into the health and well being of each family, a discussion of the weather and an opening prayer, there was a lull in the conversation.

Rabb took his cue and waited no longer. "Charlie, I think that you and the other deacons know that our daughter Clara is going to be married in June."

"Why yes Rabb, we have heard that she is going to marry a young man by the name of Kirby from down in the Yellow Creek Community. Roger there said that he knew his Daddy well a few years ago."

"Well two Sundays ago, as we sat at the supper table with Newt and his family, Clara sprang something of a surprise on us. She told us that she wants her wedding to be here in this church."

That revelation was also something of a surprise to the deacons of Zion Hill Baptist Church. Floyd the other of the two eldest deacons asked, "Wasn't it your daughter Clara who moved her letter to Shoal Creek last year?"

"It was Floyd, but we all understand the reason and cause, for Clara's change in her membership." There was no further discussion, and Clara's request was approved.

"Well brethren (Rabb intentionally used the term for personal relationships here) there is one other thing I want to talk with you about and I think you'll agree that it's as important to you as it is to me. I did what I did without your knowledge but with two things in mind, besides Clara's wedding, which will now make it three. First our Communion and Memorial Day Service in May, Clara's wedding day in June, and the Church Revival in July."

This time it was the deacon named Alton who asked, "Rabb, we know that these events are set to take place here in the church, but what is it that you have done?"

"I have taken a look at our church and there's a lot of work that needs to be done both inside and outside of the church building."

This time it was the chairman of the deacons, Charlie Latimer, who asked. "Well now, brother Rabb, don't you think that it's the responsibility of the deacons to make those decisions about the church?"

"Yes I do Charlie, and what I have said is only a suggestion from a member. But should the deacons decide that it needs to be done, Annie and I will see that the outside of the church is painted and the steps on the front and both sides of the church will be repaired."

The offer from Rabb's family was even more of a surprise to the deacons than the request for Clara's wedding to be in the church. They also soon realized that Rabb was putting them in a position of having to do what he wanted done.

"Well now brother Rabb," Charlie answered for the deacons, "That is a very generous offer for the church and we will consider your offer along with your other recommendations and give you an answer before the week is out."

"Very good Charlie, I'll be waiting to hear from you. Charlie if the deacons decide to rework the inside of the church, my advice to you is that you turn the decision on what needs to be done, over to the ladies to start with. You will save a lot of wear and tear on yourself and the other deacons because you are going to wind up doing what they want done anyway."

Rabb's advice and the deacon's willingness to take that advice was a good and timely move on the deacon's part. Early on Saturday morning six women along with Annie and Clara swung the rusty and creaking doors of the church wide open. Zion Hill Baptist Church was never again the same.

*   *   *

For those who watched it happen, and for those who participated in the work, the transformation of Zion Hill Baptist Church could best be described as spectacular. Under Rabb's instruction the exterior of the church was repaired before it was repainted. It was scraped, primed and then repainted.

On the following Monday morning Bruce Duncan, the only painter by trade in the Amicalola Community, and four men who reportedly owed Rabb an unpaid debt, showed up at the church with a variety of carpenter's tools, short and long handled scrapers and ladders.

After watching the five men scrape and hammer on the side of the church for over an hour, one onlooker stood up, dusted off the seat of his overalls and said, "Well I don't claim to know anything about painting, but I don't see how they plan on getting any painting done if they are going to spend the day scraping and scratching on the side of the church."

Another onlooker, this one sitting on the tailgate of his pick up answered, "I expect Bruce knows what he is doing. He's the only one around here who does it for a living."

Bruce and his four laborers scraped and renailed as needed, every plank on the outside of the church. They caulked the window and door frames and all the corners. One coat of primer and two coats of paint later, Zion Hill Baptist Church was not just white, it glowed both night and day.

The interior of the church also received a thorough cleaning. At the behest of the ladies, including some cunningly devised volunteer assistance, the interior of the church was washed the benches were washed and polished and the floor was scrubbed and painted. The final and finishing touch was added by two carpenters who lived in the community but were not members of the church. They reworked the pulpit by raising it a foot above the floor of the church, and they added an altar rail.

*   *   *

The word had already gone out about Clara and Rob's wedding, and while there had been some surprise at Clara's choice of Zion Hill as the location, it was soon accepted and forgotten. Everyone in the community was waiting for their own personal invitation to the wedding.

But Clara had one more surprise in store for her relatives, friends and neighbors in the Amicalola community.

The invitations were eagerly received, opened and read.

You are invited to attend

the wedding service in which

Clara Mae Turner

will be united in marriage with

Robert M. Kirby.

The marriage will be consecrated

in the sanctuary of

Zion Hill Baptist Church

on

Saturday the 6th day of June

in the

Year of our Lord 1951,

beginning at 12 o'clock noon.

"Whattttt, read that again."

"-------Beginning at 12 o'clock noon-----"

"That must be a mistake."

"It's not a mistake Mama, it's printed here in the invitation."

In another household where the invitation had just been read, "Well help my time, never in my life have I heard of a wedding being held at 12 o'clock in the middle of the day."

And in another household where a more realistic view was taken about a wedding being held at dinnertime. "Well I hope they come up with something besides cake and peanuts to eat. My belly is used to something a little bit more solid than that at dinnertime."

And that is exactly what happened. A request was sent out for the ladies to bring their favorite dessert.

Word was spread that Clete Wilkens, who usually fixed barbecue and Brunswick stew, had been hired to bring his cooker to the church and deep fry enough chicken for everybody at the wedding.

Rob had ordered four large containers of potato salad from the Pickrick restaurant in Atlanta.

CHAPTER 3

And so it was that on a beautiful blue sky and spring green Saturday at 12 o'clock noon, in early June of 1951, Clara Mae Turner and Robert Kirby were married in Zion Hill Baptist Church. The church was filled to overflowing with family, relatives, and friends of the bride and groom.

The pastor of Zion Hill was Tim Bradley, and since Clara was now a member at Shoal Creek, James McClure, her pastor was invited to participate in the taking of vow's ceremony between Clara and Rob.

After Tim had pronounced the couple as man and wife and Rob had kissed his blushing and tearful wife, Tim asked James to close the service with a prayer.

"Brother Tim if you will grant me but just a moment of time here at the beginning of Clara and Rob's life together, there is a word of assurance found in the old Bible that I would like to read to them.

"In the book of Ecclesiastes the writer, referred to as the preacher, does not promise us the happiest nor the most prosperous of conditions in which we will live out the days of our lives together.

"In the ninth chapter and the ninth verse, He does tell us to, *live joyfully with the wife whom thou lovest, all the days of the life of thy vanity, which he has given thee under the sun.*

"Rob, the Bible tells us that if we will love and cherish our wives, they will bring us great joy. I have found that to be true in my life Rob, and I doubt not you will find it to be true in yours and Clara's life."

All things considered, Clara and Rob's wedding day was a day to remember. During the remainder of that spring and summer at weddings, revivals and even funerals, it was not unusual to hear "Clara and Rob's wedding discussed."

CHAPTER 4

Frank Kirby did not care for the use of built engines in their trip cars. He tried to talk Rob out of spending the huge amounts of money required to buy a High-Compression engine and then have it installed in a trip car. Then they had to find and hire an experienced driver, like Brad Parks, to drive the car.

"Rob we are spending enough money on them big motors to buy brand new cars to haul liquor on."

"I know that Daddy, but what else can we do? We would probably lose half of our liquor if we sent it down through Forysth and Cherokee counties on a creeper. Brad hasn't lost the first gallon so far you know. Here let me knock on wood," Rob grinned as he leaned over and rapped on the wooden floor with his knuckles.

"Well, the only load of liquor that Hunt has lost was when he turned into that dead end street and they trapped him. I think he would still have gotten away if the damn policeman hadn't gotten lucky and shot one of his front tires down while he was trying to get turned around."

"Well that's right too Daddy, and I'll take part of the blame for that foul up." Rob frowned as he thought back over the morning when they lost a 1946 Chevrolet with one hundred fifty gallons of liquor on it.

Rob had always made a habit of meeting his loaded cars about three miles out from the stash, watch while the car was in the stash being unloaded, and then make sure the doors were locked after the car left. When the trip car was gone, the liquor in the stash belonged to the buyer.

Hunt was over an hour late that morning and as he came in on Howell Mill Road, he made the mistake of turning right on Bankhead Highway. When he realized his error at Maddox Park he turned left on a side street and ran up on a police cruiser.

As Hunt later told Rob, "When I drove by him, I think he recognized me and that's when all hell broke loose. They knew it was a dead end street and I didn't. When I tried to turn around they started shooting at my tires and they hit the left front one. I got out of the car and started to leave when this young hotshot jumped out of the police car and ordered me to halt, that he was going to take me in. I told him to go to hell that he wasn't taking me anywhere. Well he took out after me and I ran back down the street and turned between two houses. When I came around the corner of one of the houses I saw some clothes hanging on one end of a clothesline but the line was hard to see. I ducked and went under it, and the line must have caught him right about on his Adams apple. I heard the clothesline squeak, and then I heard him gag and start cursing. When I stopped and looked around, he was laying there flat on his back, and a woman was standing on the back porch pointing to her clothes on the ground."

Frank did not persist for long in his difference with his son over the use of built engines in their trip cars. "Whatever you think son. That's your end of the business to handle, so you know best."

Rob knew that he would have little objection from his father over Brad Parks, because Brad and Frank had taken a personal liking for each other.

On those days, when Brad was bringing an early morning load in for one of Sadie's customers, Brad would leave Atlanta by mid morning and go to Frank and Betty's house and spend the night.

Brad enjoyed working with cattle and Frank liked having someone to talk to when they went looking for a wayward calf or repaired a broken fence.

Brad of course did not forget Betty. He usually brought barbecue of some kind from Sadie's place, or a box of chilidogs from the Yellow Jacket Drive-In.

Brad spent less and less of his free time in Atlanta. It was not at all unusual for Brad to trip once or twice on Friday, and if Rob could not go with Clara to see her folks, he would pick Clara up, drop her off at Rabb and Annie's house, and then go on to Jasper to see his folks.

There was one other place where Brad began spending more and more of his time, and this time even Rob grew concerned about what affect this occurrence might have on the future of their working relationship.

At Clara and Rob's wedding Brad had been Rob's best man and Elizabeth Cochran was Clara's maid of honor. Brad had been unable to attend the only practice but Rob had assured him that being sure he had the ring and handing it to him when Tim called for it, is all you have to worry about, but you damn sure better have that ring."

To which Brad confidently replied, "I can handle it, give me the ring."

"Yeah right, you'll get this ring about two minutes before we go through the church door."

And this is what happened to Brad Parks.

"Now Brad, slip this ring on your little finger and curl it up against your hand. You won't loose it, okay, there's our song, let's go."

Brad followed Rob out into the church and they took their places, outlined in chalk on the floor. Brad remembered seeing a church filled with people but he did not see anyone that he knew. He looked at the floor, glanced to his right at Rob, and checked the ring. Lucky bastard, Brad mused to himself.

There was a change in the music that the pianist was playing, and when Brad heard and felt the change in the level of sound rush across the crowded church he stole a quick look. The aisle of the church was crowded with beautifully gowned women who walked gracefully to the front of the church and took their places. Again Brad checked his hold on the ring and glanced at Rob.

He looked across the church at the bridesmaids now calmly waiting for the ceremony to begin and that's when he saw her. She had to be Clara's maid of honor because she had come last and Brad had not seen her until now. Brad was actually shaken so hard that Rob felt him react when he saw her.

Rob knew that Elizabeth Marie Cochran was an attractive, and catchingly desirable, young woman but whoever did her hair and made up her face deserved a medal. She was stunning.

He glanced at Brad, but Brad was standing, rooted inside his chalk footprints, the expression on his usually handsome and confident face was somehow out of kilter, as if he had been hit. "Get a grip on yourself Brad, I'll introduce you ---------."

The church started rising from the back. The piano struck the opening chords of the Wedding March. Rob turned and saw the vision in white that was coming toward him down the aisle of old Zion Hill Baptist Church on the arm of her father.

To Rob's astonishment, for the first time in a long time, tears welled in his eyes, and oh the joy------.

CHAPTER 5

During Frank's early years, when he hauled his own liquor to Atlanta, he had what he called his easy load. Easy because the load of liquor only went to Cherokee County. Even though Jack Kinderick demanded and got, a better grade of liquor than Frank hauled to Atlanta, it was cash on delivery every time.

Jack ran a small country store on the road between Ball Ground and the Cross Roads Community of Freehome. His location provided him with the opportunity to be the local bootlegger. Jack did not drink himself, and he would not let those who did, hang around his place of business. "There are two things that most men want on occasion. One of them he's a lot better off if he'll get it at home. I want him to know that I keep the other one, and I'm not going to let a bunch of drunks' keep him from getting the one I keep."

When Frank stopped hauling liquor to Atlanta, Rob took over that end of their business. Frank kept his easy load to Jack Kinderick in Cherokee County. "It's not every day you can pick up a hundred dollars for a few hours of work," Frank told his son. But as Frank got older Rob began urging him to give the business to one of the younger trippers who would appreciate it.

It was during one of Brad's visits to Frank and Betty's house that Frank told Brad about the Cherokee trip and offered him the job. Brad eagerly accepted.

*   *   *

While Brad and Jack Kindrick did not form a close friendship with each other, it was a profitable relationship and one that both men wanted to continue. Besides that, the friendship of both men with Frank Kirby served as a source of trust so that neither man was particularly worried about being doublecrossed.

Unfortunately for Jack, there was a State Revenue Officer named Jeff Pope who took a safety payment from Jack once a month. Unfortunately for Brad, Jeff discovered that Frank Kirby had quit hauling liquor to Jack and Jack was now buying from Brad Parks. Worse yet for Brad, Jeff Pope had on two occasions watched Brad drive away with a loaded car and he could do nothing about it. Once from a ditch that Brad had helped him get into and another time when Brad drove his heavily loaded car up a slick dirt road while Jeff was stuck in a set of muddy and watery ruts.

Jeff discovered early on that bootleggers were easy pickings, and Jack was only one of several that made safety payments to Jeff each month. Jeff decided that now was the time to even his score with Brad and make a sizeable profit out of the operation at the same time.

"It won't be hi-jacking for an officer of the law -- I'll just be catching a load of liquor" Jeff chuckled to himself.

"I will need a place where I can carry the loaded car and keep it hid until I get the liquor unloaded off of it. Then I'll just turn the car over to the county law. They know what to do with it."

On the following Tuesday night Jeff went to see Jack Kinderick. "Listen Jack, I'll handle that end of the deal. You won't even have to touch it. You tell me what night he's coming and about what time. We know the way that Frank took, so I'm betting he'll come the same way. When he gets about half way across the Etowah River Bridge, I'll block him on my end of the bridge. There will be two deputies in the car that blocks the bridge from behind. They will snatch his ass off that load of liquor, and have him in the Cherokee County Jail before he knows where we come from. We will have his car load of liquor up there in your garage and the Cherokee County Sheriff will have Mr. Brad Parks little ass locked up in Cherokee County Jail." And that's the way Jeff Pope and Jack Kinderick's hi-jacking of Brad Parks load of liquor on Etowah River Bridge happened. ----Well almost- -but not quite, because Bradford Parks never spent a night in Cherokee County jail in his life---but he did get his leg broken.

*   *   *

Brad had already run Frank's route to Jack's place twice before tonight. Once during the day with Frank along and once at night with no one along. Brad was familiar with the roads but Frank had insisted that he drive the roads before he made the actual trip.

When you drove a trip car for Frank and Rob Kirby, you had to run the route and the alternate routes both ways at night with Rob along. "If you get jumped, how do you expect to get away if you don't know the roads? You can damn well bet they know every back road in the county."

*   *   *

Brad slowed the heavily loaded car and turned left off the Dawsonville-Tate Highway at Dug Road Store, and took the road that ran through the little community known as Pea Ridge. He passed Raeford Grant's place on the right. The front porch light was on and there were lights showing through the front windows but he saw no activity about the house. The two chicken houses were still there but they were not in use. Frank had told him that Raeford was not in good health.

He went through the intersection at Four-Mile Church and turned down the steep curves and switchbacks on Reavis Mountain Road.

Brad was driving a 1948 Dodge with a V-8 engine in it to deliver the one hundred fifty gallons of liquor to Jack Kinderick. The car ran well enough for Brad, but it was geared so high that it did not run smoothly on country back roads loaded down with and pulling over twelve hundred pounds of dead weight.

He continually had to downshift the transmission to maintain the forty to forty five miles per hour speed he wanted to travel and that was a dead giveaway, especially if you were being followed by a lawman who could tell if a car was heavily loaded.

Brad skirted the backside of Nelson and Ball Ground and turned left onto the Ball Ground highway. The Etowah River flowed under the Etowah River bridge about two miles from Ball Ground city limits. The bridge itself was steel construction with overhead girders to support the bridge below. Wide wooden tracks covered the steel support beams from one end of the bridge to the other.

It was just after 8 p.m. when Brad slowed the heavily loaded car and pulled up on the wooden entrance ramp of the bridge. Brad had absolutely no thought of trouble as he started across the bridge, but trouble was already lying in wait, and this time Brad was too late.

The lights on Jeff Pope's car came on as he pulled it across the road and blocked the bridge in front of Brad's car. "Son-of-a-Bitch," Brad spat as he braked the car and jerked it into reverse. The car did not travel more than five feet in reverse before it bumped into a car behind him. The car lights came on. Brad instantly knew what had happened.

"How in hell have you managed to let a damn bunch of cops trap you on a bridge? Any dumb asshole ought to beat that."

"Come on, let's go get him," Somebody yelled from the car behind Brad. Then Brad did two things that saved everything, himself included.

Brad had always said that if he had to run off from a car, he would take the keys out of the ignition and throw them away, but he did not do that. Brad turned off the ignition and left the keys in the ignition untouched. As he slid across the seat, in order to get out on the passenger side, his hand closed on a flashlight. He shoved it into his back pocket and reached for the door handle. As Brad opened the passenger side door and jumped out on the bridge, he came down in one of the deputy's arms.

"I've got him, I've got him right over here. Somebody come and help me get the cuffs on him," the deputy cried out.

"Who do you think you've got you, asshole? Ain't you got no handcuffs to put on me?" Brad snarled in his ear.

"After a week or two in the county jail you'll know who I am you gangling ass, little bastard," the Deputy shot back.

Brad grabbed the Deputy around the waist and pushed him back against the guardrail on the side of the bridge.

"Why you pussle gutted bastard, I think I am going to take you for a swim with me" Brad said as he began pushing the Deputy backward over the top of the waist high metal rail.

"Uh-uuh, don't do that, uh-uuh, don't do that," the terrified Deputy began to yell.

"Then keep your hands off of me you chicken shit Son-of-a Bitch," Brad snapped as he grabbed him by the collar and sent him sprawling across the hood of his car.

"Can both of you guys not manage to get a pair of hand cuffs on him?" Jeff demanded sharply.

"Just a little problem. We'll have him under control in about two shakes," the number two deputy answered as he began pulling his service revolver.

"No, No, I don't want him shot. I want him in the county jail. I'm coming to help you." Jeff called as he started running toward them across the bridge.

Brad had already made his decision if it became necessary, and now he realized it was time to make his move. Brad began running along the guardrail trying to see the water below, but in the darkness he was unable to see it. With Jeff coming fast he stooped under the guardrail and suddenly remembered the flashlight. He turned the beam of light on the water below and saw what appeared to be a swirling pool of deeper water just to the left of where he was standing.

Jeff reached the guardrail and stood with his arms over the top of the rail about five feet from where Brad was standing. "Give it up Brad, you're not going to jump. There's nothing but rocks down there." At the same time he lunged outward trying to get an arm around Brad's waist.

Brad deflected Jeff's arm and moved out of his reach. "Piss on you Pope. You ain't never been quick enough," and dropped out of sight.

"The crazy bastard has jumped in the river. Bring a light over here and see if you can't find him," Jeff called to the deputies.

Both deputies spent the next several minutes playing their lights back and forth across the surface of the water and down the river until it disappeared out of sight under the trees.

"Well he has either given us the slip or some fisherman will pull him out of the water between here and Canton in the next day or two," one of the deputies voiced his opinion to Jeff and the other deputy.

"I think you are probably right," Jeff said, "And if he has managed to give us the slip I think he will stay out of Cherokee County for awhile because he knows that I know him. One of you guys drive my car and leave it behind the jail. I have to drive this car and the illegal liquor in it to Gainesville and make a report on the whole operation. We will destroy the liquor, and I will deliver the car to the Sheriff in the morning. The county gets the car."

Thirty minutes later Brad's Dodge, with one hundred fifty gallons of liquor in it, was setting in Jack Kindericks old garage, out of sight of the road.

So far Jeff Pope's plan to hi-jack Brad's load of liquor and sell it to Jack Kinderick had worked <u>almost</u> as he had planned it … Almost, but not quite, because Brad Parks was nowhere near the Cherokee County Jail.

When Brad dropped the twenty to twenty five feet into the cold water of the Etowah River, his right leg hit the water first. Along with the big splash of water, Brad felt a sudden sharp pain in his right leg just below the knee. He knew immediately that he had hit his leg on something located just below the surface of the water. How badly his leg was injured he could not tell, but the pain was still acute as he surfaced out of sight behind a rocky overhang. Sitting waist deep in the Etowah River with an aching right leg, he was waiting for Jeff Pope and his deputies to leave with his car and one hundred fifty gallons of his liquor. Brad was sitting wet and shivering in the water, cursing his bad luck in every way that he knew how.

But as yet, and unbeknownst to Brad and Jeff Pope and Jack Kinderick, Brad Park's luck was about to undergo an unbelievable change of fortune.

When Jeff and the deputies finally left, Brad pulled himself out of the water and up the river bank onto dry ground. As he started walking the short distance toward the road, the throbbing ache in his right leg worsened. When he tried to pull his pant leg up in order to check the wound, Brad was shocked to find that his leg was swelled so badly that he was unable to get his pant leg up enough to see the injury. He shined his flashlight along the heavy roadside growth until he found an opening that let him and his aching leg through and out onto the road.

"Well at least I can still walk," Brad said to himself. "I need to get on over to Jack's house so I can tell him that I have lost his load of liquor."

Brad turned and saw a set of headlights coming toward him across the bridge.

*   *   *

"Hey feller, what in the dickens are you doing out here in the middle of the night as wet as a dog."

Brad walked over to the passenger side of the old truck and leaned in at the open window.

"Well, I was down the river there about two or three hundred yards doing a little night fishing. I was sitting on some rocks and when I stood up to change locations, I fell backwards into the river, busted my ass and lost my fishing tackle."

"That was bad luck. Might not be a bad idea to quit fishing by yourself, especially at night. Well can I give you a lift? My name is Walden and I live down close to Free Home."

"I would appreciate it Mr. Walden. My name is Parks and I know Mr. Jack Kinderick who runs the store on down the road a few miles. If you would let me off there I would be much obliged."

Fifteen minutes later they rounded a curve in the road, and Jack's store came in view. The gas tanks were still lit and several cars were parked out front.

"Mr. Walden if you will let me off at Jack's driveway, I am going up to the house and borrow some dry clothes before I go down to the store."

"I sure will Parks. Remember what I told you about fishing at night by yourself. I'm not too smart, but I quit doing that several years ago."

Brad's intention was of course to borrow some dry clothes, but also to get one of Jack's boys to go down to the store and tell Jack that he was up at the house and wanted to see him.

As Brad limped slowly up Jack's driveway, he noticed a light and heard voices coming from Jack's garage. Brad thought it strange that the doors to the old garage would be closed, with voices coming from inside the building. Wanting to know if one of the voices coming from the garage belonged to one of Jack's sons, Brad walked over to the side of the garage and peeped in between two boards having a wide gap between them.

Sitting inside was Brad's 1948 Dodge with the passenger side door open. Standing beside the open door was Jack's oldest son and a man whom Brad did not know. They had opened a six-gallon case of liquor, setting on the front seat, and removed one of the one-half gallon fruit jars of liquor.

"That is damn good liquor Don. See how long the bead holds when I shake the jar." Jack's son offered Don the jar of liquor.

"Looks pretty good. How much do you want by the case?"

"Tell you what. Let's take this jar up to the house and I'll get us a couple of glasses. We'll take a drink or two of it and you can see how good it is."

*   *   *

"The double crossing sons-of-bit-ches," Brad said to himself as he realized the extent of the swindle that Jeff Pope and Jack Kinderick had set him up for. Brad turned and started toward the store, intending to confront Jack with the plan to hi-jack his load of liquor and have him caught and jailed by Jeff Pope for hauling liquor. All of that, done to him, while they split the proceeds from his one hundred fifty gallons of liquor.

"The thieving sons of bitches," Brad said to himself, but then he realized that no one knew he was here. No one, except himself, knew that he had just found the car and load of liquor that had been stolen from him less than two hours ago. Knowing that, Brad realized that he was now the one with the options. "I wonder if they left the key in that car ------ my car."

Quietly Brad worked his way around to the front of the now darkened garage. He grinned to himself when he saw that they had left the garage doors open. "Thanks dumbasses."

Brad eased along the side of the car and carefully opened the driver's side door. (One of the first things that a driver does to his trip car, is to disconnect the dome lights, and install and off and on switch in the wiring to the tail lights) with more than a little trepidation, Brad felt for and found the switch key in the ignition.

Brad was well aware that what he was about to do, had to be done now, and done so quietly that the people in Jack's house and store would not hear or notice. Brad's leg was hurting so bad, he felt sure that it was either broken or badly fractured, but knowing what lay ahead, Brad did not wait. He knew that it was time to move.

The Chrysler engine was started and running before the starter completed one revolution. Brad engaged the transmission into reverse and barely touching the gas pedal he backed the car out of the garage just far enough to make the turn onto the driveway.

He moved the shift lever into low gear and again barely touching the accelerator he moved slowly down the driveway and turned left on State Highway 372, the Ball Ground to Crabapple Highway. Just as he turned left out of the driveway, he turned on the headlights so as not to look suspicious as he passed in front of Jack's store.

Once past the store Brad increased his speed until he was traveling near the speed limit. He watched intently out of the rear window, but he saw no cars coming from Ball Ground, nor did any cars come onto the road from Jack's store and start after him. Brad began to feel better about his chances when he crossed State Road 20 at Free Home, and continued on toward Birmingham, the first small community in Fulton County.

CHAPTER 6

There was only one place for Brad to go with his load of liquor and that was to Rob Kirby in Atlanta. There was only one hitch in that plan and that was that Rob didn't know he was coming, and as Brad knew, Rob was a stickler about knowing everything possible when he had trip cars on the road bringing his liquor to Atlanta. Worse yet, it was going to be well after midnight before he could get to Atlanta, the worst possible time.

"Well," Brad mused to himself, "There is always an exception to every rule, but I'm afraid that none of the rules apply here, this is more like a damn calamity." But when you worked for Rob Kirby, and you got in trouble, there was one thing you didn't have to worry about. Rob never left you hanging.

Just after midnight Brad crossed the Chattahoochee River on Johnson Ferry Road and entered the city limits of Sandy Springs. Brad was in extremely dangerous territory and he knew it.

"I hope to hell and back that all the blue boys are having their midnight snack."

Brad's plan was to stop at the telephone booth located on Mount Vernon Highway near Arlington Cemetery and call Rob. It was from this phone that Brad called when he was having car trouble or if he was running over thirty minutes late. He dreaded to make the call to Rob and Clara's house at one o'clock in the morning.

The phone never completed the first ring before Rob answered it with a command instead of a greeting.

"What is it?"

"Rob its Brad."

"It's Brad, Clara. Where are you Brad?"

"I'm at the phone in Sandy Springs."

"What in the hell are you doing there. We ain't got nothing going on this morning."

"I know we don't Rob, but I'm in a tight corner. I need your help."

"You have all the help I can give you Brad, but I need to know what happened."

"Rob you know that deal up in Cherokee County that Frank gave me?"

"Yeah, I know about it. I thought that was supposed to be an easy load. Did something go wrong?"

"Rob if it hadn't happened to me, I wouldn't believe it myself."

"Are you loaded?"

"I am Rob."

"So you are sitting at the phone booth on the side of Mount Vernon highway at one o'clock in the morning with a load of liquor on your car?"

"Rob I'm afraid I've got a broke leg." Rob heard the hoarseness in Brad's voice brought on by the extended time of suffering from the break of the bone in his leg. Rob knew that he had to get him in, and soon.

"Brad, you have come this far with that busted leg, can you give me another forty five minutes?"

"I think so Rob."

"Brad, take the same route in, but stay off of Northside Drive. Cross Northside and get on Howell Mill Road. I'll pick you up at the water works in twenty minutes at the most. Stay behind me about two to three hundred yards. We are going to the wooden fence on Peters Street. Park at the second light pole and be sure the light is still not working. You'll need to get out of the car and stand by the light pole where I'll pick you up. Jake will take over from there. Okay Brad, forty five minutes. Let's get started!"

Brad watched as Rob passed the light pole and turned right at the next side street. He knew that Rob would make a four block circuit and return to pick him up in ten to twelve minutes. Brad had started feeling light headed soon after he left Sandy Springs, and by the time Rob passed him on Howell Mill he was having to concentrate hard to keep Rob in view and a clear mind about where they were going and why they were going there.

When Rob flashed his lights at the second light pole, Brad braked his car and stopped at the curb beside the light pole. Waiting for Rob to return, Brad was confused about what he was supposed to do next. He was about to open the door and get out when he froze in his seat. He felt the door unlock and then begin to open. Brad turned and looked into the smiling face of the biggest black man he had ever seen.

"Do you be Mist' Brad?"

"Jake you have scared the hot scalding shit out of me."

Jake did not make an audible sound, but beginning with his shoulders his huge body shook with laughter for several seconds. "Mist' Brad, they a powlice cruizer come by heah about eva fowty-five minutes to a howa, and its now been thutty minutes. I need to be gone."

"Okay Jake, let me get out of the car. I'm supposed to stand by the light pole and wait for Rob to pick me up."

But as Brad gripped the steering wheel with the intention of swinging his legs out on the pavement his right led would not move. So instead of his legs coming out of the car first, Brad began falling headfirst out of the car toward the pavement.

"Whoa now --- Whoa now, catch on to me Mist' Brad. I've got you now. I'll just tote you ovaa by the light pole and you can stand theaa till' Mist' Rob git heah."

When Rob started to leave their house and meet Brad on Howell Mill Road, Clara refused to stay at home. "You are going to need me Rob. If Brad's leg is as bad as you say it is, you are going to need me, so don't argue with me."

When Rob turned back onto Peters Street he saw that Clara was right. He was going to need her help. Jake was carrying Brad like a small boy, one arm under his knees and one arm around his shoulders, toward the light pole.

"Oh my God Rob --- Oh my God! Surely he's not ---"

Rob accelerated his Pontiac toward Jake and instructed Clara what he wanted her to do.

"I'm going to stop right beside Jake, when I do Clara, jump out and open the back door so Jake can sit him on the back seat. Get in beside him so you can keep him from falling over. We have got to move Clara."

The exchange took two minutes and as Jake closed the door on Rob's Pontiac, he turned toward Brad's Dodge, loaded with one hundred fifty gallons of liquor, and reached for the door handle.

Rob leaned over and spoke to Jake out of the passenger window.

"Have you got me covered Jake?"

The big smile blossomed again. "Eveea things Jake, Mist' Rob, Eveea things Jake."

Five minutes later Peters Street was empty and quiet at 3 o'clock in the morning.

Ten minutes later an Atlanta Police cruiser came slowly along Peters Street headed toward Stewart Avenue. "Man I can't believe it, for a Saturday night, it sure is quiet."

"Yeah, you're right. But sometimes along about now it becomes Sunday morning. Lets go by Sadie's Place and see if she has some fresh coffee made."

*   *   *

Rob turned left off Peachtree Road going North and followed the lighted indicators around to the emergency entrance of Piedmont Hospital. He parked his car in front of the emergency entrance doors and blew his horn.

Just as Rob was getting out of the car, two orderlies came through the double doors pushing a gurney. "Do you need a gurney out here sir?"

"Yes we do. We have a man out here with a broken leg and he's also in pretty bad physical condition," Rob answered.

The two orderlies loaded Brad on the gurney and after telling Rob and Clara that he would be in room four, disappeared through the double doors.

Rob parked his car and entered through the emergency entrance doors. He saw Clara leaning against the wall sobbing into her open hands.

"Come on Clara. I know he looked bad, but he's tough enough to take it. They'll have him patched up in a day or two."

Clara turned and leaned her head on Rob's shoulder. "Oh God Rob, it was awful. They wouldn't let me go in the room with Brad. When the doctor went in the room with him I heard the nurse tell the doctor that the bone was sticking through the skin."

Rob took Clara by the arm and they walked across the hall and sat down in the waiting room. Fifteen minutes later the emergency room doctor walked into the waiting room, identified himself, and asked, "I'm Dr. Carlton Blake. Are you Rob?"

"Yessir, I am."

"He has asked for you a couple of times. I told him that you and your wife were here."

"Can we see him?"

"No, not now. We have already put him to sleep. Look, it's a pretty bad break. Can you tell me how and when this happened?"

Rob decided to tell him all that he could.

"It happened about 9 o'clock last night, Saturday night. He jumped off a bridge into the Etowah River in Cherokee County. He was unlucky enough to land on a rock just under the surface of the water. Then with his leg all busted up, he drove his car all the way to Atlanta and then called me."

The doctor looked at Rob for several seconds before he said, "I see. Are you brothers?"

"No sir, we are not brothers."

"I see. By the way, what is his name?"

"His name is Brad, Brad Parks."

"We have Brad's leg painted and sprinkled with sulfa. We have given him penicillin and we have already started IV's. Surgery is scheduled for 10 o'clock in the morning. I think we can save his leg if we don't have too much trouble with infection, but infections can be trouble."

"Doctor Blake would you let me stay in the room with him tonight. I'm afraid if he wakes up and doesn't know where he's at, he'll try to get out of bed and he might hurt himself besides tearing a bunch of equipment all to hell."

"Well okay, but they will be coming after him from pre-op sometime in the next hour or two. But speaking of staying in the hospital at night, Brad might as well get used to that, he's going to be with us for a while."

CHAPTER 7

On Saturday morning, two weeks after his fateful jump into the Etowah River, Brad was leaning against the side of his hospital bed with his new set of crutches under his arms. A new and softer cast had, just this morning, been molded on his leg. Brad kept lifting and turning his leg surprised at how much lighter and useable his leg felt.

Pale and obviously weakened, from almost two weeks of laying on his back with his leg in traction, Brad had, early this morning, realized with a feeling of uncertainty the fact that he was about to leave the safety and security of a hospital.

Dr. Carlton Blake was standing at the foot of the bed looking at Brad's chart and the record of his stay in Piedmont Hospital.

"Well Mr. Parks, I think it's a little early, but everyone else has approved your release so I guess I might as well approve it too. One reason being that you have raised enough hell wanting to go home until I guess the nurses will be glad to see you go. Let me caution you about your leg. If you should fall and break it again, you will be spending a lot more time in here than you did the first time. So be careful where you step. Exercise your leg every day and I want to see you in two weeks. One other thing Brad, you are not going to be running any foot races nor jumping off any bridges any time soon, so just go ahead and make peace with that."

Dr. Blake did not usually do so, but as he started to leave, he shook hands with Brad, Clara and Rob. Rob and Clara had come to check Brad out of the hospital and carry him out to their house until Monday. On Monday morning they were going to visit Rabb and Annie and, after a dinner, to which Elizabeth Cochran had been invited, Rob was to carry Brad on to his folks' farm in Pickens County to recuperate.

"I'm glad that Elizabeth is going to see Brad," Rob said on their way to the hospital that morning. I know he has been wanting to see her real bad, but he didn't want her to see him with his leg pulled up in all that traction harness."

"That's what he told her when she called on the Monday after the accident. She told him she would like to come and see him, but he asked her to wait until they took his leg out of traction. Then last Wednesday he called Elizabeth and asked her if she would wait until he came to see her. He told her that he would have a cast on his leg and he would be walking on crutches, but he wouldn't be lying flat on his back and he wouldn't be wearing a hospital gown. He also told her that he had something to give her if she would accept it. And, 'being the good little know it all that I am,' I found out from one of the nurses that a family friend from Jasper, who just happens to be a jeweler, visited Brad carrying a briefcase last week.

Oh yes, one more thing. Guess who Brad called, and asked if she would make the plans for Monday's dinner?"

"Well at least I know all of the plans are made, and we are in for a good meal."

"You betcha."

"By the way, since I have no doubt the plans are already made, when is the wedding going to be?"

"Oh come now, Robbie dear, there have to be a few things left for me to get excited about. Brad and Elizabeth will take care of all that in due time. But, just so you will not get in the way of those plans being made, when dinner is over you go out and sit under the shade trees with Dad. I'll bet you both have some interesting stories you can tell each other.

*   *   *

The sun was down almost to the tree line in the West when Rob came to the intersection of Highway 52 and 183, better known as the "Y" and turned his Pontiac South on Highway 183. A mile later he turned right on Burnt Mountain Highway toward Jasper.

Shortly before leaving, Elizabeth had walked with Brad to the car and after laying his crutches across the back seat, she slipped her arm around his waist and helped him sit backwards onto the car seat. Brad carefully moved his cast enclosed leg into the car and Elizabeth closed the door. They stood quietly without speaking for a long moment before Elizabeth turned away and started toward the house.

Rob waved at Clara who had been standing on the porch. "Bye Hon, I'll see you on Friday evening."

"Bye Rob, tell your Mom and Dad I said hello. I'll miss you."

Brad had not spoken since they left the Turner farm and now, as they crossed the top of Burnt Mountain, Rob decided to see if he could get him to talk about his future plans. "Well Brad how do you feel since you got out of the hospital?"

Brad sat quietly, intently staring out of the windshield, before he answered. "I'm already missing her."

"Wait a damn minute. I didn't ask you about who you were missing. I asked you how you were feeling. It's already been a long day for all of us so I figured you were about all in."

Brad grinned sheepishly at Rob and said, "Yeah, I am a little bit bushed, but this has already been the greatest day of my life. Rob, I asked her to marry me."

Rob feigned complete surprise and after a moment he said, "Why you old dog, you're not as tired as I thought you were. Well, what did she say boy, come on, fess up?"

"She said yes Rob."

"All right," Rob grinned as they shook hands.

"Does this mean that I'm about to get the chance to play payback as your best man?"

Brad looked surprised before his face broke into a wide smile. "Damn right." Then after a moment he continued, "Elizabeth is going to come up to see me on Saturday and if Nellie will let her, she is going to spend Saturday night with me – us."

Rob chuckled at Brad's quick recovery. "Well I'm glad it is 'us' instead of 'me'. You and Elizabeth would have a hell of a time of it with your busted leg and a cast on it."

"Come on Rob, you know what I meant."

"Okay, Okay Brad, just kidding. But just to put you on notice, remember how much needling I got before Clara and I got married."

Again Brad's mood turned quiet and pensive. "Rob, you know that I'm going to quit the business don't you?"

"Brad quit worrying about it. I offered you a job and you took it. I figure it's your call anytime you get ready to quit. No excuses expected."

"You know my leg that got busted is going to be a little shorter than the other one don't you?"

"Dr. Blake mentioned to me that was going to be the case. He was worried about infection and he had to do a little more work than he had intended. Listen Brad, if you and I both started worrying about your leg right now, and worried about it every day all day long, not one damn iota of good would it do. I'm carrying you home Brad. I'm carrying you to see the only two people that don't care whether or not you have even got that leg, as far as their love for you is concerned. I figure with the woman I have and with the one you're getting, we are about the two luckiest men alive. So get your head out of your ass and let's get on with it. Okay?"

*   *   *

Before Elizabeth left to return home late on Monday evening, she and Clara had made a date to spend Wednesday together. The plan for Wednesday was to go to the Shoal Creek Cemetery where they would spend the morning cleaning and planting flowers on and around Zeke's grave. They had invited themselves to lunch with Ben and Martha, then back to Wesley and Nellie's house for the remainder of the afternoon and supper with them.

As they were leaving Ben and Martha's house, Clara decided she would like to return to the Cochran's house by way of the Ridge Road, and stop at the place where the road widened into an overlook of the Old Mill Dam place on the Amicalola River.

"It's such a peaceful place Elizabeth, and when I start choking on the city of Atlanta it's one of the places I like to think about. Besides that, it's been months since we had one of our girl talks and I think it's high time we had one. So tell me, how is it between you and Brad?"

"I decided that I would keep it my secret until today. Brad asked me to marry him Monday evening before he left to go and see his folks."

"I thought so, and I was beginning to wonder when you were going to tell me."

"You mean to tell me that you already knew?"

"About ninety nine and forty four one hundredth per cent certain. Besides you had those red spots on your cheeks, and the last time I checked, I am the one who is supposed to be told."

"Oh, I'm sorry Clara, but I wanted to wait until today to tell you. I should have known. You always know everything about me already anyhow."

"When is the wedding going to be?"

"I have no idea. I am going up to see Brad and his folks on Saturday, and if Mama will let me, I am going to spend Saturday night with him --- them."

"Well I sure am glad to hear that it's them instead of him. You two would have had a hell of a time of it with Brad's busted leg and a cast on it."

"Come on Clara, you know what I meant."

"Okay, Okay kiddo, just pulling your leg a little. Come on, let's see the ring."

Then for the next hour they spent talking the senseless, erotic, meaningless and lovely talk of two girl-women whose lives were forever intertwined.

As Clara straightened up in the seat and was about to start the engine, she looked over at Elizabeth with a mischievous grin on her face and asked, "Well are you looking forward to the big bust?"

Elizabeth waited a second too long to answer so she did not have to lie to her closest friend. She looked away, but not before Clara saw the red spots appear on her cheeks, but by then it was too late anyhow.

Clara reached across the car and turned Elizabeth's face toward her. For a long moment she looked into her eyes. "I don't believe it, Elizabeth Cochran, you tell me I'm wrong. If somebody else had told me this I would have slapped the living hell out of them."

"Oh come on Clara, it wasn't like that at all."

"What wasn't like, what at all. My God Elizabeth, so it is true. What did he do, take Wesley's crowbar and pry you out of those pretty little pink drawers you wear?"

"No, but if you must know, I took them off myself."

"The Lord help, if it would do any good I would faint right here."

"For goodness sake Clara, do you think I'm the first girl to get married who wasn't a virgin?'

"No I don't, that's what makes this whole thing so unfair. There were a lot of men and women in Dawson County who thought I carried my panties around in my purse just so they would be conveniently out of my way, and I went to my marriage bed an all American virgin girl."

"We didn't mean for it to happen the way it did Clara, I swear we didn't. Everything just got out of control. It was as much my fault as it was his."

"Well I'm sure it must have been since you already told me that you took those pinkies off yourself. The only advice about that, that my Mama ever gave me was that if for some reason you ain't got your drawers on you sure better know where they are. Honest to God Elizabeth, I didn't know what she was talking about and I didn't ask."

Elizabeth shook her head and smiled for a moment before she said, "Well little Miss Tightass from Atlanta, since I have made a full and complete confession of what has happened to me since you got married and left home, how about you? Since you so graciously brought up my anticipation of the experience of the big bust, how has the experience of the connubial relationship of living and sleeping with a man affected you?"

"Oh you know me Elizabeth, I took right to it. Although I must confess that at first I did wonder if this was what all the commotion was about. But since the big C happened one night I have become a much better bedmate. Which brings me around to the one little thing I was going to tell you about today but amid all the excitement I almost let it slip my mind --- I'm pregnant. And that was what finally did it. They fell into each other arms laughing and crying and drying tears and blowing noses until all the anger and all the pretenses were washed away and gone. They were, at last, little girls again, which is what they wanted to be and feel again --- one last time.

CHAPTER 8

Finally, and yet with a great deal of resistance, the business of making, hauling and selling illicit spirituous grain alcohol (illegal liquor) began to lose it dangerous and deadly grip on the counties laying along the southern edge of the Blue Ridge Mountains. A growing economy kept more of the younger generation at home. With a better education, they became more industrious on their own. They in turn, began growing families, building homes and businesses, and creating wealth of their own.

By no means did this change in the economy mean that the liquor business in the North Georgia Mountains was about to dry up -- far from it. At best it provided an option for anyone not wanting to get involved in the liquor business to start with.

As the size of Atlanta grew, so did the demand for cheap illegal liquor grow. This time however, it was not moonshine liquor that provided the supply, but it was cheap liquor. As the need grew for a greater supply of cheap liquor, so did the need for a more convenient supply become necessary. A nearby source was needed, and the nearby counties of Douglas and Paulding on the west side, and DeKalb and Clayton counties on the east side were ready to meet the demand. Huge distilleries capable of producing a several hundred gallons of cheap liquor a day were put into operation. They were erected in basements and barns and in some instances they were put underground with an underground ventilation system installed to remove the fumes.

How did the wholesale production of cheap liquor, close to the huge Atlanta market, affect the status and output of liquor making in Dawson County? Very little. Their old customers kept coming to the mountains. They wanted liquor made from the crystal clear streams of North Georgia.

What did the skilled still hands from the North Georgia Mountains think of the large distillery operators that provided the huge amounts of cheap liquor for Atlanta? "They have been making that damned rotgut liquor down there all their lives and they still don't know how to make good liquor."

*   *   *

The first cooling breezes of early fall stirred the not yet tinted leaves on the huge oaks in the backyard of Rabb and Annie Turner's home place. The grasses and weeds of late summer had wilted and died in the searing heat from the long days of July and August.

The deep red foliage on the small sumac bushes held onto their leafy trim, but the golden yellow leaves on the limbs of the sassafras began dropping as soon as they began turning. On past the barn and down along the field road toward the creek a few yellow and brown leaves were beginning to drift away from the tall poplars. The colorful days and cool nights of autumn were once again returning to the North Georgia Mountains.

The wives had prepared the huge after church dinner, and, during the meal, they all joined in the lively conversation about life and death and living in their community. The wives would cover all the local gossip that was not acceptable for mixed company after the men left for the shade trees out back.

There was, by now, one other topic of which most of their talking and joviality was about. It was their grandchildren, and according to Annie, Rabb's grandson was making an absolute fool out of him.

"He had not been to Atlanta since he quit hauling sugar and cans from down there, but the day our grandson was born, we stayed at the hospital all day and all night. He would not leave until that baby was born and he got to hold it."

*   *   *

Besides our adoration of them, is it not true that we think of our grandchildren as an extension of ourselves, since we so quickly attach ourselves to them and they to us.

*   *   *

They were of course older now, Wes, Nellie, Ben and Martha were in their mid-fifties while Rabb and Annie were nearing sixty.

These latter years of midlife were more relaxed and, except for the

342

usual array of aches and pains, they were in reasonably sound health. For the most part they were enjoying these years that would soon lead them into the final stage of their lives.

The three old friends sat together now in their favorite after dinner (the noon meal) resting place and relaxed in the shade of the spreading oak trees in Rabb and Annie's backyard.

The three wives were already engaged in the harder and hotter work of clearing the table and washing the dishes. It was not an enjoyable job but they accepted it as part of a woman's housework to do. Besides that, the men were out of the house, and there were happenings and a few delicate occurrences they wanted to discuss.

The conversation of the three men moved easily along as they discussed what each man felt was of some interest to the other two. It was, in reality, dull conversation until Wesley asked, "Rabb, I hear that you are out of the sugar business, is that right?"

"Yeah, that's right Wes. I have sold everything I had, lock, stock and barrel. I'm out of it."

"Well is it true that Luke Gayton was the one that bought you out?" Ben asked.

"Yeah it was Luke."

While we have all been talking and sitting on our backsides, old Luke has been doing right well for himself."

Their talk fell silent for a few minutes before Ben said, "Well I'm glad for him. If there was ever a boy that made it the hard way, it is Luke. I'll never forget the night that Doc Holden brought him to the house after his Mama died. I had my doubts he would ever get over it. Luke's Daddy was a sawmiller and he was gone a lot. Luke and his Mama was mighty close."

The three wives came out of the kitchen onto the back porch, laughing and talking with the eternal optimism that wives and mothers seem to be blessed with. They walked across the yard and joined their husbands in the shade of the trees. The lateness of the hour and the slight breeze moving through the trees lent just a touch of coolness to the air.

They chatted among themselves for a short time, mostly about their day together, to Annie about the delicious meal she had prepared for them, about their children and grandchildren and when their next visit was expected to be. Then came the invitations and promises to return the visit, then the good-byes and soon the visitors were gone. Annie sat down in one of the recently vacated chairs and for a while they enjoyed each other's familiar company. They both agreed that it had been a good day.

Ben and Martha drove home through the changing colors of the coming fall season. Martha commented on how pleasant it had been to spend the afternoon with their closest friends. She also mentioned that she was encouraged to see that Annie seemed to have regained some of her strength and vitality since the family's terrible ordeal. Martha was immediately sorry that she had alluded to Zeke's death in any way. Lines of anger deepened across his forehead and the muscles hardened along his jawline. Moments later she was relieved when Ben's face relaxed again into his usual appearance of good humor. A short time later and in an easier frame of mind Ben turned to his wife and said, "You know Martha, I don't believe the liquor business back here in these mountains would have ever amounted to much of anything if the government had kept their noses out of it."

Martha was surprised that Ben seemed to be trying to justify Dawson County's only "claim to fame" that it was moonshine liquor capital of Georgia. She turned and looked at her husband for a long moment before she answered. "That may be true Ben, I don't know. I do know this though, for I have lived through it. All of the trouble put together that the government has caused people in the liquor business doesn't compare with the trouble that people in the liquor business have caused themselves."

"Well I guess that's all true Martha. I certainly know that the liquor business has caused me a lot of trouble and it's caused you a lot of worry and care. I'm mighty sorry about that. I think you know that's the main reason I quit. But I have never been ashamed of anything I did in order to make a living for us."

Martha reached across the car and laid her hand on her husband's arm. "I know Ben, I know."

Here ends my story about the life and times of Ben McClure, his family and friends. I shall miss them for they have also become friends of mine. Along the way we lost some of them. I grieved for each of them. They all mattered to me. I hope in some way they did for you also, because I wanted them to be like us.

God-Fearing Criminals
Glossary

1. **Battlin board-Battlin stick** – used in days of washing clothes by hand. Clothes were spread on the board and beaten with a stick to loosen heavy soil.
2. **Boiling spring** – cold water bubbles up out of the ground.
3. **Coke** – coal with most of the gases removed by heating; it burns with intense heat and little smoke.
4. **Disremember** – to be unable to recall. (A colloquialism in the area)
5. **Dinner** – the main meal in the country and eaten about 12 o'clock noon.
6. **Grip** – suitcase.
7. **Heater** – heats still beer causing the beer to steam more quickly.
8. **Hog Still** – a huge aluminum vat with wooden heads that contain several thousand gallons of still beer. The still beer is fermented and distilled in the same vat.
9. **Mash Stick** – used to stir the still beer.
10. **Pottail** – the remains after the still beer has been run thru the still.
11. **Shack & Shack Truck** - an illegal distillery and the vehicle which carried supplies to the Shack.
12. **Stash** - a secure location where illicit liquor is stored.
13. **Supper** - the last meal of the day.
14. **Temper** - reduce alcohol to 90 proof.
15. **Thump barrel** - an additional wooden barrel between the still and the condenser.
16. **Trippers, Trip Car** - those who drove the trip car used to haul moonshine.
17. **Tripping** - the actual job of hauling the moonshine to customers.
18. **Worm** - condenser.

About the Author

J.M. Burt was born in 1928 in Dawson County, Georgia. After serving in the Air Force, he worked for Lockheed Martin Company in Marietta, Georgia, retiring in 1987. He and his wife, Marie, have three children; Jonathan, Noel and Karen. They currently live on a small cattle farm in Cherokee County, Georgia.

LaVergne, TN USA
07 January 2010
169207LV00002B/15/P